Troublemaker

ALSO BY LINDA HOWARD

Shadow Woman

Prey

Veil of Night

Ice

Burn

Death Angel

Up Close and Dangerous

Cover of Night

Drop Dead Gorgeous

Killing Time

To Die For

Kiss Me While I Sleep

Cry No More

Dying to Please

Open Season

A Game of Chance

Mr. Perfect

All the Queen's Men

Kill and Tell

Now You See Her

Son of the Morning

Shades of Twilight

Mackenzie's Magic

Mackenzie's Pleasure

After the Night

Dream Man

Loving Evangeline

Heart of Fire

A Touch of Fire

Mackenzie's Mission

Angel Creek

The Way Home

A Lady of the West

Duncan's Bride

Mackenzie's Mountain

White Lies

Bluebird Winter

Heartbreaker

Diamond Bay

Midnight Rainbow

Almost Forever

Sarah's Child

Troublemaker

Linda Howard

HARPER LUXE

An Imprint of HarperCollins*Publishers*

This book is a work of fiction. The characters, incidents, and dialogue are drawn from the author's imagination and are not to be construed as real. Any resemblance to actual events or persons, living or dead, is entirely coincidental.

HarperCollins books may be purchased for educational, business, or sales promotional use. For information please e-mail the Special Markets Department at SPsales@harpercollins.com.

FIRST HARPERLUXE EDITION

ISBN: 978-0-06-246635-8

HarperLuxe™ is a trademark of HarperCollins Publishers.

Library of Congress Cataloging-in-Publication Data is available upon request.

16 17 18 19 20 ID/RRD 10 9 8 7 6 5 4 3 2 1

To all the beloved dogs
who have enriched my life

Troublemaker

Chapter 1

Washington, D.C., Area

It was one of those bright, early-March days that made you think spring had to be here, even though you knew the winter bitch wasn't yet ready to loosen her grip and move completely out of town. Morgan Yancy sometimes lost track of what season it was anyway. He'd have to stop and think: was he in the Northern Hemisphere, or the Southern? His job demanded that he travel to hellholes at a moment's notice, so he could find himself going from the Arctic to the Iraqi desert, from there to South America—wherever it was in the world that his talents were needed.

Thirty-six hours ago he'd arrived at the small condo that passed for home these days, slept the first twenty-four hours and awakened to the discovery that his days and nights were mixed up. Wasn't the first time, wouldn't be the last. So he stayed up a while, ate some peanut butter smeared on stale crackers, worked on his gear, ran seven miles in the dark city to tire himself out, then conked out again.

When he woke, it was spring—or as good as.

He took a cool shower to blow the rest of the cobwebs out of his head, then rummaged in the refrigerator and found that his last bag of ground coffee had enough in it to make half a pot. Good enough. He opened the carton of milk, sniffed, winced, and poured it down the drain. There was some fuzzy green cheese in the fridge too, so he tossed it. No doubt about it: he had to do some grocery shopping while he was home this time. He could do without cheese and milk, but things got dicey if he didn't have coffee. Funny how he could go days, weeks, without it, drinking whatever was handy, but when he was home he damn well wanted his coffee.

The bright sunlight lured him out onto his postage-stamp patio. Coffee cup in hand, he stepped out and assessed the situation.

The weather was perfect: just cool enough not to classify as warm, but warm enough that he was comfortable without a jacket. There was a light breeze, and a few cotton-ball clouds floated by.

Well, fuck; life was tough sometimes. He didn't have a choice about it: he had to go fishing. He'd lose his man-license if he let a day made specially for fishing slip by without taking his boat out.

Besides, the old *Shark* needed to have the cobwebs blown out of the motor every now and then. He did upkeep on it whenever he was home, but it hadn't had a good run in about five months—which, come to think of it, might have been how long it had been since he'd had more than a day at home. The team sure as hell had been on a grueling stretch.

He fished his cell phone from the cargo pocket on his right thigh, and called Kodak, a buddy from his GO-Team. Kodak's real name was Tyler Gordon, but when you have eidetic memory, what the hell else could people call you besides Kodak?

Kodak sounded a little groggy and froggy when he answered, not surprising considering he'd been on the last job with Morgan. "Yeah, wassup?" The combination of hoarseness and borderline consciousness made the words barely intelligible.

"Fishing. I'm taking the *Shark* out. Wanna go?"

"Fuck, don't you ever sleep?"

"I've been sleeping. I've slept for most of two days. What the hell have you been doing?"

"Sometimes not sleeping. I'm sleeping now. Or I was." There was the sound of a huge yawn. "Have fun, buddy, but I won't be there having it with you. How long you going to stay out?"

"Until about dark, probably." He should've expected this; Kodak was a horn dog, pure and simple. He'd have thought about getting his rocks off even before putting some decent food in his belly. Not that Morgan hadn't thought about getting his own rocks off, but that had come *after* food, and he hadn't gotten any further than the thought.

There was another yawn. "I'll give it a pass this time. Catch you later." The air went dead as Kodak disconnected.

Morgan shrugged and slipped the phone back into his pocket. So he'd be fishing alone today. He didn't mind. Most times, he preferred it. The sun, the wind, the water, the blessed solitude—it was great, especially when he was unwinding from a job.

Within five minutes he'd downed enough coffee to get him by, pulled on a shirt and some socks and boots, and was in his truck heading for the marina. Breakfast came from a fast-food drive-through, but hell, it wasn't as if he didn't eat crap most days of his life anyway.

Besides, in his opinion America had some great-tasting crap. If the fat police really wanted to complain about food, they should go to some of the shit-holes he'd visited; after that, then maybe they'd have a deeper appreciation for tasty crap.

The marina where he kept the *Shark* was on the old, run-down side and a fairly long stretch down the river, but he liked it because it was small, and he could keep better track of any new boats or any suspicious vehicles in the parking area. If he were able to get the boat out on anything resembling a regular schedule, he'd be able to keep better vigilance, but so far he'd never had any trouble—no reason he should, just that habit was habit—and he had a talent for spotting vehicles that were out of the ordinary for their surroundings. Nothing stood out today, though he did take the precaution of driving up and down all the aisles before stopping. There were no vehicles parked facing out and no rentals or anything else suspicious.

He backed his truck into a parking slot, got out and locked it, then double-checked that it was locked. It was second nature; he double-checked everything when it came to security. As he stuck his key into the padlock on the security gate that blocked entrance to the docks, the marina owner, Brawley, stuck his head out of the shack thirty yards away and shouted, "Been a while! Good day for fishing."

"Hope so," Morgan replied, raising his voice to cover the distance.

"You heading out to the bay?"

"Don't think I'll go that far." The Chesapeake was a good forty miles down the Potomac; he'd use up most of his fishing time running there and back.

"Catch one for me," Brawley called, then ducked back inside the shack. Through the glass, Morgan watched him pick up the phone, an old-fashioned corded job that had probably been there since the day the marina was built, and cradle it on his shoulder as he dialed. You didn't see many of those phones these days.

Morgan snapped the padlock closed again, then continued down the dock to the slip he rented under the name of Ivan Smith, which he'd chosen because the name amused him, Ivan being the Russian "John." Hell, this was D.C.; probably half the population expected that the other half was using aliases.

He scrutinized all the boats he passed, looking for anything unfamiliar—not so much the boats themselves, though a small, out-of-the-way marina like this one tended to have a slower turnover rate than the bigger marinas—but equipment, such as an expensive radio array on a shit-can boat, or people who didn't quite fit in. Maybe their shoes were hard soled, or maybe they were armed, anything like that.

Nothing. The place was just as it should be. The smell of the river, the sound of the water lapping against the boats, the creak of the docks, the gentle bobbing of the boats—all of it soothed his soul, and he felt his permanent reservoir of tension emptying just a little. He'd definitely been born with an affinity for water. Once, noticing that he was doing something with his left hand, a teammate had asked him if he was ambidextrous, to which an instructor standing nearby had retorted, "No, he's amphibious." That was close to God's truth: give him gills, and he'd have been a happy camper.

He'd grown up around Pensacola, so he couldn't remember a time in his life when the ocean hadn't felt as if it were a part of him. The Potomac was a far cry from the Gulf of Mexico, but any water would do. Hell, he'd be content paddling around a lake in a canoe—for a little while, anyway; then he'd start itching for some action. There was nothing like blowing shit up or getting shot at to give a man a real jolt of adrenaline.

He went onboard the *Shark*, feeling the familiarity of the boat wrap around him. Because he respected the water as much as he loved it, he checked the gas and oil, the battery, the radio, and the bilge pump. He got his tackle from the locked storage and checked it. He checked that he had his cell phone, though he knew damn well that he did; same with the knife in his pocket, the pistol in the holster at the small of his back, plus the backup on his right ankle and the backup to the backup in the bottom of his tackle box. Everything was a go.

He freed the *Shark* from its moorings, then slid into the seat and turned the ignition key; the reliable motor fired up immediately. He turned his cap around backward on his head, reversed out of the boat slip, and turned the steering wheel toward freedom. The choppy water reflected the blue of the sky today, with murky green depths sliding along below him. He felt every bounce and slap of the hull on the surface, then the ride smoothed out as he gained speed.

Man, this was the life. Now if he could just haul in some fish—for bragging rights if nothing else, so he could rub his success in Kodak's face—he would count this a damn good day.

Even though he was just going fishing, he couldn't turn off the habits ingrained by sixteen years of intensive training, live combat, and plain old feral instinct. He hadn't reached the age of thirty-four without learning how to stay alive. He gave the water the same attention he'd given the parking lot; his head constantly swiveled back and forth as he studied everything rushing by on both sides of the boat. He noticed every craft

TROUBLEMAKER • 9

on the water, who and how many were on board each craft, what they were doing, how fast they were going and in what direction. He noticed if anyone paid any particular attention to him, which almost no one did, because there was nothing flashy about the *Shark*.

The water traffic was heavier than he'd expected, given that this was a weekday—maybe. He was halfway certain this was . . . Wednesday? Thursday? Damn. If this was Friday, he'd seriously lost track of when he was. Changing time zones was one thing, but when you backtracked across the IDL a couple of times, everything kind of went twilight zone on you, when tomorrow became yesterday, and today hadn't happened yet. Stretching out his leg, he fished his cell phone out of the cargo pocket and swiftly glanced down to check the day. Thursday. Okay. He'd been in the ballpark, which was all he asked after a long mission.

The Potomac was a big river, almost eleven miles wide in places as it worked its way southeast to the Chesapeake Bay. Avoiding the other boats should have been easy, but it seemed as if most of the people out today had no idea what the rules of the road—or river, in this case—were. Boats ran at angles, cutting in front of other boats, some deliberately throwing up water on other boaters. Wet-suit-wearing idiots on WaveRunners darted back and forth, in and out, seemingly oblivious to the topography of the river and whether the boats they were meeting had a choice of either hitting them or running aground. The wonder was that someone hadn't gotten shot. After two close calls—and the second time, having discarded the idea of doing some shooting himself, he almost chose hitting the idiot on the WaveRunner over scraping the bottom of his lower unit in the mud—he gave up and took to the middle of the river. To hell with it; let everyone else steer around him. He might earn some dirty looks and cuss words, but at least he wasn't in danger of tearing up the *Shark*.

Because he was in the middle of the river instead of running along the right side, when he glanced at a cabin cruiser anchored about a hundred yards to his left, his sharp eyesight picked up the sun glinting on a shock of silver-white hair as the wind blew back the hood of a black rain jacket. There were a couple of people on the deck, one in a blue shirt, and the other in the black jacket. The hair struck a chord of recognition with him, and on impulse he turned the wheel of the *Shark* toward the cabin cruiser; if the person with the silver-white hair was who he thought it was, he wanted to make certain everything was all right.

The hull bounced across the water; as he got closer he saw the person in the blue shirt go belowdecks. Then the woman—because it was a woman—with the silver-white hair started waving at him, big, side-to-side enthusiastic come-here waves, and he knew he'd guessed right.

He waved in return, then a few moments later throttled back and eased the *Shark* alongside the cabin cruiser; he cut the engine off and moved up to lower the electric trolling motor into the water so he could hold his position. "Congresswoman," he said in greeting to Joan Kingsley, twelve-term member of the House of Representatives and a leading member of the House Armed Services Committee. They'd initially crossed paths the memorable time when the Kingsleys' son had been kidnapped in Venezuela, and Morgan's GO-Team had been dispatched to rescue him. Congress-woman Kingsley had insisted on personally thanking all the men involved in saving her son's life and had even thrown a lavish backyard barbecue at a private location for the team. Normally, acceptance wouldn't have been possible, but because she was on the HASC, an exception had been made. You didn't snub someone who held the strings to the money bags; Mac, the head of the GO-Teams, was way too savvy for that, so he'd given the go-ahead.

To Morgan's surprise, he'd liked her. She was un-doubtedly a politician, alert to all angles, but she'd also struck him as not just grateful, but genuinely friendly.

She had a warm, open smile and seemed to meet every-one on the same level. Her husband, a D.C. lawyer, was friendly enough, but unlike hers, his friendliness came across as more calculated. Well, hell, given that he *was* a D.C. lawyer, what else could be expected?

"I didn't recognize you at first," she said, leaning over the railing and smiling down at him. "I wondered who on earth was barreling toward us."

"Sorry. I didn't mean to alarm you."

"I wasn't worried," she said, and laughed. "After all, my boat is bigger than yours."

"Yes, ma'am, it certainly is" was all he allowed him-self to say as his sharp gaze roved over the boat. Every-thing seemed to be okay, and given that no one else was on deck, she could have given him some kind of sign if there was any trouble.

She was an important person in Congress; she should have exercised better security, but he wasn't about to lecture her on that. He'd satisfied himself that there wasn't any trouble, which was what he'd set out to do.

"Come aboard and have a drink with us," she in-vited. "We're just having a relaxing day." She turned her head as the man wearing the blue shirt reemerged from the cabin. "Dex, it's Morgan Yancy."

"So I see." Dexter Kingsley was buttoning up his shirt over his white tee shirt as he approached the rail.

A practiced smile was on his evenly tanned face—a tan that said it was either sprayed on or he'd been in a tanning bed. "It's a good day to be on the water. Want to come up for a drink?" The invitation was the same as his wife's, but somehow lacked the underlying sincerity.

Morgan wasn't even remotely tempted. Making polite small talk wasn't his strong suit, even if he hadn't had the prospect of fishing pulling at him. "Thanks, but I'm heading to one of my fishing spots. When I saw the congresswoman, I just came over to say hello." He pulled the trolling motor out of the water and leaned over to put his hand on the side of the cabin cruiser and push himself away, then settled himself in the driver's seat. "Y'all have a good day."

"You too," Congresswoman Kingsley said and turned away from the railing with a smile and a wave.

Morgan turned the ignition key, his big motor roared to life, and he idled away from the cabin cruiser until he was far enough away that his wake wouldn't violently rock their boat. He lifted his head into the wind and let the combination of water and leisure time pull him in.

It was dark, the other side of nine-thirty, when he pulled into his parking slot at the condo. It had been late when he'd docked the *Shark,* then he'd cleaned his tackle and locked it away before heading home. He'd also made a brief stop at a grocery to cover his basic food needs; he hooked the plastic bags on his fingers and dragged them with him as he slid out of the seat. A click of the remote locked the truck.

The condos were at least thirty years old, six rows of two-story buildings made of brick and pebbled concrete. He supposed the effect was supposed to be modern and uncluttered—and maybe it had been thirty years ago, but now it was nothing more than butt-ugly. Each ground-floor unit, like his, had its own little patio, while the upper-story condos had balconies that struck him as fairly useless but that were used a lot during the summer for grilling and such.

The plastic bags rustled and banged against his left leg with every step, reminding him of why he hated buying groceries. After the fact, he always thought that he should throw a backpack in his truck and leave it there for hauling in what few groceries he bought, but he wasn't home often enough for it to be a habit so he'd forget about the backpack. He'd also almost forgotten he didn't have any coffee left, but the grocery's sign had caught his eye and he'd whipped into the parking lot without time to signal, resulting in a few indignant horn blasts. Couldn't be helped; he had to have coffee.

A concrete support pillar and some tall shrubbery partially blocked his view of the condo building, something that grated but the homeowners' association wasn't willing to do away with part of its mature landscaping and shady trees just because he didn't like it. He couldn't explain that the greenery provided points of ambush because civilians simply didn't get shit like that, so he dealt with it. It wasn't as if he had a lot to worry about; the crime rate in these units was very low, and was in fact a selling point for the young families who made up the majority of residents.

Still—habits were a bitch, but he couldn't ignore half a lifetime of training. To keep from walking around a blind corner, he swung wide into the street the way he always did so he was approaching straight on; there wasn't a lot of traffic in the condo development, and he didn't often have to wait until a car passed.

But even with a direct approach, he still didn't like it. Sometimes, such as now, he liked it less than at other times, and he couldn't have said why. He didn't have to; instinct was what it was.

He stopped in his tracks.

Sometimes . . . such as *now*.

The sudden surge of awareness was like an electric shock, sending all of his senses into hyperalert. He instinctively moved his right hand to the pistol snugged into the holster at the small of his back even as he tried to pick up any movement in the shrubbery that shouldn't have been there, anything that was responsible for making the back of his neck suddenly prickle. He couldn't see anything, but still his senses were screaming. *Something* was there, even if it wasn't anything danger—

The thought hadn't completely formed when the shadows of the shrubbery moved slightly, black on black. More adrenaline shot through his system, and Morgan acted without thought, training taking over as he dropped the plastic bags and dove to the left, leaving his right hand free as he pulled his weapon.

His body was still airborne, stretched out, when he saw a faint flash and a sledgehammer hit him in the chest.

He had two distant but clear thoughts: *Suppressor. Subsonic round.*

He slammed to the ground, the impact almost as jarring as the sledgehammer to the chest. He rolled with it, the pistol grip fitting into his palm as if his hand and the weapon had been made together, one functioning unit. One part of his brain knew he'd been hit and hit hard, but the other part stayed ruthlessly focused outward, intent on doing what he needed to do. He fired toward where he'd seen the flash, the sound sharp in the crisp night air, but he knew only a rank amateur would stay in the same place so he tracked his next shot away from the shrubbery, following the barely seen black-on-black shadow, and pulled the trigger again.

His mind disconnected from the shock waves of pain rolling through his body because that was the only way he could function. His thoughts raced, analyzing probabilities and angles of fire, selecting the best option even as adrenaline overrode the devastation and kept his body moving. Without being aware that he was moving, he rolled behind a fireplug, and didn't realize where he was until he was already there. A fireplug wasn't much cover, but it was some.

His vision was wavering, things rushing at him then drawing back, as if pushed and pulled by an invisible tide of air. Peripherally, he was aware of entrance lights coming on, of curtains being pulled back as his neighbors peeked out to see what the hell was going on. He blinked fiercely, trying to stay focused. Yes—the increase of light brought a man's form into dim view and he fired a third shot, controlled the upward kick of the muzzle, fired again. The dark form toppled to the ground and lay still.

God, his chest hurt. Shit. This had really fucked up his tattoo.

His vision wavered again, but he grimly held on, keeping his weapon trained on the downed threat.

"Down" didn't mean "out." If he let go, let the darkness come, the other guy might get up and finish the job. Dead didn't count until it was confirmed dead, and he couldn't confirm shit right now.

But doors were opening, people were shouting. The sounds were distorted and strangely far away, the lights fading. Through the growing shadows he thought he saw some of the braver souls venturing out, investigating the gunfire. Words swam at him, around him, and some of them sank into his consciousness.

"Shawn! Are you *crazy?*" A woman's voice, both angry and afraid.

"Just call the cops," said a man—maybe Shawn, maybe someone else.

"I already did," said a third voice.

"What the hell is going on?"

More noise, more voices added to the chorus as people began approaching, cautiously at first, then with more confidence when nothing else happened. Morgan tried to call out, say something, make any kind of noise, but the effort was beyond him. He could feel his breath hitching as the distant pain rolled closer, like a tidal wave that was about to swamp him.

This might be it for me, he thought, and was almost too tired to care. He tried to control his breathing because he'd heard that hitching sound before and it was never good. He didn't have to hang on long, he thought—maybe half an hour, if people would get the lead out of their asses and get him to the hospital. But half an hour seemed like an eternity when he wasn't certain he could hang on even one more minute.

He rested his head on the concrete sidewalk, feeling the chill of it. His outstretched hand was just resting on the winter-dead grass at the edge of the sidewalk and he had the distant thought that it was kind of nice to be touching the earth. If this was it for him, well, it sucked to go, but all in all this wasn't too bad, considering all the grisly ways he could have gone.

But, damn it, he was fucking *pissed* because if he died, he didn't know who had killed him or, more importantly, *why.*

Someone bent over him, a vague shape swimming out of focus. He had to send MacNamara a warning, and with his last ounce of strength he gasped out, "*Ambush.*"

Chapter 2

Consciousness—or the lack of it—was a strange thing, fading from one to the other and back again without a line of demarcation and without any direction by him. Sometimes he surfaced a few degrees from total nothingness to a vague and distant awareness of *being*, and the same vague and distant acknowledgment of the black nothing, and even knowing what it was, distinguishing between the two. Then he'd sink back down, and there was nothing until once again the tide of consciousness floated him upward like a piece of trash in the sea.

Once there were a lot of bright lights, and warmth, and a sense of well-being, but then that too vanished.

I'm not dead.

That was Morgan's first coherent thought. Though he'd occasionally been aware of other things: pain, noise, indecipherable voices—sometimes one he almost recognized—as well as an annoying beeping, none of that had really meant anything to him; they were simply there, at a distance, like a pinpoint of light at the top of a deep, dark well. There came a time, though, when he drifted high enough that he realized what it meant that he could feel the pain and hear the noises: he was alive.

Time was meaningless. People talked to him. He couldn't respond even when he could understand, but they seemed to know this. They handled his body, doing things to him, explaining every step of the way. Sometimes he didn't care, a lot of times he did, because, *hell*, some things just shouldn't be done to a man. Neither seemed to matter. They did what they came to do, and that was that.

Moving wasn't an option; he not only seemed incapable of it, he wasn't interested in trying. Simply existing took all of his strength. His lungs pumped at a strange rhythm that he couldn't control, there was a tube down his throat, and damn, maybe living wasn't such a good idea.

But dying was out of his control too. If he'd been given a choice, he might have stayed down in the darkness because whenever he surfaced, the pain was an ugly motherfucker that slapped him around and made it look easy. He'd have kicked the bastard's ass if he could have, but it won every battle. At other times the pain was more distant, as if a layer of wool protected him from it, but it was always *there*. Eventually, and laboriously, he decided the layer of wool was really drugs . . . maybe.

His only weapon against the pain was stubbornness. He didn't like losing. He fucking *hated* losing. A vestige of will, of sheer bullheaded stubbornness, made him focus on the pain; it was his target, his adversary, and he kept coming back for more. It might knock him down, but by God, it couldn't keep him down. Even when he felt like doing nothing more than howling in agony—if he'd been able to howl—he fought for awareness, for each increment of improvement.

On a very basic level, fighting was what he knew, what he was, so he fought everything. He didn't fight just for awareness; he fought the tube down his throat that kept him from talking, the needles in his arms that kept him—in his own mind, at least—from moving. They—the nameless *they*—promptly strapped him down so he couldn't move a muscle, not even his head.

Rage joined the pain. He was so damn mad he thought he might explode, and what made it even worse was that he had no way of expressing his absolute fury at being so helpless, while every inch of his body and all of his instincts were abused.

Then, exhausted, he would sleep—or sink into unconsciousness again. Maybe they were one and the same. He sure as hell couldn't tell the difference.

One day he opened his eyes and focused—actually *focused*—on the middle-aged woman who was standing beside him fiddling with the lines coming from multiple plastic bags hung on a metal tree. For the first time he thought, *Hospital,* which meant his torturers were actually taking care of him, but that didn't help his feelings. He put all of his animosity into the glare he leveled at her.

"Well, hello," she said, smiling. "How are you today?"

If he'd been able to talk he'd have told her exactly how he was, and his language wouldn't have been pretty.

She seemed to know exactly what he was thinking because her smile widened as she patted his shoulder. "The tube will come out pretty soon, then you can tell us all about it."

He tried to tell her all about it right then and managed only some faint grunting noises, then he humiliated himself by promptly going back to sleep.

When he woke again, he knew immediately where he was . . . kind of. Moving nothing but his eyes—because he fucking couldn't move anyfuckingthing else—he took stock of his surroundings. His vision was blurry, but he was trained to observe and analyze and after an indistinct length of time, he fuzzily came to the conclusion that though he was in a hospital bed with raised rails on each side, and he was obviously in some sort of facility, he definitely wasn't in a hospital. The room, for one thing—it was painted blue, there were curtains over the windows, and it had a regular door with a regular doorknob instead of the massive doors found in hospital rooms. It seemed to be an ordinary bedroom that had had a ton of medical equipment shoved into it and positioned however it would fit into the room.

Then there were the nurses—damn their sadistic hides—who tended him. They sometimes wore colorful uniforms, but sometimes not; the middle-aged woman who had been there the last time he woke up was always dressed in jeans and sneakers and a sweater, as if she'd just come in from a farm somewhere. Sometimes when his door was opened, he'd catch a glimpse of someone armed standing just outside, and it was never anyone he recognized.

All of his thoughts were blurred, his memories even worse. He had a *very* fuzzy memory of Axel MacNamara being there a couple of times when he'd awakened, asking insistent questions—not that MacNamara ever asked any other kind—but the best Morgan had been able to do was blink his eyes a few times and he wasn't sure what the hell he was blinking his eyes for, so eventually MacNamara went away.

But even as he fought through the fog of sedation and trauma, anger still burned deep and bright inside him. When he could think, he remembered what had happened, though the ambush kept getting mixed up with the aftermath and sometimes he'd have shot the nurses if he'd had a weapon in his hand. He couldn't formulate all the ramifications of his ambush, but he knew they had to be bad, and no matter how unfocused and helpless he was, he was still damned and determined to find out who had done this and what their goal was. A more naive and protected person might think the goal had simply been to kill him, but Morgan had stopped being naive somewhere around the age of three, and "protected" wasn't in his job description. Killing him had to have been part of a larger plan—the question was what plan, and who was behind it?

He could think that, but he couldn't communicate well enough to transmit. His helplessness was so galling he'd have wrecked the place if he'd been capable of moving, but the way he was strapped down, he couldn't even press the call button for the nurse—if he'd wanted to call, which he didn't, because whenever they showed up they did stuff he didn't like.

One day, though, when he woke up he felt as if he'd turned a corner. He didn't know which corner, but with it came a sense that his body had decided to live. The medical staff must have come to the same conclusion about his physical state of being. An hour or so later a doctor—he guessed the guy was a doctor, though hell, maybe he was someone they dragged in off the streets because he was wearing jeans and a flannel shirt—came in and cheerfully said, "Let's get that tube out of your throat, get you talking and drinking and eating. You ready? Cough, that'll make it easier."

One second Morgan was looking forward to having the tube out of his throat, and the next his body was in total rebellion against what was happening to it. *Bullshit!* The only thing that could have made it easier was if he'd been unconscious. It felt as if his lungs were being dragged out with the tube, and his chest was being hacked in two. His vision blurred and darkened, his body arched involuntarily, and if he'd been able to, he'd have done damage to the son of a bitch, because if that was "easy," then "hard" would have killed most people.

Then the tube was out and he was breathing on his own, shaking like a leaf in reaction and soaking wet with sweat, but at least he could talk—sort of. In theory, anyway. His throat felt as if it had been scrubbed with sandpaper, and his mouth wasn't in any better shape. It took him three tries to get out one raspy, almost inaudible word:

"Water."

"Sure thing." A smiling woman with salt-and-pepper hair poured some water into a cup and held the drinking straw to his mouth, and he managed to get some water down his raw throat. He could practically feel the membranes of his mouth absorbing the moisture, and he greedily sucked down two more swallows before she moved the cup away.

He gathered his strength for more words. "No more . . . dope." He needed his head clear. He wasn't sure exactly why, but instinct was driving him hard.

"Don't go too macho on us," she replied, still smiling. "Pain puts stress on your body and stress will slow down the healing. Let's reassess every day, okay?"

Meaning they were going to give him more dope whether he wanted it or not. He was fairly sure in a regular hospital his wishes couldn't be ignored, but this was obviously not a regular hospital. They were going to do whatever they thought needed doing, and he could just live with it. The pun wasn't lost on him. But then everything else was because, damn it, he went to sleep again.

The next time we woke up, Axel MacNamara was there.

The visit must have been timed to coincide with the downswing of effectiveness of whatever drugs they were giving him, because Morgan felt at least halfway alert. Yeah, MacNamara thought of things like that. The bastard planned everything, probably down to how long he chewed each bite of food.

Morgan wouldn't have said he was clearheaded, just that the mental fog wasn't as thick. He was clear enough to be aware of a vague sense of fear, one he couldn't analyze—hell, he could barely identify it. He'd trained himself to ignore fear's existence, settling instead on "alarm" as his fight-or-flight trigger. But now he was afraid, though he couldn't have said of what. Maybe it was that this fogginess, this sense of disconnect from everything except pain, would become permanent. Maybe the damage was too great to heal completely. Maybe this was his new reality. But—no. He could sense his own improvement, though from "near death" to "really shitty" wasn't that long a road.

To hide his unease, he said, "Hey," to MacNamara, then scowled because the word sounded mushy, his voice thin and weak. He shifted himself around, intending to reach for the foam cup sitting on the rolling table beside him, only to discover that he was still strapped down—and that pain meds on the decline also meant he had to deal with his shot-up and patched-together body that protested every movement. Both the pain and his helplessness pissed him off.

"Get these . . damn straps . . . off me," he rasped, anger lending some strength to his voice.

Axel didn't budge. "You gonna try to rip the IV lines out again?"

The idea was tempting, but he knew if he did, the straps would come back. He wanted to be in control of his body.

"No," he said grudgingly.

MacNamara deftly released him, then pressed the button that raised the head of the bed. Morgan got dizzy for a minute, but he took deep breaths and willed himself not to show any sissy-assed weakness such as passing out. He'd never live that down.

"You up to answering questions?" MacNamara asked in that abrupt way of his, no time wasted in pleasantries or even asking how Morgan was feeling.

Morgan kind of half-glared from bleary eyes, mainly because his default mood was that deep and festering rage. "Ask," he said, reaching again—this time with results—for the foam cup, which he sincerely hoped held some water. The movement was just short of agonizing; his chest felt as if someone were hacking at it with a cleaver. He ground his teeth together and kept stretching his arm out, partly because he was damned if he'd give in to the pain and partly because he really wanted that water.

Anyone else would have gotten the cup for him, but not MacNamara. Right now, Morgan appreciated the lack of sympathy; he wanted to do it himself. He closed his shaking hand around the cup and lifted it. There were a couple of inches of water in the cup and he sucked it dry, then fumbled the cup back onto the table. He sank back against the pillow, as exhausted as if he'd just finished a twenty-mile run.

"Do you remember what happened?"

"Yeah." Maybe he was mentally fuzzy, but he wasn't amnesiac.

MacNamara pulled a chair around and dropped into it. He was lean to the point of spareness, just a little above average height, but no one would ever mistake his lack of size as a lack of power. He was intense and ruthless, just the kind of guy the GO-Teams needed to watch their backs.

"Do you know who shot you?"

"No." Morgan drew a breath. "Do you?"

"He was Russian mob."

Morgan blinked, flummoxed as much as he was capable of being flummoxed. Russian? Mob? What the hell? He didn't have anything to do with the Russian mob. "No shit?"

"No shit."

"I don't know . . . anyone in the Russian mob." He'd started to say he didn't know any Russians, but remembered that he did in fact know a number of Russians— none of them in the mob, though. "What's his name?"

"Albert Rykov. Was. He's dead."

Good, Morgan thought. He didn't have a lot of forgiveness for people who shot him . . . none, in fact. "I've never heard of him." A sluggish thought occurred: "Maybe he was after someone else?"

"No." Axel's tone was flat, certain. He wasn't entertaining any doubt whatsoever.

"Why would the Russian mob target me?" That didn't make any sense at all. He scrubbed his hand over his face, felt the rasp of whiskers even though he had a vague memory of one of the nurses shaving him at one time or another . . . maybe. Then he stared in shock at his own hand, at how thin and almost translucent it was, not like his hand at all though he knew it was because it was attached to the end of his arm . . . which also looked freakishly thin. For a minute he fought a sense of disconnection, fought to bring his thoughts back on track. What had they been talking about? Right—the Russians.

"They didn't. Rykov was attached to the mob, but this looks like an independent hit. Someone outside hired it done."

In that case, the possibilities were legion because he still couldn't think why anyone would want him dead, which theoretically left the world's entire population in play.

"Walk me through everything that happened after you reached stateside," Axel said, leaning back and crossing his arms.

"I debriefed"—he figured that was already known, given that Axel would have all the paperwork— "grabbed a bite to eat at a McDonald's, went home, took a shower, and went to sleep. Slept a full twenty-four. Then I worked on my gear, took a run in the dark, came home, went back to sleep." The simple statements were punctuated by pauses to catch his breath.

"Anything happen at the McDonald's? Or during your run? Who did you talk to?"

"No, no, and no one, other than the cashier who handed my order out the drive-through window."

"Did you recognize the cashier?"

"No. It was some kid."

"Did you see anything inside the restaurant?"

"No." He was sure of that because he remembered being a little uneasy by his restricted line of sight. After a mission, it always took a while to decompress and ease out of combat mode.

"Then what?"

Morgan blew out a breath, tried to whip up his rapidly flagging energy—not that he'd had much to begin with. He was so weak he didn't recognize his own body, which made him feel even more disconnected than maybe was accounted for by the drugs. "When I woke up, I wanted to go fishing. I called Kodak but he was otherwise occupied, so I went alone."

Axel nodded. Morgan figured he already knew that, just as he'd known about the debriefing. "Did you talk to anyone?"

"Congresswoman Kingsley and her husband. They were on the river."

"Anyone with them?"

"No, they were by themselves."

"Anyone else?"

"Not to talk to." A memory niggled at him. "Brawley—the marina manager—said hello."

Axel was a master at reading nuances of expression. "And . . . ?"

Until he heard the "and," Morgan hadn't been aware there *was* an "and." He took a deep breath, cut it short when the pain in his chest cut into him. "Could be coincidence, but he made a call after talking to me."

"How soon after?"

"Immediately."

"Cell phone?" If Brawley had used a cell, Axel could use the time and the cell towers to get a bead on the possible call recipients.

"No." Very clearly, Morgan saw in his mind the old-fashioned corded phone Brawley had used. "Corded landline."

"Shit." Frustration was clear in the word. Getting the info wasn't impossible, but it would require a warrant. Technology would let them bypass that little detail if the call had been made on a cell.

But, regardless of the phone call, Morgan couldn't think of any way Brawley would know where he lived or, more importantly, *why* he would need to set up a hit.

The effort to sit up and answer questions was wearing on him hard. He didn't have much more juice left in him. "No reason," he muttered, letting his head drop back. His eyes closed automatically, and he fought them open again.

"What?" Axel demanded.

Morgan focused, laboriously reconstructed his thoughts. "No reason for Brawley," he finally said, or thought he said. Maybe his mouth wasn't working. His eyes closed again. But he didn't care because darkness was rising up and swallowing him whole, and there was nothing he could do to stop it.

The next time he saw Axel, Morgan was actually sitting up under his own power. It was almost three weeks since he'd been shot; he knew because he'd asked. Sitting up wasn't all he could do. Twice a day for the last couple of days he'd taken a few steps across the small room, bracketed on each side by nurses so he didn't face-plant. He was eating halfway-solid food now, and he'd never before in his life been so grateful for mashed potatoes, or oatmeal. He didn't even like oatmeal. Tomorrow, they'd told him, he could have eggs. He'd requested steak with those eggs, and they'd laughed at him. Hands down they were the meanest nurses he'd ever been around.

Even more disturbing, he was beginning to love them.

He didn't know how long it had been since Axel had been there, but he figured it was about a week. The only surprising thing was that Axel hadn't been there every day to badger more details out of him.

Sometimes Axel's persistent nitpicking was a pain in the ass, but now Morgan would have welcomed it because he wanted to get the bastard or bastards who had set up the ambush. It was typical of Axel that he'd chosen that time to stay away.

"About time," Morgan said by way of greeting.

"I've been busy, running down details and setting things up."

"What things? What details?"

"That's what I'm here to tell you," Axel snapped as he dropped into the visitor's chair.

Being snapped at was good; if Axel had tried to be kind—with emphasis on the word "tried," because he'd never really succeed—Morgan would have suspected he wasn't recovering as well as a few steps and mashed potatoes would indicate.

"So, talk."

"You were located by your boat registration. We've found where someone hacked into state records and got your info off your registration form."

There was something wrong with that. Morgan said, "I use my post office box as my mailing address."

"Yes, but the form also includes your Virginia driver's license number and your social security number. Those were both traced, and that's how they got your address."

"The big question is why."

"Yeah. But there's another wrinkle, one that's even more serious."

It was almost amusing that Axel would think something was more serious than one of his operatives being targeted. Well, given that he dealt with global issues, he was probably right; Morgan had to give him that.

"When you were first brought in, we didn't know what was going on, if an orchestrated attack was being made on GO-Team members or if another attempt would be made on you personally. I loaded up the hospital with men to guard your ass, but the logistics were a nightmare, too many stairwells and elevators, too many people coming and going. As soon as you were halfway stable, I had you loaded up and brought here. I'm the only one who knows where you are."

"Other than the people who transported me here."

"I changed transport teams three times."

Yeah, that was Axel, paranoid and cautious to a maddening degree. "So what's this new wrinkle that has you worried?"

"The GO-Team files were hacked after I had you moved."

Shit. Morgan frowned, working it through. Obviously, whoever had tried to kill him was still after him. Just as obviously, whoever it was knew what he did.

"It's the security breach that worries me more than anything," Axel said, and Morgan stifled a wry smile. Yeah, the loss of one of his men would definitely rank below security in his book. "After I had you moved, I let it be known that you had some memory problems but were recovering, and the doctors saw no reason why you wouldn't regain all your memories."

That was cold, even for Axel. Morgan growled, "Well, hell, why not just paint a target on my back?"

"The target's already there," Axel pointed out. "My job is to find out who and why. Unless you're fucking someone else's wife, the strong possibility exists that this is work related."

"I'm clear on the domestic front."

"Then it's related to the GO-Teams."

There was no arguing with that. Still—Morgan shook his head. "But *why*?"

"If I can figure that out, then I'll know *who*. And vice versa. All I need is something to point me in the right direction."

"So what's your plan?" Because Axel always had a plan; Morgan might not like it, but he had no doubt the plan existed.

Axel said, "I'm going to bury your location under enough security that whoever wants to find you will really have to dig to find it, and that'll trip an alert I've had set up. But I can't make it easy to find, or whoever it is will know it's a setup and won't bite."

"That's it? What do I do in the meantime?" Other than work at being able to walk for longer than thirty seconds at a time, that is.

What could only be described as a truly evil smile spread over Axel's face. "I'm sending you to my ex-stepsister."

Whatever Morgan had expected, that wasn't it. "What?"

Axel obligingly repeated himself, word for word.

"You're involving civilians?" That was what startled him the most. What they did was kept away from normal people, though of course there was civilian support staff, but they had signed on knowing what the work involved. Deliberately throwing innocents into danger wasn't something they did.

"I don't expect any real problems. I've been doing some digging, getting things set up. No reason any civilians should be involved, other than her giving you a place to stay."

"And your ex-stepsister has agreed to this?"

"She will," Axel said carelessly. "Once the alert is tripped, we'll move in."

"The alert won't tell you *who*."

"It'll give me a direction, but best of all, I'll be able to put some people in place to catch any threat coming after you."

"How in hell will you do that?"

Axel ticked off the reasons. "It's a very small town, small enough that any strangers will be noticed. It's relatively close to D.C., in West Virginia, which means no airports or trains or bus lines involved; whoever comes after you will come by road, and the number of roads I'd have to cover is very limited." He paused and gave what could only be described as a satisfied sigh. "And best of all, it'll really piss her off."

Axel MacNamara didn't give a shit about most people and most things, but he did give a shit about his country and the operatives on the GO-Teams he oversaw. Every mission they went on, they put their lives on the line, and he not only respected that but he was sworn, both professionally and privately, to do his best for them regardless of the context. Sometimes it was fighting tooth and nail to make sure they had the best equipment available, sometimes it was smoothing the political way, sometimes it was polishing and spinning certain events so pertinent details were either distorted or hidden completely. They did the jobs they were tasked with doing, and if any shit rolled downhill, he wanted it to stop at the people in charge, not the men he regarded as his.

Generally he hated politicians, but he was a lot like them and by the very nature of his job had to associate with them.

It was a bunch of bullshit, but he played the game.

The situation with Morgan Yancy was worrisome—not because of the threat to Morgan's life, though he would hate to lose such a skilled operative—but because the GO-Teams computer system had been hacked. Their missions were highly classified and extremely sensitive politically.

He had to move very cautiously; if he was too obvious, he might frighten off his prey. If he wasn't obvious enough, the wrong conclusions could be drawn and the bait ignored. That was why he dropped a few tidbits of information here and there, but never much at any one time, and sometimes he didn't say anything at all.

A few days after talking to Morgan and laying out the basics of the plan, he managed to maneuver himself into position at one of D.C.'s endless parties, where Congresswoman Joan Kingsley was in attendance. Her husband, Dexter, was absent, but she had navigated the capital's social waters for so long that she was perfectly comfortable on her own. As politicians went, she was very likable—even to him, and he didn't like anyone. He tolerated her much better than he did a lot of others, though he never let himself forget that she was a politician first and an ally second, even if Morgan's team *had* saved her son's ass. Gratitude went only so far in D.C.

Inevitably, she and her husband were both on the list of suspects. They'd had contact with Morgan that day.

Maybe she was clear and her husband wasn't, or vice versa. Maybe they were both clear, or both guilty—he didn't give them the benefit of the doubt because he didn't *know* and therefore assumed they were both guilty. Regardless, Congresswoman Kingsley had contacts and avenues of information, both going and coming, that he himself didn't have, and she was a good conduit for getting out the word that he wanted out.

He didn't approach her, though she was very easy to spot with that striking white hair. She made a practiced circuit of the crowded room, chatting with everyone, smiling the warm smile that charmed almost everyone she met. Axel was immune to charm. He started every day assuming most people were up to no good and the others simply hadn't thought of it yet.

At one point he lost sight of her—though he was careful not to let her know he was watching—but she reappeared in about ten minutes with freshly applied lipstick, so his best guess was a trip to the ladies' room. She could also have been meeting a lover, exchanging information, or making a private call. Without any evidence to the contrary, though, he was going with the ladies' room theory.

They were an hour and a half into the party when their circuitous routes around the room brought them together. He tilted his glass toward her in acknowledgment but didn't interrupt his current conversation with a senator's aide even though it was deadly boring and he'd have liked to cram a pair of dirty socks down the pompous jackass's throat. Let her come to him. He wasn't approaching anyone.

Finally the senator's aide paused when he stopped a passing waiter to deposit his empty glass on the man's tray. Congresswoman Kingsley smoothly slid in and said, "Hello, Karl, Axel."

"Congresswoman," Axel replied in acknowledgment, and watched in amusement as the senator's aide struggled with his ego and the pecking order on Capitol Hill. The congresswoman was an important personage, but Karl looked on the House as inferior to the Senate; therefore his position as chief aide to a senator *should* be superior to hers. Then his ego butted into the unfortunate fact that Congresswoman Kingsley had been elected—several times over—while he was a hired aide who hadn't been elected to anything..

"Congresswoman Kingsley," Karl finally muttered, using her title while she'd used his first name. Oh, the slings and arrows, Axel mused.

She gave Karl one of those smiles and said, "Would you excuse us? I'd like to discuss a few details with Axel."

There was nothing Karl could do except say, "Of course," and take himself away.

Axel sipped his drink—sparkling water on the rocks because when you were wading in a pool of sharks, you needed all your wits about you—and waited for her to steer the conversation in the direction she wanted, though he did paste a faintly questioning expression on his face.

"I heard something disturbing," she said, pitching her voice low so only he could hear her.

He gave a slight lift of his eyebrows that invited her to continue.

"I heard Morgan was killed."

"Not so," he promptly replied.

Relief flickered in her eyes. "Thank God. But—was he hurt? My source was very specific about the victim's name."

He'd like to know exactly who her source was, but he didn't waste time trying to dig that info out of her. She was a seasoned veteran of the dance.

"He was shot—and I won't lie, it was serious. But I have him in a protected location while he recovers."

"What happened?"

"Assassination attempt. The problem is he can't tell me why."

"He doesn't *know*?"

Axel rocked his hand back and forth. "He thinks he does. He suffered a serious concussion and he's having a few memory problems, but he says he knows what's going on if he can just remember it. There isn't any permanent brain damage, and the doc says that he'll remember when all the swelling is gone."

"For goodness' sake! When will that be?"

"No definite date, everyone heals differently. He has pneumonia now and that's a setback, but the docs say he's already getting better. I'm thinking a few months, most likely, before he's back to normal."

"That must be difficult, being grounded until then. I don't know him as well as you do, but I suspect he isn't a good patient."

"Understatement," Axel said.

"I'm so glad he'll be all right. We'd all be devastated if anything happened to him. Give him our best when you see him."

"I will," he replied, holding back the information that he wouldn't be seeing Morgan at all until and if his trap was sprung. He'd spread these seeds of information in several venues around town; now he had to wait and see if any of them sprouted. Morgan had been targeted for a reason; that reason *had* to be rooted in something he'd seen or done that day. Maybe the threat he was looking for was several layers deep, not Congresswoman Kingsley herself, or Brawley, or even Kodak, but someone who knew them. He wouldn't know until someone acted.

Chapter 3

Chief of police Isabeau Maran looked up from an annoying pile of paperwork as the door to the police station opened, letting in a brisk dose of early spring air. Her golden retriever, Tricks, was snoozing on a comfy fleece bed on the floor beside the desk, but at the disturbance the dog opened her eyes and lifted her beautifully shaped golden head. She didn't thump her tail in welcome because this was Tricks, and she didn't know who was coming through the door; therefore, she wouldn't waste the effort until she knew whether or not the new arrival was worthy of a welcome.

Bright sunshine glared on the worn tile and Bo narrowed her eyes against it as Daina Conner carefully stepped inside. The intruder's identity established, Tricks gave her tail two thumps, which signaled a moderate degree of pleasure but not enough to bring her to her feet, then lowered her head back onto her paws to resume her nap.

"What's up?" Not that Bo wasn't glad to see Daina, because there weren't *that* many unattached women roughly her own age in Hamrickville, West Virginia, but they usually did their socializing outside the police station. They looked like polar opposites: Daina was curvy and blond and blue-eyed, Bo was dark-haired and dark-eyed, and the only curves she owned were in her driveway. But they both enjoyed the same type of movies, liked the same jokes, and had each other's back.

"I had one beer too many at lunch," Daina announced, plopping her butt into the cracked and duct-tape-patched chair across from Bo's desk. Her stylish blond hair flopped over her eyes and she carelessly pushed it back. "I don't have another appointment until three, so I thought, what better place to sober up than here? I can have some coffee, chat with you, then you can give me a Breathalyzer after a while and tell me whether or not I'm okay to drive." Daina owned the local beauty shop, The Chop Shop, a couple of miles out on the main road into town. It was a short enough drive that Bo thought it wasn't fear of driving while tipsy that had brought Daina by, but rather a way of killing time until her next appointment.

Which meant she could kiss good-bye the idea of making any real headway on the paperwork, Bo thought as she pushed back from her desk and went to the Mr. Coffee sitting on top of a double-drawer filing cabinet in the corner, which was located there for the sole reason that there was an electrical outlet behind the cabinet. There was about half an inch of dark sludge left in the carafe from . . . this morning, maybe. Hard to tell. It had been there when she arrived a little after noon, so for all she knew, it could have been there since yesterday afternoon.

She took the carafe into the bathroom, dumped out the sludge, rinsed, then ran fresh water. Coming back into the main office, she began the process of making coffee. "So who were you having beers with?" she asked, not bothering to point out that if she were a real stickler about things, she'd arrest Daina for public intoxication because obviously she *wasn't* a stickler. From her point of view, it wasn't as if Daina was staggering drunk, and she'd done the responsible thing by *not* driving and electing to come here instead. Bo's philosophy was don't bitch about what works.

"Kenny Michaels. I've decided to go ahead with remodeling the kitchen, and we were going over what I want, paint colors—my gawd, I think I've looked at a gajillion paint chips. Stuff like that."

"So what colors did you decide on?" While the coffee was brewing, Bo stepped into the so-called break room—it was originally just a large closet—stocked with a refrigerator, microwave, tiny table, and two chairs squeezed into the space. She opened the top freezer compartment of the avocado-green refrigerator, which of course refused to ever give up the ghost the way any decent-colored refrigerator would have, and took out a pint of ice cream. Well, it had originally been a whole pint, but now it was down to half that. She didn't know if Daina liked vanilla ice cream; tough cookies because it was all she had. She levered off the top, found a spoon, stuck it in the ice cream, and set the cardboard carton in front of her friend. "Eat."

Absently Daina obeyed, her thoughts elsewhere. "A sort of pewter-ish gray, with a grayish blue," she replied, still on the color theme. "Not very kitcheny, but that's the whole idea. I don't want anything that stimulates my appetite or makes food look good. I want something calm and soothing . . . you know, so I'll stay away from it." She stopped, pulled the spoon from her mouth and stared at it. "The hell? This is ice cream," she said, frowning down at the carton as if she had no idea how it had come to be in her hand.

"Five points for observation powers." Bo resumed her seat. "Kenny Michaels, huh? He's kind of cute."

And he was, in a construction, hammer-hanging-from-a-loop-on-his-pants kind of way. Not tall, but not short, a muscular kind of stocky. Divorced, late thirties, one son who was a senior in high school. She didn't know anything bad about him, which meant there probably wasn't anything bad to know.

"Of course. Why else would I renovate my kitchen? And why am I eating ice cream?" Daina still looked perplexed, but she dug the spoon in and lifted a bite to her mouth. "Not that I'm complaining, but I just had dessert at lunch."

"It helps sober you up."

Daina's eyes went wide. "No shit." Awestruck, she lifted the carton and stared at it again. "A legitimate reason for eating ice cream? There *is* a God!"

At that moment Tricks was evidently struck by the abrupt realization that someone in the room was *eating,* and it wasn't her, because she surged to her feet and planted herself directly in front of Daina, her extravagantly plumy tail gently swishing, her dark gaze locked on the carton of ice cream.

Daina froze with another bite halfway to her mouth. "Oh my God," she breathed, as motionless as if she were being confronted by a cobra rather than a golden retriever. "What do I do?"

Bo hid her amusement. "Tell her no. She can't have ice cream."

"No?" Daina said weakly, her tone of voice making it more of a question than a statement. Tricks sensed an advantage and moved closer, laying her head on Daina's knee and giving her the full, soulful stare that had turned rough men, much less a half-drunk friend, to putty in her paws.

Bo sighed. You couldn't give in to Tricks because she then concluded that if she just kept after you long enough, you'd eventually give in, and she was relentless in her efforts to get what she wanted. "Tricks, no," she commanded. When Tricks didn't move, she said, "Young lady, I said *no*." She clapped her hands twice. "Go back to your bed right now."

Reluctantly, Tricks moved away, her expression as mutinous as that of a thwarted toddler, but she padded back to her bed and lay down with a huff . . . and with her back turned toward Bo to show her indignation.

Bo barely swallowed a snort of laughter. Dealing with a canine diva—moreover, a very intelligent diva—was never boring and definitely kept her on her toes. She was the only person Tricks would obey when it didn't suit her, which meant Bo pretty much had a constant companion. She didn't mind; she adored her dog, though during that first tumultuous year she'd often felt like tearing out her own hair in frustration. As alpha as Tricks was, Bo had had to prove over and over that she was even more alpha, and only the fact that she controlled the food had won the day.

Daina hurriedly downed more ice cream. "She scares me," she confessed.

"Yeah, that's why you're down on the floor playing with her so often."

"I didn't say I don't love her. I said she scares me. If she lived with me, I'd be her slave."

"Probably." Reluctantly, Bo turned her attention back to the stack of papers on her desk. "Do you want to take a nap, or do you want to interrupt me while I'm trying to wade through this paperwork?"

"Anything I can help you with? Read reports and give you the gist of them so you can put your initials at the bottom?"

"You're tipsy. Would your gists be reliable?"

The coffeemaker was making the sputtering and spitting noises that signaled it was near the end of its process, so she poured some into a polystyrene cup and pushed it toward Daina. Daina said, "I like sugar and cream in my coffee."

So did Bo, but somehow the supplies of both tended to disappear and she'd learned to soldier on without if she had to. "So put some ice cream in it. Problem solved."

"Good point." Carefully Diana put a healthy dollop of ice cream in the hot coffee and took a cautious sip. She considered the taste, then tipped her head and said, "Not bad." After that judgment, she added two more dollops and likely would have emptied the rest of the carton into the cup if it wouldn't have made the coffee spill over the sides. "Why are you still doing paperwork, anyway? Isn't everything computerized?"

Bo glanced at the old-fashioned monitor sitting on her desk. "Kind of. Maybe. On some days." The antique—meaning it was over ten years old—computer system desperately needed updating, but paying the policemen ranked higher on the scale, something she agreed with. She could get by with doing real paperwork, and take some of it home to do on her own computer system, as long as the guys had a fairly decent salary, dependable vehicles, and the equipment they needed. She and Hamrickville had an unconventional but symbiotic relationship going, so she wasn't going to scream about getting a new computer.

She switched the topic back to Daina. "So, this thing with Kenny Michaels—are you seriously interested?"

"I could be." Daina drank some of her ice cream coffee. "But not yet. I'm still in the intrigued stage."

Still lying with her back to them, Tricks let out a long moan that hovered about halfway between a whine and a gripe. Daina froze again, her expression guilty as she stared at the dog. "Ignore her," Bo said. "She's telling on me for not letting her pester you."

"Who's she telling?"

"You. You're her only hope. If she can make you cave, she figures she'll get some ice cream before I step in and stop it."

"How about if I just give her one little bite to make her happy—"

"No."

"Just one—"

"*No*. This is Tricks. Do you know what that would do? You'd never again be able to eat in her presence, anything, period. She'd be in your lap. I'd have to lock her in another room, and then *I'd* be mad at you."

Another long moan. The dog sounded as if her heart had been broken. Daina gave Bo a pleading look. Bo said, "Don't make me lock you up."

"Oh, all right. But you could at least give her one of her own tr—" She started to say the word "treats," but stopped in mid-word at the fierce glare Bo gave her. Tricks understood a lot of words, and that particular word would have her on her feet looking for what she considered the promised goodie. Even worse, after hearing the word spelled a couple of times, Tricks had figured out what was being spelled, so she couldn't be fooled that way. "Sorry," Daina said again, wincing. "I forgot. Say, have you ever thought about having her tested? I'm pretty sure she's, like, a doggie genius, or something."

"I know she is, and no, I'm not having her tested. Why would I? It isn't as if it would get her into a better college."

Daina laughed, leaning back in her chair and digging into the remaining ice cream. "I think she'd do well. Look, put me to work. Until I'm sober enough to drive back to the shop, the least I can do is help you out. Nothing's confidential, is it?"

"No, everything here is a matter of public record."

"Well, shit. There goes my motivation."

Bo laughed and went back to reading while Daina finished both the ice cream and the coffee. Even with the interruptions of occasional conversation, she made a sizable dent in the stack of papers. The interruption she couldn't ignore—but thank goodness it came just as she finished—was when Tricks got up, fetched her tennis ball, then patted Bo's knee with one of those big paws. Actually, it was more like a swat than a pat.

"Time for a walk, princess?" She rubbed behind the silky ears, then stood. "Want to walk with us?" she asked Daina, who checked the time on her cell phone.

"Sure, why not? How far are you planning to walk?"

"About half a mile."

"Half a mile!" Her friend skidded to a halt, looking dismayed. "How long will that take?"

Bo hid her amusement. She walked Tricks several times a day, so half a mile was nothing to her. To Daina, however, who thought walking from her car into the shop was all the effort she should expend—and who was wearing platform heels—half a mile likely seemed unreasonable.

"Fifteen, twenty minutes, depending on how much nosing around Tricks does."

"No can do. Sorry. Get your trusty Breathalyzer and see if I'm okay to drive."

Bo would almost have guaranteed that she was, but in the unlikely event Daina had an accident, the town would be liable, so she paused to do exactly as requested. Tricks didn't take kindly to the delay and swatted her several more times, then butted her leg.

"All right!" she said to the dog. "Hold your horses." She checked the display and told Daina, "You're good." Another head butt knocked her leg sideways. "Okay, okay, I'm coming. You must really need to pee."

Daina left and Bo locked the door behind her, then took Tricks out the back way. Tricks immediately dropped her ball at Bo's feet and took off running.

Taking the hint, Bo threw the ball as hard as she could—which, after two years of training, was a decent distance. Thanks to having a dog who loved chasing a ball, she had nice throwing muscles. Tricks caught the ball on the first bounce and immediately paused, posing with her head lifted in a beauty-queen tilt, waiting for the praise she expected when she made a good catch. "Perfect! That's a beautiful catch!" Bo called. With a wag of her tail, Tricks abandoned the pose and trotted back, joy in every line of her body. Despite Trick's insistence that she needed to pee, Bo had to throw the ball three more times before the dog finally squatted and did her business.

Bo dug her keys out of her pocket and unlocked her seven-year-old red Jeep Wrangler. Tricks bounded up into the passenger seat and happily waited until Bo had buckled her special doggie-harness seat belt.

As she was leaving the parking lot, her second-in-command and the true heart and soul of the police department, Jesse Tucker, pulled in and stopped his squad car beside Bo's Jeep. Both of them lowered their windows so they could talk.

She hung an elbow out the window and squinted against the afternoon sun, which was shining directly into her eyes. "I'm finished with the paperwork," she said. "Unless something has come up, I'm going home to do some work there." She was a freelance technical writer, and that was where the bulk of her income came from.

"Everything's as quiet as it ever is," he replied. "Weather report said it's going to turn cold again tonight, maybe some snow."

"I'm keeping my fingers crossed we dodge this one."

Spring wasn't in a hurry, that was for certain. Starting in February they'd had the occasional bright, warm(ish) day like today, giving everyone hope that they'd seen the end of snow for this year, but despite the calendar saying it was spring, they hadn't turned that corner yet. Snow wasn't unheard of in April, and her day would be the same regardless of what the weather did; that didn't stop her from feeling disgruntled.

"I'll check in before I head home," he said, which he always did anyway. He pulled the squad car into a parking slot, and Bo pulled out onto Hamrickville's main street, which was named Broad instead of Main. Several people waved at her as she passed: Harold Patterson in the Broad Street Barbershop, Doris Brown as she entered the bakery she owned and operated, as well as Mayor Buddy Owenby, who was walking well now after having broken his ankle this past December while deer hunting. The mayor kept curtailed hours, too; his was a part-time job like hers, and he owned the small grocery store that served the town. Bo was fond of Mayor Buddy; he'd served four terms and was in large part responsible for keeping the little town as viable as it was. It had been his idea to turn over running the town as much as possible to the younger generation, thereby keeping them involved and, most of all, *there*. Hamrickville hadn't seen a large drain of its younger citizens toward greener pastures.

As many people as waved to her, twice that many waved to Tricks. She knew who they were waving to because they yelled, "Tricks!" as the Jeep rolled by. It seemed as if everyone in town knew her pet. For her part, Tricks sat in the passenger seat with her tongue lolling out and a big, happy golden-retriever smile on her face. For all her diva ways, Tricks had the typical retriever nature, sunny, without a lick of dignity, and always ready to play.

Several miles out of town, Bo took a secondary road and drove a couple more miles before she reached her driveway. Her mailbox was on the opposite side of the road so she drove past the driveway, checked for any traffic either behind her or in front of her before swerving onto the right shoulder to give herself a wider turning axis, then left across both lanes of the road to pull onto the opposite shoulder just short of the mailbox. She'd performed that maneuver so often there was a crescent-shaped track worn out in the shoulder on both sides of the road.

The mailbox was set far enough off the pavement and the shoulder was wide enough that other vehicles had plenty of room to get past. And if anyone didn't like it—well, tough shit; she was the chief of police, and even though she lived in the county instead of inside town limits, no one in the sheriff's department was going to hassle her over something as mundane as how she collected her mail. She didn't get a whole lot of perks with the job, but she'd gladly use the ones she did.

She put the transmission in park and got out, tugging hard on the door of the battered mailbox because it was slightly warped from being attacked by a couple of teenagers with a baseball bat. She pulled out the usual assortment of sales papers, flyers, a bill or two, and one thick oversized envelope that didn't have a return address. *Huh.* Bo eyed the envelope, examining the postage—just the right amount, a post-office sticker rather than extra stamps—and the location and date. It had been mailed three days before from New York City.

Double huh. She didn't know anyone in New York City—or state, for that matter.

Common sense told her a mail bomb would come in a box, not an envelope, even if she had any reason to

be wary of a mail bomb, which she didn't. Hamrickville wasn't exactly a hotbed of crime, or of anything
else.

She flipped the envelope over and looked at the
back. Blank. The envelope was a heavy cream-colored
paper, about the size for a largish birthday card. And it
was definitely addressed to her, using her formal name
of Isabeau instead of just Bo.

It wasn't her birthday. Nowhere close.

A pickup truck blew past with a *toot-toot* of the
horn and a wave: Sam Higgins, school bus driver. She
returned the wave, then curiosity got the better of her
and she put the rest of the mail on the Jeep's hood so
she could open the envelope.

The card she extracted did indeed say *Happy Birthday*. In full, it said *Happy Birthday to a Wonderful
Sister*. What the hell? She had a couple of half-brothers
and/or -sisters whom she'd never met; she considered
herself an only and liked it that way. It had to be a case
of mistaken identity, but how many Isabeau Marans
could there be? There was only one in Hamrickville,
West Virginia, that was for certain.

She opened the card. Glued to the interior was a
small photograph of someone she definitely recognized,
because a shit turd was always recognizable as what he
was even though it had been years since she'd seen him

and with luck it would be many more, as in the-rest-of-her-life more.

Underneath the photo was written, "Hope you enjoy the present I sent. Take good care of it." There was no signature, but she didn't need one.

"You didn't send me a present, you asshole!" she snarled at the photo. Even if he had, she'd have burned it.

As soon as she had that thought, a small yellowish flame flashed across the card. She yelped and dropped it; the whole thing turned black and dissipated into thin ash before she could even stomp on it. She stomped anyway, just for good measure. Just thinking about her asshole former stepbrother could make her temper flash almost like whatever chemical he'd used to treat the card. If that thing had dropped into her lap she could have been incinerated too—not that he'd have cared. He'd always thought crap like this was funny.

She didn't know why she'd been so abandoned by good fortune that he'd get in contact with her now, after all these years—if a flash-burning card could be called "contact"—but he'd succeeded in putting her in a foul mood. She was so angry she stomped the ashes another couple of times.

Breathing hard, she looked down at the ashes. If she could have gotten her hands on him, she'd have tried to strangle him. He'd always had that effect on her. She'd had the same effect on him. It had been mutual hate at first sight when her mother had married his father, but thank God the union hadn't lasted very long. If it had, she had no doubt that either she or Axel would now be in prison for murder. Well, that was the past, even if the jerk had for some ungodly reason thought sending her a booby-trapped birthday card was funny. How in hell had he known where she was, anyway? It wasn't as if they'd kept in touch.

She grabbed the remainder of the mail and slammed into the Jeep. Tricks immediately sensed the change in her and gave her a quick, sympathetic lick on the hand as Bo refastened her seat belt. "Everything's fine," she said, rubbing behind Tricks's left ear. And it was. The jerk's lunatic card had made her mad, but it was just a card and she'd already indulged in a mini–temper tantrum. That was enough; he didn't deserve the effort of more.

After checking for traffic—none—she pulled across the road to her driveway, which cut through a stretch of woods, curving up and away from the road; the house was a half mile away, perched on the flat top of a small rise and hidden from view from the road. She had no close neighbors; the nearest house was a mile back down the road toward town. The isolation of her home wasn't ideal, but she hadn't had any other option so she dealt with it. At least she had plenty of room for Tricks to romp and play, and that wasn't a small thing.

It was a pleasant drive; she'd become accustomed to it and even enjoyed a sense of homecoming now. For a few years she'd resented having to live here, resented the havoc the housing crash had caused in her life and her plans, but after a while she'd become more philosophical about it. She had her own share of blame in the state of affairs, after all. If she'd taken others' advice, she wouldn't have been landed in the predicament of sinking all her funds in a house and then having the buyer walk away, leaving her broke with a house she didn't want and couldn't sell.

That house she hadn't wanted was now home. She was comfortable there, even though hands-down she would have preferred a condo in a city. The lemons-to-lemonade theory had given her friends, a surprising sense of belonging, and Tricks. She glanced at the dog and had to smile at the expression of bliss on the furry face. Tricks loved riding anywhere, but she knew she was going home; she recognized the routine with the mailbox, and the drive. Home meant comfort and familiarity and all her toys, as well as a late-afternoon romp and then supper.

Bo rounded the last curve, and the house came into view. An unfamiliar vehicle, a new-looking black Chevy Tahoe, was sitting in the driveway. She stopped the Jeep, then had a horrifying thought: My God, what if *Axel* had come to visit and that nasty surprise card was his way of announcing himself? She narrowed her eyes; if it *was* Axel, he could leave the same way he got here, and the sooner the better. He wasn't welcome in her home.

But it wasn't Axel who slowly exited the SUV. A quick look was all she needed to know this was a stranger, a tall man with somewhat shaggy dark hair. She reached into the glove compartment and pulled out the pistol Jesse had insisted she get. Beside her, Tricks's attention was riveted on the stranger, and she gave an excited "Woof!" She was leaning against her harness, eager to exit the Jeep. In her world, strangers were someone new to play with her.

Bo's world wasn't as optimistic. She didn't turn off the ignition, in case she needed to get away fast; instead she lowered the window and called out, "May I help you?" The words were courteous; the tone was the one Jesse had taught her to use, louder than a woman would normally speak, and more authoritative.

The man put his arm on top of the SUV. "Are you Isabeau Maran?"

"I am." The fact that he knew her name didn't mean she was any less cautious. Besides, he looked like a ghoul, with a dead-white face and sunken eyes ringed with dark circles.

He wiped a hand across his face. "My name is Morgan Yancy. Your stepbrother sent me to you."

Chapter 4

I don't have a stepbrother," she said flatly, completely unappeased by the obvious conclusion that this man was the "present" Axel had sent. She didn't know what he'd meant by that and didn't care. She wasn't having anything to do with Axel or his present—not that this guy looked like any kind of present other than a gag gift, and she wasn't laughing.

"Axel MacNamara," he clarified. His voice sounded funny, kind of thin and breathless. He was a big guy— tall, anyway, because his head was well above the top of the SUV, so the thin voice was out of place.

"I know who you were talking about. Doesn't matter."

"He said you'd feel that way." The man looked around, his gaze moving slowly from object to object as if it was an effort to move even his eyes. She got the impression he was buying time more than anything else. Suddenly she realized that he didn't look ghoulish, he looked *unhealthy.* A sheen of sweat coated his face though the day was too cool to warrant sweating from just sitting in a car.

"He was right."

Then something clicked in her brain, and Bo narrowed her eyes, studying him. People who were sick and weak had that thinness to their voices, as if they didn't have the strength to draw a good breath. The pallor of his skin emphasized the stark angles of his face and the dark stubble of several days' growth of beard, the dark circles under his sunken eyes.

She got the sudden impression that his outstretched arm on the top of the SUV was all that was keeping him upright. She looked at his hand. Yes; the tips of his fingers were white from pressing hard against the metal. He was sweating from the effort he was making to stand upright.

"What's wrong with you?" she demanded, her tone still wary but underlaid by a note of concern she couldn't help feeling.

He raised his other arm, wiped his shirt sleeve across his face. "Got shot." He gave her a hard look that she felt even across the distance between the two vehicles.

"It wasn't fun, don't want to do it again. So I'd appreciate it if you'd put away that weapon."

He couldn't see the pistol in her hand, but he must have seen her lean over and accurately guessed she was getting a weapon from the glove compartment. Mindful of their isolation, she wasn't scared but that didn't mean she had to abandon caution. With a touch of irony she said, "I'm sure you would, but I'll hold on to it for now. What are you doing here?"

"I told you. I was sent."

"For what reason?" Not that she didn't have an idea, simply because she knew how Axel's perverted brain worked.

"Recuperation, and under the radar."

Beside her, Tricks had evidently decided she'd been patient long enough. She butted Bo's arm and woofed again; her ears perked up and her dark eyes locked on the stranger she hadn't yet been able to greet properly. The man gave her a brief look and then dismissed her as no threat. Well, Tricks *wasn't* a threat—except to clean clothing—but Bo didn't trust people who didn't like animals, so her misgivings swelled higher again.

"I don't think so. I don't know you. I don't want to know you, and I sure as hell don't want you as a roommate."

"*Paid* roommate," he qualified. Slowly he pulled a cell phone from his pocket. "Here, call Axel. He'll explain."

"I don't want to talk to the asshole."

"I don't expect he wants to talk to you, either, but he does what needs to be done."

Meaning she didn't? Bo gave him a hostile, distrustful look. It was wasted because he chose that moment to close his eyes and swallow, as if he were fighting to stay conscious.

He might be a good actor, but even an Oscar winner couldn't make his face go gray. She had the alarming conviction that he was about to face-plant right there in the gravel driveway.

Shit!

Swearing under her breath, she put the Jeep in park and shoved the door open. Tricks bounced as much as she was able, wanting to get out. "Stay," Bo said firmly as she got out and slammed the door shut. Her boots crunched on the gravel and a chilly breeze blew in her face, bringing with it the sharp, clean scent of impending rain or snow. Tricks began barking, keeping up the doggy litany of displeasure at being left behind as Bo rounded the Tahoe SUV, the pistol still in her hand and a sharp eye on her unwanted visitor.

She might as well have saved the effort. She doubted he'd be able to hit anything other than the ground.

He was literally clinging to the vehicle, his right knee braced against the frame, right arm across the roof, left hand clamped on the door.

"Sit down," she said sharply. "*Sit.*" It was the same tone she used on Tricks when Tricks decided—as she did on a regular basis—to test whether Bo was still boss.

The tone worked on men as well as it did on dogs—either that, or he didn't have any choice. He let out a shaky breath and all but collapsed into the driver's seat, half-sprawling before he gathered himself and managed to sit upright.

In the Jeep, Tricks gave the bark that signaled she was really running out of patience, that she was deeply unhappy about being kept harnessed now that she was *home,* where she normally had the run of the place.

Bo ignored the bark. "Let me see your ID," she commanded and stood at a safe distance while he placed the cell phone on the dash and laboriously fished his wallet out of his back pocket. Taking it in his left hand, he extended his arm back toward her, evidently intending that she take wallet and all. She did, stretching out and snagging it, then moving farther away in case he suddenly recuperated and jumped at her. She didn't think he would, or could, but that wasn't a chance she was willing to take.

There was cash in the wallet, enough to make a nice thick bulk, some credit cards, and a driver's license. Looking back and forth between him and the wallet, she saw that the Virginia license did indeed say Morgan Yancy. The Morgan Yancy in the photograph looked much healthier than the one sitting in her driveway. The face had the hard, sculpted look of a man who kept himself in peak physical shape—not a handsome face, but definitely a masculine one. Brown hair—check. Blue eyes—check; she was close enough to see that. They were a particularly striking shade of blue, fierce and icy, as if an eagle had been born blue-eyed. Six-foot-two, check. Two hundred thirty pounds? No way in hell. He was at least thirty, forty pounds shy of what the license said, which explained why his clothes hung on him like shapeless bags.

On the plus side, the ill-fitting clothes were clean and in good shape, nothing fancy, just jeans and boots and a flannel shirt. On the not-so-plus side, Ted Bundy had been clean-cut and nicely dressed, so that didn't prove anything.

Tricks barked again.

He retrieved the cell phone from the dashboard and tossed it to her; startled, she juggled the wallet and made a one-handed catch of the phone that she considered nothing short of miraculous, given that she'd never played any kind of sports. She should have let it drop in the dirt. Who threw cell phones around? "Call him," he said, leaning his head back against the seat and closing his eyes again. He was breathing kind of heavily.

"I don't know his number."

"It's the only number programmed into that phone."

Well, wasn't that all special and spy-ish? And useless, because—"I haven't talked to him in seventeen years. I wouldn't recognize his voice." Besides, she didn't *want* to hear Axel's voice again—ever.

"So work it out." The guy didn't open his eyes. "Maybe he knows something about you that no one else does."

He was taking a lot for granted, she thought with resentment, a complete stranger showing up uninvited and evidently expecting her to take care of him. Or maybe he was at the end of his endurance and didn't have the energy to move on down the road. From the way he looked, she had to reluctantly go with that last conclusion.

Damn it. She didn't want to get hooked into anything, but at the same time she didn't see how she could send him away when he was incapable of going.

She took a few more cautious steps away from him, just in case he was faking and tried to charge her while she was distracted by the phone. She didn't think so, but yeah, she was cautious—and suspicious. Looking back and forth between him and the phone, she examined it; it was a cheap dumb phone, keypad instead of a touch screen. She pressed the call button and put the phone to her ear.

There was some unusual clicking. She waited and was beginning to think the call hadn't gone through when there was another click and a man's voice said, "Yes."

She said, "Who is this?"

"Nice to talk to you, too." The voice was male, mature, and no way in hell could she tell if it belonged to her former stepbrother.

"Sorry," she said briskly. "You won't be talking to me a second longer unless you tell me something that identifies you."

He snickered. "One word: *stripes.*"

Dismayed, she shook her head. Even if *"stripes"* hadn't verified his identity to her, the adolescent snicker would have. She was caught: this was indubitably Axel MacNamara. No one else, not even her mother, had known that when Bo was thirteen, for some unknown reason she had decided having tiger stripes on her legs would be cool and make her stand out in a crowd. In retrospect, she could only wonder at herself, but maybe being thirteen was answer enough.

She had painted stripes of sunblock on her legs, then lain out in the sun. The resulting effect had made her look as if she had a skin disease. The only remedy then had been to paint the tanned portions of her legs with sunblock—which had taken a *long* time, which was why Axel, the stepbrother from hell, had caught her at it—and try to tan the pale stripes to their surrounding color. That had ended up being the summer she never wore shorts.

"Okay," she said grudgingly. "I know who you are. What the hell do you think you're doing, sending a stranger here and expecting me to—"

"Cut the dramatics," he said with the cool disdain that had always set her teeth on edge. "Even I wouldn't have sent anyone dangerous. Let me amend that: he isn't dangerous to you. He needs a secure place to recuperate until I can handle a delicate situation. I don't know how long it will take."

"So I'm just supposed to house a stranger for an unspecified length of time?" She cast a weather eye at the stranger in question. His eyes were still closed. He was still sitting mostly upright, but she wasn't at all certain he was conscious.

"Yes. Feed him and do his laundry, too, because he sure as hell isn't up to it."

She could feel her blood pressure rising and was seized by the urge to bang her head against something.

Axel had always affected her that way. "What makes you think I would ever do you a favor?" she asked furiously.

"I don't. That's why I'm offering you a hundred thousand smackeroos, tax free, to do this. All you have to do is say the word and the money is yours."

She stilled. Her heart rate, her breathing—everything seemed to slow. A hundred thousand—a *hundred thousand*. It wasn't a fortune, but it was a great big turnaround in her financial situation. Though that amount wouldn't pay off the house, it would knock a sizable hole in the loan, give her more breathing room, and relieve a great deal of stress. She was making do now, her head was above water, but she'd like better than simply making do.

Then she took a deep breath and forced herself back into the real world, rather than jumping headlong at what seemed like a great deal. She no longer leaped before she looked. "Uh huh. Exactly how would it be tax free? Paid under the counter? You do know the IRS tracks every deposit that's more than ten grand, right? Whatever crooked thing you're into, I don't want any part of it. And is it true he got *shot*?" Now that she thought about it, she couldn't believe she hadn't reacted to that tidbit of information when Morgan Yancy had said that. Only now was the outlandishness of it hitting her.

"Yeah," the stranger said wearily from the front seat of the Tahoe. "I got shot." At least that proved he was still conscious.

"In the chest," Axel said in her ear. "Damn near killed him. He coded twice. Look, he can't go back to his place because we don't know who targeted him or why. He isn't in any shape to look after himself right now anyway, but I had to get him out of the system in a hurry and to a place where no one will look for him. On the other hand, I'd like to keep him fairly close by. Your place is perfect on both counts."

Bo shook her head, in denial of everything he was saying. "You do know you're on a cell phone, right? And that it's likely being monitored?"

"These cells aren't. They're encrypted, the calls were bounced around and they're burner phones anyway." He paused, then said, "You'll actually be paid enough to cover the income tax on the hundred thou. Don't worry, you won't be audited because of it. Come on, yes or no."

She didn't want to make an immediate decision. The worst financial mistake of her life had come from her leaping before she looked. "I need to think it over."

"Sorry. It's now or never. Like I said, these phones won't be used again, and it's too dangerous to contact me by normal means."

The day was long past when she could be rail-roaded into making decisions before she had answers. "Hmmm. Point one: I don't like being pushed. Point two: I don't trust you, which makes me think you're afraid I'll see what's off about this if you give me time to think about it. So, okay, here's your answer—"

"All right, all right!" He sounded grumpy, which she enjoyed. Given the age difference between them, in their admittedly juvenile arguments during the brief time their parents had been married, she had never gotten the best of him. But she wasn't thirteen now, and she knew her own mind. "A hundred and fifty thousand."

"I'm not bargaining for more money, but thank you. I'll keep that number in mind *if* I agree," she said coolly.

"Look." For the first time in her memory, there was a tone in Axel's voice as if he were addressing her without mockery, with dead seriousness. "I know this is an unusual situation. Your particular circumstances make it ideal for my purposes, though. No one would tie us together—"

"Thank God," she said, unable to resist the admittedly juvenile verbal jab.

"Ditto. But you have resources, you're isolated without having to move him too far away in case I need him, and most of all, you need the money."

There was that. Since her colossal career misjudgment seven years ago, money—or the lack of it—had been behind every decision she'd made. She'd learned how to make smart choices financially, to be an adult and do what had to be done, which was work two jobs. Occasionally part of her still yearned for the heady feeling of taking risks and coming out on top, but at the same time she was mostly happy where she was. It was a learned happiness, but happiness nevertheless.

She wasn't embarrassed by her financial situation. It was much better now than it had been, and she'd dug herself out the pit. Still, how did *Axel* know anything about her life at all, much less her finances?

As if he'd read her mind, he said, "I did some deep digging on you."

"If you're so anxious to hide him, wouldn't that leave a trail?"

"If one knew where to look, yes, but I went through intermediaries, in-person and verbal instruction only. There are a lot of layers between us. I made sure you're protected and anonymous."

It wasn't like Axel to be conciliatory or even agreeable, which told her how important this was to him. Being safe would definitely be important to Morgan Yancy, at least while he was in his current condition. She wasn't a bleeding-heart-type person, but neither was she callous, and she already knew she couldn't send him away for the simple reason that he wasn't in any shape to drive. He'd be spending the night here, regardless. Whether or not he was any stronger tomorrow remained to be seen.

A hundred and fifty thousand dollars . . .

Then she sighed. No matter how much money he was offering, she had other people to consider. "It won't work," she said flatly. "If he has a killer stalking him, I won't endanger the people around here. I just won't."

"You won't be," Axel assured her. "There's no connection to make, no way of tracing him to you. Just give him a place to hide out. I guess I could send him to a safe house, but security has been breached so none of those would be safe—and that's why I'm contacting you out of network. The problem is internal."

The dilemma was immediate, and maddening. She needed the money, but she didn't trust Axel. She didn't want a strange man—and a wounded one, at that—staying with her, but he wasn't capable of leaving. So he was staying for at least a short while, whether she wanted him to or not, unless she called Jesse or an ambulance and had him hauled . . . where? There was a local doctor, but as far as she could tell, Morgan Yancy didn't need medical care, he needed time to heal and regain his strength. If she had him taken to a hospital, he'd be in the computer system, which meant that if she believed Axel even a little bit, she'd be endangering the man's life.

Okay. She didn't trust Axel, though to be truthful she didn't know if that was because he truly wasn't trustworthy or if it was simply because she disliked him so much. He evidently had some kind of government job but, considering the government, that wasn't really much of a recommendation.

She said, "Hold on," and held the phone down against her thigh to cover up the speaker so Axel couldn't hear. Approaching the SUV, she said, "Yancy?"

He opened his eyes halfway, a gleam of blue in the grayness of his face, and muttered, "Yeah?"

"Axel said there's no way to trace you to me."

He took a deep breath, or tried to. She caught the sudden hitch, as if his chest muscles protested. His throat worked as he swallowed, then he said, "That's why I drove. No record, and the Tahoe is clean, can't be linked back."

"Drove from where?"

He gave a small shake of his head, meaning he wasn't going to tell her. Given his condition, he had probably come a fair distance, either that or—*Damn it!* "Exactly when did you get out of the hospital?"

"This morning," he said, and let his eyes close again.

Double damn it.

She might regret it, almost probably she would regret it, but a hundred and fifty thousand was a lot of money and even though she didn't trust Axel, she could see for herself that the man in front of her wasn't a threat—not now, at least. Even more, he was relying on Axel not to betray him, and presumably he knew her former step-brother better than she did, which really wouldn't take much at all because his father and her mother had been married a grand total of eight months. Morgan Yancy was betting his life he could trust Axel.

She lifted the phone to her ear again. "All right," she said, keeping it brief. "But if the money isn't in my account in two days, I'm putting him on the road."

"It will be," Axel said. "It'll be there tomorrow."

Now that the decision had been made, for good or ill, Bo turned her mind toward practical matters. "Let me get my bank account routing number."

"Please." The word was full of disdain. "I already have it." The phone clicked and the connection was gone; he'd hung up.

She thumbed the button to cut the connection on her end, then stood looking at the phone. "Now what?"

Yancy shifted in the seat and lifted his head slowly, as if the effort was almost more than he could manage. He held out his hand, and Bo placed the phone in it. He deftly took the phone apart and removed the battery, as if it were something he'd done a thousand times.

Having decided enough was enough, Tricks gave another bark, this one special. She had a whole repertoire of different sounds she used to bend humans to her will, and the plaintive, high-pitched puppy bark was her ace in the hole. It was her "Mom, help me!" call, and even though Bo knew she was being manipulated, she was usually so amused that she did whatever Tricks wanted. Right now, Tricks wanted out of the Jeep, which was simple enough.

"I'll be right back," she said, leaving him where he was and walking back over to the Jeep. She began shivering and pulled her denim jacket closer around her. The temperature had dropped easily ten degrees just since she'd pulled into the driveway. She opened the passenger door and put the pistol in her jacket pocket while she freed Tricks from the harness. She was no longer afraid Yancy was going to jump her, but, hey, it didn't cost anything to be careful.

Tricks grabbed her tennis ball and bounded out of the Jeep, her whole body wiggling with joy. Before Bo could grab her collar, she was gone, racing over to the Tahoe and around to the driver's side. Tricks loved to meet people, but Morgan Yancy might not be an animal lover or in any mood to be licked and nudged to throw the ball, which to Tricks was the greatest honor she could grant someone.

"No!" Bo said, running after her pet though she knew it was already too late. She just hoped Tricks didn't climb into the guy's lap.

She rounded the rear bumper of the Tahoe and skidded to a halt. Tricks was right there in the open door, of course, standing on her hind legs with her front paws braced on the door jamb and her face right up at the man's. He'd opened his eyes and turned his head so that they were almost nose to nose. Before he could react, though, Tricks lowered her muzzle and sniffed at his neck, then moved slowly down his chest, pausing in one spot as if she'd found something interesting. Bo stilled, wondering if that was where he'd been shot.

Tricks moved her nose around and over that one spot, never quite touching. He sat very still while she gave him what was probably the most thorough smelling he'd ever experienced. Then she very gently licked his shirt, on that same spot, and lowered her front paws to the ground before laying her head on his thigh.

Bo sighed. She'd seen it before; Tricks always seemed to know if anyone was sad, sick, or wounded, and would offer the comfort of her company. "Come on, princess," she said gently, putting her hand on Tricks's head. "Back up, okay?" She nudged Tricks back, put herself between dog and man. "Is that where you got shot?" she asked Yancy, her tone more brisk than when she'd been talking to Tricks.

"Yeah," he muttered. "She zeroed right in."

"I'll try to keep her away from you; she can make a pest of herself until she gets used to you." Bo looked at him—he truly looked awful—and at the door. Under normal circumstances the distance wasn't long at all, maybe twenty yards, but these weren't normal circumstances because he looked as if he'd need help to go twenty feet. He couldn't make that distance. She could, however, get him closer.

"If you can get into the passenger seat, I'll pull the Tahoe up to the patio so you won't have to walk so far." She'd agreed to this; now she had to be practical about the logistics of getting him inside and taking care of him because one thing was for sure: he couldn't do it on his own.

"I can walk from here," he said grimly, lifting his gaunt face and staring at the house as though it were an enemy to be conquered. Her stomach clenched at the fierce determination she saw there. He'd try, she thought; even knowing he couldn't, he'd try anyway, and keep trying until he was unconscious on the cold ground. She couldn't get her mind around that kind of steely willpower.

She didn't let even a hint of sympathy leak into her voice. "No, you can't. You can barely stand up. If you can drive it yourself, fine, just pull up and around so the driver's side is as close to the patio at you can get. If you can't, then move over so I can do it. Your only other option is sitting in the car all night because if you face-plant, I won't be able to get you up."

Not the most diplomatic way of presenting the options, she thought, but what the hell; even though she'd agreed to take care of him, and even though she was getting paid well for it, she was still disgruntled at having her home essentially taken over by someone she hadn't invited—hence the no sympathy. Besides, she didn't think he'd respond to sympathy—not that she knew him or could begin to gauge his personality or what he'd been through, but if she'd been shot and was in the shape he was in, she thought by now she might be fed up with being *helped.*

"I can drive," he muttered.

"Fine," she said, and closed the door. She put Tricks safely in the house, closing the door to keep her in; Tricks, of course, darted to the window and stood with her front paws on the windowsill, tilting her head from side to side as she alertly watched these unusual proceedings. Bo waited on the patio as Yancy started the engine and slowly steered the Tahoe in a wide circle in the yard, stopping when the driver's door was even with her front door.

Before Bo could reach him, he hauled himself out of the vehicle and struggled to stand upright. He'd pushed himself so far that now every move was costing him. "Do you have luggage?" she asked as she deftly slid herself between him and the Tahoe and wedged her left shoulder under his right arm.

"Duffle bag," he replied, his thin voice so utterly exhausted the words were almost soundless. "In the back."

She wrinkled her nose. He felt too hot, and he smelled . . . sickly. That was the only way she could describe it, a blend of sweat and medication, maybe an antibiotic swab for his wound, even a whiff of adhesive tape.

"I'll come back for it." Given the way he looked, she figured the faster she got him inside, the better. She tried to support him as much as she could, but it wasn't easy. While she was a little above average in height, he was at least a head taller, and even though he'd obviously lost weight, he still outweighed her by quite a bit. He was noticeably weaker, leaning heavily on her, barely able to shuffle his feet along the concrete patio. There was only a small step up from the patio into the house, thank goodness, because she didn't think that even with her help he could have managed more than that.

Tricks ran over and bounced around them, generally getting in the way and making a nuisance of herself, as Bo maneuvered him toward the sofa. "Move," Bo admonished. "Where's your ball?" Distracted, Tricks dashed off to find her tennis ball. It wasn't in the first place she looked and she began hunting for it, which gave Bo a few extra seconds to get him settled on the sofa.

"Go ahead and lie down," she instructed, positioning a throw pillow for his head. A look of resentment flashed across his face, followed just as fast by resignation. Slowly he eased down, stretching his long form out. He was taller than her sofa was long, his feet hanging over the other end, but there was nothing she could do about that. A long sigh eased from his chest and he closed his eyes. Bo paused a few seconds, then, because he looked uncomfortable with his legs in that position, she pushed another pillow under his knees for support. He didn't stir.

She straightened and rolled her shoulders, loosening the muscles. The effort of getting him inside had made *her* sweat, too.

Tricks had found her tennis ball and brought it to Bo, nosing it into her hand. "Good girl," Bo praised, rubbing behind the silky ears. Tricks sniffed at the man on the sofa, then gave a joyous whirl because someone new was in the house. She bounced up and down, woofed softly to Bo, then began racing back and forth from her toy box to the man, bringing toy after toy until there was a heap of stuffed animals, chew sticks, and balls in front of the sofa.

His breathing had deepened. Maybe he'd gone to sleep. At any rate, he was oblivious to the growing heap of offerings, but bringing her toys was keeping Tricks occupied. "Go to it, girl," Bo said to Tricks and left her still fetching toys while she herself went out to fetch the heavy duffle.

She grunted from effort as she dragged the duffle out of the Tahoe; it was so heavy she couldn't prevent it from thudding to the ground, so she knew he hadn't lifted it into the SUV himself. Probably he hadn't even packed it himself.

Huffing and puffing, she lifted one end of the duffle and dragged it to the house and inside the door, where she let it drop with a thud. She looked at the flight of stairs going to the loft bedrooms, pondering the further logistics of her houseguest. She doubted he could make it up the stairs to the guest bedroom, so that meant he'd be sleeping on the sofa. There wasn't any point in trying to wrestle the heavy bag upstairs when he'd need it down here. At least there was a full bathroom on the ground floor, or they'd have a serious problem. For now, the best she could do was shove the duffle close to the sofa so he could reach it if he needed anything.

His eyes were still closed despite Tricks's bouncing back and forth. Bo hesitated a minute, thinking of all that needed doing, such as feeding them both and probably taking care of somehow getting him to the bathroom. Testing the waters, she asked, "Are you conscious?"

No answer.

Damn. She didn't know if that was good or not. If he was just asleep, that was good. On the other hand, if he was *unconscious,* that could be very bad. She shouldn't disturb him if he was sleeping. If he was unconscious, not doing something could kill him.

This was a bona fide dilemma.

Better to make a mistake and ask forgiveness than do nothing at all, as the saying went. She leaned over him and gently shook his right shoulder. "Hey—" That was the only word she got out because his eyes flared open and his right arm shot out, his hand clamping around her throat, fingers digging deep and cutting off her air. For a split second all she could see was the blazing blue of his eyes, filling her own vision as it rapidly began dimming. Panic shot through her, hot and acid; the abrupt certainty that she was going to die blurred into an instinctive fury and without thought or even being able to see what she was aiming for, she struck, putting all her strength behind her right fist as she drove it toward his face. The impact jarred her arm all the way to her elbow.

He grunted, *"Fuck!"* and released her throat.

She staggered back, gasping for air, her hand going to her throat to massage the aching tissue. As soon as she could suck in some air she gasped, *"Shit!"*

They stared at each other from a safe distance of several feet.

Whoever had said it was better to make a mistake and ask forgiveness, blah blah blah, had been full of shit.

He'd been in the house fewer than five minutes, and he'd already tried to kill her. This *couldn't* be good.

Chapter 5

She should have known Axel would lie. "not a danger to her," *hah!*

Bo eyed him as she gingerly shook her hand; punching someone in the face *hurt.* Probably it hurt him, too, but that was his problem. He struggled to a sitting position and felt his nose. A little bit of blood trickled down and he wiped it away with the back of his hand.

Guilt almost—but not quite—assailed her for punching a wounded man. Common sense told her not to be angry, but he'd been trying to choke her and she didn't feel very sensible about it. She wasn't the instigator here. Even as weak as he was, she knew in her gut that he could easily have killed her, likely would have if he hadn't realized what he was doing and who she was.

She didn't want him bleeding all over her sofa. Silently she fished in her pocket for one of the clean tissues she always carried, in case Tricks gave her a drink of water she hadn't asked for, and held it out to him. He took it and wiped at the blood, then looked down at the smear of blood on his hand and wiped it away too. He didn't seem to want to look at her.

Tough.

"What the hell?" she demanded and left it to him to decipher her meaning, not that he needed to be a mental giant to do so.

"Sorry," he muttered, holding the tissue to his nose. "Just . . . don't shake me, okay? Yell, or throw something at me."

"You can bet I'll throw something at you." Annoyed, she realized she was as much as admitting she wasn't tossing him out on his keister. She'd made a deal with the devil, and she was getting paid for it.

Besides . . . she wasn't stupid. The man had been shot, after all, and she could add two and two. She said, "Combat?"

He hitched up his right shoulder, then froze as the movement evidently pulled on things that didn't want to be pulled. After a moment he said, "Of a sort."

She didn't see how there could be a "sort" of combat; you either fought, or you didn't. Still, enough said. She got it. She was still grumpy about the incident, but she got it. She stood with her arms crossed, half-glaring down at him. "Okay," she finally said. "But don't choke me again."

Blue eyes flashed up at her. "I'll try not to." He dabbed at the slowing trickle of blood from his nose. "You have a good punch. How's your hand?"

"Hurts."

"So does my nose."

"Good."

He sat there looking as if he might keel over again, which made her wonder if she'd try to get him up or just let him lie there. No, she'd have to get him up, or Tricks would go bonkers with joy thinking a human on the floor was some new game. Thinking of Tricks made her look around in search of her pet, and she heard the big slurps from the kitchen as Tricks got a drink of water. She looked back at her guest to find him slowly surveying the mound of stuffed animals and squeaky toys in front of the sofa. His chest rose and fell as he took a cautious breath. "Booby trap?" he finally asked.

As if she knew they were now talking about her, Tricks abandoned her water bowl and grabbed another toy before trotting over. This one was a squeaky rubber chicken which she had never played with a lot, but now she bit the squeaker and made what was supposed to be a clucking sound, then deposited it in his lap.

"Bribes," Bo said. "She's trying to entice you to play with her."

He looked down at the rubber chicken draped across his leg. Tricks nudged it as if urging him to pick it up. "She's gotta do better than a chicken."

"She won't give up until you give in, so my advice is to go with it."

He scowled at her, the expression on his rough face both annoyed and exhausted. "Can't you keep her in a crate or something? I'm really not up to this."

He was only telling the truth, and ordinarily Bo would have already been making Tricks behave, but she was still pissed so she wasn't inclined to cut him any slack. "I'd put you in a crate before I would her," she snapped. "Here, baby." She clapped her hands and Tricks came to her, nuzzling her knee. She bent to stroke her dog and narrowed her eyes at the human interloper. "This is her home, not yours. You're here on sufferance."

His glance was cold, telling her that despite his condition, he wasn't about to back down. "I'm here because you need the money."

Knowing he was right didn't help her temper any. On the other hand, continuing to argue with him would be childish. She clenched her teeth, then grudgingly said, "You're right, and this isn't getting us anywhere. I'll try to keep her away from you. Before you pass out again, you need to eat something. What would you like?"

"I'm not hungry."

"Okay, I'll fix you a smoothie."

An appalled expression crossed his face before he quickly blanked it and said, "No, thanks, I'm really not hungry."

"I didn't ask if you were hungry." Her tone was curt. "If you don't have something, you'll just get weaker. It's common sense. If you aren't up to solid food, I can throw together a smoothie with some peanut butter, milk, banana—things like that. That way you'll at least have something nourishing."

"How about just some milk?"

"Fine with me, as long as it has peanut butter and a banana in it."

He muttered something under his breath, but her own expression must have said he'd drink it or wear it, so he finally said, "I don't care, make what you want."

She intended to. She turned and went to the kitchen, which meant the middle section of the wide-open bottom floor plan. She lived in a barn—a real, honest-to-God barn, one that she herself had overseen the design and renovation of, though it hadn't been for herself because she'd never wanted to live in a barn. She'd done it for a client who had then backed out on her, leaving her saddled with debt and a barn dwelling she didn't want in a location she hadn't picked for herself.

But it had worked out. She couldn't say it hadn't. The barn had become hers, and she had made a life for herself here in this little corner of West Virginia, with the mountains and rivers and plenty of space for Tricks. She had friends, she had a job—two of them— and damn if she wasn't content with it all.

The kitchen was a brightly lit square, framed by posts that set it off, and the flooring was slate while the rest of the first floor was plank hardwood. It was so open that she could keep an eye on both Tricks and Yancy while she threw things into the blender: milk, yogurt, peanut butter, a banana, vanilla flavoring. She kept the portions small, because she didn't think he'd be able to down very much. That was guessing on her part because she'd never been seriously ill or injured, but she imagined his appetite would be slow to return. The trick was to keep enough nutrients in him that he'd get better. The deal was to give him a safe place to recuperate, right? Once he had recuperated and could take care of himself, he'd be gone; therefore, the better care she took of him now, even if she had to bully him to eat, the better the deal for her.

Besides, she liked the idea of bullying him. He'd not only tried to choke her, but he didn't like Tricks. She found the second charge the most damning. Okay, so a lot of people weren't animal lovers, but considering his position in her house he'd been damned rude about it. He wasn't even allergic because he hadn't started sneezing or anything even when he was lying on the sofa, where Tricks liked to lounge. Some people were just butts, with no other explanation needed for their behavior.

She added ice to the blender and turned it on, running it until the contents were smooth. Then she poured it into a glass, stuck a straw in it, and took it to the sofa. "Here," she said, setting the glass on the end table. "Cheers."

Reluctantly he picked up the smoothie and sipped at it. It must not have been as bad as he'd anticipated, because he took a few more sips, then sighed and set it down. "Thanks," he said, and though the word was grudging at least he said it.

"You're welcome. I need to take her for a walk—" At the word "walk," Tricks grabbed her tennis ball and went to the door where she stood fairly vibrating with anticipation. "—and I'll be gone about twenty minutes, maybe a little longer. Do you want the TV on?"

"No, I just want to lie down and rest for a while."

"Okay, then. Drink the rest of that smoothie."

She started to leave the door unlocked, but realized that when she left, he would likely go back to sleep, which was the equivalent of leaving the house unprotected. Without saying anything, she got her keys and pistol as usual and grabbed a heavier coat on her way out the door, flipping the hood up to cover her head. The wind was now downright icy, and the low dark clouds pressing down on the hills looked as if they might start dropping snow any minute.

She locked the door and started off across the yard. Tricks dropped the ball at her feet and, as usual, took off running, certain Bo would throw the ball in the direction she'd chosen.

They had a route they walked, a path that had been tramped down over the many walks she'd taken since getting Tricks. The path wound around the edge of some woods, and Bo stayed well away from the small hidden lake where she sometimes let Tricks swim in the summer. Going to the lake was a treat, not a routine. Beyond the woods was a meadow, and beyond that more woods where the trail climbed a decent hill. When she'd first started walking Tricks, Bo would be out of breath by the time they reached the hill, much less climbed it, but now she crested it without any problem. She threw the ball for Tricks the whole way, with Tricks racing back and forth.

This was the best part of every day, out walking with her dog, her boots making rustling noises in the fallen leaves, watching Tricks's joy as she dashed back and forth.

She would have liked to stay out longer than usual in case the weather turned especially nasty during the night, and she wouldn't be able to walk Tricks tomorrow as often as normal, but her other work waited for her at home and she couldn't prolong the walk forever. She said, "Let's go home, girl," and, with a happy wag of her tail, Tricks reversed her course.

They were about halfway back when a hush fell around them. The wind died and fat, silent snowflakes began drifting down on them, the flakes decorating Tricks's pale golden fur like confetti. Bo took out her cell phone and snapped a few pictures of the dog with snowflakes on her head because she looked so pretty with the swiftly melting decorations. Tricks was a camera hog who stopped and posed, dark eyes bright and smiling, every time she saw a camera, as if she knew what a picture she made. "Good girl," Bo crooned, bending down to nuzzle the top of her head. The dog cuddled against her for a minute, always happy for a snuggle, then they continued on the trail. The flurry stopped before they reached the house again, but given how cold it had gotten, Bo expected there would be more snow coming.

When she unlocked the door and went in, she saw that her "guest" was stretched out on the sofa, sound asleep. Tricks trotted over to him and began a head-to-toe sniffing exploration. Bo watched to see if he was disturbed, but he didn't stir, and after a minute Tricks abandoned him for one of the stuffed animals still piled in front of the sofa, shaking it, then trotting with it to her own bed where she beat it against the floor a time or two before dropping it and selecting another.

Bo checked the smoothie. He'd drunk about half of it, which she guessed was about as good as she could expect this first time. She poured the rest of it down the sink.

She had some time before feeding Tricks and herself, so she went to the small office area she'd set up under the slant of the stairs and opened the file on her computer. Her current project wasn't all that interesting, converting technical language on how to operate a camcorder into language the average person could follow, but it was something she was good at. It helped to have the actual product in her hands, but if that wasn't possible, she could make do with diagrams. As long as she could visualize the action, she could describe it.

One of the deals she'd made with the town was that it provide Wi-Fi to her house, meaning she could now send and receive all the data she needed to work without having to drive into town to use the library's Wi-Fi. Just that convenience had made a big difference in her productivity. She always had proposals out, and she worked hard at delivering her projects by deadline or ahead of time, so over the years her business and income had grown—but not grown enough to keep her afloat after getting saddled with the barn and all the personal debt she'd stupidly piled up getting *that* project done. With that one blow her fledgling business in house flipping had died a gruesome death, and she'd returned to the tech writing to keep herself in food.

Sometimes Bo could only marvel at how her life had turned on that one bad deal. At the time she'd been panic-stricken, but if the client hadn't left her holding the bag—or, in this case, the barn—she'd have moved on to another town, another house, and she wouldn't have the roots she'd eventually put down here. "Roots" had been an alien concept to her; she'd moved around, not getting attached to any place or any person, then life had happened and here she was. She had a place that had become home, she had friends—good ones—and she had Tricks. All in all, she thought she'd gotten the best part of the deal. Sure, sometimes she wished she could take in a concert or wander through a museum, eat at a restaurant with a decent wine list—and someday she might take a vacation and do just that—but she was oddly content where she was. No one could have been more surprised than she was at herself.

Tricks curled up on the rug beside Bo's chair and took a nap. With dog and man both asleep, Bo got in a couple of hours of solid concentration, finishing one project a week early and getting started on another. When her stomach reminded her that it was time to eat, she pushed back from the computer desk and stretched. Tricks immediately looked up, her expression one of happy anticipation because she too knew it was time for food.

She went over to the sofa and checked on Yancy, who still hadn't stirred. Did she wake him and try to get food down him now, when it was most convenient for her, or wait until he woke naturally? He'd been exhausted, so he'd probably sleep for quite a while, maybe even through the night—which brought up another possible problem.

What if she let him sleep, eventually went to bed herself, and left him alone down here? She tried to anticipate what might happen if he woke, groggy, in a strange place without a light to guide him to the bathroom if he needed to go. Come to that, he didn't know where the bathroom was, and she didn't know if he had the strength to wander around looking for it.

She doubted he'd think it was funny if she set an empty bottle beside the sofa with a note that said, *Use this.*

Where was a potty chair when she needed one? She would take delight in setting it out for him, knowing she would be enraged and humiliated if someone did that to her, but hey, she was still miffed about the whole choking thing.

She sighed; she had to be an adult about this. Too bad, though. On the other hand, he *had* said to throw something at him. She could do that. Boy, could she do that.

He was lying on the sofa's throw pillows, but Tricks's stuffed animals were soft, and she'd conveniently piled them in front of the sofa so Bo wouldn't even have to fetch them. She selected a teddy bear from the pile and tossed it onto his stomach. "Hey!"

Nothing. He didn't even twitch.

Tricks's head shot up, though, and her attention riveted on the new game. She trotted over, every muscle alert with eagerness. To head her off—because she was completely capable of leaping onto his stomach after her bear—Bo dropped the duck she'd picked up and said, "Come on, sweetie, let's get you fed." Only food would derail Tricks's attention from playing.

With Tricks prancing along beside her she went back into the kitchen, opened the plastic bin of dog food, and dipped out the appropriate amount. Because Tricks liked treats to enliven her meal, she chipped up a little bit of sliced turkey into the dry food, then set the bowl down in the raised feeder.

Tricks looked at the food, then up at Bo. She waited.

"Okay, it's one of those nights," Bo sighed. Having fought the food wars for all of Tricks's life, she knew the battles to pick. This wasn't one of them. She bent down and selected a piece of kibble, offered it to Tricks. Tricks turned her head away, as if the kibble wasn't worthy of being considered and she was offended that Bo had offered it.

Bo dropped the kibble back in the bowl, then rubbed behind Tricks's ears and crooned to her how pretty she was, that she was the prettiest puppy in the world, and sometimes she needed her head pinched off for being such a PITA, but it was said in that loving croon and Tricks ate it up. Bo selected another piece of kibble, offered it for inspection. This time Tricks sniffed at it as if this one had possibilities, then turned her head away again. Bo once more went through the ear-rubbing and love-talking routine, then picked up the third piece of kibble. Tricks sniffed it, thought a minute as if weighing whether or not she'd been praised enough, then daintily took the kibble from Bo's fingers. It passed muster because she gave a pleased wag of her tail and without further ado lowered her head to the food bowl and began eating.

Bo rolled her eyes at her canine diva and while Tricks was occupied, hurried back to her guest/patient. Hands down, he was more trouble than the dog.

She grabbed the stuffed duck from the floor and tossed it at him. It landed on his stomach. He didn't wake.

"Damn it," she muttered, and pick up the one-legged giraffe. Tricks had torn off the other three legs but used the remaining one to sling the giraffe from side to side when she was "killing" it. Now that Tricks had started eating, it wouldn't take her long to finish, and Bo needed to get him awake before that happened. She wound up and put some muscle behind the throw. The giraffe hit him full in the face.

He started awake pretty much the same way he had before when he'd choked her, except this time his attacker was a mangled stuffed animal. She saw the fierce glitter of his eyes as he lunged upward, then he gave a deep groan and collapsed back onto the sofa, his free hand going to his chest and his expression a grimace of pain.

Horrified, Bo's eyes widened and she clapped one hand over her mouth, then immediately removed it to say with fervent guilt, "I'm sorry, I'm so sorry!"

He fought off the pain and opened his reddened lids. "What the hell?" he rasped, breathing hard.

It was almost a replay of the choking episode, with some aspects swapped. Apologetically she said, "I was trying to wake you up—again. I tried calling, but that didn't work. You *said* to throw something at you," she added, then winced. "In practice, not a good idea."

Cautiously, moving as slowly as a ninety-year-old, he levered himself to a sitting position. The bear and duck fell from his lap to the floor. He looked at them, then at the one-legged giraffe still clutched in his fist in a death grip. Loosening his fingers as laboriously as if the joints had frozen, he dropped it to the floor with its fellow toys, his expression carefully blank. Bo had the chilling memory of that same grip clutching her own throat. This guy obviously lived dangerously, given that he'd been *shot,* but it struck her like a punch in the stomach that what she knew only scratched the surface. The back of her neck prickled with warning, as if she'd been caring for what she'd thought was a dog only to realize it was really a wolf.

"The bear and duck didn't work," she said uncomfortably, lacing her fingers together in front of her and pushing away the unsettling comparison. She felt awful; she simply hadn't considered how much pain he might be in, especially if he moved without thinking.

He rubbed his face, then let his breath out in a sigh. "It's okay. How long was I asleep?"

"About two and a half hours."

"Sorry," he muttered. "I didn't mean to sleep so long. I guess the drive took more out of me than I expected."

"I imagine so, since you just got out of the hospital," she said, keeping her tone neutral though she personally thought he needed his head examined for pushing himself that hard. The long nap didn't seem to have done him much good; his color was still an awful shade between gray and dead white. "The reason I woke you up is, you need to eat, even if it's just a little, and you can't let yourself get dehydrated. Then there's the practical stuff: can you make it up the stairs to the guest bedroom—"

He looked chagrined, as if just now considering the matter, but shook his head.

"I didn't think so. That means you're going to be sleeping on the couch, though I guess I could make a pallet on the floor if you'd rather be able to stretch out, but in my opinion you wouldn't be able to get up and down by yourself."

"I can," he muttered. "But I'd rather not."

"Got it." Oddly, she did understand what he meant. If he had to, he would. If necessary, he would crawl up the stairs, or do whatever circumstances called for, but that gritty determination would cost him in pain. "In that case, I need to show you where the bathroom is, which I figure you need by now. And if you don't, then you're definitely dehydrated and I'm going to start pouring liquids down your throat."

"I do," he said. "Need the bathroom, that is."

"Then let's get you there." She frowned, thinking. "I wonder where I can rent a wheelchair."

"No," he half-snapped. "I'm walking. I've had enough of wheelchairs. The only way I'll get my strength back is by pushing myself."

She started to argue with him about how ill advised that was but bit back the words. Stubbornness went hand in hand with gritty determination, and if she told him he was stupid to try doing something, he'd probably half-kill himself to prove her wrong. Instead she asked, "Are you healed enough yet? How long has it been since you were shot?"

"About a month." He wiped the sweat from his forehead, sweat caused by the exertion of fending off a one-legged giraffe and then sitting up.

"Not that I know anything about gunshot wounds, but yeah, it does seem you'd be in better shape by now."

He snorted. "The open-heart surgery was worse than getting shot."

She blew out a breath. "That would certainly explain it. They saw your sternum in half, right?"

His mouth quirked in a kind of ghastly humor. "That was almost the least of it, but yeah, I don't guess the bone has completely knitted back. Then I got pneumonia. The docs didn't want to let me go, but I'd been in one place too long. Mac and I decided it was time to move." As he spoke, he began the struggle to get to his feet. Bo moved to one side to try to help him but the angle was awkward and she moved to the end of the sofa, where she could at least get her left arm hooked under his right armpit and help lever him upward.

"Mac" was obviously Axel, and the pneumonia on top of open-heart surgery definitely explained why he was so weak. "Are you still on any medications?"

"No antibiotics, my lungs are clear." He was finally standing upright, though he was breathing hard and swaying back and forth.

Something about the phrasing caught her attention. Chief of police was an administrative position, not a real one, but she had still picked up on some things from Jesse. "That's good about the antibiotics, but what about other prescriptions?"

His red-lidded blue eyes sparked with irritation. "If you mean dope for pain, why not ask outright?"

If he thought she'd back down, he was about to embark on a learning curve. "Okay. Are you supposed to be taking any dope for pain?"

"Forget it. I'm not taking any more of that sh—crap. It makes me woozy."

"So?" A thought occurred, and suspicion gnawed at her. She narrowed her gaze. "Unless you think you have to be alert because this location isn't as secure as Axel said, though why I'd believe anything he said is a question for the ages."

He said tersely, "I have to get around by myself now. There aren't any nurses or orderlies to get me up if I fall. So if it's okay with you, I'd rather be steady on my feet."

Her suspicion faded because that was completely logical, not to mention he'd probably been increasingly annoyed by his physical condition and dependence on others. "I wouldn't call this *steady*," she pointed out.

"Steadier than I would be if my head were floating off."

That was true, but also alarming. With her shoulder jammed under his arm and her left arm around his waist while she used the right one to grasp his belt, she led him past the kitchen toward the bathroom in the back. He gripped her right shoulder with one hand, his weight bearing down on her as he shuffled his feet forward. Thank goodness the downstairs bath wasn't a large one, even though it was a full bath with a shower/tub enclosure. He could easily reach things on which to brace himself: the vanity, the toilet, the doorknob. She guided him in, braced his hip against the vanity, and said, "I'll be in yelling distance if you need me."

"Thanks," he said and didn't sound as surly as usual.

She gave him his privacy, retreating to a distance where she couldn't hear him pee. Okay, so it was as much about her privacy as his, but she didn't want to listen to a stranger taking a leak.

There was no telling how long it would be before he was strong enough to climb the stairs, or even step into the tub to take a shower. Showering was going to be an immediate problem—not tonight because he was exhausted from the day's exertions, but definitely to-morrow. He needed one of those shower stools to sit on, but she didn't have one. She did, however, have some of the lightweight plastic porch chairs stacked in the storage room at the back of the house, and maybe one of them would fit inside the tub. If not, she'd find something.

After a couple of minutes she heard the toilet flush—hard to miss that—then the plumbing in the walls noti-fied her that water was being run in the sink. Good; at least he was a hand washer. She grinned to herself. She could just see his face if she'd sent him back to wash his hands.

Then the bathroom door opened and she went to meet him, taking up the same position as before. "Let's talk supper," she said as she helped him back to the sofa. "I think you should eat something solid, but if you still don't feel up to it, I'll make another smoothie for you."

"What are you having?" He sounded only minimally interested.

"What I usually have: I'll nuke a frozen dinner." Sometimes she cooked, but that was the exception, not the rule. Cooking wasn't her forte. She could get by, and maybe she'd make some spaghetti tomorrow if he felt like eating that, but she was tired and didn't want to bother with anything tonight.

His chest rose and fell. "Got anything with beef in it?"

She ran a swift mental inventory of her selection of frozen dinners. "Sorry. I have chicken and turkey." Tomorrow she'd go shopping, but he'd been dumped on her without warning, and for tonight he'd have to make do with what she had.

They'd reached the sofa, and she braced his weight as best she could while he half-sat, half-collapsed onto the cushions. She wracked her brain for some suitably macho food. "Or I can make you a peanut butter and jelly sandwich." Maybe that wasn't macho, but at least it wasn't girl food.

His head shot up. "No shit? Uh—sorry."

"That's okay. I've said 'shit' a time or two in my life."

"A peanut butter and jelly sandwich sounds great." He almost sighed the words, as if grateful he wouldn't have to eat yogurt or sprouts.

The choice wasn't the most nutritious, but at least it was solid food. Going on a hunch, she made him half a sandwich; if he managed that and wanted more, she'd make another for him, but she doubted he'd want anything else. When the sandwich was made, she considered what he might want to drink. Her options were water, skim milk, and beer. "Water or milk?" she called. She wouldn't tell him about the beer.

He evidently knew something about women, because he said, "What kind of milk?"

"Skim."

"Water, please."

She snorted and got him a glass of water, put that, a napkin, and the small plate containing his half sandwich on a tray that she took to him and placed on his lap.

"If you can finish this half sandwich, I'll make you another," she said to head off any comment.

She didn't linger and watch him eat, though Tricks had no such compunction. The dog had been on her best behavior, staying out of the way and not demanding attention, but food knocked that notion out of the park. She positioned herself directly in front of him, dark eyes fixed on the sandwich, following every move he made as the sandwich moved from plate to mouth and back again. About every ten seconds she scooted a little closer to him, in case distance was causing him to misinterpret what she wanted. Within a minute, she was practically sitting on his feet, her muzzle resting delicately on the edge of the tray.

Bo bit the inside of her cheek to keep from laughing and watched to see how he dealt with the power of the eyes.

He'd eaten about half of the half sandwich when he asked warily, "Is she going to attack?"

"I wouldn't put the sandwich anywhere close to her mouth," Bo replied, then relented because she didn't want Tricks to startle him into any sudden movement. She'd already done that herself, and she still felt guilty. The least she could do was afford him some peace to eat his pitiful meal.

She opened Tricks's treat jar. "Want a treat?" she asked rhetorically because Tricks had abandoned him as soon as Bo reached for the jar. She trotted over, eyes bright, and from the corner of her eye Bo saw Morgan hurriedly stuff the rest of the sandwich into his mouth.

She crouched down and gave Tricks the treat as well as a good rub behind her ears and a kiss on top of her head. "Want another?" she called, feeling as if she was offering a treat to the man as well as the dog.

"No, thanks," he said. "That was enough."

After collecting the tray and setting the glass of water beside him so he could have a drink if he needed one, she nuked a turkey dinner for herself and ate in silence, sitting at the kitchen bar. Only when she'd finished did she think to ask him if he wanted the TV on.

"Sure," he said, though he didn't sound very interested. At least sound, rather than silence, would fill the air. She usually read or watched TV or surfed the web at night, but she didn't want to sit with him and had already spent enough time today on the computer; she didn't want to spend more. That left reading, or going up to her bedroom to watch the small TV set she had up there.

But it wasn't late enough to go to her room; it wasn't even quite dark yet, given that it was April and daylight savings time had pushed sundown to around eight. The clouds made things darker, and glancing out she saw that a thin layer of snow was on the ground, looking more like frost than snow. "It's been snowing," she said, just to make conversation. "Nothing heavy, at least not yet."

"It's April." He scowled at the window. From his seated position he couldn't see the snow on the ground, but there were a few flakes swirling in the almost-twilight.

"We've had snow in April before." Every April, it seemed, even if it was just a light covering to remind everyone Mother Nature could hammer them at any time.

"I'm from Florida. Snow sucks."

"I got used to it," she said. She'd grown up in several different places and hadn't called any of them home until she'd landed in West Virginia.

The time crept on, and Bo became more and more uncomfortable. She didn't like having her home, her privacy, invaded by a stranger. She'd deal with it, but she didn't like it. What little conversation they had was as brief and stilted as the snow conversation. She put on a coat and took Tricks out one last time and came back in to find in that short length of time her guest had gone to sleep.

She took that as a signal to fetch a couple of blankets and a pillow from the guest bedroom. To wake him up, she stood at a safe distance and yelled at the top of her lungs, which sent Tricks into a barking frenzy and definitely woke him up, though without the violent reaction of the first two times.

She helped him make another trip to the bathroom, refilled his water glass, made up the sofa with blankets and pillow, and once he was sitting down she pulled off his boots and set them aside. "Do you want to keep your pants on?" she asked, keeping her tone prosaic. She didn't care if he took them off or not—she had zero interest in his body—but he might have a preference. "Do you have any pajama bottoms in your duffle?"

"I'll keep them on," he said, which in a way answered her question about the pajamas.

She thought a minute, then took out her cell phone and called her landline number. She had both as a redundancy in case of emergency, one of the requirements of the town fathers. She had a phone in the kitchen, and one in her bedroom. As soon as it rang, she disconnected the call, then handed the cell to him. He looked at the phone and back at her. She explained, "If you need me, just call up the last number. I have a phone in my bedroom. That's if you don't have your own cell phone—" She stopped. "Do you?"

"I have another burner, in the duffle."

She shrugged. "I'll deal with it tomorrow. Just keep mine tonight."

"What if someone calls you?"

She opened her mouth to tell him that wasn't likely, then stopped. "Right. It's snowing, so there's no telling what some idiot might do on the highway."

"The phone is in the end zip pocket on the left."

She got out the phone, identical to the one she'd used to call Axel, and programmed her cell number into it. Then, with a sense of relief, she said good night and bolted with Tricks up the stairs to the privacy of her room.

She hadn't realized exactly how tense she was until she closed the bedroom door and felt her shoulder muscles relax. She and Tricks were always here by themselves, and it felt *wrong* to have to work around someone else's presence. Having him here meant she couldn't wander downstairs in her underwear to get her first cup of coffee, meant she and Tricks couldn't have a rousing game of Hide the Ball, meant she had to consider all sorts of demands on her time that she wasn't used to having. She had to close her bedroom door in her own house, not for her privacy because she knew he wasn't able to come up the stairs, but to protect him from an inquisitive dog in the middle of the night. She shuddered to think what would happen to Tricks if he was awakened by a cold wet nose shoved into someplace sensitive.

No doubt about it: she'd had all the company she could stand for one day.

Chapter 6

M organ woke and didn't immediately know where
he was; he lay very still, instinctively reaching out with his senses to locate any danger, anything
wrong. Then the particular scent of his surroundings
registered, and everything clicked into place.

He was at Isabeau Maran's place. The scent was
great, a mixture of wood from the barn structure, the
leather of the sofa he lay on, some sort of perfumey
stuff in a bowl . . . what was it . . . yeah, potpourri.
Silly-ass name. But most of all he could smell her. This
was her place, and the scent of her was everywhere.
He'd gotten up close and personal with that scent when
she'd helped him into the house . . . barn . . . whatever it was. He'd been so exhausted yesterday that now
he'd be hard put to physically describe her, other than

attractive, skinny, with long dark hair, but she smelled great—not because she smelled like a woman, which he guessed she did, but because she smelled nothing like disinfectant.

If he never smelled that particular hospital scent again, he'd be deeply grateful. The whole past month was tied up in a nightmare ball of pain, drugs, uncertainty, fear, anger, a disconnect from reality, and he didn't want to be reminded of it in any way.

He blew out a breath. He needed to take a piss, and the hell of it was he had to assess the situation. He hated it, hated every second of feeling this weak, but it was his new reality. He could make the trip on his own, or he could call her. She'd already had to help him to the bathroom twice; everything in him rebelled at the idea of asking her for help again. It wasn't as if she were a warm and fuzzy person who made offering aid seem like nothing, the way his nurses had. She seemed to like her dog much better than she did people, which, okay, given that she'd dealt with Mac at any early age wasn't so unreasonable. He still needed to piss. For a few minutes he lay there dreading the effort it would take to accomplish that simple task, but damned if he was going to call her for help. Even if he had to crawl, he'd get to the bathroom under his own steam.

The house wasn't dark. The TV was still on, though the sound was turned off because the noise had annoyed the hell out of him. A lot of things annoyed the hell out of him now because nothing was normal. He eased to a sitting position, relieved that the ache in his chest was nothing more than that. Pneumonia had been a bitch; the coughing had nearly killed him figuratively, while the pneumonia had almost done the job literally. He sat for a minute to make sure he wasn't dizzy, then braced his right hand on the arm of the sofa and levered himself up.

Okay. Not too bad. He was a little light-headed, but as he stood there the sensation faded.

His steps as he crossed the open space were slow. He couldn't do his normal confident stride; the best he could do was kind of shuffle his feet along. His body had always been a powerful machine that did his bidding, and now he didn't recognize himself in this weak, aching shell. Maybe the worst part of this whole shitty situation was the uncertainty that he'd ever get back physically to what he had been before being shot.

He took the time to look around, noticing details that he hadn't before. There was a keypad beside the door, and a red dot glowing on that told him she had a security system, and at some point had activated it. Guess it was a good thing he didn't need to go out to the Tahoe to retrieve anything.

The barn was uncluttered, except for the dog's toys strewn around. There was furniture—the living room area, the kitchen area, the dining area, and what looked like a small office space—in the whole open space that was the downstairs, but the furniture was only what was needed. The whole vibe was kind of barn mixed with industrial, which was weird for a woman. He didn't know shit about decorating, but he knew women and how they liked to surround themselves with *stuff.* Isabeau Maran evidently either didn't have a lot of stuff, or didn't like stuff.

He was relieved that, however slow he might be, he made it to the bathroom without any real problem. At least he could walk it under his own steam. Driving all day had knocked him flat for a while, which was humiliating in and of itself. Before being shot, he could and had swum and/or run for miles, but now just sitting upright for a few hours had done him in. That last hour of driving had been accomplished by sheer determination, and he'd made it by the skin of his teeth. By the time he'd parked in the driveway in front of the barn, he'd been glad no one was there because the best he could do right then was lay his head back and take a nap. He'd been there about forty-five minutes before his hostess arrived.

Mac had neglected to mention that his ex-stepsister was a crazy dog lady, which Morgan supposed was better than a crazy cat lady. At least there was just one dog, and dogs were easier to corral than cats. He liked animals in general, just not right now. He didn't have the energy to play, pet, or fend off an overly friendly retriever. Ms. Maran had made it plain where the dog was in the pecking order, and that was above him.

Okay, he got that. His presence was an unpleasant surprise. He was a stranger, and an imposition. He was as uncomfortable in this situation as she was.

They'd get through it though; he because he didn't have any choice in the matter right now, and she because she needed the money. Despite the fact that she was being paid well to house him, he was grateful she'd accepted. From what he'd overheard when she was talking to Mac, she'd been on the verge of refusing even after the money had been offered. She'd been adamant that no one here be endangered by his presence. Morgan was fairly certain no one would be, but he couldn't swear to it. Even the best of plans tended to get hiccups, or fall apart entirely when something unforeseen fucked up everything. He'd keep that to himself, though, or he'd likely find himself on the road in the morning, with nowhere to go and unable to get there under his own steam anyway.

He made it back to the sofa, stared without interest at the silent TV for a while, then got the remote and clicked the *off* button. The room went dark, a dark he found soothing. A hospital room—even one that was makeshift—was never dark. Once he had regained consciousness, the constant light, even a dim one, had become so annoying he'd have shut off every machine, smashed every light, and sealed the door . . . if he'd been able. He hadn't been, but now he could certainly turn off the damn TV. He knew that once his eyes adjusted, he wouldn't be in complete darkness; clocks on the microwave and the oven in the kitchen would be pinpoints of light, but *normal* pinpoints, not on machines that were hooked up to him. It hadn't been only the light that had bothered him; the unceasing *noise* had too, the sounds of the machines running, conversations outside his room, people walking.

He drew a deep, cautious breath—everything in his chest still protested the expansion of muscles and rib cage—and felt something in him relax at the silence, the darkness.

Bo didn't sleep well because she knew there was a stranger in the house. Sharing space wasn't something she liked or was accustomed to. Her bedroom door was closed, and Tricks was accustomed to having the run of the house so *she* was restless. Tricks got up on the bed, she got down on the rug beside the bed, she went to the door, she nosed around the bedroom. Finally Bo sat up and said, "Get up here and go to sleep." Tricks made the throat noises she did when she was arguing, but she jumped up on the bed and finally settled down. Bo thumped her pillow and tried to settle down herself.

She did finally go to sleep, but woke up annoyed—with herself, with Axel, with the man downstairs for getting shot in the first place. If he'd been more careful, he wouldn't be in this shape. On the other hand, neither would she be making a hundred and fifty thousand—!!!—for taking care of him, so from that point of view, she was grateful he'd been careless.

As she threw back the covers, Tricks jumped up as bright eyed as ever, ready for her first trip outside. She dashed to the door and stood there with her tail wagging, looking expectantly from Bo to the doorknob, as if trying to show her how to open the door.

Normally Bo didn't bother getting dressed, but now she did. She hit the bathroom herself, stopped to drag a brush through her hair and drink a glass of water. By the time she was dressed, Tricks was going back and forth between her and the door, letting her know this delay was unacceptable. Bo forcibly shoved her annoyance away. This was the way things would be for a while, she'd agreed to it, so she'd damn well be an adult about the situation. She wouldn't blame Morgan Yancy for being careless; instead she would do her level best to take care of him and actually earn the money Axel was paying her.

She thought of his gray, exhausted face, and her conscience twinged. She'd let her massive dislike for Axel color her interactions with a man who was barely hanging on.

With that in mind, she'd have clipped a leash to Tricks's collar if she'd had it with her, but the leash was downstairs. All she could do was do her best to keep Tricks from bounding up in his lap and generally making a nuisance of herself. Bracing for whatever Tricks might do, she opened the bedroom door and said, "Let's go outside."

No matter what, watching Tricks greet the morning always made Bo smile. Tricks never just *walked*. She pranced, she danced, she all but skipped. She was overjoyed with the prospect of going outside, of having her breakfast, at life in general. Bo also suspected Tricks got up every morning plotting a world takeover, because she never stopped trying to arrange everything to her liking.

The broad, industrial-type stairs were open to the floor level, and she could see that Morgan was still stretched out on the sofa, though the blanket that had covered him was now on the floor. Poor guy, as tall as he was, the sofa couldn't be all that comfortable. Until he could make it up the stairs under his own power, though, the options were limited.

Tricks immediately started for him, of course, and Bo said again, "Let's go outside," and grabbed the tennis ball from the floor. Immediately distracted, Tricks began bouncing in anticipation. Bo detoured through the kitchen to hit the magic button on the K-cup coffeemaker and slide a cup into place, grateful that the cup would be full when she returned. After disarming the alarm, she opened the door, and Tricks shot through the opening.

The ground was white but it hadn't been a heavy snowfall, probably no more than an inch. That was good because the sun was trying to break through the low gray clouds and the snow should melt quickly. For now, the day was cold but not icy. All in all, not bad. The year before, they'd been hit with a big snow in the middle of April, and that had been such a downer because it had seemed as if winter would never let go.

She had to throw the tennis ball for Tricks a few times before the dog settled down to do her business. Then Tricks ran around sniffing things, as if checking whether or not any strange creatures had invaded her territory during the night. She found a stick and romped in the snow with it, twisting and jumping and prancing. Finally Bo called her in with "Ready for breakfast?" Tricks was always ready for breakfast, or any other meal; she immediately came trotting over, a look of canine glee sparkling in her eyes. Bo retrieved the tennis ball from the yard—who, exactly, was the retriever here, and who was boss? She didn't care. She and Tricks had their routine, and they were both happy with it.

As they entered the door, she smelled the delicious scent of coffee at the same time she noticed Morgan was now awake and sitting up. He looked marginally better than he had yesterday, despite the growth of beard darkening his jaw. At least he didn't look as if he were about to die.

His gaze was blank and guarded as he looked up at her. Considering how welcoming—*not!*—she'd been the day before, Bo didn't blame him. She hung her jacket on the hook beside the door and asked, "Are you a coffee drinker, or would you like something else?"

Relief flashed across his face and was gone before she was certain she'd read him correctly. "Coffee," he said immediately.

"Cream or sugar?"

"No, just black."

She really, really wanted that first cup of coffee, but she thought he probably wanted it more. She did take the time to slide another K-cup into the machine and another mug under the dispenser, and press the button before taking the steaming hot coffee to him. His blue eyes focused on the cup as if she were bringing him ambrosia. "Thanks," he said, reaching out with both hands. He had big, rough-looking hands, scarred in places, bruised from needles and thin from the ordeal he'd been through, but she knew for a fact how strong they still were because she'd felt one clamped around her throat.

She watched his eyes close briefly as he took that first sip—she knew how *that* felt—and asked, "Didn't they let you have coffee in the hospital?"

"Once I could eat, yeah, but this is the first cup today. I was afraid I'd have to settle for skim milk." His voice was still thin and kind of scratchy, his eyes swollen from sleep, but she got a sense of increased energy from him. Not a lot, but anything was an improvement.

"I'll pick you up some he-man milk today. My pantry is empty even for me," she admitted. "I haven't had time to do much food shopping lately." Between her chief-of-police duties and the technical-writing projects, she'd been hustling, which was good for her bottom line but hell on her schedule. Going back into the kitchen, she got her own coffee and took a few blissful sips before setting it aside to dip some dog food into

Tricks's bowl, and put out fresh water for her. Tricks rushed over; she never had to be enticed to eat first thing in the morning; that routine was only for dinner, when she wasn't as hungry.

Feeding the dog was easy; feeding the man was a problem.

"I'm at a loss for breakfast," she confessed. "I have the aforementioned skim milk and cereal—Grape-Nuts, if you're interested." She knew she wasn't. In her mind, cereal was for when there was nothing else in the house. "I also have instant oatmeal, and I can throw in some raisins to make it more hearty. Other than that, we're back to the PB&J, or another smoothie. Or—" Thinking of something, she quickly opened the refrigerator door and checked the contents. Yes, she had cheese. "—a grilled cheese sandwich."

"I'm fine with just coffee," he said. "I'm not hungry."

"We went through this yesterday. You have to eat."

"Sandwich," he said grudgingly. "Peanut butter."

"I'm sorry for the pitiful selection, but like I said, I haven't been shopping." She felt chagrined by her lack of options, even though she hadn't had any warning. "What would you like while I'm shopping? Eggs, sausage, pancakes?" She pulled a notepad toward her and began scribbling down a list. Eggs, breakfast ham, salsa, fresh fruit, whole milk—

"Yes," he said, evidently to everything.

The enormity of feeding him dawned on her. It wasn't just breakfast; it was three meals a day, every day, for an unspecified length of time. Her scribbling got faster. Steaks, though maybe he wasn't up to that yet. She could put them in the freezer until he was. Salad fixings. Hamburgers, potatoes, frozen hash browns.

This was going to cost a fortune. Good thing Axel was paying her well.

Food wasn't the only problem. She couldn't hide him away out here for any length of time. For one thing, her grocery bill would give her away, and Hamrickville was small enough that things like that got noticed. For another, she didn't *intend* to hide him. That was a scandal waiting to happen. She'd tell Jesse that Morgan was out here, and the basic truth that he'd had open-heart surgery and needed a place to recover.

She couldn't tell Morgan's real name, though, given that he was in hiding and Internet searches were like taking out an electronic billboard.

She thought about that as she slapped peanut butter and jelly between two slices of bread—he got a whole sandwich this time—and when she took the sandwich to him, she said, "What name will you be using?"

Evidently he and Axel had already covered that base because he said, "I have a second ID that'll past muster in case anyone checks."

"Oh, it'll be checked. As soon as my chief deputy finds out you're here, he'll be all over it."

He showed no surprise at her having a chief deputy, which told her that he already knew her circumstances here, and the setup she had with Hamrickville. She cocked her head, eyeing him. If he so readily had a fake ID, how did she know he'd shown her his real one? On the other hand, did it really matter?

"Yes, I told you my real name," he said tersely, correctly reading her expression.

She shrugged. "It doesn't matter if you did or not, because I wouldn't know either way. I don't know you. All I know is that Axel sent you, you're in sorry shape and obviously need help, and a big payment is supposed to be deposited in my bank account today. You can call yourself Lady Gaga, for all I care."

"I'll stick with Morgan," he said drily. "My second ID is for Morgan Rees, R-E-E-S." He didn't pronounce it *Reece*, but rather the way it was spelled. "Middle name Allen."

"Is Allen your real middle name?"

"No."

"Okay. Morgan Rees. I got it. And if Jesse asks, I don't know your middle name, because it isn't as if we hooked up in the past or anything."

"Jesse is your chief deputy?"

"He is. Jesse Tucker. You'll be meeting him, probably some time this afternoon."

"Why?"

"Because when I tell him you're here, he'll have to check you out himself."

"Is he your boyfriend?" The blue eyes narrowed, his gaze drilling into her and the intensity in his gaze taking her aback.

"Lord, no!" she said, startled. What had made him ask that, unless he was weighing the possible complications of jealousy and prolonged contact? She supposed that was reason enough, given his circumstances.

"But he'll come out here to check for himself whether or not I'm on the level?"

"He's a good cop. He's also a friend, though not romantically." And Jesse was somewhat protective of her, not because of any romantic feeling but because he was afraid being chief of police would make her a target for people who didn't know the position was administrative and wanted to show up the "lady chief." She lived alone in an isolated area, something she still sometimes felt uneasy about, so she was grateful for the attention he paid to her welfare.

Come to think of it—Jesse always checked in when he left for the night, and last night he hadn't. The omission was so unusual Bo swiftly got her cell phone and called Jesse's cell, her brow knit with worry.

Jesse answered on the second ring. "Mornin', Chief."

She blew out a breath of relief. "I was worried. You didn't check in last night, and I just realized it."

"Ah . . ." Jesse fell silent, as if he couldn't think what to say. Bo could practically feel his embarrassment.

"What happened?" she demanded. "Is anyone hurt?"

"Hurt? No! No, it isn't anything like that."

Now it was her turn to say, "Ah." Jesse was crazy about one of the stylists, Kalie Vaughan, at Daina's salon. Lately Kalie had been saying yes when he asked her out, and she suspected Jesse's forgetting to check in had something to do with Kalie—either a fight, or *not* a fight. She smiled, because she strongly suspected the situation was *not* a fight. She said, "Okay. Tell Kalie good morning for me."

Startled, Jesse yelped, "How did you—" and she laughed and pumped a fist in the air in victory at guessing right. Not only that, she and the rest of the town had been rooting for them; they were both very well liked, and just *fit* together, as if they'd been made for each other and were only now realizing it.

"Okay, you got me," he said sheepishly.

"Yes, I did." She didn't try to keep the smugness out of her tone. "I'll be in around noon unless you need me before then."

She clicked off the call and found Morgan watching her as intently as ever, his gaze so sharp and focused that it made a chill race up her spine as she saw again what a dangerous man he was when he wasn't recovering from being shot. No, he was *still* dangerous, and she'd felt his hand around her throat as evidence of that. He was a wounded predator, but a predator still.

"What's going on?" he asked, his muscles tense as if preparing to swing into action, though what he thought he could do considering how weak he was—

He'd do whatever was necessary. She knew it without question, though she had precious little to go on other than the direct fierceness of his gaze, and his explosive reaction when he was startled out of sleep.

"Nothing," she said, then when his gaze flashed she amended, "Nothing of an official nature, anyway. Jesse has been seeing someone we all really like and she's why he forgot his check-in call last night."

He relaxed against the back of the sofa to finish his sandwich. Bo picked up his empty cup and indicated it. "Want another?"

"Please."

Bo went back to the coffeemaker and did the routine, grabbing some more of her own coffee and looking around for Tricks while the cup filled. Tricks was in the corner nosing through her toy box, though most of the stuffed animals were on the floor in front of the sofa. She found a dirty chewed-up old bone; it was covered with hair from where she'd wallowed on it, and some of her fur had gotten stuck on the rough places. All in all, it was a disgusting sight, but not to Tricks; carrying it proudly, she pranced over to the newcomer, where she laid it on the sofa beside his leg, then backed up a few steps and watched him with bright eyes, obviously waiting for something. Her plumy tail wagged gently back and forth, as if encouraging him.

"What does she want?" he asked, raising his voice a little.

"For you to either throw it, praise her for having such an excellent selection of toys, or play tug of war. Or, if she really likes you, she brought it to you for you to chew on. She's generous that way."

He made a rough, kind of gasping sound that could have been almost a laugh, but she wasn't certain. "Do I get to pick?"

She took pity on him; she delivered the fresh cup of coffee and grabbed the bone from beside his leg before Tricks could snatch it up to prevent her from getting it. "Never show weakness," she advised. "If you do, you're beyond human aid."

He snorted. "She's a retriever, not a tiger."

"She's a force of nature, and don't forget it." Bo's tone held humor, but she was also serious. She was the only known human whom Tricks acknowledged in any way as being in charge—not that she wasn't fond of other people, because Tricks loved people in general, but she tended to think they existed to pet her, praise her, and give her anything she wanted. Bo worked hard to keep Tricks from being a pest—unless she was pissed off at the person in question, in which case she let Tricks be as much of a pest as she wanted, which could be awesome.

To prove she could be single-minded, Tricks began trying to butt the bone out of Bo's hand. "You can have it," Bo said, relinquishing the bone, "but you have to go lie down to chew it. Go on, go lie down."

Tricks turned her head away, as if she couldn't believe she was hearing such nonsense.

"Go lie down," Bo repeated. Tricks went back to the sofa and hit Morgan on the knee with it. Bo said, "*No*," and took the bone away from her. Without another word she put the bone back in the toy chest, and closed the lid.

The dog actually made a huffing sound. Bo ignored her and focused on Morgan. "When you finish that cup of coffee, do you want to try for a shower? If you don't feel like standing up, I can get a plastic chair and put it in the tub."

"I can stand up," he said, his tone gruff.

"Great. Do you want me to get anything out of the duffle for you? A change of clothes, bandages?" She was fairly certain bandages should be involved.

"Just a change of clothes."

"No bandages?" she pressed.

"The surgery was a month ago. All of that has healed."

"Uh huh. What about any incisions for tubes, things like that?" She didn't bother keeping the suspicion out of her tone.

"Healed enough," he said flatly. "I'm through with that."

She could scarcely hold him down and bandage him against his will, especially since she didn't know exactly where he might need a bandage, so she shrugged one shoulder. "It's your call. Anything in particular you want to wear? Sweatpants, anything like that?"

His face was impassive. "A change of underwear, socks, shaving kit. The rest doesn't matter. I'm not going anywhere."

He didn't like the idea of her going through his duffle; she knew that because she wouldn't like it either if she were in his position.

"If you'd rather I not prowl through your things, just say so."

"I would have. I don't care." His tone was flat.

"Good enough."

"There's a weapon in there, though."

"I'm not surprised. Are you licensed?" Even if he wasn't, this was another of those instances, such as not booking Daina for public intoxication, where she'd use her own judgment rather than strictly follow the law.

"I am in Virginia."

That, too, was good enough. Virginia and West Virginia had reciprocity laws regarding concealed carry permits. Then she had another thought. "Under which name?"

There was still no expression on his face. "Both."

Man, she would sure like to know what organization he was with. Government for certain, but which of the myriad alphabet agencies? But going on the theory that in this case ignorance might be the best policy, she didn't ask. He was covered in case Jesse did some investigating, and that was the important thing.

She pulled the duffle around so he could see what she was doing, then crouched beside it and unzipped it. Finding his shaving kit was easy, because it was on top. She set it aside. Under the shaving kit was a pistol case for a Glock 41, Gen4. It was heavy and in the way, so she pulled it out and set it aside too; likewise with the three boxes of ammo. "You think three is enough?" she asked, wondering exactly what he was worried about in Hamrickville.

"If I didn't, I'd have more."

His socks and underwear were neatly rolled. Socks, tee shirt, and boxer briefs were set aside. A quick feel through the duffle unearthed one pair of sweatpants, which she selected on the theory he'd be more comfortable in them than in either jeans or tactical pants, which constituted the rest of his pant selection. He had tee shirts, a few flannel shirts, and one faded red sweatshirt. He wouldn't need anything that heavy unless he was going outside, something she didn't think he'd be doing today. "Will this do?" she asked, indicating his selections. "Do you have any other shoes? Sneakers, maybe?"

"I think there's a pair of sneakers in one of the side pockets."

"Do you want them?"

"Yeah. Socks on a hardwood floor can be tricky."

That was the truth. She noted the size of his sneakers—eleven and a half—and made a mental note to pick him up some socks with no-slip strips on the bottoms. He might sneer at them, but they'd be here if needed. And if he never wore them, she wouldn't be out anything more than a couple of bucks.

She took the selections into the bathroom and got a couple of towels and a washcloth from the linen closet, laying those out for him too. There was shower gel in the shower, a non-slip pad in the bottom of the tub, and a rubber-backed bath mat for him to step onto. There was also a towel rack he could use to balance himself while stepping in and out of the tub, though she hoped he didn't put a lot of weight on it or he and the rack would both go down.

By the time she was finished delivering and checking, he'd made his slow way to the bathroom. He moved carefully and he had his left arm kind of braced over his chest, but he'd made it and didn't look as if he'd die any moment.

"Just yell if you're too worn out to make it back to the sofa." She kept her tone brisk and matter-of-fact. "I'll be eating my oatmeal."

"Thanks, but I'm good," he said, and she figured he'd rather punch himself in the face than ask for help again.

She sat on one of the stools at the kitchen counter, eating her nuked oatmeal and sliced banana, but mostly sucking in another cup of coffee and listening to the sound of the shower. After a while the shower cut off, then another running water sound took its place; he was standing at the lavatory, shaving.

Bo had finished, rinsed her bowl and spoon and put them in the dishwasher, and was thinking about a third cup of coffee when he left the bathroom. Steam and dampness spilled out of the open door, though he'd had the ventilation fan running. His dark hair was wet and looked as if he'd combed it by running his fingers through it, but he was freshly shaved, and his expression drawn as if the exertion had sapped him. Both sweatpants and tee shirt hung on him. He slowly made his way back to the sofa and eased down.

"Do you want another cup of coffee?" she asked.

"No, thank you. Two was plenty."

Two was probably the limit of what he needed to drink, too, considering what an effort it was to get to the bathroom and back. That didn't need saying, though. She collected his cup and dealt with it, then said, "All right, I need to get moving. I'm going to town to stock up on groceries, then I have to be back in town by noon. Will you be all right here by yourself?"

He glanced up at her and the same thought shimmered between them: He had to be. He didn't have a choice. "I'll be fine." Then he glanced at Tricks, who was being good and playing with her stuffed animals. "What about Princess?"

Bo's mouth curved with amusement as she realized she'd never told him Tricks's name. "Her name is Tricks. T-R-I-C-K-S."

"I thought it was Princess. That's what you called her yesterday."

"Princess is her title, but her name is Tricks. Besides, I call her a lot of things. For the first year of her life she thought her name was No No You Little Shit."

His eyes lit, and something remarkable happened. Mr. Stoic tilted back his head and laughed.

Chapter 7

Bo made a mad dash to town and supermarket with Tricks riding shotgun. She was uneasy about leaving a stranger alone in her house though, really, what was he going to do? Go through her kitchen cabinets? He might crawl up the stairs but he sure couldn't climb them, and there was nothing more interesting there than her underwear drawer if he got his jollies that way. She doubted he'd make the effort, though, even if he were capable of it. He hadn't even wanted the TV on. She suspected he'd gone back to sleep as soon as they left.

The thin layer of snow was already melting and the roads were in good shape. She left Tricks in the Jeep, with the windows down a little for some cold fresh air, and made a record-breaking trip through the supermarket.

First, because it was most important, she restocked on food and treats for Tricks. Then she backtracked to the front of the store and began loading up on fresh fruit and some veggies, though fresh vegetables generally needed some sort of cooking and she didn't do much of that, but maybe she'd throw together a loaded salad, or something. She got frozen pizzas, he-man milk, bacon and eggs, canned biscuits, frozen pancakes and waffles, anything she could think of that was fast, easy, and something a guy might eat. Pancake syrup. The makings for hamburgers. Chips and salsa. Cheese, cheese, and more cheese. Olives? Did men eat olives? But olives reminded her of Italian food, so she got some frozen lasagna and the makings for spaghetti, which called for garlic bread. My God, feeding the man was likely to eat up everything Axel was paying her!

She didn't take the time to edit her selections or plan any meal in particular because she was in a hurry. When she was checking out, the tiny white-haired cashier, Miss Virginia Rose—a retired schoolteacher who hadn't taken well to retirement so she'd gotten a job at the supermarket where she could keep tabs on the whole damn town—raised her eyebrows at the mountain of food Bo loaded onto the conveyor belt. "Goodness, I've never seen you buy so much food."

Miss Virginia wouldn't directly ask, but she would certainly set the table for confession.

Bo was happy to oblige. The best way to avoid the appearance of guilt was to be up front with as many details as possible. "An old friend is staying with me for a while. Can you say 'junk-food junkie'?" She pushed two packs of Oreos forward, oné regular and the other golden so he'd have a choice. She might snag one or two of them herself.

Miss Virginia might have wanted Bo to enlarge on the old friend, but she was in a hurry and resisted. News would get around town soon enough. She couldn't hide him, didn't intend to try. If people thought there was a mystery, they'd start trying to solve it, and nothing good would come of that.

She paid cash for the mountain of food, her normal procedure these days. Once she'd have swiped a card without thinking, but when she'd hit her limit on multiple cards while she was renovating the barn, she'd had to learn different habits. The grand total on the bill made her wince, which reminded her she needed to check her bank balance some time today to make certain Axel had deposited the promised funds. What time did banks credit electronic transfers, anyway? Her inquiring mind really wanted to know.

She loaded the groceries into the back of the Jeep. Tricks had been perfectly content watching people come and go, though Bo received a welcome lick when she slid behind the wheel. She scratched behind Tricks's ears and said, "Let's go, sweetie. I want time to take you for a nice long walk before we head to the station."

Her tire tracks when she'd left were the only ones on the snowy driveway, meaning her guest hadn't changed his mind and driven away during the not-quite hour and a half she'd been gone. The Tahoe was still in the same place, its windshield still covered with snow. There were no tracks leading from the house to the SUV, so he hadn't even gone outside.

She let Tricks out of the Jeep and watched as she dashed around, smelling things, peeing, and smelling more things. She let the dog nose around while she got one bag of groceries out of the back and unlocked the door to take them in.

Morgan was asleep, one leg stretched out and his right foot on the floor. His left arm was curled across his chest, his right arm dangled. The blanket was kind of over him, but mostly not. If the noise of her entry hadn't wakened him, she saw no reason why he shouldn't continue sleeping. His body needed the rest.

Hurriedly she brought in the rest of the groceries, put them away, then grabbed Tricks's tennis ball and headed out for their walk. By the time they returned, she had just forty minutes before she was supposed to be at the station.

She hesitated, glancing at the sleeping man. Let him sleep, or wake him up for a quick sandwich? He needed to eat, but he also needed to sleep or he wouldn't be doing so much of it. What did she know about taking care of invalids? Not much, obviously. Now, if he were a dog, she'd be much more adept. When she'd gotten that little ball of fur she'd named Tricks, she'd been so terrified of her own ignorance that she'd read every article and book she could find on taking care of dogs. She'd never been the warmhearted, nurturing type, so it was ironic she'd landed in this role.

She hesitated for a minute, then slapped together a ham and cheese sandwich, put it in a sandwich bag along with some chips, and set them as well as a glass of water on the coffee table where he'd see them when he woke up. That would have to do.

She and Tricks drove back to town. On the way, she called the bank to ask about electronic transfers, and after a few minutes of holding, the head cashier picked up again and said, "Chief, we had a transfer come in overnight for you. It's already been credited to your account."

"That fast?" Bo asked, her heart rate suddenly doubling. Until then the money had been a possibility rather than a reality, and the realization that she was no longer mostly broke was so startling that she stammered something about her share of an inheritance and hung up.

Good lord! What a turnaround! For seven years she'd been digging herself out of a deep hole, then like a lightning bolt she was once more secure and solvent. The relief was so overwhelming she felt giddy and pulled to the side of the road until she'd settled down some. She hugged Tricks, which earned her a lick. "Guess what, baby girl," she said as she stroked the dog's lush fur. "You're going to be getting a new stuffed toy to play with. How does that sound, huh? Do you want a new baby?"

Tricks tilted her head back in enjoyment of the stroking, her eyes half-closed and a blissful golden-retriever smile on her face.

Bo's mind whirled with things she *could* do, one of which was buy a new vehicle that was more suitable for her, but the past seven years had taught her a lot and she immediately rejected the idea. No way. She didn't need a new car. She might want one, but she didn't *need* one. The Jeep was running fine, and it was paid for. No, it wasn't the most comfortable or practical choice for her, it had some miles on it, but she was used to it and she couldn't see spending money she didn't need to spend. That was how she'd gotten into such a financial mess to begin with. Likewise, she didn't need a new wardrobe. Or jewelry. Or a bigger TV.

Everything she needed—a home, friends, a job, Tricks—she already had.

Buying Tricks a new stuffed animal sounded like a great way to celebrate. Other than that, she'd use the entire hundred and fifty thousand to retire the last of her credit-card debt and make a big payment on her mortgage. She might refinance, she thought—but if she did, it would be for a shorter length of time. With the credit-card debt gone, she could easily pay extra on the principal as well as start saving for when she actually *needed* a new car.

With seven years of hard work she'd bought herself some wiggle room and relief, finally. It was kind of annoying that Axel, of all people, had provided her with the means to jump out of the hole.

Never mind how annoying it was. She'd jump anyway.

When her heart rate settled down, she pulled back onto the highway and finished the drive to town. The light snow had melted into the occasional white patch, and a weak sun was trying to break through the dismal gray sky. Traffic was on the light side; evidently people were waiting until the snow was completely gone, and the temperature more than two degrees above freezing before they ventured out on their Friday errands. She passed a few people heading out for lunch a little early and greeted them with a honk and a wave. She made it all the way to the second traffic light before someone yelled, "Tricks!" and the royal procession began.

Tricks ate it up, beaming and giving the occasional happy "Woof!" when her name was called. She knew the routine and was more than happy to play her part.

The school principal, Evan Cummins, was leaving the bank where his wife, Lisa, was a vice president of commercial loans. The bank was small enough that she was likely *the* vice president of commercial loans, but the title was nice and Lisa well liked. Evan waved his arm to flag Bo down, and she pulled to the curb and rolled down her window. Evan darted across the street and leaned down to look in at her and Tricks. "Morning, Chief," he said cheerfully. "Hi, Tricks."

"Good morning," Bo replied. "Is anything wrong?"

"No, everything's okay that I know of, which usually means something will blow up in my face as soon as I get back to the school. I just wanted to ask you if it would be okay for Tricks to ride on the Seniors' Float in the Heritage Parade. She was the kids' number one pick."

The mental image tickled Bo, and she began laughing. "Will she have to wear a tiara?" The Heritage

Parade was an annual event put on by the town, held in May just before the end of school so they could guarantee the kids' participation. They got out of school to decorate the floats, and the competition between the classes was fierce. The day included an antique car show, a crafts fair, and different food vendors set up in the small town park so people could picnic without having to bring their own food. There were, of course, a Heritage King and Queen picked from the senior class.

"I wouldn't be surprised," he replied. He was a pleasant-looking man in his mid-forties, brown hair and brown eyes, with a dimple beside his mouth when he smiled. All the kids and teachers in their small school seemed to like him, with the occasional hiccup in popularity whenever some of the kids got in trouble. He was a local, which to her way of thinking was a big plus because he knew everyone and the current set of parents were likely his own schoolmates, which meant he got more trust than an outsider would have.

Bo thought about it. Tricks loved attention, but she loved it only when Bo was nearby. "I don't know that she'd stay on the float if I weren't there. And, no, I don't want to ride on a float. She might do okay if we practiced, but more than likely she'd jump off the float and start looking for me."

Evan made a series of thoughtful expressions as he ran possibilities through his head. "How about if you're hidden where no one can see you? On the float, I mean. I don't want her to get hurt jumping off a moving flatbed trailer. The kids really want her there. I think they'd crown her queen if she attended school."

When Tricks was just a year old, Evan had talked Bo into attending Career Day at the school and bringing Tricks along. The gregarious dog had pranced into the redbrick building as if she owned it, bestowed her tennis ball on select students for them to throw for her, cuddled, licked, and generally charmed all the kids.

Bo hesitated. "Let me think about it." She really didn't want to spend an hour or so crouched on a slow-moving float, especially when there wasn't any guarantee Tricks would sit prettily even with Bo nearby. She sighed. Oh hell, of course she'd do it, if Tricks would cooperate. "We'd need to do a practice run or two, to see if she'd do it. She might hate the commotion."

Then again, when had Tricks ever hated being the center of attention? Nevertheless, Bo wasn't going to spring anything on her that was that far outside her experience.

"I'll get something set up," he promised and lightly slapped the door frame as he straightened. "Thanks,

Chief. I'll tell the kids it's a maybe, and it depends on Tricks."

She rolled up the window and continued down the street toward the police station, but before she reached there she saw Jesse's patrol car come racing up the street and slide to a stop in front of Doris Brown's bakery. He leaped out of the car and ran inside.

Unless he had a cake emergency, Bo thought, something was wrong. She pulled to the curb on the opposite side of the street, let the window down a couple of inches so Tricks would have fresh air, and dashed across the street to join him. Had someone had a heart attack? Just as she reached the sidewalk, she heard a scream and a loud crash and her heart jumped; she jerked the door open and rushed inside.

At first the scene was too chaotic to make sense. Jesse and a man were rolling on the floor, throwing punches. Miss Doris stood behind the counter, her hands clapped to her cheeks with her eyes wide and panicky while she emitted a series of little cries like a squeaky car alarm going off. Her granddaughter, Emily, sat crying on the floor with a hand held over her left eye. The glass in one of the counters was broken, as was a table. A customer, Brandwyn Wyman, had grabbed up one of the chairs and was circling the two men fighting, ready to clobber one of them in the head if she got an open shot.

All Bo knew was that if a fight was going on, she was on Jesse's side. Without giving herself time to think and chicken out, she gulped once and threw herself into the fray and locked her arm under the other guy's chin, pulling back as hard as she could. If nothing else, at least she could distract him and give Jesse a chance to get him handcuffed.

The man bucked and threw himself sideways, trying to dislodge her. The impact with the floor jarred her, hard, made her vision blur and sound fade. She'd never been in a physical fight before and wasn't prepared for the shock of impact—it was, well, *shocking*—but she tightened her arm and held on, reaching over his shoulder to clamp her free hand around her other wrist to keep him from breaking her grip. Another scream split the air, Jesse was swearing like a sailor, and then she felt the guy's muscles tightening as he gathered himself and lurched to his feet with her clinging to his back for all she was worth. He punched blindly over his shoulder, catching her on the right cheekbone. A series of things happened almost simultaneously:

She saw stars. Literally.

Fury swamped her, a red, all-encompassing fury that blotted out reason and felt as if her entire body had expanded from the force of it. She heard someone roaring, "I'll tear your fucking head off!" and to her horror realized it was *her* because she was suiting action to words and had her knees braced against his back while she hauled back with all her body weight behind it.

Jesse came off the floor like a tiger, reaching for them.

And Brandwyn stepped in, a five-foot-two, red-haired avenging angel with purpose in her eyes as she swung the chair with the precision of a professional baseball player, missing Bo's head by inches but clobbering the hell out of her target.

The guy went down like a fallen tree. Not being an experienced rider of either horses or humans, Bo couldn't launch herself free fast enough to evade yet another impact with the floor. The back of her head slammed against wood, her right shoulder slammed against something else, and there was a brief moment of silence.

"Holy shit."

Again, the voice was hers, faint and astonished now. She blinked up at the ceiling and tried to make her surroundings snap into place because they seemed to be doing crazy stuff such as whirling and dancing. She heard Jesse on the radio, his tone sharp and urgent, then Miss Doris's round face swam into view as she knelt beside Bo. She was saying, "Oh lordy, oh lordy," over and over.

Bo took a deep breath, and her surroundings did indeed snap back into place, with an audible *pop!* She turned her head and saw Jesse efficiently handcuffing the guy and rolling him over as he cast a swiftly assessing look at her.

"Get some ice, Miss Doris. For both Emily and the chief."

Miss Doris scrambled to her feet and hurried away, and her place was taken by both Emily and Brandwyn. Emily's left eye was swollen and rapidly bruising, but she seemed otherwise unhurt. She grabbed some napkins from the holder on one of the tables and gently pressed it to Bo's cheekbone. Brandwyn squatted beside her, her attention darting from Bo to the unconscious man as if prepared for him to recover and cause more trouble. If so, from the fierce expression on her face, she intended to be prepared.

"What the hell?"

Bo wondered who was controlling her tongue, because the last three sentences out of her own mouth had been swear words. Not that she didn't cuss a bit now and then, but she'd always been careful not to say the F word now that she was chief. That ban had now been broken, and she had no doubt the entire town would know her utterances, verbatim, before the day was over. Mayor Buddy might feel he needed to have a word with her over her public use of foul language.

"Shit," she said, in response to her own thought.

"Damn it!" She'd just done it again. "Will someone please put a gag on me?"

Jesse joined the squat club. He looked a little worse for wear himself, with his shirt torn and his nose dripping blood. Emily handed him a napkin and he made an effort to clean it away, then simply clamped the napkin over his nose. "The medics will be here soon," he said, his tone nasal but comforting. "And half the county, I expect."

Bo began cautiously moving her arms and legs, checking herself out. She didn't think there was anything broken, but she was kind of addled and couldn't be certain. "Why?"

The three squatters looked at each other in alarm.

"I'm not concussed," she said a bit irritably. "I don't think so, anyway."

"You did hit your head kind of hard on the floor."

Yeah, she remembered that. "Okay, okay. I see your point." Nevertheless, she got her left elbow under her and levered herself to a sitting position. If the medics and half the county were on their way, she at least wanted to be sitting up, preferably in a chair.

"Take it easy," Emily said, her soft voice worried. She was a pretty, gentle young woman, very much like her grandmother both in sweetness and in her master's touch with baking.

"That was wild," Brandwyn said, awe in her tone. "You jumped on his back like a monkey on an elephant."

That was kind of how she'd felt, too, and not in a good way. The elephant had definitely been in control. Groaning a little, she hauled her butt into a chair just as Miss Doris hurried back with not two but three bags of ice. One went on Emily's eye, the second one on Bo's cheekbone, and the third on Jesse's nose.

She felt strange, kind of disconnected from everything, even the throbbing of her cheekbone and shoulder. This was the first violence she'd ever encountered, and she hoped it was the last. The altercation felt as if it had lasted for half an hour at least, but it had to have been—what?—a minute, tops? She patted her coat pocket for her cell phone but came up empty.

"I've lost my cell."

Brandwyn looked around and said, "Here it is," as she stooped to pick up the phone from where it had skidded under another table. Bo took it and pressed the home button to bring up the time. Yes, less than five minutes had passed since she'd spoken to Evan in front of the bank. And what the hell difference did it make anyway?

It didn't. Checking the time was just more of that sense of disconnection, trying to find something solid, something normal.

Maybe the best way was in conversation. As soon as she had the thought, she realized the rest of them *were* talking, Jesse asking questions, Brandwyn and Miss Doris talking over each other, Emily starting to cry.

Bo said, "Who *is* that?" and pointed at the handcuffed man on the floor, because she didn't recognize him.

The four of them stared at her. "That's Kyle," Emily said, sniffling. "My husband."

"What? Kyle? What happened to his hair?" She'd met Kyle once or twice; she'd always thought Emily had married the pick of the Gooding family, but maybe not. When she'd seen him before, he'd worn his hair buzzed, been clean shaven; now his light brown hair was long, almost touching his shoulders, and he had the scruffy three-day beard a lot of guys were wearing to show how cool they were.

"He's been growing it out," Emily replied unnecessarily.

Kyle began shifting and making sounds that were a combination of grunts and groans. Following hard on that were some slurred curses, including "Stupid bitch, you'll pay for this."

"Are you threatening your wife?" Jesse asked in his cop voice, setting the ice bag aside and gripping the front of Kyle's jacket with both hands to haul him to a sitting position. As he did so, the first of the sirens became audible, coming in stereo from both ends of town.

Kyle wasn't stupid; his father had always paid to make trouble go away whenever any of his kids misbehaved, but Miss Doris and Emily were both well liked, and some trouble trumped money. Not only that, he was beginning to realize he'd been in a fight with two law officers, and that wasn't good. "No," he said sullenly. "I'm talking about a divorce."

"Praise the lord," said Miss Doris, glaring at him. "You're so low-down, you'd have to grow ten feet taller before you could lick the soles of Emily's shoes."

"Miss Doris, how about you and Emily, and Brandwyn, move to the other side of the room, please." Jesse cast an encompassing look at both Kyle and Bo, decided one wasn't going anywhere and the other was doing okay, and he began herding the ladies along.

Kyle slanted Bo one of those sullen looks.

"I didn't know it was you," she said, though it wouldn't have made any difference if she had. "I haven't seen you since you grew your hair out."

He didn't look apologetic, but again, he wasn't stupid. "I didn't know it was you either," he mumbled, and that was likely true given that she'd jumped him from behind. "Sorry." After a pause, "You okay?"

She didn't answer because the medic truck screeched to a stop outside the shop, followed by a county car coming from the opposite direction. They parked nose to nose, and two medics and a deputy bailed out. Other sirens were wailing as more patrol cars descended on them.

The medics came first to her, for reasons unknown. The attention was overwhelming, swamping her with the sense of being out of control as well as disconnected. She wasn't hurt all that much, a little bruised and sore, while Jesse was actually bleeding, but then she realized all the others were on their feet while she was sitting down—well, except for Kyle, but considering he was handcuffed, evidently sympathy for him was running low. One of the medics finally peeled off to check out Jesse and Emily, while the other checked her pupils, which appeared to be normal.

Maybe they were reacting to the novelty of the "lady chief" being in an altercation, but the small bakery was soon filled to bursting with county deputies and other official types, as well as the town's other four police officers, two of whom were off-duty. For God's sake, even the coroner showed up; it must have been a slow day for bodies. Several of the town council members arrived, as well as Mayor Buddy. Kyle Gooding was hauled to his feet, his head examined where Brandwyn had clobbered him with the chair, and taken away to the hospital in the next town over for checking out. He wanted to have whoever hit him arrested, but that didn't fly considering he'd been in the process of attacking two law officers when Brandwyn brained him. After he was checked out, assuming he wasn't admitted, he'd be taken to the county jail because the town didn't have a jail and all their arrestees were put in the county facility. Even after Kyle was gone, people *still* stood around, laughing and retelling the fracas.

Bo instinctively retreated behind her mental walls, where she always went when she was in protective mode. She'd learned to do that at an early age as a means of coping with her mother's parade of boyfriends and husbands, constant relocating, and a father who appeared to forget about her for years at a time. What had worked for the kid still worked for the adult. She didn't like being the center of attention, and if the attention wouldn't go away, then she would, at least inside her head.

Mayor Buddy came and patted her hand. "Quite a bit of excitement," he said kindly as he pulled a chair around and sat down beside her, his pleasantly homely face caught in an expression halfway between concern and laughter.

Bo roused herself to reconnect. "I want to apologize for my language," she said because she'd heard the phrase *"tear your fucking head off"* several times during the past half hour or so. The deputies had gotten a kick out of it, but she didn't know how the town elders would feel. No one would care if she cussed like a sailor in private, but public perception was a different animal.

He chuckled. "Don't worry about it. It makes such a good story most everyone in town will likely tell it themselves. The few that get puckered up about it will be outnumbered. I swear to you, I never thought this kind of thing would be in your job description."

"I didn't either." She'd thought it was administrative, all the way. And it would have been; jumping in had been her choice, no one had told her to do it.

"Kyle's daddy will likely kick up a fuss."

"I know." Warren Gooding owned a couple of prosperous sawmills in the area, which meant he employed some of the townspeople, and he liked to throw his weight around because of it. He'd always stepped in whenever his kids did anything wrong, blaming everything on someone else, so she expected him to follow pattern. Still, he didn't live within the town limits, so he couldn't even vote in elections, and considering the circumstances, she thought he'd concentrate his efforts on finding Kyle a good lawyer and maybe trying to get the prosecutor not to press charges.

If it were left up to her, she'd let bygones be bygones; she wasn't really hurt and neither was Jesse. Hitting Emily, to her, was the big deal, but whether or not Emily pressed charges was up to her. But there would be charges because no one wanted people to get the idea they could get away with resisting arrest and assaulting officers of the law. This whole thing was going to get very messy before it was over; Miss Doris was beloved in the town and the Goodings weren't, but the Goodings were influential, strident, and persistent.

She caught a glimpse of the big school clock on the wall behind the counter, and saw that almost an hour had elapsed. Aghast at her own negligence she said, "Tricks!" and surged to her feet. As cold as the day was, she knew overheating wasn't a problem, but it was definitely time to get her out of the Jeep.

"Where is she?" That was one of the county deputies; she thought his name was Mayhew, or Mayfield, something like that. It didn't surprise her that he knew who Tricks was.

"In the Jeep," she said as she started to the door.

"You stay here, maybe drink some tea and get settled. I'll get her."

"Tea!" said Miss Doris, her eyes lighting. "That's a good idea. All three of you need something to drink." She dashed behind the counter and went to work.

Bo watched as the deputy crossed the street and opened the passenger door of the Jeep, then released Tricks from her harness. He wasn't fast enough to catch her leash, though. Tricks jumped down and immediately trotted to the curb, her expression a little anxious as she searched for Bo. As always, she stopped at the curb and looked both right and left, a trick that delighted all the kids in town whenever they saw her do it, then she dashed across the street, leash trailing, and came straight to the door of the bakery, with the deputy in hot pursuit as he made repeated grabs for her leash.

Ignoring any health department regulations about animals in a food establishment, another deputy opened the door and let Tricks in. She darted to Bo, her whole body wagging with joy at being reunited. Bo received a thorough sniffing from her feet up, then a lick on the hand, then she was abandoned because the smells of food captured Tricks's interest. Tricks made a beeline for the display cases and stood in front of them, her tail swishing back and forth as she seemed to peruse the baked goods.

"I'm going to take her out back," Bo said to no one in particular and took Tricks out the door and around the side of the bakery to the patch of grass behind the building.

The brief period of solitude felt like an escape. She stood in the cold air, watching Tricks nose around and choose the optimal spot to pee, and relished the quiet and aloneness. She wasn't a recluse by any means, but the whole slightly farcical situation was too chaotic and intense for her to quite get a handle on it. She needed time to regroup, just a little, to settle herself down.

When she and Tricks went back inside, Miss Doris was waiting with a cup of hot, sweet tea. Emily and Jesse also held cups, though Jesse looked a bit self-conscious at holding the dainty teacup. He'd probably have preferred coffee, but Miss Doris thought he needed tea, so he'd drink the tea and thank her for it.

Things began winding down. Statements were taken from all involved, the medics pronounced her good to go but with the warning that she should get a friend to stay with her overnight, just in case there were any delayed symptoms.

Despite Miss Doris's rejuvenating tea—which had indeed helped settle the jittery feeling—Bo felt tired and drained. She'd had no idea brawling was such hard work. She was able to make her escape and go to the police station, where she could do normal things such as feed Tricks, give her some water, then kneel on the floor and bury her face in the dog's plush golden fur as she hugged her and apologized for letting her stay in the Jeep for so long. Tricks didn't care; she was happy to be hugged and doted on, regardless of the reason.

She didn't have the police station to herself, of course; the dispatcher, Loretta Hobson, had to get the lowdown on what had happened, the phone rang, both off-duty officers came in just to check on things, Daina heard about what had happened and called to see if she was okay, a couple of the town's nosy old men came by on trumped-up excuses so they could see what was what and make a report at the daily gathering of the Liar's Club at the diner, where they sat and drank coffee and chewed the fat for hours at a time.

All of that felt somewhat normal, though she began to realize she'd never live down the tale.

Dutifully Bo made herself sit down and start on the never-ending paperwork generated by even a small-town police force. That was her job, after all. She'd been at it for maybe half an hour when Jesse came in and dropped into the visitor's chair in front of her desk.

"Sorry about that," he said gruffly. He looked chagrined that she'd been involved in a violent situation. Jesse loved being a cop, had never wanted to be

anything else, but he despised paperwork and administration to an intense degree. It had been his idea to hire
her as police chief to handle the administrative side
while he handled the enforcement part of it, so he was
feeling guilty that she'd been hurt, however slightly.

She shrugged and felt the soreness in her right shoulder. "No one made me jump in, I just did it. I'm okay."

"I let him take me by surprise. I know how do-
mestics can blow up on you, and I let my guard down
anyway." His cheekbones flushed with color. Failing to
meet his own standards as a cop would eat at him, and
he'd make sure he never made that mistake again. He
looked like such a Boy Scout with his short dark-blond
hair, blue eyes, and square jaw that if someone didn't
know him, it was easy to underestimate his dedication
to the job. "Are you really okay? I know the medics
told you to have someone stay with you tonight."

With an inner start, Bo remembered her houseguest.
His presence would be convenient tonight, and though
she didn't think there was any need, neither would she
take any chances with her health.

"Someone is staying with me," she said.

"Who?"

"An old friend. He showed up unexpectedly yesterday afternoon."

"He?"

"Morgan Rees. He's in bad shape and needed a place to stay."

Pure cop flowed over Jesse, hardening his gaze as he considered what "bad shape" could mean, and the reasons behind it, such as drug addiction. "Bad shape how?"

"He's had open-heart surgery, then pneumonia, and he literally doesn't have anyone to take care of him. Poor guy looks like death warmed over."

"He's an old boyfriend?"

"Not even that." She could see where it was unusual that she'd open her home to someone with whom she didn't have any real links. "He was a friend of a friend, originally. We've never even dated. But we got along, and he's desperate, so . . ." She let her voice trail off and shrugged. "At least I won't be by myself tonight."

"Do you mind if I meet him?" That was Jesse, direct and determined.

She smiled as he hit right on her prediction. "I told him you would. Sure, come out whenever you want." Even if that wouldn't be the surest way to allay any of Jesse's suspicions, she'd have wanted him to meet anyone staying with her as a safety measure. She wasn't a scaredy-cat, but she was definitely a cautious one. It struck her that she'd never before had an overnight visitor, of either sex, and it was seldom that anyone came out to her place. That was fine with her because she liked her own space and her privacy and wanted to be able to leave any situation and go home.

"I was planning on following you home anyway to make sure you got there okay. Head injuries can be tricky."

"I appreciate it," she said, and meant it.

Chapter 8

Morgan was half-asleep when he heard the Jeep return; he'd already learned its sound, but there was a second car following close behind. He sat up, glad he'd made the effort to drag some clothes out of the duffle bag and get dressed. He didn't have on shoes, but at least he had on pants, socks, and a tee shirt. Through the windows he saw her and the dog, followed by a guy in a police uniform. This must be the famous Jesse, come to check him out.

Fine. He'd expected it, they'd prepared for it. He wasn't worried about the cops; he knew his forged background would stand up to inspection. He'd play his part, though God knows acting weak and sick was reality, not acting—and it grated.

The door opened and the dog dashed in, straight to him. She gave him a lick on the hand, then turned her attention to the half-eaten sandwich on the coffee table. At least he'd slid it back into the sandwich bag, so she couldn't wolf it down. He leaned over and retrieved the bag, zipped it up. If he let the dog have the sandwich, he imagined his hostess would tear him a new one.

She closed the door and turned around. "Jesse, this is Morgan Rees," she said. "Morgan, Jesse Tucker."

She kept the introduction tight and brief. Morgan glanced at her to see if he could read anything in her expression and immediately saw the swelling bruise on her cheekbone.

Alertness zinged through him, adrenaline sharpening his gaze, straightening his spine, tightening his muscles. He found himself on his feet, though the process of getting there was slow enough that it chafed. "What happened?" he demanded, his tone rough.

She looked briefly puzzled, then realized where he was looking and touched her cheekbone as if she'd forgotten about it. "Oh, that. There was a fracas in the bakery. Much fun was had by all."

"Bo—I mean, the chief—helped me subdue a suspect," Jesse supplied. Morgan had already made a swift appraisal; the cop looked like the prototype for "straight arrow," in good shape, posture military-erect, eyes clear and direct. He'd just made a tiny slip, one that Morgan immediately caught. So she was called "Bo" instead of "Isabeau?" Good thing he hadn't used Isabeau, or the cop might get the idea they didn't know each other very well at all, and that could open up a can of worms. Why hadn't she told him that? Because he hadn't called her by name when they'd talked, after first asking if she was Isabeau Maran. She wasn't accustomed to subterfuge, so the difference between her given name and the name she used simply hadn't occurred to her.

"I hope the jerk paid for it," he growled, directing a piercing look at Jesse.

"He paid, and he'll pay some more."

He gave a brief nod. His ire was reluctant but it was real. The bruise on her face wasn't bad; he got worse on almost every mission. But he was trained for it, and he was built to take physical punishment. She wasn't. She was an ectomorph, long arms and legs without much muscle mass, her bones thin. There was no extra weight on her and never would be. Her facial structure was faunlike, with big brown deer eyes and a delicate jaw; fracturing it would be easy, and his hands curled into fists at the idea of some jerk punching her.

"It's just a bruise," she said and looked at the sandwich in his hand. "Want me to take that? Jesse, you want something to drink?" Meaning the subject was closed, and she didn't want to be fussed over.

"I'm good, thanks."

Morgan gave her the sandwich bag and she went over to the kitchen, leaving the two men alone, though since it was all one big open space he guessed "alone" was stretching it a bit.

Jesse's stare was unwavering. "The chief says you guys are old friends."

That part could be a little sticky. He had to make it sound as if they'd known each other well enough that he could show up at her house and reasonably expect her to let him crash here while he healed, but not so close that they'd kept in touch or knew everything about each other.

"Yeah, we met years ago, had some mutual friends. No relationship or anything like that, just friends."

"But you know each other pretty well."

"If you're asking were we close enough that I could just assume she'd take me in, the answer is no. I wanted out of the hospital and didn't want to go into a rehab facility. Enough was enough." He scowled. "After a month—God almighty. I'd have crawled out if I had to."

"So you just decided to come here."

In a flash Morgan saw the fabricated background wasn't going to hold up under this cop's nosiness. He'd dig deeper than most, and the logic wasn't there. Other people might accept the glossed-over version, but Jesse Tucker wouldn't. He gave Jesse a shrewd look, sizing him up. Maybe the best thing was to come clean—not completely clean, not his real name or the full circumstances, but enough to have the cop back off. That wasn't what he and Axel had agreed on, but he'd always had autonomy in the field, so he could make any adjustments he thought were warranted.

"I got shot," he said baldly.

From the kitchen Bo said, "I thought you weren't going to tell that." Her tone was both interested and absent, which was exactly the right note to hit. Maybe she was better at this than he'd assumed. Her little comment let Jesse know that she wasn't being lied to, that her eyes were open and she didn't need protecting.

"He needs to know," Morgan replied. "So he doesn't do any digging that might give me away."

Jesse was standing ramrod straight, his gaze hard and level. His hand was resting on the butt of his service weapon, a completely automatic move he probably wasn't aware of making. "Give you away to who?"

"Whoever did the shooting," he said tersely, which wasn't the truth but close enough. They knew who'd fired the shots; they just didn't know who had aimed the shooter. "That's why I couldn't stay in my own place."

Jesse mentally chewed on that a minute, then said, "Why don't you tell me exactly what's going on."

"I'll tell you as much as I can. Do you mind if I sit?" He hated to admit his weakness, but it was either do that or start wobbling on his feet. Without waiting for the answer—what did he care anyway?—he eased down on the sofa, using his right arm to brace himself so no sudden movement pulled on his chest muscles. "First, I'm government. That's pretty much all I'm going to tell you. If you start digging and trip any electronic wires, you can get me killed."

"But you brought your trouble here without thinking about the danger to my town?" There was fire in the cop's eyes, fire that was justified. But Jesse also sat down, and that was progress. He was at least willing to listen and, because of Bo's response, was already inclined to believe what he was told.

"You think I'm stupid?" Morgan shot back. "There are layers of protection. Rees isn't my real name. We went out of our way to make sure Bo is in no way linked to what happened. My backstory is solid, I'm off the grid. No one digging from the other end is going to find me unless you blow my cover by making inquiries from this end. What we're waiting for is whoever was behind the shooting to trigger their own alarms by trying to find me. Then we trace it back, identify, and handle." He didn't say how the situation would be "handled," but he didn't have to.

"I've already asked all those questions," Bo added as she rejoined them. "Jesse, I wouldn't have let him stay if I hadn't satisfied myself it was safe. I talked to his . . . supervisor, I guess. The way this was handled, without any kind of electronic or paper trail, there's no way he can be connected to us. His supervisor, him, me, and now you—we're the only ones who know."

Except that wasn't quite true, Morgan thought, though he kept his expression veiled. The connection to her was going to be difficult to find, difficult enough that no one would think they were *meant* to find it, but the whole point of this was that he could eventually be located. Then the shit would hit the fan, for the guilty party at least, and afterward he'd get back to his real life kicking terrorist ass.

Jesse didn't like it, didn't like anything about it; that was plain. He looked back and forth between Morgan and Bo, weighing, considering, but finally his trust in Bo outweighed his reservations. "If you're satisfied, boss," he said.

She rocked her hand back and forth to indicate she hadn't one hundred percent bought in. "I'm satisfied enough, for now. But I know for certain Morgan isn't in any shape to leave, so that's that."

That too was a good note to hit. She was aware of the possible danger, but also of reality. If Jesse thought she was being reckless, that could tip the scale the way they didn't want it to go, but she'd just reassured him she was on guard.

"I wouldn't have come here if I thought there was any danger to either Bo or the town," he said, putting a thumb on the scale to tip it even more in his favor. "If it helps, I'm armed."

"Got a permit?"

"One that covers every state. But I also have one issued by West Virginia, so I'm covered there."

"Mind if I see them?"

Axel had covered that too, getting him concealed carry licenses in the Morgan Rees name. He hitched his left hip up and retrieved his wallet from his back pocket, extracted the permits and handed them over.

Jesse's eyebrows rose as he looked at them. "They're issued to a Morgan Rees. I thought that wasn't your name."

"It isn't; if you thought you'd find out my real name by this, it won't work. I do this shit for a living, and the agency paperwork behind me is solid. These will stand up." They weren't legal, but they'd stand up.

Morgan could see the ire and frustration in the cop's eyes; he knew what Morgan was admitting and didn't like not being able to investigate something his instincts told him he should. He had no reason to believe anything Morgan was telling him, but he also realized that it could be true. Jesse glanced at Bo, and once again his trust in her was the deciding factor.

"If you're okay on this, boss, then I guess I am too."

"Even though I think it's okay," she replied, "I also think we should be smart about this. We won't let our guard down."

That seemed to settle the matter. After a few minutes Jesse left, not satisfied but reassured anyway. Bo immediately put on her coat and took Tricks for a walk. Morgan watched out the window as she and the dog disappeared into the tree line, the dog all but bouncing around her as she chased the tennis ball Bo tossed underhanded—and with her left hand, which struck him as odd—and brought it back to her with a happily wagging tail and an eager expression that was easy to read even from that distance.

He clicked into analysis mode, going over every nuance of Jesse's tone, exactly what he'd said. He thought the cop would be a good ally despite his misgivings. To cover the bases he needed to let Axel know exactly what had been said and that the cop had been partially read in on the situation, but he wouldn't call again unless it was an absolute emergency because he had no way of knowing where Axel was, or with whom. Any contact would have to wait until Axel initiated it.

He got to his feet and walked around, knowing he had to start pushing his body to do a little more each day. The hours of driving the day before had unexpectedly knocked him flat, telling him he still had a long way to go before he reached full recovery. He could wait patiently in ambush for days at a time, but this physical incapability was maddening. There was no way of knowing when whoever was behind his shooting would find his location, so he had to be ready.

Bo and the dog returned in about half an hour. The dog looked happy, and Bo's cheeks were flushed from the cold. She used her left hand to open the door.

By then he was back on the sofa. He said, "What's wrong with your right arm?"

"Shoulder," she corrected, her tone matter-of-fact. "I banged it in the fight. It's just bruised."

"Did you have it checked out?"

"It's just a bruise. I'll ice it down before I go to bed."

"Is it swollen?"

He saw a flash of annoyance in her eyes, then she smoothed it away and pulled her emotions back, hid them. "No, just sore."

She did that a lot, he thought. Most women were naturally more open with their emotions than men, but not her. She battened down the hatches and let very little show—except with the dog. She was as open as a book when she was dealing with her pet. Her expression both lit up and softened then, and her voice took on a subtle croon. With people—or at least with him; she might be more open with her friends—she was brisk and businesslike.

Maybe she didn't like being fussed over. Maybe she had a hard time admitting to any weakness. He could understand that because he was right there with her. He was so damn tired of being fussed over he sometimes thought he'd punch the next person who tried to plump his pillow or adjust a blanket over him. Thank God Bo didn't seem to have any instinct to fuss, such as when she'd simply put a sandwich in a Ziploc bag for him, along with a bottle of water, and left him alone for the day. The solitude had actually felt good.

Despite her reserve there had been an ease between her and the cop, one that said they worked well together, and, yes, a real friendliness. Morgan supposed he couldn't blame her for any reserve, given the situation and that they had just met.

"Let me see what I can scare up in the way of food," she said, changing the subject. "I bought some guy food today. I'm not much of a cook, but I can do basic stuff like spaghetti."

The mention of spaghetti made his mouth water. His food for the past month had been so bland he'd had a hard time working up any interest in it. Where was the logic in trying to stimulate someone's appetite with food that tasted like paste? "Spaghetti? With garlic bread?"

She actually smiled. "I guess that's the answer to my question. C'mon, Tricks, let's get you fed before I get started on the people food."

He wasn't surprised that the dog came first.

She went through some weird routine with the dog while she was feeding her, something that involved a lot of sweet talking and a couple of "Let's try this ones." He didn't turn around to check it out. She was feeding the dog—how interesting could it be? Not very.

She slapped the spaghetti dinner together pretty fast, but from what he could tell, she opened a jar of sauce and didn't bother fancying it up with extra meat and spices.

Trays were another thing he was ready to do away with, so he made his slow way to the small table and sat opposite her. She poured a glass of real milk for him. He'd have preferred a beer or even a glass of sissy wine, but at least the milk wasn't skim. The pasta was a little chewy. The spices and the garlic bread, though, were like heaven. The only thing that came close in taste was the fast-food hamburger he'd stopped for on the way down to West Virginia. He'd managed only a couple of bites, but, *hell*, the ketchup and pickles and onion had almost made him moan as the taste exploded on his tongue.

"You've had a rough twenty-four hours," he finally said after they'd eaten in silence for a few minutes. The truth was, he was already full, but maybe if he wasted a little time in small talk, he'd be able to eat some more. Besides, he was reluctantly curious about her. This whole setup she had, the chief-of-police thing, was interesting.

She looked up, mildly puzzled. "I have?"

He ticked the items off: "Choking, hurting your hand when you punched me, getting punched in the face, hurting your shoulder."

"Oh." Her face cleared. "Also banging the back of my head on the floor. I have a knot back there."

"That type of thing happen very often?"

"Brawling in the bakery? First time for everything."

"I'd expect the police force to be small enough that you'd be called in on almost every arrest."

"I'm administrative, not enforcement. I was hired as someone to do the paperwork and handle the work schedule."

He frowned, forked up another bite of spaghetti. "But you had to have training to qualify for the job."

"Not in West Virginia, you don't. It's a small state with a small population, so I guess there had to be other options or half the towns wouldn't have adequate staff. The position of chief can be purely administrative. Jesse didn't want to deal with the paperwork or headache of scheduling, so Mayor Buddy worked out something else. He knew I'm fairly tech savvy because I do technical writing, and he offered the job to me. I took it. It's part-time, and it's a good deal for both me and the town."

He grunted. That meant she'd thrown herself into a fight without any idea how to protect herself; she was lucky to have come out of it as well as she had. Part of him was appreciative of the guts, while another part of him was a little pissed off she'd been put in that position. *None of his business.*

No sooner had he told himself that than he asked, "So you jumped into a fight without any training?" He tried to keep the pissed-off out of his voice but a little bit leaked through.

If she heard it, she ignored it. She shrugged. "Dumb, huh? Jesse insisted on teaching me how to shoot, some, and showed me a few basic self-defense moves, but that's about it. I know I took a risk. It worked out okay, but I'll sure think twice about trying that again."

She was so damned reasonable about it that he was frustrated in venting his unreasonable ire. He had to tell himself again that it was none of his business. On the other hand, if she landed herself in the hospital, he'd be in a touchy situation, so he'd rather she stayed hale and hearty. That made it very much his business.

"I can teach you more," he said.

"You can barely move."

The accurate assessment pissed him off even more because it was so true. "I'm better today than I was yesterday. I don't have to be in great shape to show you how to disable someone."

"We'll see," she said, but he got the feeling the non-committal reply meant she had no intention of following through.

Yes, they *would* see.

Having someone else in the house was an ongoing irritant, like hearing a mosquito buzzing but not being able to locate it to smash. Regardless of that, over the next few days Bo found them settling into a kind of routine. She didn't go into town on the weekends, so she spent most of those two days working on her tech-writing projects, and doing her regular stuff with Tricks.

She didn't put in any time at the station, but she heard plenty from both Jesse and Daina about the Emily/Kyle situation. The judge had conveniently—and probably deliberately—been out of touch, so Kyle's bail hadn't been set until Saturday afternoon, meaning Emily had time to do whatever she wanted to do. What she wanted to do was file for divorce (which she had), get a restraining order against Kyle to keep him away from her and her family (which she had also done), and pack up Kyle's clothes and personal effects and take them to his father's house (which she'd also done, with Jesse's presence to make sure all went well). Emily was acting with a purpose, getting things done and forging ahead.

The entire Gooding family was occupied in trash-talking Emily and her family. Her uncle on her daddy's side, Harold Patterson, owned the barbershop and of course the barbershop was a hotbed of gossip. The Emily/Kyle scandal was going hot and heavy, with half the town taking sides as Bo had known would happen. Most of them were on Emily's side because Warren Gooding had never endeared himself to anyone, but there were a few who thought Emily was being a bitch.

From Daina came the information that Mrs. Gooding had been in and said that she suspected Emily was running around on Kyle. Also from Daina was the report that the whole bakery incident had started because Emily found out Kyle was cheating on her and told him to get out.

There was going to be bad blood over this for a long time to come, Bo thought. She might have to arrange a police presence at athletic games and such, anywhere members of both families might come into contact with each other.

But that would remain to be seen; maybe Kyle would move away. Emily might meet someone, and *she* could be the one who moved. Life happened. Bo had enough on her plate at the moment without looking for more.

The weather cooperated by turning sunny, if still cool, so she and Tricks had their long walks and plenty of playing. Spring was finally showing signs of coming to stay, and just in time; she and everyone else had had all of winter they could stand. The trees spent the weekend exploding in buds, as if they knew something humans didn't. The air was filled with a kind of vibrancy as if every plant was humming with activity.

Morgan wasn't a demanding patient. He didn't ask for anything extra, and he wasn't exactly a patient. He didn't have much strength and he still hadn't attempted the stairs, but he could get himself to the bathroom for his needs, take a shower without aid, and she kind of got a kick watching his laser focus as he watched her approach with the morning's first cup of coffee for him. He stared at that cup as if willing it into his hand.

He was walking around more. He slept, he read, he watched some TV but not much. On Sunday afternoon, for the first time he went outside, onto the concrete slab porch. He moved one of the chairs into the sunshine, where he sat for a while.

That threw Tricks into a tizzy. Someone was outside who could throw the ball for her, even if that someone wasn't Bo, but she wasn't outside to take advantage. She went from window to window, to the door, got her tennis ball and went to Bo, then back to the door. She dropped the ball and barked, then picked up the ball and started the whole rotation again.

Bo was trying to work, and knew how relentless Tricks could be in getting her way. Giving in would be a tactical mistake. She checked the clock, but it wasn't quite time to take Tricks out so she said, "No," and kept working.

Tricks trotted over and butted her leg.

"No." This time she said it sternly, and raised a warning finger. Tricks huffed, dropped the ball, but gave up for the moment and curled on the rug by the desk to pout.

That was all Bo needed, for Tricks to give up for just a minute so she wouldn't think she'd won. She let a couple of minutes lapse, saved her work, then stood up and said, "Let's go outside."

Tricks jumped up, grabbed her ball, and raced to the door. She was dancing with excitement, whirling with her feet patting up and down.

A couple of days of rest and the application of ice packs to her right shoulder had done wonders, and Bo was able to throw the ball without pain. As soon as she stepped outside, she wound up and let it go, and Tricks took off in joyful pursuit.

"Good arm," Morgan commented.

"I've been doing this almost nonstop for two years, as soon as she got big enough to get the ball in her mouth."

Tricks caught the ball on the second bounce and brought it back for a replay, dropping it at Bo's feet and racing off. "Cheater," Bo said, bending down to retrieve the ball. She threw it over Tricks's head, but this time it was caught on the first bounce. Tricks stopped, posed, and Bo said, "Good catch!" in an admiring tone. One tail wag, and they did it all over again.

Then Tricks took the ball to Morgan, dropped it beside his chair.

Bo started to go after it, but he leaned down and got the ball, gave it a sidearm toss. He got good distance on it—too good, because it rolled to a stop before Tricks could get there. The dog gave him a disgusted look and took the ball back to Bo.

She had to laugh. "You failed the ball-throwing test," she said.

He scowled. "It was a good throw."

"It went too far. She likes to catch it on the bounce."

"She told you that, huh?"

The mild skepticism in his tone put her back up a little. "Watch her. A two-bounce catch is acceptable, but she likes the one-bounce catches. She'll stop, pose, and wait until I praise her. She gave you the honor of throwing her ball and you failed."

He snorted.

Bo threw the ball, and Tricks caught it on the second bounce. She brought it back, dropped it, took off again. Bo picked it up and heaved it over her head. It was a one-bouncer, and as soon as Tricks caught it, she froze in a proud, head-high pose. Bo let her hold the position for a few heartbeats before she said, "Beautiful catch!" Tricks acknowledged the praise with a quick tail wag, and brought the ball back.

Bo laughed. "I don't know if I've trained her or she's trained me, but I've learned not to underestimate her ego, vanity, persistence, or intelligence. She'd be a pain in the butt if she wasn't so happy and loving."

He just shook his head. He looked as if he thought Tricks was a pain in the butt regardless of how happy she was, but so what? Tricks would be here long after he was gone.

"She's two years old, then?"

"About two and a half, now. She was originally bought—and registered—by old Mrs. Carmichael. I couldn't have afforded her. But about two weeks after Mrs. Carmichael got her, the old lady had a heart attack on the way to visit a friend and crashed the car. Tricks was with her, in a travel crate, thank God. Mrs. Carmichael died from the heart attack." Bo watched as Tricks sniffed around, found a suitable place, and finally deigned to empty her bladder. "The puppy was terrified and trembling. I took her with me to the station while Mrs. Carmichael's son was notified and just held her in my arms. Then it turned out Mrs. Carmichael's son didn't want her and told me to give her away to anyone who wanted her."

"That would be you."

"Yes, indeed," Bo said ruefully. "I didn't know anything about puppies, I'd never had a pet, but by then I'd been holding her for a few hours and I suppose she'd imprinted on me. The son went to his mother's house and gathered up all Tricks's food and toys and brought them to me. He was sleepwalking from shock, but he knew his wife didn't want a dog. I brought Tricks and

all her stuff home with me and did some panicked re-
search on how to take care of a puppy. She was still terrified, in a new place, and wouldn't stop shaking unless
I held her. When I put her in her little crate that night,
she cried. It broke my heart. So I got her out and let her
sleep curled against me. That was that."

"Pushover." His mouth quirked with humor.

"You think you could have resisted a little ball of
white fur? She looked like a baby's stuffed animal, or
a cotton ball with big feet." A *demonic* cotton ball, at
that. The first year had been hell on wheels until Tricks
decided she had to defer to the human who controlled
the food.

"We always had pets when I was growing up," he
said, which didn't really answer the question. Then he
shrugged. "Now, I'm not at home enough to take care
of a cactus."

"Didn't you say you're from Florida?" She thought
he had, but she'd had other things on her mind that
afternoon.

"Yeah. What about you? That isn't a West Virginia
accent."

"All over. I was born in Arizona, but I don't remember it. Mom moved a lot." And married a lot, hence
the moving. Morgan was good, spotting the difference
between her accent and Jesse's. Over the years, she

thought her speech had modified. In the rare instances when her mother got in touch—both times—she'd said something about how "hick" Bo sounded now. Maybe the accent was a good mother-repellent because she hadn't heard from Rebecca in a few years now. She loved her mother, but she loved her best at a distance.

"How long have you been here?"

"Seven years."

That seemed to dry up their small talk for a while. He sat quietly in the sun, looking at the greening grass, the budding trees. Whatever he did for a living was obviously hazardous, so Bo guessed he wasn't accustomed to either the quiet of country living or his current state of inactivity. She threw the ball some more for Tricks, who joyously retrieved for a good forty-five minutes before going to the bowl of water Bo kept outside, getting a good drink, then flopping down on the concrete to pant and bat the tennis ball back and forth with a paw.

After watching Tricks for a minute, Bo said, "You must be getting a little bored."

"I'm feeling better," he replied, which she supposed was an answer. If he was feeling better, of course he was bored. While he hadn't been able to do anything much more than eat a little and sleep a lot, boredom hadn't factored in.

"I can't offer you much to do. Some books to read, the laptop computer. I don't usually need the laptop for work, so you're welcome to it."

"Computer," he instantly replied. "Thanks."

She stretched her legs out, rubbed Tricks's back with her toe. "Afraid they'd be girl books?" At the touch, Tricks rolled over on her back and lay there with her legs in the air and her tongue lolling out, the very picture of canine bliss.

"I wouldn't care about that." He paused, and she saw a glint of blue as he slanted a cautious look her way. "Are they?"

"Some. But I also have some mysteries, some suspense, a couple of Stephen Kings. They're upstairs in my room. I'll bring a few down, and you can let me know when you need more."

She didn't think she'd ever before been able to satisfy a man with some books and a computer, she thought, and hid a smile as she got to her feet and went inside, Tricks at her heels.

Chapter 9

On Monday morning when Bo left her bedroom and looked down on the whole lower floor from the stairs, she realized that she was becoming accustomed to seeing the tall man sprawled asleep on her sofa. "Sprawled" was the operative word; he slept with one long leg draped over the sofa back, and the other either stretched out or with that foot planted on the floor. Given his height and the length of the sofa, he didn't have much choice. It would be a red-letter day when he was able to climb the stairs and sleep in the guest room, in a real bed.

She thought he looked some better—not a lot, but some. His color wasn't as gray, and though he'd slept a long time after sitting out in the sunshine yesterday, at least he'd been able to make the effort. Just two days before he'd had difficulty shuffling to the bathroom and back.

His appetite was improving, too. Every day he was able to eat a little more. She was beginning to feel a bit invested in his condition, and that disturbed her. She didn't want to get to know him on anything more than a superficial level. She wanted him to get well and get gone with as little impact on her life as possible other than the very welcome addition of a hundred and fifty thousand to her bank account.

She had to admit he was playing it smart, keeping things low-key. She thought he was normally a take-charge guy accustomed to command, but he was careful to not be demanding. Though occasionally some impatience leaked through, he never let it become more than a leak. Likewise, several times he was a tad grouchy, but the grouch never escalated into anger. After the choking incident, they both worked to keep things under control, and she was appreciative of his efforts.

Tricks, however, knew no boundaries. He was a new playmate in her world, and she was determined to make him play. She bounded down the stairs now, full of energy and enthusiasm, and raced to the sofa to push her nose into his armpit before depositing her tennis ball on his chest. The ball rolled off and she pounced on it with joy.

He groaned and swung his legs down as he eased to a sitting position. "Hey, girl," he croaked in a rough morning voice, giving Tricks a quick rub behind the ears as she brought the ball back to him. This time it landed between his spread legs. He quickly grabbed it before she darted her nose toward the ball to show him where it was. Bo stifled a snicker. He'd learned the hard way.

He got up and headed for the bathroom as she started the coffee. They muttered "Morning" at each other, then Bo took Tricks out. Coming back in, she opened the refrigerator to stare at the contents, wondering what she was going to prepare for breakfast. She'd spent a small fortune on groceries just three days before, so why was she having this problem? Because she didn't usually cook breakfast, that was why. Normally she'd eat some granola and drink coffee while she worked.

Okay, something that didn't take a lot of time, because she had work to do. She threw some bacon into the microwave, scrambled some eggs, and slapped slices of bread into the toaster. Breakfast would take ten minutes, max.

As she was plating the eggs, reality hit her smack between the eyes.

She'd been busy, pressed to lay in adequate supplies for him, and she'd been cooking for him, doing his laundry. She'd been knocked off her stride by his arrival, then the bakery incident, and all the extra work that taking care of him entailed. That was the only explanation she had for the fact that she'd asked almost *no* questions, had no idea really who she'd let into her house, knew nothing about him other than the scant information he and Axel had given her at the very first.

Well, that was easily remedied. As soon as he came out of the bathroom, freshly showered and shaved, dressed in an olive-drab tee shirt and black cargo pants that barely hung on him even with a belt, she said, "Are you a spy or something?" What he was was important because that was the reason why he was so thin, why he was *here*.

He flicked a glance at her but didn't pause as he went to the counter and picked up the cup of coffee she'd set aside for him. "Starting to have some questions, huh?" He leaned one hip against the cabinet and eyed her over the lip of the cup as he sipped.

"A bit late, but yeah." She wondered if he'd answer any of her questions, or if she could believe him if he did. Spies lied for a living, right?

"No, I'm not a spy."

"If you were, you'd lie," she pointed out as she divided the slices of bacon onto their plates, then got out another plate and began buttering the toast and stacking the slices on it.

"True. Though if I were, you'd be smarter not to point that out."

His calm admittance was either annoying or gratifying, and she couldn't decide which. She wanted to believe him; she wanted to think she was doing a good thing, even if she was being paid well to do it. Too bad there was literally no way she could know for certain; all she could do was go with what she thought was most probable. "I think it's too late for smart—you're already here. But if you aren't a spy, then why were you ambushed?"

"That's the sixty-four-thousand-dollar question. We don't know."

She put down the butter knife for a sip of her own coffee while she considered that. "You work for the government, so you assume it's job related. Could it be personal?"

"Not likely."

"You've lived such a pristine life, huh?"

Amusement quirked his mouth. "I didn't say that. But I don't have any psycho exes, haven't gotten into any fights with the neighbors, anything that could be a trigger. I'd been out of the country for a few months, and after I caught up on my sleep, I went fishing.

Someone hacked the state files and tracked me using my boat registration number. Let's eat while we talk; our food is getting cold."

He set down his coffee and picked up the plates of eggs and bacon, taking them to the table. When he'd first arrived he'd looked like a wreck, not anyone's idea of a James Bond type, but with just a few days of recuperation and steady food he was moving better, she thought, still slow but with more confidence. She was beginning to see an animal grace in the way his muscles worked that reminded her all over again that this man lived a life that was totally alien to hers.

She pushed away the thoughts about how he moved and worked through what he'd said. If the attack had been personal, then almost assuredly the attacker would have *known* where he lived and wouldn't have had to hack any files. "Okay, so it's the job."

"Yeah. And the shooter was Russian mob, but he'd hired out for an outside job."

That stopped her. She set down her cup and stared accusingly at him. "You said you didn't know who shot you."

"Clarification: we know who did the shooting because I nailed his ass. What we don't know is who hired him. Whoever it was could get inside state files, which in itself isn't that hard, but our—ah—agency files were also hacked, and that not only took a high level of expertise, but also knowledge that the files even exist."

That information gave her pause. "Nailed his ass" was a euphemism, she assumed, for "killed." This man had killed. Deep down she'd known it, simply from the way he'd gone for her throat when she'd startled him, and also because *he'd* been shot. She'd never before known anyone who was shot. Accidents happened, and people were shot because they were involved in crime or someone close to them was, but she got the feeling firearms and violence were a constant part of this man's life.

She blew out a breath. "You said you aren't a spy, but you said 'agency.' Are you freakin' CIA, or not?"

"Not."

"Then what are you? Or is this one of those 'I could tell you but then I'd have to kill you' deals?"

"No, I'm not covert, or black ops. I'm former military—"

Boy, was that a surprise. *Not.*

"—but now I'm paramilitary. More freedom to act. We're organized into teams, government sanctioned, and we handle crises before they blow up into catastrophes." While they were talking, she'd gotten the plate of toast and jelly, and he'd made a return trip for the two cups of coffee. He set hers beside her plate. She took the seat she always took; he slid into the one he'd appropriated, to her right. For the first time she wondered if he'd deliberately selected that particular seat because it faced the windows and door. He was unarmed so she didn't know how much good it did to be able to see any approaching danger—not that they had to actually see if anything or anyone was outside because they had Tricks, who could hear things way before they could. She was an excellent alarm system.

The alarm system, attracted by the food, came to the table and curled up on the floor beside Bo's feet.

"So do you think this was connected to your last mission, whatever it was?"

"Not likely."

Impatiently she said, "Do you have *any* idea?"

"No. I've been over and over everything I did that day, and nothing pings. I talked to four people, unless you count the cashier at the supermarket where I stopped, which would make five. There was nothing unusual about the four, nothing that has shown up in Mac's investigations. But because the agency files were hacked, that means someone knew what I do for a living and where I work."

His delivery was calm and analytical, punctuated by bites of food. He sounded more as if he were discussing an academic problem than something that had almost gotten him killed.

She didn't understand that perspective, unless being shot at was so commonplace he took it for granted. She couldn't imagine that kind of life, or the type of person who deliberately chose it. "If it isn't personal, then it's either something you did, or something you saw— either on the mission or after you got home. Common sense."

"I know, but I got nothing. If I saw something, I didn't know what I was seeing so it didn't register. Nothing about the mission was unusual. There were screw-ups, but there are always screw-ups, and none of them were major. We went in, we got the job done, we were sent to another hot spot, then to another, and seven weeks after we left, we made it home, everyone alive and in relatively good shape."

She was operating from a position of ignorance, so there was nothing she could offer him in the way of possibilities that he hadn't already thought of—he, and Axel, and probably a whole bunch of other people. She was also not entirely accepting of everything he told her, and she saw no reason to be coy about it.

"You could tell me anything," she pointed out conversationally. "I have no way of telling whether or not you're lying. For someone in your occupation—if that really *is* your occupation—you're being very open about it, not just with me but with Jesse too."

He sipped his coffee, then shrugged. That was twice he could have been using the coffee as a blind to hide his expression, or as a subtle diversion. She'd never before thought of drinking coffee as an evasive action, but with him she was beginning to think she needed to view everything through that filter. "You're not very trusting," he finally said. Evidently she wasn't as good at those diversions and hiding her thoughts as he was.

"That's a good thing," he continued. "You'd have to be a fool if you took everything at face value. What you said is true enough. But as a team leader, I have both the authority and the training to make field decisions. If I hadn't brought Jesse into the loop, he might have triggered some alarms by poking where he shouldn't have—am I right? He didn't seem like the type to give up if he wanted to know something unless he had a compelling reason *not* to."

She wrinkled her nose. "No, you pegged him right."

"As for you—Mac and I discussed how much you could be told, and he said he'd leave it up to me." He reached for the jelly to slather some on a second piece of toast, the first time he'd eaten extra. His forearm brushed her arm and automatically Bo drew back, a frisson of alertness shooting along her nerve endings.

She couldn't have said why; she'd touched him before, helped him into the house, but—that was her touching him. This was the first time he'd touched her.

On one level, her alarm felt silly. She wasn't afraid of him, didn't think he was a rapist or anything like that; if she had, no way would he be staying in her house. But on a very basic level her instincts told her some-thing else, that he was like a tiger in a zoo: under control at the moment, but still a wild animal.

She glanced up and saw shrewd awareness in his blue-lightning gaze, as if he'd correctly tagged her re-action. This could get awkward, considering he'd be living in her house for an unspecified time—if she let it. She was more inclined to be up front.

"Don't take it personally. I'm cautious that way." In her experience, romantic entanglements were un-reliable and more trouble than they were worth. Her parents' examples were proof enough, but she'd tried marriage herself only to have it fall apart within a year. She'd learned her lesson; she was better off on her own, relying only on herself.

"So you aren't afraid I'll try to jump you?"

Humor was in his eyes now, and she snorted. "The shape you're in? I could take you."

"As humiliating as it is to admit, yeah, you could." His gaze darkened. "I hate being this weak. I'm working on it, though; I estimate it'll be another two or three weeks before I can start any real workouts."

Was that a warning, or casual conversation? If she'd ever had any real skills at deciphering personal dynamics, they were rusty now from disuse. She'd be on firmer ground if he were a dog. She opted for casual conversation. "There's a gym in town. Not the best, but at least it's a gym. And I have a treadmill tucked in the storage under the stairs; I can get it out when you think you're ready."

"Thanks. For now, my next goal is climbing those stairs. No offense, but your sofa is killing me."

While Bo was doing her morning work, Morgan walked outside, both to give her room to concentrate and for the joy of getting out in the fresh air and sunshine and pushing his body a little. Getting back into shape wasn't going to just happen; he'd have to work for it, maybe harder than he'd ever worked before, because he couldn't remember ever being this weak before. He was already getting stronger, probably because he was eating more. Bo wasn't a fancy cook, but he wasn't a fancy eater; give him a good hamburger or spaghetti dinner any day, rather than some frou-frou arrangement of two green beans, a mushroom, and an ounce of sautéed chicken.

Because it would only be fair, when he was able, he intended to take over some of the household chores. He could vacuum with the best of 'em, and do laundry. From what he could see, she had almost no down time, unless you counted when she took the dog for walks.

Carefully he walked to the edge of the woods, then turned and looked back at the barn—house. It was an unusual place for an unusual woman. He was a man who liked women, so he pondered his hostess. She had walls—*serious* walls. Some women had walls because they were afraid, but he didn't sense any timidity or uncertainty in her. She was self-contained, confident in who she was and the choices she made, alone and happy to be that way.

He liked that about her because clingy, dependent people annoyed him. His own nature was to take charge and get things done, which was why he was in the GO-Teams to begin with. He liked the adrenaline rush, but he also liked the sense of accomplishment, of being able to do things the ordinary person couldn't do. He put his ass on the line every time he went on a mission; nothing about indecision and weakness appealed to him, no matter how it was packaged.

Bo's packaging was on the skimpy side, but appealing for all that. She was a little taller than average, thin, with long arms and legs, and no boobs to speak of. If she was bigger than an A-cup, he'd kiss her ass—and enjoy doing it, because though she might be skinny her ass had a definite curve to it. Her face was faintly exotic, all big dark eyes and a wide, soft mouth, more appealing than pretty. There was that word again: appealing. And he didn't need to think about how appealing she was. He was here to recuperate and wait for Axel's trap to be sprung, then he'd be gone. He'd enjoy some flirtation, the zing of sexual attraction, if the circumstances were different. They weren't. There wasn't any point in thinking about Bo's curvy little ass.

Instead, he should spend his time going over and over everything that had happened the day he'd been shot, trying to spot the pertinent detail that had so far eluded him. Being relegated to the position of bystander rubbed him wrong. He was accustomed to swinging into action and doing what needed to be done, to being the bullet instead of the bait. He wanted to be doing something, anything, other than sitting with his thumb up his ass. He felt useless. Hell, he *was* useless. If anything happened, he wasn't certain he could save himself, much less anyone else.

Look at him now: he'd walked maybe fifty yards, and he was exhausted—though that was an improvement because when he'd arrived last Thursday, he'd needed help just getting into the house, and to the bathroom. It galled him that he needed to rest before he could make the return fifty yards.

At least he was upright, and in the sunshine. The bright heat felt good on his skin. He stood there listening to the birds singing as boisterously as if they were drunk, and his mind slipped back to that day.

Congresswoman Kingsley was at the top of his list for somehow being behind all of this, but he had to admit she was there solely because she was a politician. Other than that, he couldn't think of anything she'd said or done that was out of the ordinary. There was also her husband, Dexter the lawyer. Politician, lawyer to the power brokers—was there much difference between them? Again, Dexter hadn't done anything other than become a lawyer.

He replayed his chance meeting with them, everything they'd said, anything he'd seen, and nothing popped.

Next on his list was Brawley, who had made that phone call immediately after seeing him. But Axel had managed to trace the call, and the only call Brawley had made in that time frame had been to his wife. After checking out both Brawley and the wife, Axel had found nothing. They were regular citizens, with nothing suspicious in their backgrounds. They'd raised a couple of kids, had a few grandkids, went to church.

The last person on Morgan's list was the one he was most reluctant to think about: Kodak. He and Kodak had been in so many firefights together he couldn't say who had saved the other's life the most times. Kodak knew where he lived, wouldn't have had to hack any files to get his address . . . and yet, Kodak was sharp enough to have done exactly that as a means of throwing suspicion away from himself.

But then he came back to the same bottom line he'd reached on the others: he couldn't think of any reason why. From Axel's interrogation of Kodak after the ambush, he knew that Kodak had indeed had a lady companion that morning, that he'd spent the day with her. She'd gone home after an early dinner. Everything looked normal; there were no suspicious calls made to or from Kodak's cell—or even his lady friend's cell—and no sudden transfer of funds from his bank to that of Albert Rykov.

They hadn't even been able to track the money backward. Rykov had made a sizable deposit, but it had been in cash at the Bank of America ATM on Pennsylvania Avenue. Security cameras had recorded it; Rykov had been alone. The money was a dead end. It wasn't even gratifying to know that someone had paid twenty thousand in cash to have him killed.

Everything led to a dead end. No one he'd seen that day had said or done anything suspicious. He was no closer to figuring out who'd tried to kill him now than he had been when it first happened.

He heard a muffled but happy bark and turned to see Tricks barreling toward him, tennis ball in her mouth, which explained why her bark had been muffled. Bo was following behind. Tricks reached him and dropped the ball at his feet, then took off running. Careful to keep his balance, he bent to pick it up and hurled it over her head. It bounced, she leaped and caught it, and immediately she froze in place with her head proudly lifted, waiting to be praised.

"Good girl!" Bo called, clapping her hands. "That was a beautiful catch." She reached him and said, "You've been out here a while. Are you okay?" Her dark eyes were calm, revealing nothing more than a casual concern.

"Yeah, just thinking."

"You didn't move for a good forty minutes. Do you want to go back in before I take Tricks for her walk?"

Meaning she wasn't certain he could make the short trip on his own and didn't want to leave him there until she got back. The reminder of his weakness frayed his temper, and he started to snarl an answer before catching himself. Snapping at her wouldn't help him recover any faster, no matter how much it galled him to have to accept her help.

On the other hand, maybe there was an upside to this.

He said, "My knees got a little shaky. I thought I'd rest a while before trying to get back to the house."

Strictly speaking, none of that was a lie. His knees *had* gotten a little shaky when he'd walked out. He'd also rested. But he could easily make the return trip to the house—okay, if not easily, at least without falling on his face.

"Lean on me," she said without hesitation, though again there was nothing to read in her face that hinted at any great concern. She stepped close and shoved her shoulder against him the way she had the day he arrived, her right arm around his waist. He looped his left arm around her shoulder and let a little of his weight rest on her as they slowly walked back to the house, Tricks prancing in escort.

He looked down at the top of her head, at the sun gleaming on the thick, rich darkness of her hair. She didn't do anything special, he didn't think; her hair reached the middle of her back and all she did was pull it back and clip it at the base of her neck. If she wore any makeup, he couldn't see it, though he wasn't exactly an expert in the makeup department. He noticed lipstick, or if a woman wore enough eyeliner that she looked like a raccoon. Other than that, he was a guy, which meant he was fairly oblivious.

Her skin was smooth, with a healthy sheen to it. A faint peach-hued flush had warmed her cheeks. Beneath his hand the bones of her shoulder felt fragile, not much thicker than a child's. There was nothing childlike about her, but the feel of her shoulder clasped in his rough fingers made his stomach tighten because it reminded him that she had jumped headlong into a fight without regard for her own safety, that she'd been punched in the face by some low-life son of a bitch who needed to be shown a thing or three about what happened to jerks who hit women.

"Are you okay?" she asked again, frowning as she slanted a look up at him, and he realized his breathing had gone deeper and faster as anger bubbled his blood.

"I'll make it," he said roughly, sidestepping the question. Yeah, he was okay. He made himself a promise: Before he left this place, he'd make it his mission to track down that bastard and make him wish he never saw Hamrickville again.

Chapter 10

When Bo stepped into the station with tricks beside her, the first person she saw was Warren Gooding. If he hadn't seen her too, she'd have silently backed out and not returned until after he left. Unfortunately, he *did* see her, so she was denied the coward's way out. Her stomach tied in knots at the thought of the coming confrontation because it wasn't going to be pretty.

Loretta, the dispatcher, peeked out from around her cubicle and mouthed "*Sorry*" at her. Bo gave a slight nod to let her know it was okay. What could Loretta have done, thrown the man out? She only wished. Physically Loretta could have, because she was a big woman, but that would only make the inevitable meeting that much more hostile.

"Mr. Gooding," she said calmly. She didn't feel calm, but she could act calm. Telling him he was a jerk and his son was a jerk wouldn't accomplish anything. She tried to picture the path she walked with Tricks, the peacefulness of the trees and wind and sun. Maybe that happy-place stuff really worked; it was worth a shot.

"I'd like to talk to you in private." His tone was curt, his scowl saying that he wasn't in a placating mood. He was a tall, heavyset man, and would have been good-looking if his discontent with the world and everyone he knew wasn't evident in his expression.

"Certainly." If she'd been a betting person, she'd have bet every cent Axel was paying her that she knew what he was going to say. He thought he was a special snowflake, that the rules that applied to everyone else didn't apply to him. She wasn't looking forward to his outrage when he found out no snowflakes were special, that they all melted.

The station house was a mostly open floor plan, with a few desks and chairs scattered around. The town's money could only go so far, so functionality was the name of the game, with decoration and status far behind. The best that could be said of her area was that she had the newest office chair, which was to say it was less than ten years old. Maybe. She led the way to her desk, indicated the visitor's chair. He glared around as if the layout of the station was her fault. "I said *private.*"

"I heard what you said, but this is as private as it gets. I don't have a private office. Our only other option is to step into the bathroom, and no offense, but that isn't going to happen." She could just see that, yelling back and forth over the toilet—though she hoped it wouldn't come to the yelling part. The hope was a small one, but miracles did happen every now and then.

His head swiveled back and forth as if looking for an office to appear out of thin air. Frustrated, he turned back to glare at her some more.

"Please, have a seat." She indicated the visitor's chair. After hesitating a minute, not wanting to give in but having no other option, Mr. Gooding dragged the chair over so he was mostly sitting beside her, rather than in front of her. She slid her own chair back and swiveled it so she was facing him. They weren't meeting as equals, and she didn't want him to think they were.

Tricks had gone to greet Loretta and now came prancing toward the new person. When she was a few feet away, however, she got a distinct look of doggie distaste on her expressive face and came to a halt. Bo kept watch on her, ready to intervene if

Tricks decided to greet Mr. Gooding with her usual enthusiasm, but after studying him for a second Tricks backed away and went to her bed. Evidently ill temper smelled bad.

Good girl! There was no evidence that Tricks was telepathic, but Bo sent her the approving thought anyway.

Mr. Gooding scowled at Bo as if she were the cause of all his problems. "I want you to drop the charges against Kyle," he said abruptly.

A lead-in exchange of pleasantries would have been nice, but so much for that. She suspected Mr. Gooding wouldn't know "pleasant" if it bit him on the ass. "Why?" She kept her tone calm, the word faintly puzzled.

His face got red and his voice got loud. "Because that bitch he married—"

She held up her hand, cutting off his outburst. "I'm not involved in his marriage. Whether or not Emily presses charges is up to her. The only charges I'm involved in are those of assaulting a police officer and resisting arrest."

"He said he didn't know it was you."

"Yes, I know. I didn't know it was him, either, when I entered the bakery and found him in a fight with Officer Tucker. How is that pertinent?"

"He'd never have swung at you if he'd known," Mr. Gooding charged. His face was still red, and his fists were clenching and unclenching.

"Doesn't matter."

"The hell you say it doesn't matter!" His voice rose again.

"Mr. Gooding. Even if he didn't know who *I* was, he definitely knew who Officer Tucker was."

"We don't live in this town, we don't know every half-ass cop by sight."

"That's possible," she allowed. "However, I assume you and your son both know what a police *uniform* looks like. Officer Tucker was in uniform." God, this was unpleasant. The knots in her stomach were turning into faint nausea; that happy-place stuff wasn't working. She didn't enjoy confrontation, but neither did she back down from it. All she had to do was remain calm.

"My boy could do time over this when it doesn't amount to a hill of beans. Neither you nor your deputy are hurt. There's no point in dragging this out, in ruining his life because he and his sorry-ass wife got in an argument. Tell me what this department needs and I'll make sure you get it. A new squad car? An add-on to the building so you'll have an office?"

Well, that was brazen, even for him. Outraged, she sat there for a minute. He probably thought she was weighing the offer; instead she was wondering how hard it would be to hook her feet under the railing of his chair and tip it over backward. Maybe he'd bang his head as hard as she'd banged hers during the scuffle with his son.

No, she couldn't do it. That way lay madness— intensely satisfying, but still madness. When she could control her tone and keep it even, she said, "Are you seriously trying to *bribe* me? Because if you are, hold on while I get my phone so I can record all this." She did just that, fetching her phone out of her bag and tapping a few icons. She laid it on the desk. "Would you repeat all that, please? About buying us a new squad car or adding on to the station building if we'll drop our charges against Kyle?" She lifted her brows in inquiry.

He looked in real danger of exploding, or maybe stroking out, but he saw the quicksand at his feet. "I categorically deny I was trying to bribe you! That's ridiculous! These charges against Kyle are ridiculous—"

"Don't bother recording it," Loretta said laconically from behind her partition. "I *heard* it."

His head whipped around; in his choler, he'd forgotten about Loretta, perhaps because she was out of sight and no calls had come in. The red color in his face deepened into puce. Before he could dig himself in any deeper and the situation became even more of a powder keg, Bo took a deep breath and willed herself back from the edge.

"I suggest we let this case play out within the confines of the law. Kyle has no prior charges—or any that stuck, because you're always buying him out of trouble, which should tell you something right there"—she had to put that in, accompanied by a flinty-eyed look, but then she pulled herself back to calm—"so I doubt he'll do any hard time, though the judge might give him some short time in the county lockup. I doubt even that. Likely he'll end up with probation. I don't know, but it's my best guess."

Instead of seizing the opening, Mr. Gooding went on another angle of attack. "But he'd still have a *record*. My boy has all he can handle, with his slut of a wife taking everything he has. He can't even get his own stuff from his own house because she's got a restraining order against him. She'll probably sell all his guns—"

Please, Jesus, let it be so, Bo silently prayed. Aloud she said, "I understand Emily packed up Kyle's things and sent them to your house. What else does he need? Make me a list and I'll make sure he gets it. And don't say guns, because I'm sure you don't think Kyle needs access to any weapons until he's calmed down."

"Those guns belong to him."

"Then they'll be granted to him in the divorce settlement. Don't worry about the guns. It isn't hunting season, and if he did something so stupid with one that even you couldn't buy his way out, he'd go away for a long, long time. Hard time, too. The best thing you can do now is sit on him and keep him out of trouble so things can calm down."

His fists were still clenching and unclenching. Unable to corral his fury at being at a disadvantage, he jumped to his feet so violently the chair fell over backward anyway. Tricks gave a startled yelp and shot off her bed, darting to Bo and pressing against her legs.

"I'll be pressing charges against *you*, missy!" Savage outrage thickened his tone. "You made threats against my son—"

"You mean that part about tearing his fucking head off?" put in Loretta, still hidden by her partition. There was a snicker. "Yeah, everyone took that real serious, considering he weighs about twice what she does."

"*Shut up!*" he roared, pivoting and taking a threatening step toward the partition. "This stupid town is taking orders from two ignorant pussies and I—"

Loretta slowly stood up, all six-feet-one and two hundred seventy-two pounds of her rising from behind the partition. Her chin was tucked, her eyes bright as she eyed him as if he were steak tartare and she was a starving lion. "I'll bet my pussy against yours any day, hoss. If you want to know who I am, the name's Loretta Hobson, from out Lister Road. You've probably heard of my family? The Mean-As-Shit Hobsons? I'll take you on any day."

His head jerked back. Everyone in the county had heard of the Mean-As-Shit Hobsons. Cross a Hobson, and you were likely to find your house burned down—and that's if they were in a good mood. The worst part of it was they were pretty damn smart and had never been caught at anything.

In a very level tone, Bo said, "Mr. Gooding, I think it would be best if you leave now. Just be patient, tell Kyle to act smart for once in his life, and let things settle down. I'll forget this one time that you tried to bribe me, but if you try such a thing again, I'll arrest you on the spot. Are we clear?"

He was still watching Loretta as if she were a cobra and had him hypnotized. Loretta barked, "Are we clear?" and he visibly jumped, his head swiveling toward Bo. His cheeks had lost all their color, but malice burned in his eyes.

"I'll have your job for this," he uttered almost soundlessly. "Wait until the town finds out you're shacking up with some guy who turned up out of the blue."

That hadn't taken long, she thought. Morgan had been at her house for a whole four days. "Oh, you mean my old friend who *just had open-heart surgery* and can barely walk? That guy? Sure, go for it, but be prepared to be laughed at."

That information was almost too much for him to process. He teetered on the verge of a violent explosion, but self-preservation kept him from going there because he seemed to sense that Bo and Loretta were a hair's breadth from putting handcuffs on him. He couldn't bear to admit defeat but had no other option. Finally he simply turned and stomped out, leaving the door standing open in his wake.

Blowing out a breath, Bo closed the door and turned back to Loretta. They grinned at each other and met halfway across the office for a high five and a fist bump. "I'm so glad you're a Hobson," she told Loretta.

"It comes in handy." Loretta blew on her nails, buffed them on her shirt. "I can't wait to tell my brothers. They'll get a kick out of it. You really got a man living with you?"

"For now, poor guy. He just got out of the hospital."

It was the description of "poor guy" that did it because no woman described a romantic interest that way. Losing interest, Loretta said, "Hope he feels better soon," and dropped the subject.

The excitement over, Loretta returned to her cubicle and Bo sat at her desk. Tricks sniffed around before deciding to take a nap. After thinking the situation over for a few minutes, Bo called Mayor Buddy and filled him in on her encounter with Warren Gooding.

He sighed. From the sound, she could just see his face, homely but pleasant, settling into lines of concern. "I knew he was going to be a problem. Still—he did just give us leverage, and we might be able to work it to our advantage."

"I'm torn," she admitted. "I dislike him so much I'd love to file bribery charges against him, but overall that wouldn't be good for the town. If the sawmills closed because he wasn't there to run them, that would hurt some innocent families who depend on the jobs."

"It's your call. If you want to file charges, I'll back you up."

Letting go of the vision of Warren Gooding behind bars, Bo gave her own sigh. "Strategically, I think we'd be better off not filing charges, but not letting him know."

"I agree. I'll talk to the town council about this whole situation. I don't want everyone getting sucked into what should be a private divorce situation. Bad blood can cause trouble for years. Harold Patterson"—that was the barber—"is already up in arms because he's been sweet on Miss Doris for years, not that she's having any of it, but he thinks he can impress her by taking up for her and Emily."

Bo rubbed her forehead; she could feel a headache coming on. The way the lives of people in small towns were woven together was foreign to her, but over the years she'd gotten sucked into it anyway, and damn it, now that she knew these people, she *cared*, however reluctantly. It was disturbing that she even *knew* this many people. If she'd known this would happen, she might never have taken the job of chief.

"I need a vacation," she said aloud.

Mayor Buddy chuckled. "I know the feeling. Small towns, huh?" He paused, then with a faint undertone of guilt said, "Come to think of it, have you ever taken one? Vacation."

Mortified that he might think she'd been asking for paid time-off, she said, "I was joking. I have too much on my plate to even consider a day off. Not only do I have a boatload of tech projects lined up, I have a friend recuperating at my place."

"I heard about that. When he's feeling better, bring him to town so people can meet him. I bet Miss Doris would bake something special for him."

Oh, yes, she definitely had a headache. When Morgan was feeling better, he wouldn't look so sick.

That stood to reason, didn't it? What would people see when they met him? Would they see what she saw, a man who chose to live his life on the razor's edge of danger, a man who could and had killed in a number of ways? Perhaps it was because she knew he'd been shot, knew—vaguely—what he did for a living, but to her it was evident in the sharpness of his gaze, in the way he moved, the intense alertness about him even when he was doing nothing more dangerous than watching TV. Who would be so oblivious that they'd look at him and think he was nothing out of the ordinary?

Now Mayor Buddy was wanting to enfold Morgan in the town's embrace, which to her was a little like putting a tiger in a petting zoo. And Miss Doris would bake the tiger a special cupcake.

God in heaven. She couldn't keep Morgan secluded, or everyone would die of curiosity and she could just see a regular parade of visitors to her house on a pilgrimage to see the man she kept hidden there. Small towners were both nosy and brazen; they wouldn't care if their excuses were flimsy as long as their goal was accomplished. Sooner or later—probably sooner—she would have to bring Morgan to town. What better way to spike Warren Gooding's charges than to let people see for themselves what shape Morgan was in? Sooner would definitely be better, while he still looked sickly.

When she got home, Morgan was outside on the porch again, his chair in the sunshine. The late afternoon was feeling cool to her, but he didn't have a jacket on over his tee shirt. Her laptop was open in his lap, and he was tapping at the track pad. Tricks woofed happily as soon as she saw him, and when Bo released her from her safety harness, she bounded out of the Jeep and raced to him, her tail wagging madly, her whole body wiggling in delight.

He stopped what he was doing to scratch her ears with both hands and ask how her day had gone. After a minute of that Tricks abandoned him to do some investigative sniffing. "Hi," he said, glancing at Bo, and went back to the laptop.

Two seconds later he muttered, "Shit!" and closed the laptop.

"What's wrong?" she asked, going to stand beside him while she kept an eye on Tricks.

"I saved seven of the little fuckers, you'd think that would count for something," he growled. He shoved his hand restlessly through his hair. "Sorry. That slipped out."

She had to laugh. Dragging another chair around, she sat and stretched out her legs. "Playing Pet Rescue, huh?"

"For about three hours now. I run out of lives, I play something else until I have more lives." He slanted a look of blue fire at her. "No offense, but I'm going crazy with boredom. I'm not good at doing nothing."

"None taken. I'd be bored too." Privately she thought the timing couldn't have worked out any better. "If you feel up to it, want to go to work with me tomorrow? I can't guarantee sitting in the police station will be any more interesting than playing Pet Rescue, but it'll be a change of scenery."

"God, yes."

"Things got a little interesting today." She told him about Warren Gooding's visit, and the standoff with Loretta, which elicited one of those rusty-sounding laughs from him. "Evidently people are already curious about you, so you can expect a steady parade of people coming by to look you over. But Mayor Buddy also said Miss Doris would probably bake something special for you, so I'd say it'll be worth being stared at."

"Hasn't anyone in your town ever seen a stranger before?" he muttered.

"It's a small town. Being nosy is required." She smiled as she tilted her face toward the sun. The down time was . . . relaxing. It was oddly companionable, sitting here with him in the late afternoon, chatting while she watched Tricks. She never would have described him as companionable, but there it was.

"How did you end up here? This isn't exactly on the beaten path."

"Hubris," she replied. The story wasn't a pretty one, but what the hell, she wasn't ashamed of it. She'd made some mistakes, and she'd worked hard and dug her way out of a hole. "I teamed up with a friend in California and flipped a house. It seemed like a fun thing to do, real estate was booming, and we each cleared about thirty thousand profit from it. In hindsight, that was the worst thing that could have happened because I decided I liked flipping houses better than tech writing and could make a lot more money from it. My friend didn't like the work so much, though she did like the money, so she opted out of going in with me on the next house. I made money on it too. I thought I was an expert. The people who bought it had a friend who hired me to convert an old barn where he grew up, and here I am."

"Weaseled out on you, huh?"

She appreciated his quick comprehension. "It got so I couldn't get in touch with him very easily, and whenever I did he'd tell me to keep going, and he made the decisions on lighting fixtures, flooring, high-end kitchen appliances. To keep construction flowing, I used my money, and when that got low, I switched to my credit cards. Dumb. Real estate was tanking, big time. The barn was almost finished when he told me he couldn't get financing, and on top of being stupid enough to use my own money, I hadn't gotten a signed contract from him. He walked away clear, and I had a barn to live in and a mountain of debt."

"Which explains why I'm here. If it hadn't been for that, you'd have told me tough luck and put me on the road again."

"The money was definitely a big consideration. But I've worked hard, whittled the debt down, and it's all manageable now. At least my head is above water, thanks to my deal with the town. Besides, I wouldn't have put you on the road right away. You were pitiful."

He winced at her less-than-complimentary description, but it was accurate so he shrugged and let it go. He surveyed her for a minute, his thoughts hidden. She was unprepared for what he finally said. "I can get Axel to pay you more."

She blinked, astonished, then laughed. "Not necessary. When I say it's manageable, I mean it. I'll use the money to knock a big hole in the remaining mortgage and either pay it off early or refinance for a lower payment. I'm good with the deal as it is." She hauled herself out of the chair. "I need to get busy. How does pizza sound? You do eat pizza, don't you?"

"Pizza sounds like heaven. Any kind of pizza. I even ate vegan pizza once. Not willingly, but I ate it." He stood with improving ease, holding the laptop in one big hand.

"C'mon, Tricks," Bo called, then looked up at him with a smirk playing around the edges of her mouth. "By the way, it would help if you could look really pitiful tomorrow, because the rumor's already going around that we're shacking up."

Chapter 11

*P*itiful. The word clanged angrily around inside Morgan's skull. She thought he was *pitiful.* Maybe he wasn't as okay with it as he'd thought. Even worse was the accuracy of her assessment; his ass had definitely been dragging the ground when he'd arrived here, but he was doing a lot better. Some, anyway.

He'd try his ever-lovin' best to look *pitiful* for her tomorrow, so no one would think he could possibly get it up or that she would even consider crawling between the sheets with him. After tomorrow, though, he was going to start getting back in shape. He knew how. He'd gone through training that broke most men. Tomorrow would be pushing it some, so he'd have to be smart about it. His sternum and chest muscles were still healing, and he didn't want to tear anything loose.

Then he considered the almost military straightness of her back as she walked into the house ahead of him, and he had to wonder if she'd used the word deliberately to alienate him. No man liked being described as pitiful. The tactic would have worked on most men, but he wasn't most men. He was aggressive, intelligent, and he didn't say, "Oh, well," when presented with a problem or a challenge; he met the challenge and solved the problem.

Yes, she had chosen that word with, if not malice, definite intent. He knew it instinctively. It was those walls again; he had been careful not to make a comment that could in any way be regarded as sexual, but she'd still felt the need to reinforce the distance between them. Was it simply because he'd been here for several days now and was a part of her home life? She'd wanted to make certain he stayed a temporary intrusion.

From what he'd seen so far, her home really was her sanctuary. Officer Tucker had followed her out to interrogate him, and also to make sure she got home safely after bumping her head, but no one else had visited. No one had even called, other than Officer Tucker's nightly check-ins, which were very brief.

She was a solitary person; he got that. She was also candid and open about her past, how she'd ended up here, what she was thinking. Maybe being so candid was another defense mechanism: tell people so much that they wouldn't suspect she was hiding anything, such as a key part of herself.

She turned on the top wall oven to start preheating and got out Tricks's food. He eased onto one of the stainless steel and wood bar stools at the counter, watching as the dog excitedly pranced around her. When she had it prepared, with little pieces of turkey on top, she set it down and he waited for the weird ritual he'd noticed at every one of the dog's dinnertimes. Tricks didn't do it any other time, but at dinner she had to be coaxed to eat.

This time, however, Tricks ignored the food bowl and came to lie down beside the stool where he was perched. She crossed her front paws and appeared to be waiting.

Bo made an exasperated sound in her throat and picked up the food bowl. "Yes, your majesty," she said, as if the dog had spoken. As she approached, Tricks uncrossed her paws. Bo placed the bowl between them, right in front of her. Tricks wagged her tail and began eating.

Morgan had to laugh. She and the dog were a never-ending comedy act. "Exactly which one of you is trained?"

"I am, up to a point," she admitted without hesitation, slanting a quick smile at him. "She's done this her whole life. She eats without a problem the rest of the day, but she wants her supper how she wants it. Sometimes she wants to be praised before she'll eat. Every so often she'll pick out the spot where she wants to be, and I have to put the bowl in front of her or she won't eat." She bent and gently caressed Tricks's head. The dog stopped eating to give Bo's hand a lick. "She's worth the trouble."

Straightening, she washed her hands and got a pizza pan out of the cabinet, then extracted a large frozen pizza from the freezer. "It's a supreme. Want me to pick anything off it before it cooks?"

"No, I like it all." Except for anchovies. He'd tried them, though in his opinion whoever had come up with the idea of a fish pizza should be taken out and shot. Some things just shouldn't be.

The oven beeped, signaling that it was hot, and she slid the pizza pan into it. He watched her for a minute, liking how fluid her movements were. She moved like a dancer, each step precise and graceful.

He could have silently watched her until the pizza was ready, but he wondered if she'd be as candid about the rest of her life as she had been about her stab at flipping houses. Maybe he could learn some more about what made her tick. The only way to find out was to do some verbal poking around and see if she'd answer. "What's the deal with you and Mac? Axel," he amended.

"He's a jerk," she said without hesitation.

"Yep. Not arguing that. I mean, what's the history?"

"My mother and his father got married. I wasn't thrilled. Neither was he. We hated each other on sight."

"How long were they married?"

"Seven—no, eight—interminable months. Interminable for all four parties."

"Not a long time to develop an undying hatred for someone."

She leaned against the cabinet on the other side of the bar. "It was plenty long where Axel is concerned. I was thirteen and insufferable, he was eighteen and insufferable. At least I had the excuse of being thirteen. I gather he's still insufferable."

"He has his good points. Not many, but some. He isn't good with people, but he's damn good at his job. When my life depends on good intel and good equipment, I appreciate the last part."

She gave a small grunt of acknowledgment. "I guess so."

"Trust me—I *know* so. Axel's father was your mom's second husband?" He kept his tone casual, wondering how much more she'd divulge.

She had a variety of noises that expressed a lot of feeling, and this time she used a snort. "Second? More like fourth. I think." Looking at the ceiling, she counted them off on her fingers. "Dad, Wilson, Hugh, Douglas—yes, he was the fourth."

"Damn. Four marriages and you were just thirteen? That's rough." He still kept it casual because he suspected she wouldn't appreciate sympathy.

"Mom is a serial bride. She's on number seven now, but she's getting older so she may hold on to this one for a while—unless she's divorced him since the last time I heard from her, which has been a while. We aren't close. Not enemies, just not close. She's got her own thing going on, and I'm here in West Virginia. She likes big cities."

The scenario was getting clearer. Bo had had no stability in her life, no one on whom she could rely, so she'd learned to count on herself and no one else. His psychology skills weren't even at armchair level, but it didn't take a genius to figure out how disruptive the musical-chair stepfathers had been in a young girl's life. His own childhood had been steady, thank God.

"After Douglas she was single for a while—long enough for me to finish high school without moving *again*, though she had a couple of steady boyfriends.

After I started college, she married . . . Adam. I think. He didn't last long, so I never met him. Adam, Alan, something with an A. I'm not sure about number six, either. Number seven is William, and I've actually met him. They've been together a few years and live in Florida."

"How often did you change schools?"

"Every time she married, but after Douglas I was in the same school until I graduated. I was able to join the swim team. I love swimming. All of the apartment complexes we lived in had pools, and that's where I spent my summers."

Yeah, he could see her as a swimmer, with her aerodynamic build. She'd be the sprint swimmer, while he was an endurance swimmer, able to swim for miles. That is, *normally* he could swim for miles; now he'd probably drown after twenty yards.

"What about your dad? You close to him?"

"No. He pretty much forgot about me when he left. He remarried, adopted his new wife's kids, had a couple more of their own, and that's his family now. I think they're living in Sacramento, but that was years ago so they may well be somewhere else by now."

He got the picture. It wasn't awful, but neither was it pretty: ignored, abandoned, jerked around from place to place. No wonder she had walls.

"What about you?" she asked, slanting him a sideways glance from those dark eyes, turning the tables on him. "Have you been married? What about your family?"

"My dad is dead, from a fall in the kitchen. He hit his head on the corner of the cabinets. That was almost fifteen years ago. My mom remarried year before last, to an okay guy. He loves her and takes care of her, and that's good enough for me."

She waited a minute, probably to see if he'd answer her first question. "What about marriage?"

"Never been married, no kids. I came close to getting hitched once, but it didn't work out. It's hard on a wife when the husband is in my line of work. I'm out of the country more often than I'm in it." His heart hadn't been broken either, because the truth was he could remember his fiancée's name, but not really how she looked.

"I can see where that would be a problem," she admitted.

"How about you? Ever been married?"

"Once. I tried it when I was twenty-one, fresh out of college. It lasted less than six months before he cheated."

"Ouch." He'd been keeping an eye on the clock and he had a good idea how long frozen pizzas were supposed to heat, having eaten more than a few of them in his life. He slid off the stool. "Sorry I haven't been paying more attention, but I don't know where you keep stuff. Point me in the direction of the plates and things and I'll set the table."

She looked surprised, dark brows arching. "Are you sure you're up to it?"

"Carrying two plates?" he asked testily. "Yeah, I'm sure."

"Don't get cranky about it. The plates are there—" She pointed toward one of the cabinet doors. "The glasses are there, and the silverware is there."

"Why do we need silverware?"

She chuckled. "I don't guess we do."

As he collected the plates and glasses he said, "I like the barn. You did a good job." The kitchen cabinets were kind of beat up, but it was like they were supposed to look that way. Big industrial-looking lights hung from the high ceiling, as well as steel ceiling fans. Considering how high the ceiling was, the fans were a necessity. The layout was open from one end to the other, the only real privacy either in the bathroom or the rooms upstairs. It would be a great bachelor pad, out here in the middle of the country, nothing restricted or fussy about the building.

"Thanks. It wasn't renovated in my taste, but I suppose over the years it's become mine. It's my furniture, and that helps. Plus no one else has ever lived here, and in a way that makes it more mine."

"Except for the cows."

That got a smile from her. "Cows don't count."

He set the plates on the table, added napkins. As he headed back to get the glasses he said, "What do you want to drink?"

"Grab a couple of beers from the fridge."

His head came up, his attention laser-focused on her. "Beer? You have beer?" She'd been giving him *milk* when there was beer?

"If you're steady enough on your feet to carry crockery, you're steady enough to have a beer. Plus you aren't on any pain meds; I wouldn't let you mix them."

"Beer," he muttered, opening the refrigerator door and yes, thank you, Jesus, there were five dark brown bottles there. He hooked his fingers around the necks of two of them and pulled them out. They weren't Bud or Miller; there was a pig on the label. He tilted the bottles up to look at them. "Naked Pig? Never heard of it."

"Back Forty is a little brewery in Alabama. One of the guys in town is a truck driver and every time he goes through there he stops and picks up an order for the devotees here. I like Naked Pig."

She was into microbreweries. He didn't care. She was a beer-drinking woman, and life was looking better by the minute.

She pointed toward a bottle cap opener that was stuck on the stainless steel refrigerator by a magnet. He popped the tops off, tossed them in the trash. "You want yours in a glass?"

"Yes, please."

"Girly."

She grinned. "That's my beer, so watch your mouth or you won't get any."

He chuckled and poured the beers into glasses—his, too, though he'd have been just as happy to drink it out of the bottle. Her beer, her rules. He'd buy the next delivery.

He almost moaned aloud as the first cold sip slid down his throat. The bubbles snapped on his tongue, and the crispness of the taste made him want to down the whole glass at one go. "Damn, that's good," he sighed.

She checked the pizza. "Just another minute or so." Tricks had trotted over when she opened the oven door and stood looking up, hope in every line of her furry pale gold body. "No, nothing for you," Bo said. "You've already had your dinner. I'm not baking cookies."

He said, "You bake cookies?"

"She gets cookies for her birthday."

"That's tomorrow, right?"

"No, it's quite a while until her birthday."

"Mine's tomorrow," he lied.

"It is not. I saw your driver's license, remember?"

"It's a fake."

"I'm not baking cookies."

Morgan consoled himself with the beer, silently pleased at how well the last half hour of conversation had gone. They'd teased each other—a little—and she'd given him an insight into what had made her so reserved and self-protective. He hadn't made a big deal of it, she hadn't made a big deal of it, but he knew damn well it *was* a big deal because it had to be. Kids needed stability, and she hadn't had that.

She took the pizza out of the oven and briskly zipped the pizza cutter through it, then brought the pan to the table and set it on a pot holder. As she sat down, she turned her head to check on Tricks, and the late afternoon light fell on her right cheekbone. It looked as if she had a faint smear of dirt on her face. He started to say something, then realized she'd done a damn good job of covering the lingering bruise. Some of the makeup had worn off, or he might not have noticed either. Then he realized she'd been covering up the bruise all along because he hadn't noticed it since Friday night.

She didn't want people fussing over her, or thinking she was anything except one hundred percent okay.

She could have been milking it for all she was worth, and he knew a lot of people who would have. Instead she preferred to be left alone.

They concentrated on the pizza and beer, and for the first time since he'd been shot, Morgan felt as if he was himself again, rather than a patched-up wreck. Did things get more normal than beer and pizza? He was still a patched-up wreck, but he was a wreck who was starting to get back to being human.

After dinner, she cleaned up and headed out with Tricks for their last walk of the day. He stood in the large windows and watched until they were out of sight, partly to make certain he knew in what direction they'd gone and partly because he liked looking at her curvy little ass.

While he had some privacy, he decided to test the limits of his strength. He wasn't expecting miracles, but he wanted some kind of parameter he could judge his progress by. Going over to the stairs, he held firmly to the steel banister and began climbing.

The first step was okay; the second one was okay. The third one was mostly okay, but by the sixth one his knees were weak and he was breaking out in a sweat, which he took as a signal not to push his luck. He eased back down while he could still do it without having to scoot on his ass like a toddler. Tomorrow he would try it again, and maybe he could make the seventh step.

When he was back on the ground floor, he turned around and counted the steps. It was a long flight, more than a standard floor. There were twenty steps. If he could improve one step a day, in two weeks he'd be sleeping in a bed.

It was ridiculous how much he looked forward to going to Hamrickville. It was a small town—a very small one. But he'd spent five nights here, and he needed a change of scenery to relieve his growing boredom. Bo had lent him her laptop, yeah, but he couldn't electronically check on the things he wanted to check on without tripping an alert, so he was reduced to checking regular news sources and playing dumb-ass games that he wasn't any good at.

When it came time to leave, Tricks bounded out and raced madly around the yard as if she was overjoyed he was going with them. Bo unlocked the Jeep and called Tricks to her; while she was clipping on the harness, Morgan slid into the passenger seat. She led Tricks around to the driver's side and said, "Tricks, up."

The dog didn't move.

"Tricks, up."

No response.

Morgan glanced over at the dog standing motionless in the open driver's side door, staring at him with what he could only describe as an appalled expression, if a dog could be appalled.

"Tricks, come on," Bo said, then she too froze and stared at him.

"What?" he asked, impatience leaking into his tone. He didn't know what was going on, but he knew he wanted to be on the road.

"Oh, my God."

"*What?*" He looked around for a threat, any threat, reaching for a weapon that wasn't there in the holster he wasn't wearing.

"You're in her seat."

He went still. Had he heard that right? He looked at the woman. He looked at the dog. She had to be shitting him—the woman, not the dog. But Bo's expression was earnest and kind of deer-in-the-headlights as if no way had she anticipated this, and Tricks was still looking appalled as she stared unblinkingly at him. The two pairs of dark eyes were unnerving.

What was he supposed to do? Obviously, even on short acquaintance he knew Bo placed the dog way above most, if not all, humans, but still—he looked at the backseat. The Jeep wasn't the four-door model.

The backseat was small, and just the idea of contorting himself to get back there made his chest hurt.

"I know," she said helplessly. "I wouldn't ask you to try."

That was something, at least. Or he could drive and she could get in the backseat, since Tricks obviously wasn't going to, but he was supposed to look pitiful—just thinking the word grated on his nerves—and pitiful people didn't drive. But the Tahoe was sitting right there, and it was a four-door. "We can go in mine. Will it matter to her which seat she's in then?"

"It shouldn't," Bo replied, though there was a tiny hint of doubt in her voice.

He got out of the Jeep and she went back inside the house to get his keys. She used the remote to unlock the doors and he got into the passenger seat before Tricks could beat him to it, just in case. Bo retrieved her weapon from the Jeep and circled around to the driver's side, where she opened the back door and said, "Tricks, up."

Thank God, Tricks bounded up into the backseat and sat down as if she were Queen Elizabeth in the royal carriage. He looked back at her, and she turned her head away. Outrage was in every line of her furry golden body.

Bo stifled a laugh as she fastened the harness to the seat belt. "You are so on her list."

Tricks was an intelligent dog, no doubt about it, but dogs didn't plot vengeance so he wasn't worried about it. Besides, he'd sneak a treat to her and all would be forgiven. He wouldn't tell Bo about the treat, though; he knew better.

He'd bypassed Hamrickville on his way to her house, so he paid attention to the route she took, noting the highway numbers and landmarks. The Tahoe had GPS and a navigation system, but he'd rather rely on his own knowledge than that of a bunch of people he didn't know, who might or might not have been paying attention to detail when this section of the country was mapped. As it turned out, the drive was a grand total of twelve minutes, not bad at all. If he were driving in D.C., twelve minutes might take him a couple of blocks, depending on the direction and time of day.

There was no hint of civilization to come; she rounded a curve and there it was, compact, most of the buildings looking as if they'd been built in the 1940s or '50s, sidewalks, no parking meters. Most of the intersections just had stop signs. He saw a bank, a hardware store, a barbershop, other small shops, and the bakery that must have been where the fight took place last week because he couldn't imagine the town could support two bakeries. Some of the shops had flowerpots in front of them, or little bushes, but for the most part it wasn't a fussy town.

"The school is about a mile in that direction," she said at one intersection, pointing south.

He was a little surprised the town was big enough to have a school. He kept that thought to himself. They passed city hall, a compact, one-story redbrick building with white columns by the double doors. Then he saw the sign that said HAMRICKVILLE POLICE STATION on another redbrick building without any columns to fancy it up. She parked in back beside a white Dodge pickup with rust spots on it. "That's Loretta's truck," she said as they got out.

He couldn't wait to meet Loretta. He was also aware he had a part to play; he'd been playing it since he arrived at Bo's house, and that was to dial back the acuity of his senses, intellect, personality—everything that made him a lethal weapon. He'd slipped up when Bo had startled him awake, but since then he'd kept himself at a simmer instead of the rolling boil at which he normally functioned. He had to convince the good townsfolk of Hamrickville that he was Bo's weak and sick old friend, and that he was essentially harmless. The weak and sick didn't need much exaggeration, though it was mostly just weak; the harmless required concentration, and his audition was with the infamous Loretta Hobson.

She lived up to her billing. She was damn near as tall as he was, and outweighed him; she was built like a tank. But she had a sweet smile, and it was evident she liked Bo. Tricks, who was still ignoring him, bounced into Loretta's cubicle for some petting and sweet talk from the dispatcher. Bo had to tell about him getting into Tricks's seat, and Loretta sorrowfully shook her head. "She'll make you pay." She eyed him, as shrewd a look as he'd ever received before. "I heard you've had some health issues."

"Some," he said, admitting to it but not going into details because hell, he was tired of thinking about it.

"You've come to a good place to get some rest. The folks around here will take care of you. I reckon you're here this morning because you've got cabin fever?"

"You'd be right about that," he admitted.

"It's usually pretty quiet around here, last Friday and yesterday being the exceptions rather than the rule. Still, it's a change of scenery."

He agreed and took a seat in the visitor's chair by Bo's desk. She asked if he wanted coffee and took some to Loretta before bringing a cup to him. Then she got a bottle of water for herself and settled in front of an ancient computer, one so old the monitor was a separate unit and was half the size of a footlocker. It had been a while since he'd seen one of those, but she booted it up and after what seemed like half an hour of clicking and whirring, it was good to go.

He stretched his legs out and crossed them at the ankles. "What happens if this thing crashes?" he asked, indicating the computer. "Are parts still made for it?"

"No, but so far we've been able to scrounge spare parts from other old units. Our luck is still holding."

She dove into a stack of paperwork, and he shut up so she could concentrate. The quiet Loretta had touted didn't last long. Officer Jesse came in the back door and said, "Hey, Chief. Hey, Morg. How're you feeling?" Which played well to the impression that Morgan was an okay guy in Officer Jesse's book. The guy was sharp. Mentally Morgan elevated him to Officer Tucker, because he was no one to dismiss or underestimate. He'd have fit in on any big-city force if he'd wanted to.

"Better," Morgan replied. Then followed the usual male stuff about baseball; he normally didn't follow sports much because he was so often out of the country, but he'd been watching some baseball in the few days he'd been at Bo's house so he could hold up his end of the conversation. So far, so good.

Then, by some kind of osmosis, word spread through town that he was in Bo's office. He didn't know how because he could hear every word Loretta said and it wasn't her. Bo hadn't called anyone. Jesse hadn't called anyone. The only explanation was that someone had seen them arrive even though she'd parked at the back of the station.

The door opened and a short, plump, white-haired woman with bright eyes and a beaming smile came in, bearing a covered platter and accompanied by the smell of heaven.

"Miss Doris," Jesse said, springing to his feet to take the platter from her.

"I heard your visitor came to town with you," Miss Doris the baker said to Bo, her cheeks flushing pink as she looked pointedly at Morgan. Maybe she was excited because there weren't many strangers who visited Hamrickville.

"He did. Miss Doris, this is Morgan Rees. Morgan, this is Doris Brown, the owner of the bakery and the best cook in the county." By now, Morgan knew Bo well enough to hear the amusement in her tone, though no one else appeared to notice. Maybe they were too interested in the platter. God knows, his own interest was high.

Miss Doris's cheeks flushed even pinker. "Oh, I don't know about that. But I'm pleased to meet you, Mr. Rees. I brought you a welcome basket—actually it's a platter, but I didn't have any baskets. Maybe there's something there that'll tempt your appetite."

Morgan could feel the saliva gathering in his mouth. Damn, he was all but drooling at just the smell coming from that platter. "Ma'am," he said, "I got tempted the minute you walked through that door." He didn't clarify, letting the comment stand as it was. Miss Doris got so flustered she couldn't talk, and her flush deepened all the way into a full-out blush.

Bo made a low sound in her throat that could have been either laughter or a muffled snort. He suspected the latter, but he ignored her and took Miss Doris's hand, lifting it for a light kiss on her knuckles. "Thank you, ma'am."

Her mouth was an O, and she blinked several times. "Oh," she said weakly. "Oh, my. You're so welcome, Mr. Rees."

"Call me Morgan," he invited. "When you feed a man, first names are called for."

Bo planted her hands on her hips and said, "Just when did you start kissing hands, Morgan Rees? You never did before."

Again, she'd hit just the right note that spoke to old acquaintance. In return he managed a little smirk while still striving to look "pitiful." "You were never around when circumstances called for hand-kissing."

"Stop talking, and let's see what's on that platter," Loretta ordered. The woman was sensible.

Miss Doris removed the cover and revealed several cupcakes, individual little fruit pies, a lumpy something that turned out to be monkey bread—he knew because Bo said, "Oh! Monkey bread!"—and some cream-filled doughnut holes. There were also several bone-shaped treats that she told Bo she'd baked just for Tricks, using only stuff that was good for dogs. Tricks's sense of smell was much better than theirs, of course, and she was dancing around the platter, her doggie expression one of great happiness and expectation.

"Here's one for you, darling," Miss Doris cooed; for a shocked second Morgan thought she was talking to him. Shit, had she taken his flirting seriously? But no, she was talking to the dog. He should have known.

Tricks gobbled down the offered treat and immediately looked for more. Bo said, "You can have your chew bone while we have our treats." She produced what looked like an antler from her desk and gave it to Tricks, who pounced on it and immediately took it to her bed, where she lay down and started some serious gnawing.

Everyone—except Tricks—seemed to be waiting for Morgan to make his selection, given that the platter had been brought in his honor. He wasn't much of a cupcake guy; they seemed kind of sissy to him. He wanted one of those pies. But the lumpy brown thing was interesting. "What's monkey bread?" he asked.

"It's like a bunch of little cinnamon rolls stuck to-gether," Bo replied.

All right! He liked cinnamon rolls. Miss Doris pulled off a few of the lumps and put them on a paper plate that she'd been thoughtful enough to also provide. Miss Doris was rapidly becoming his favorite person in the town.

Coffee was poured for those who wanted it—that would be him and Loretta—and they all made their choices. For a few minutes the only sounds in the office were chewing and a few little *mmm*s of appreciation. Jesse went for the pies, Bo for a cupcake, Loretta for the monkey bread, while Miss Doris looked on with a beaming smile.

For a few minutes Morgan was too taken up with the melt-in-your-mouth cinnamon-y lumps of monkey bread to notice anything else, but when he did look around it was to see Bo delicately licking the icing off her cupcake.

A savage kick of lust almost paralyzed him. He froze, every muscle locked on target. He managed to look away and pretend he was concentrating on his monkey bread, but fuck, all he could see in his mind was the pink tip of her tongue licking almost gently at the icing. His skin was too hot and tight, his breathing restricted. Holy shit. Just like that, he had a hard-on like iron, and he needed to sit down before someone noticed, if he could only fucking move.

He did, somehow. He all but collapsed in the visitor's chair, which was the best he could do because his hard-on made it impossible for him to sit down normally without making some major adjustments in his pants, which he wasn't about to do in front of the ladies. Loretta and Bo might take it in stride, but Miss Doris might faint.

"Are you okay?" Bo asked, her attention snapping to him.

"Yeah, fine," he muttered. Maybe they'd think he was embarrassed by how weak he was. He set his paper plate on his lap to cover the evidence, and prayed a sudden throb didn't knock the plate sideways. Damn it, didn't women know better than to lick things in front of a man?

There followed a flurry of attention from Miss Doris and even from Loretta, who volunteered her brothers to help him with some workouts when he felt better, to rebuild his strength. He had to verbally appreciate Loretta's offer and fend off Miss Doris's intention of slapping a cold wet cloth over his face. He was sweating, but not from sickness. At least all that took his attention off Bo's tongue and gave his hard-on time to give up and start subsiding.

Miss Doris had to get back to the bakery, and she left in a flurry of thank-yous. Jesse had another pie, though he did slant a look at Morgan that made him think maybe the officer had seen enough that he had a good idea about the true cause of Morgan's "weakness." Probably every man alive had had the same thing happen to him. Unruly body parts in your pants just came with the territory.

Thank God, Bo didn't want to lick a second cupcake; she didn't even eat the cake part of the first one. A call came in about a four-year-old stuck in a tree, and Jesse left to go do some tree-climbing. Bo began wading through all the paperwork on her desk, and Tricks napped, worn out from her antler-gnawing.

A pretty blonde, who was introduced as Bo's friend Daina, dropped by with slushies for them all as an afternoon treat. Morgan began to feel as if he was going to die from sugar overload. Daina was there purely out of curiosity, of course. She didn't stay long, but long enough to get in a little impersonal flirting.

Then a bunch of vehicles pulled to the curb outside, several pickup trucks and cars. A gaggle of high school kids exited; the door opened and the whole gaggle poured in, all of them talking at once. "Chief Bo! Mr. Cummins said we needed to practice driving Tricks around."

On the face of it that didn't make sense because he doubted Bo would let them practice their driving with Tricks on board. But she seemed to know exactly what they meant, because she said, "What do you have?"

"We thought we'd start off with a pickup," one of the boys said. "Get her used to riding in the open. If you get in back too, we know she'll stay."

Tricks had jumped up when the kids entered and was in the middle of the group, getting her required petting. One of the girls said, "We even have a tiara and a feather boa for her."

"She'll do okay with the boa, but I don't know about the tiara," Bo said, not blinking an eye. "I tried putting a cap on her once and she wouldn't have it. But she did like the Christmas bow I stuck on her head."

Morgan kept his mouth shut. The conversation was getting weirder by the minute. What the hell were they doing?

"Let's get her loaded up and see what she'll do," the boy said. "I'll drive really slow, Chief."

Bo and Tricks and the whole group went outside. Loretta left her cubicle to stand on the sidewalk and watch, so Morgan joined her. The boy lowered the tailgate of his truck and tried to get Tricks to jump up in the bed, but she was too busy with the petting. Bo said, "Tricks, up," and patted the tailgate. Tricks obediently jumped up, then immediately jumped down again.

"Tricks, up."

Same result.

Sighing, Bo climbed into the bed of the pickup, sat down, and said, "Tricks, up."

With the center of her life sitting there, Tricks jumped up and covered Bo's face with a mad flurry of licking. A couple of the girls climbed in the back with them. One had the aforementioned tiara and boa. She looped the pink boa around Tricks's neck, and carefully set the tiara on her head. With one shake, Tricks had the tiara off. It was tried again, with the same result.

"I think there's a sticky bow in the break room," Loretta said, and went inside to see if she remembered right. She didn't bother explaining why a sticky bow might be in a police station.

She returned with a slightly crushed and mangled glittery green bow. The backing was peeled off and the bow carefully stuck on top of Tricks's head.

The boy closed the tailgate and got into the cab. Bo scooted against the back of the truck bed, and the two girls flanked Tricks in the middle, each with an arm around her. "Go!" the boa girl said, and all the vehicles slowly pulled into the street like a parade, their lights on, and blowing their horns.

Morgan looked around to make sure he was still on Earth. Or maybe this was just some weird small-town custom; his small-town experience was thin, so he had to allow for that. "What the hell is going on?" he asked Loretta.

"They're practicing for the Heritage Parade," she explained. "The junior and senior classes get to each decorate a float for the parade. The seniors this year want Tricks to ride on their float, but the chief said she probably wouldn't unless they got her used to it first, so they're practicing with her. The real floats aren't ready yet, not that they'd show them ahead of time anyway. My guess is the next time they'll use a hay-hauling trailer, get her used to the size."

Well, that explained the tiara and boa.

The sidewalks began filling as shopkeepers and customers came outside to watch the little parade. People began bellowing, "Tricks!" and waving. The two girls flanking Tricks waved, practicing their parts. Tricks woofed left and right, her doggy face beaming.

"She looks like a homecoming queen," Loretta said happily, stepping into the street so she could continue watching. Bemused, Morgan went to stand beside her.

A few blocks down, at the traffic light, some man stepped into the middle of the intersection and stopped traffic coming from all four directions, not that there was that much, but still. Waving, he directed the little procession to make a U-turn so they could head back toward the police station. The kids, driving carefully with their precious cargo of police chief and dog, sedately swung around in the intersection to reverse course.

As they neared, he could hear the happy "Woof! Woof!" and see the golden head adorned with a bedraggled green bow turning from side to side with each woof, as Tricks accepted the applause and cheers of an entire town.

Somehow, Morgan thought, getting shot had thrown him into the fucking Twilight Zone.

What the hell. Might as well fit in.

He began waving and clapping too.

Chapter 12

When they got home, Bo let tricks out of the Tahoe while Morgan followed more slowly. He hated to admit it, and he'd certainly enjoyed the trip to town, but the unaccustomed activity had tired him. Normally he still napped during the day, or whenever he got tired, but today he hadn't had that luxury and it was telling on him. He thought of the sofa with longing, wanting nothing more than to stretch out and close his eyes.

Bo unlocked the door, and the dog darted inside. She looked back at him. "Today was more of an effort than you thought it would be, wasn't it?"

"Yeah," he admitted.

"You can put your feet up and relax while I'm throwing supper together." She stepped aside and waited for him to enter, then closed the door behind them. Morgan headed for the sofa, then stopped dead in the middle of the floor.

Tricks sat in the middle of the sofa, the extravagant, long white feathery strands of her tail draped over the cushion like a fringed shawl. She was looking off, as if she had no idea they were on the premises.

"Or not," Bo said, standing as still as he was. "Oh, dear. You got her seat, so now she's got yours. I'm not getting into the middle of this. You have to handle it, make it up to her somehow. I'm warning you, she holds a grudge."

Evidently. On the other hand, she was a dog. Morgan said, "Is it all right with you if I give her a treat?"

Tricks's eyes flicked toward him at the word "treat," but she didn't abandon her post.

"Bribing her isn't a good idea. She remembers, and then you'll have to bribe her every time."

"Okay, no bribery. I won't try to get her down. I'll just give her the treat, and go sit somewhere else. Will that work?"

"Maybe. It'll go a long way toward getting back in her good graces. Also, you should probably apologize."

The idea was so outlandish that he laughed out loud. "C'mon, that's carrying things too far. She understands food. What's she going to understand about an apology?"

"You'd be surprised. You can take my advice or not."

Bo went to the refrigerator and got out a slice of sandwich turkey. "Here you go," she said, giving it to him. "Hope it works."

He rolled up the slice and went to sit beside the dog. As soon as the cushion compressed under his weight she glanced at him, alerted by the smell of the turkey, then looked away again. "Good girl," he crooned. He tore off a piece of turkey and offered it to her. "You were a champion, riding in that pickup today."

She looked at the turkey, and delicately took the offering from his fingers.

"That bow on your head suited you." Another piece of turkey, another acceptance. Figuring that was enough buttering up, he gave her the rest of the turkey and let her sit there. He'd definitely have liked to lie down but instead turned on the TV and stretched out his legs while he let his head rest on the back of the sofa. It wasn't lying down, but it would do.

Tricks didn't get down, but after a minute she too lay down, and put her head on his thigh. He let his hand rest on her side, feeling the plush silkiness of her fur, her warm body, and the strong beating of her heart. Good enough.

Though the trip to town had been amusing as hell, Morgan elected to spend the rest of the week at what he'd started thinking of as "home." Once Bo was gone for the day, he worked on his endurance. He walked around the yard, even ventured into the woods a short distance as his legs got stronger. Being outside felt good. The belated arrival of spring had brought with it an abundance of good weather, warm without being hot, everything turning green almost overnight. He'd always been a man who preferred being outdoors, so though the circumstances were far from ideal, at least he was outside and he was moving under his own steam.

Late Friday afternoon when Bo got home, she said, "Mayor Buddy has called an emergency town council meeting tomorrow morning. Something's come up with the Gooding situation. I have to be there."

"What's he done?"

"I don't know, but this is the first time Mayor Buddy's ever called an emergency meeting, so it must be serious."

"Can he do anything to hurt the town?"

"Several townspeople work for him, and if he fired them or laid them off, it would sure hurt their families."

"Is he threatening to do that?"

"I guess I'll find out tomorrow."

Morgan was a little disappointed because he'd been looking forward to having her at home the entire weekend, but what the hell, he'd use the opportunity to push himself a little more. He'd been working on those stairs. He could make it to the twelfth step now before his legs got shaky. He didn't push the stairs; the last thing he needed was to pass out and fall down them. But in just a week he was feeling more human instead of a physical wreck. The soreness in his chest, while still there, was better. His legs were stronger. He was eating more. No way to tell, but he figured he'd gained a good five pounds this week.

He was bored with his own company, yeah, but he had another reason for not going with her to work every day: he didn't want to wear out his welcome, which was tenuous to begin with. Bo wouldn't want him around every minute of every day. She was becoming easier with him—not that she'd acted overtly uncomfortable, but not many people would be completely at ease with having a stranger dumped on them. Any discomfort she'd felt had been hidden behind her inner walls, but he figured it had to be there. She was too private, too emotionally shielded, to not feel stressed by his presence.

If she'd had any idea he'd got a raging hard-on from watching her lick the icing off her cupcake, she'd stay as far away from him as possible, maybe even put him on the road despite her agreement with Axel. As far as he knew, she hadn't spent any of the money Axel had deposited in her account, and though she could definitely use it, she didn't *have* to have it. She was free to get rid of him and wouldn't worry about hurting his feelings by doing so.

He didn't want to leave. Not yet, anyway. He wanted the mystery of who had tried to kill him solved, yeah, but that was in the future and he couldn't do anything about it. What he could do something about was his physical condition, and his growing attraction to Bo. She was a challenge, and he liked that but it wasn't *just* that. He couldn't nail down exactly what it was about her that interested him so. She seemed to be content with who she was, how she looked, her life in general. It was nice being around a woman who didn't need to be reassured about anything.

After breakfast on Saturday, she took Tricks for a long walk, then went upstairs to get ready. When she came down again, Morgan had to fight to keep from staring. She was wearing a simple skirt and blouse, nothing fancy, but the skirt was just tight enough to cup her curvy ass, and my God, her legs went on forever, and he broke out in a sweat as he pictured them hooked over his shoulders. *Down, boy,* he silently ordered his dick. *Don't point.*

He sat down because the fool was pointing anyway. To distract himself he said, "It's a dress-up type of thing?"

She looked down at her skirt. "Not dress-up, exactly, but I don't want to show up wearing jeans or anything like that. Jeans are fine when I'm on the job, because I never know what I'll need to do, but a town council meeting is different."

Instead of wearing her thick dark hair in its usual low ponytail, she'd twisted it up so the nape of her neck was bare. If he hadn't already been sitting down he'd have gotten weak-kneed at the sight of the delicate furrow. What the hell? He'd never even noticed a woman's neck before, but the sight of Bo's, with wisps of dark hair framing the slenderness of it, made the bottom drop out of his stomach. So much for distracting himself.

Tricks was dancing around Bo, delighted they were going for a ride. The dog was delighted about everything: going, coming, mealtime, her walks, playing ball, and life in general. The only thing she hadn't greeted with joy was the sight of him in "her" seat, and even with the offering of turkey it had taken a couple of days before she'd forgiven him enough to let him throw her ball. He was back in her good graces, though, so he said, "Why not leave Tricks with me? Do you take her into the council meetings?"

Bo glanced worriedly at Tricks. "Usually, but the normal meetings don't last over an hour. I don't know about this one."

"Then leave her here. I can take her out and throw the ball for her, and feed her lunch if you aren't back by then."

She still looked undecided. He said, "I can handle her. Is she likely to run off?"

"No. She won't be happy that I left without her, though."

"So what will she do? Throw a temper tantrum?"

She smiled at that. "No, but—once she stops pouting, just explain to her that I had to go to town and I'll be back as soon as I can, okay?"

He must have looked incredulous—this was a *dog* they were talking about, not a kid, and this was taking things pretty far even for her—because she said, "I know it sounds silly, but you know how they say a dog is about as smart as a two-year-old? She's as smart as a four-year-old. She understands a lot of what you say."

She understood the speaker's tone of voice, yeah, but most dogs did learn and respond to that. "She'll understand she hasn't been abandoned, and she knows time?"

"Yes, she knows time." Now Bo scowled at him. "Never mind. I'll take her with me."

"Fine," he said testily. "I'll explain it to her. I promise. Now go, before you're late."

She didn't want to, he could tell, but it was concern for Tricks if the meeting ran long that settled the matter. She bent down to nuzzle the top of Tricks's head. "You stay here this time, sweetie. You'll be a lot more comfortable here than you will be in an old meeting room. I'll be back as soon as I can."

She straightened and left without looking back, though he could tell she wanted to. He and Tricks stood at the window watching as she left, he because he got a glimpse of her long legs when she got into the Jeep, and Tricks because she probably couldn't believe she was being left behind.

As the Jeep went down the driveway, Tricks whined plaintively. "It's okay, girl," Morgan said, bending down to stroke her. "She'll be back before you know it." Then, because he'd promised even though he felt like a fool for doing it, he added, "She's got a meeting to go to that could last a long time, and she didn't want you to have to wait if you need to take a leak, or whatever. She'll be back, probably by lunch. I can't imagine any of their meetings taking much time even when they're talking about assholes."

Tricks whined again, then licked his cheek and trotted off to find a toy.

He checked the news and played a game or two on the laptop before restlessly putting it aside. It was good to feel restless; when he'd been in such bad shape, he hadn't had any interest in doing anything other than lying right where he was, but now he wanted to move.

He did the stairs, and this time made it to number fifteen, almost to the top. He rested a bit—damn that fifteen steps could make him tired—then decided to do some light calisthenics. Stretching and gently getting his heart rate up would be a good thing. He got down on the floor and stretched, cautiously testing the limits of his stiff muscles.

Of course the dog bounded over, thinking it was a game because he was on the floor and all but danced on top of him. He told her no a couple of times, told her to move a couple of times, then gave up. So much for her understanding almost everything that was said to her. Everyone tended to act like she was the second coming of Air Bud, but when all was said and done, she was a dog. A pretty one, he had to admit, and smart enough, but still a dog.

He gave up on floor stretching, got to his feet, and tried putting his palms flat on the floor to stretch his hamstrings. His hamstrings did fine. His lower back, though, seized in a spasm that almost put him on his knees.

Spitting out curses between his teeth, he managed to straighten. Shit! The muscle spasm eased, and he stood there for a minute while he got his breath back, furious at this new reminder of the sad shape he was in. Six weeks ago he'd been in top physical form, able to run and swim for miles, carry a hundred pounds on his back while trekking through all kinds of miserable shit, and still kick ass in a firefight.

He might never be in that kind of shape again. He had to face the fact that he could be looking at a new reality. The docs had repaired him, but the human body wasn't like a car, you couldn't slap a new piece of sheet metal in place and call it done. His heart might never be as strong again. He wouldn't know unless he worked his ass off trying to get to that point. What if he couldn't do it, though?

He'd quit the GO-Teams, that what. All the guys' lives depended on each man being able to do his job. He wouldn't jeopardize any of them because of his ego, because he couldn't let go. He could probably still be involved, maybe in training, maybe logistics, but if he wasn't a hundred percent he wouldn't go back out on a job.

Tricks got her tennis ball and came to stand in front of him. She put a paw on his knee, then looked at the door.

"Time for a pee break, huh? Okay, let's go."

She pranced to the door. She never just *walked* anywhere, like normal dogs. It was as if she knew how pretty she was, and that the world as Bo Maran had structured it revolved around her. "Spoiled brat," he muttered, but then he smiled because yeah, he remembered her riding in the back of the pickup with a green bow stuck on her head, woofing like a homecoming queen—if homecoming queens woofed, that is.

They stepped outside and she dropped the ball at his feet, then took off running. Morgan bent to pick up the ball, and the muscle spasm knifed him in the back again. He cussed and groaned and gradually managed to get upright again, though sweat was running down his temples. Fuck, that hurt! It wasn't the all-consuming pain of being shot and the following surgery, but it was sharp and paralyzing in its intensity. He wasn't sure he could even walk right now. He took a few deep breaths, willing the pain away.

Tricks trotted back to him, an accusing expression on her face.

Bo had insisted that the dog understood most of what people said. What the hell; it was bullshit, of course, but—"Tricks, I hurt my back and I can't bend down. If you want me to throw your ball, you'll have to put it in my hand."

She pounced on the ball like a cat, picked it up, and nosed it into his palm before taking off at a run again.

He stood there, stunned. No. Fucking. Way. It was a coincidence. She stopped when the ball didn't bounce in front of her the way she liked and looked back at him. He didn't dare try twisting his torso to throw overhand but he gave it a good underhand toss so it bounced in front of her, and she caught it on the first bounce. She stopped, posed, and he rolled his eyes even as he said, "Good girl."

She brought the ball back and put it in his hand. He tossed it, she brought it back and put it in his hand. She did it a fourth time.

He was so astonished he forgot about his back and strolled toward the woods with her. As long as he kept his pace slow and even, as long as he didn't twist, he was fine. He tossed the ball, and Tricks brought it back. That wasn't coincidence; he'd never seen her do it before, she'd always dropped the ball at the feet of the person she'd chosen to honor. But she put the ball in his hand every single time after he told her what he wanted.

Eventually she got tired, stopped to pee. He was tired too, and his back was aching so he said, "Let's go, girl," and they headed back inside. A glance at the clock told him it was almost time for her lunch, as if her standing beside her bowls and staring at him wasn't clue enough. In case he didn't get the hint, she looked at the bowls, then back at him.

"Not yet. Your mom keeps you on a strict schedule."

With a sigh, she lay down beside the bowls to wait.

Was it possible she really understood him? Bo thought so and talked to the dog as if she were indeed a four-year-old child. He wasn't convinced, but damn, he was wavering.

He waited until Tricks's exact lunch time before squatting to dip the proper amount of food from the container into her bowl. Squatting didn't hurt his back, though he had a bit of difficulty in standing up again; he had to hold on to the counter top and pull himself up.

Tricks showed her appreciation with a wag of her tail and paused in her eating to bestow a lick on his knee. That was normal, he thought; dogs liked being fed.

He needed to eat, too; the council meeting was obviously running longer than Bo had thought it would, but he'd lived most of his life feeding himself. He was better; he didn't have to have food brought to him. He slapped together a sandwich and ate it standing up. He even drank milk because it was better for him than beer. He didn't want to drink her remaining Naked Pig beer when he didn't know how long it would be before the next delivery.

He sat at the table to read for a while because the chair had a straighter back, and that eased the ache in his own back. After letting Tricks rest and nap, he said,

"Hey Tricks, want to go outside?" Let's see if she'd do that again, or if it had been a fluke.

Tricks retrieved her ball and went to the door, tail wagging in enthusiasm, feet dancing. They stepped out into the sunshine. She dropped the ball at his feet and took off running.

"Yeah, that's what I thought," he muttered. Raising his voice he said, "Tricks!"

She stopped and looked back at him, surprised and displeased that he hadn't thrown the ball, but she trotted back to him. Come to think of it, she had the most expressive face he'd ever seen on a dog; reading her was as easy as if she could speak.

"You have to put it in my hand," he said because, hell, if she understood that much, she should remember what he'd said about his back—assuming she knew what a back was.

She picked up the ball, put it in his hand, and took off.

Morgan looked down at the fuzzy, dirty, much-used yellow ball. "I'll be damned," he said softly, and tossed it over her head so she could catch it on the first bounce and pose, waiting for his admiration.

When Bo entered the room in City Hall where the town council meetings were held, she was surprised to see that both Miss Doris and Emily were there, as well as Jesse. Then she realized she shouldn't have been surprised because the meeting revolved around the Goodings and what meanness they might unleash on the town, which meant Emily, Jesse, and she herself were at the heart of it. She and Jesse took seats at the back of the room but didn't have time to chat.

Mayor Buddy called the meeting to order, then gave Emily the floor.

Emily was young, just in her mid-twenties, but self-possessed. She said, "First, I want to apologize to everyone that my personal life is causing problems for the town."

There was a rumble of voices assuring her that the fault wasn't hers. She flushed and said, "I had the bad judgment to marry Kyle, so it goes back that far. This past week has been like a war. He and his daddy are threatening everything they can think of if I don't just sign over everything to Kyle and drop the domestic violence charges. I have to tell you, some of those threats involve the town."

Miss Virginia Rose, the cashier at the grocery store who was also on the town council, said, "What kind of threats?"

Emily twisted her hands. "Well, it isn't just the people who work at the sawmills. Mr. Gooding said if he shut down the sawmills, the town would lose a lot of its revenue because the people who work there do most of their shopping here. And he's right."

"I doubt he'd shut down the sawmills," Mayor Buddy said. "That's his livelihood, too."

"All I can tell you, Mayor, is that he's always talking about his investments and how much money he's got tucked away, and he said he can survive shutting down the sawmills for a few months, but the town and the people who work for him can't."

The meeting erupted into a flurry of angry comments until Mayor Buddy gaveled it back to order. This was indeed a problem because the town operated on a shoestring budget with no surplus to tide it over. The loss of those sales taxes for even a few months would be catastrophic.

Bo and Jesse sat quietly listening. Everyone had a different idea about what to do, including Miss Virginia Rose's suggestion that some of the townsfolk take the Goodings out somewhere and beat the shit out of them. Bo could tell several of the council members thought that was a good idea, which was problematic with her and Jesse both sitting there.

Time ticked by. She checked her phone; this was taking far longer than she'd anticipated. She was glad Tricks had stayed with Morgan, she thought, because otherwise she'd have had to interrupt the meeting at least a couple of times to take Tricks out. Plus she would have had to go down to the police station to get some of the food she kept there. On the other hand, this might be the longest she'd ever been away from Tricks other than the one time when she'd had bronchitis and Daina had kept Tricks while Bo miserably waited her turn to be seen in a doctor's office. Tricks had been about six months old and hell on wheels; easygoing Daina had been no match for her, and still wasn't.

"We're going to have to arrest most of the people here," Jesse muttered to her because the talk had segued from prevention to vengeance, which included hiring the Mean-As-Shit Hobsons to deal with the situation. Considering Mr. Gooding's reaction to Loretta, Bo thought that idea had some merit.

On the other hand, she also remembered how vehemently Mr. Gooding wanted Kyle out of this situation without a criminal record.

She held up her hand. Mayor Buddy banged his gavel and said, "Chief Maran has the floor."

Bo got to her feet, and everyone in the room looked at her expectantly.

"Emily, which would you rather have, Kyle prosecuted for hitting you, or him signing the divorce papers and just going away?"

"Divorce and going away," Emily said promptly. "I know I'm supposed to prosecute but I gotta say, he never beat me or anything like that, he slapped me that one time in the bakery and I'm ashamed to admit it, but I slapped him that morning before I left the house. He could file charges against me, too, couldn't he? But he hasn't."

"Yes, he could," Bo said. "I don't know if the mayor has told everyone, but Mr. Gooding came to see me on Monday and he's very concerned about Kyle having a criminal record. I think we can use that as leverage and work out something between the town and the Goodings, and that includes Kyle signing the divorce papers and leaving Emily alone."

It took a while to hammer out a plan. As Mayor Buddy put it, the Goodings were bitter, vindictive sons of bitches who never forgot a slight unless "we make it in their best interests to do otherwise."

The plan revolved around Emily, and she was all in. Only a week had passed, but she could push hard to have a divorce granted immediately, if not sooner. She could light a fire under her lawyer, they could get the papers ready, they could get Judge Harper lined up. The linchpin was getting Kyle to sign. The proposal they came up with was that if Kyle didn't give Emily any more trouble, if he agreed to the divorce settlement, which was simply that he kept his stuff and she kept hers and they sold the house and split the profits, assuming there were any, the charges against him would be dropped. He also had to stay away from her and get on with his own life without interfering in hers. If he couldn't do that, all bets were off. And if she started having any mysterious troubles, such as her car getting keyed or her tires knifed, the Hobsons would be sicced on him. That last wasn't legal, but what the hell—maybe none of it was.

Jesse was the law-and-order person there, and he didn't have any problem with it. He was for whatever served the community best rather than going balls-to-the-wall for the few misdemeanor charges that were all they had on Kyle. "I'm okay with all this," he said. "Kyle didn't get off without catching some good licks himself, including Brandy braining him with the chair. If everyone else is on board, I am too." That pretty much sealed the deal as far as everyone else was concerned.

Then they had to decide who would make the proposition to Mr. Gooding. Mayor Buddy volunteered, and everyone heaved a sigh of relief. Mayor Buddy was as wily as they came; he'd make it sound as if they were doing the Goodings a favor and be damn convincing about it. The town lawyer said he'd draw up some papers because they had to have signatures on the deal or the Goodings wouldn't take it seriously. Whether or not the papers would stand up in court was something else entirely, but from the conversations around her Bo thought that if the Goodings reneged, court would be the least of their worries because the Hobsons would be called in.

Finally—*finally*—she was on her way home. She was starving but didn't take the time to stop and get a hamburger because she was anxious about how Tricks and Morgan had fared together. Tricks would be okay; Morgan's welfare was the most at risk. If Tricks felt put-upon or insulted, she might well refuse to come back inside, and Morgan was too weak to chase after her. He could fall and hurt himself if he tried to push too far.

She didn't exactly lock the brakes and sling gravel when she slid to a stop beside the Tahoe, but it was close.

The good news was that there was no one lying on the ground unable to get up, and no annoyed golden retriever refusing to obey "Come here." Maybe they had rocked through without any major problems.

Silly, but her heart was beating a little faster as she opened the door, braced for whatever scene greeted her there. No, it wasn't silly because she knew Tricks.

Still, she wasn't prepared. Nothing could have prepared her.

Morgan was sitting on the sofa, all in one piece. Tricks was standing on her back legs in front of him, her front legs braced on his chest, looking up at him with an expression of pure delight while he scratched behind her ears and crooned to her in a deep, soft tone. They were all but nose to nose. At Bo's entrance Tricks turned her head to look at her, giving her one of those joyous looks that always melted Bo's heart because she'd never before seen such a happy creature. Tricks looked back up at Morgan, and he bent his head to gently touch his forehead to hers. "There's Mom," he said unnecessarily, and Tricks took that as her signal to go greet the center of her life.

She raced over and began dancing around Bo in an excess of joy. Bo knelt and indulged in a frenzy of petting, but she barely knew what she was doing. She felt as if she'd been hit between the eyes with a two-by-four, or maybe punched in the stomach. Something. Even her lips were numb.

No. Oh dear God, *no*.

Chapter 13

She didn't want to be attracted to him. She shouldn't, *couldn't,* be attracted to him. There was no point in it, it was stupid, it was a total waste of time and emotional effort. She knew better.

Yet here she was, almost melting because he was snuggling with her dog. Well, not that exactly; Tricks had a way of making everyone eat out of her paw. It was *him,* specifically. She wasn't wearing rose-colored glasses when it came to seeing him for what he was. For the most part he had kept himself very low key, and she appreciated the effort he'd made, but she hadn't forgotten that he was here because he lived a very dangerous life, one so different from hers she couldn't begin to relate. He was also a temporary fixture; when he was well, he'd be gone. He wouldn't stay.

She'd never before been attracted to overt masculinity, the kick-ass-and-take-names mentality. So why him? Her ex-husband had been better looking; feckless, but better looking. Morgan's features were rough, carved by hard experience. A woman would never look at him and think "Pretty!" but she would definitely look at him and think "Man." Maybe that was it; maybe it was a chemical reaction, and she was responding to all that testosterone.

Her heart was pounding way too fast, perhaps in panic. She'd been *aware* of him from the beginning, and it had been easy to delude herself into thinking it was nothing more than his unaccustomed presence in her home making her on edge. She had tamped that awareness down, controlled it, rationalized it. What she hadn't been able to do was destroy it. The awareness had waited, ticking away like a time bomb; perhaps she'd let herself get too comfortable because the bomb had just exploded in her face and she didn't know what to do, how to handle it.

He'd changed. If he'd stayed the way he was, she'd be okay because she'd be in caretaker mode. He'd arrived a physical wreck, but now he wasn't. He'd been here just a little over a week, and though she saw him every day, she was still aware that his color was better, he was stronger, he was gaining weight. Without knowing for certain, she guessed that when she was gone he worked at building his stamina because she couldn't imagine a man who did what he did for a living being content to simply wait and let his body heal on its own. No, he'd be pushing himself beyond what an ordinary person would, fighting back against weakness, which was further evidence of who and what he was.

He was far from recovered, but in that one week he'd improved enough that he could manage by himself. In the name of self-preservation she should insist that he leave. Doing so would undoubtedly cost her what Axel had already put in her bank account, but she hadn't spent any of it so she wouldn't be any worse off than she had been before. It wasn't as if she'd be destitute; she was okay financially.

But where would Morgan go? He couldn't go home. He'd have to contact Axel, get some other arrangements made, and on that first day he'd made it plain any further contact could paint a target on his back. He had some money, he had credit cards, he was undoubtedly capable. She *could* tell him to go.

But what kind of person would that make her, if she put her emotions above his life? This wasn't a game he was playing. He'd already almost died. Axel had said he'd coded twice during surgery.

She would be endangering his life if she made him go.

She would be endangering her heart if she didn't.

All of those thoughts and realizations were racing through her mind like strobe flashes. The inner turmoil of realization was so great that she felt the blood draining from her face, literally felt her flesh contracting. Morgan must have seen it because he started to his feet, caught himself and winced in pain, then forced himself upright. He moved fast, was beside her in three long strides. "What's wrong?" he asked, cupping her elbows in his rough palms to catch her if she staggered.

Bo fought down her reaction, conquered it, regained her mental balance. No way would she let him guess what she was thinking. She had too strong an instinct for self-preservation for that. She blew out a breath. "I just got woozy. Low blood sugar, I guess; I didn't stop to get anything to eat."

He was frowning with concern. "Sit down, and I'll get you something. What do you want? A sandwich?"

"Just a yogurt. It's too close to dinner to eat a sandwich." Dinner wasn't the only thing that was too close; *he* was too close, too warm, too big. She didn't want to notice that the top of her head didn't reach his chin, or how broad his shoulders were. She didn't want to see the faint line of a small scar on his jaw, or smell the hot man-scent of his skin. He was still holding her elbows, and she liked the feel of his hands on her skin, the heat of them. Oh, damn, this was bad. He needed to release her. She needed to move away.

Thank God, he let her go and went to the refrigerator to fetch the requested yogurt and a spoon. Bo went to the bar and eased onto one of the stools. She was shaking, both inside and out. He couldn't know. He could never know. She had to suck it up, hide her feelings—no, she had to ignore those feelings, box them up and seal it tight, until even she couldn't tell they were there.

He opened the yogurt container for her before he placed it in front of her, the piercing blue fire of his gaze searching her face. Keeping her expression bland, she said, "Thanks," and put a spoonful in her mouth. Never before had she been so grateful to have something so ordinary to do.

"I've never got what it is women like about yogurt," he commented, leaning his hip against the counter on the other side of the bar. He was still thin, but he had the easy grace of an athlete, someone who had trained his body far beyond the capabilities of most humans. What was he like when he was at full strength?

Don't think about it, don't think about it. She wrenched her thoughts from that path and made herself shrug. "The texture is creamy. It's easy, nothing that has to be prepared. When you don't want a lot, it's just enough."

"The same can be said for peanut butter."

"Do you like beef jerky?"

"Yeah. So?"

"So what's appealing about gnawing on something with the texture of leather?"

He grinned, his ice-blue eyes crinkling at the corners. "When you finish, you feel like you've accomplished something. Why didn't you stop to eat? Worried about Tricks?"

She scoffed, rolled her eyes. "I knew Tricks would be fine. I was worried about *you*. I just could see you doing something when you were outside that pissed her off, then she'd get all huffy and not come back inside, and you'd hurt yourself trying to catch her."

He laughed as he looked at the dog, who was lying on her back with all four feet in the air while she enthusiastically chewed on the bedraggled one-legged giraffe. "Yeah, she's a terror." He rubbed the side of his nose, his expression suddenly a little abashed. "You were right. For a dog, she's damn brilliant."

"I know," she said smugly. "I've been dealing with her for two and a half years now." Tricks's intelligence wasn't due to anything Bo personally had done, but she was still proud of the dog. She paused, and curiosity got the best of her. "What did she do?"

"I was trying to do too much and got a muscle spasm in my back. She wanted to go outside, and I couldn't bend down to pick up her ball so I told her she'd have to put it in my hand. She did." He slowly shook his head in amazement. "Every time. How did she understand that?"

"I don't know. All I know is, she does. If she could talk and had opposable thumbs, she'd rule the world." She finished the yogurt, slid off the stool to put the carton in the trash and the spoon in the dishwasher. "How's your back now?"

He turned to face her, lounged against the counter again. "Better. I borrowed her ball and used it to work the kink out. She thought that was a hell of a lot of fun, trying to get the ball from under my back."

Bo laughed because she could just picture it. Having someone on the floor on her level was one of Tricks's favorite things. She would light up with glee . . . right before she pounced.

"So how did the meeting go?" he asked. "Given how long it took, I'm guessing not well."

"Pretty good, actually. It was about the Goodings, of course, but we worked out a plan to handle the problem. Mayor Buddy is going to make Mr. Gooding an offer he can't refuse."

"Does it involve a horse's head?"

She stifled a laugh. "Only if the Hobsons get involved. I hope it won't come to that. We're offering to drop the charges in exchange for Kyle signing the divorce papers and leaving Emily alone."

Morgan slanted another of those blue-lightning looks down at her. "What will prevent him from going back on his word once the charges are dropped? Can you trust him?"

"Not one bit. That's where the Hobsons come in. If he doesn't honor the agreement, we turn them loose on him."

He chuckled. "I like the idea. Every town should have the equivalent of the Hobsons."

"They probably do, but it's our good luck that Loretta and her husband both work for the town. Charlie is in the water department."

"She's married?"

"To her high school sweetheart. Their son is in Morgantown, in his junior year."

"Is he a Hobson too?" Morgan asked, looking a little puzzled.

"No, why? Oh—her name. Loretta was already working for the town when they got married, and she said it was too much trouble to change everything."

"I guess keeping Hobson has its advantages."

"Oh, yeah." It struck her that their easy conversation was *too* easy. She'd become too comfortable with him, and he was already too familiar with the town and her life. Time to get out. She bent down and scratched Tricks's silky belly. "You want to go for a walk, sweetie? I've been cooped up in a meeting room all day, and I could use some exercise."

Tricks released the giraffe and jumped up, racing for her ball. As she passed by him, Morgan caught Bo's arm, his clasp light, his expression serious. "Do you feel up to a walk? I can take her."

Part of her was warmed that he was concerned enough to ask; another part of her panicked at both his touch and the close attention he was paying to her. She didn't want him to notice her, didn't want him to think twice about her or anything she did. She hid her reaction with a casual, "I feel fine now." And she did—physically, at least. Her reaction before hadn't been physical to begin with, not that she wanted him to know it.

"Where do you go?" he asked, looking through the windows at the woods on the right. "I figure I need to know, in case something happens and I have to call in the rescue squad."

"I just follow the path through the woods, up the hill, and back. It's about a mile and a half, enough to give her a good walk." Tricks brought her ball up, and Bo stroked her head, then said, "I need to change clothes, I guess. Hold on, sweetie, it won't take but a minute."

She hurried up the stairs with Tricks right behind her. As soon as the bedroom door was closed behind her, Bo blew out a long breath. She needed the walk more than Tricks did, needed the time away from him to give herself a good talking to, to put her dumb-ass reaction in that mental box and seal it tight. She didn't rule out maybe someday finding someone and getting married again . . . not completely, anyway. That was okay. That was normal.

Falling for a man she *knew* was going to leave was just plain stupid. She learned from her mistakes; she didn't keep making the same ones over and over.

He was leaving. She had to keep telling herself that, because the minute she let herself forget, she was in real trouble.

The following Tuesday, after dinner, Morgan said, "I climbed the stairs today. I'm ready to graduate from the sofa to a real bed."

"That's good." Bo kept her tone absent though her stomach tied itself in knots at the idea of him upstairs, so close to her while they slept. Yes, he'd be in the guest room, and each bedroom had its own en suite bath so they wouldn't be sharing space, but still . . . she'd liked the sense of distance, the barrier of the stairs. Now he'd conquered that barrier, and he'd be upstairs with her at night. "I think there are sheets on the bed but I'll check to make sure, and put towels in the bathroom."

"I've already taken my duffle up."

She straightened to stare at him, almost dropping the plate she was putting in the dishwasher. He'd managed to lift that heavy thing? *How?* She'd had to drag it inside. Sure, some of his clothes were in the laundry, but still. "How did you manage that?" she blurted. And how had she missed its presence? The duffle was big, and the only place to put it where it was out of the way but still easily accessible was behind the sofa. The duffle was gone—but now that she was looking she noticed the big Glock was on the lamp table beside the sofa.

He smirked, leaning against the cabinet beside the dishwasher and crossing one booted foot over the other. "The smart way. I unpacked half of it, took it up, then came back down for the rest of the stuff. Which means I climbed the stairs *twice*." He chuckled at her expression. "I never thought I'd be proud of just being able to go up a flight of stairs."

"Considering your condition when you first got here, you've come a long way." He was still thin, still didn't have a lot of stamina, but both his weight and his strength seemed to be increasing every day. "Exactly how long has it been since you were shot?"

"It'll be six weeks on Thursday. I'd be in better shape if it hadn't been for that damn pneumonia, but it kicked my butt big time."

Just six weeks. To her that seemed like a very short time, considering how severe his wound had been, but here he was grousing because pneumonia had held him back.

She nodded at the Glock. "Are you feeling the need for protection?"

"Not particularly, but you can never tell. Besides, now that I'm stronger, I can take Tricks out if you're busy. I've noticed that you've started taking your pistol with you when you walk her."

She had; now that the weather was warm, snakes were coming out. She wasn't optimistic about being able to actually hit a snake with a shot, so she also carried a walking stick, and kept Tricks closer to her.

"Common sense," she said.

After she took Tricks for an extra-long walk in the fragrant spring evening that they both enjoyed—and, yes, she took her pistol—she made certain the guest bedroom and bath were ready for an occupant. His clothes were already hanging in the closet, so he'd not only taken everything upstairs, he'd had enough energy to unpack.

She went out on the balcony that ran the length of the upstairs and called down over the railing, "Have you been sandbagging?"

He was watching TV with his long legs stretched out and feet crossed at the ankle. Instead of turning around he simply tilted his head back. "How so?"

"You hung up your clothes. After climbing the stairs—*twice*—you should have been exhausted."

"I managed," was all he said, then he went back to watching TV.

Meaning he'd pushed himself, the way he'd been pushing since that first awful day, because that was what he did. Most people would rest when they got tired; he took it as a sign to do more.

She hid her antsiness by following her regular routine. Morgan had a beer, one of the six-pack of Miller he'd given her the money to buy to tide him over until her truck driver friend made another run through Alabama and could pick up some Naked Pig. After that first grocery run she'd made when he first arrived, he'd insisted on paying for all the groceries, and she'd let him. She liked that he'd thought about it.

She did some work, but she'd so devoted herself to staying busy these past several days that after an hour she finished the project—*very* early—and didn't have another one ready to start yet. In the name of staying busy, she'd inadvertently worked herself into having some down time.

Now what?

She did some busywork. Then Tricks wanted to play her version of soccer, and after a minute or two of watching, Morgan took over the game, which freed her to do something else, meaning busywork in the kitchen, neatening the silverware drawer.

He played "soccer" with her for so long that Tricks finally called a halt and ran to her water bowl. Morgan said, "I guess she's finished," and resumed his seat on the sofa.

Tricks drank long and deep, then immediately trotted to Morgan. Bo was a few seconds too slow to react. She started to say, "Don't let—" but it was too late. Tricks had held extra water in her mouth and taken it to Morgan, where she gave it to him right on his knee.

He jumped up with a muffled "Shit!" Tricks backed up a few steps and sat down, looking incredibly pleased with herself because she'd shown her new friend how much she cared for him by taking him some water.

Having been the recipient of Tricks's water gifts many times before, Bo succumbed to a fit of the giggles. She tried to stifle them, but the look on his face was so funny and helpless she couldn't help it.

"Why did she do that?' he demanded.

She coughed and fought down any further giggles. "My best guess? She was thirsty from playing so long and thought you must be thirsty too, so she brought you a drink. She's done it before, but only to me and a few other people she really likes."

He looked down at his wet jeans, then at the dog sitting there beaming at him, if a dog could be said to beam. He muttered, "This better not be a joke." Then he cleared his throat, leaned down to stroke her and rather gruffly said, "Thank you, Tricks. That was very thoughtful of you."

She gave a doggy grin and wagged her tail, as if she knew how clever she was.

At bedtime, they all went upstairs together, which felt so weird Bo could barely say good night. If he'd gone upstairs ahead of her, or come along later, it would have been okay. The together thing was as if they were a family, which made prickles of alarm explode all over her body. They weren't even friends. They were acquaintances who happened to be temporarily living together, emphasis on *temporarily.*

She firmly closed the bedroom door behind her and considered locking it, but she refused to be silly about the whole situation. He was now able to climb the stairs, so whether or not he slept on the sofa or upstairs in the guest room made no difference. If she'd thought he was a threat to her that way, she'd never have allowed him in the house to begin with.

She got ready for bed, petted Tricks and told her to go to bed, and turned out the lamp. She knew she was too edgy to go to sleep right away, but she could try.

Within a minute Tricks was whining, going from the bed to the door and back again.

"No. Don't start this crap," she muttered. "Tricks, go to bed!"

But Tricks had an eerie way of identifying the arguments she could win and the arguments she couldn't because she persisted. Back and forth, from the bed to the door, back again to whine and poke Bo with her nose in case the whining hadn't gotten the message across. She knew Morgan was upstairs, and that was something new and exciting. She wanted to go visit. If Tricks had done the same thing during the day, Bo would have been stern with her, but it was bedtime, she was tired and wanted to go to sleep, and the whining was annoying.

After five minutes of relentless whining and poking, she surrendered.

"All *right*!" she groused, throwing back the covers and getting out of bed. The room was dark, but there was still enough light coming through the windows, and from the electric clock, that she could see Tricks bouncing up and down with joy that her hardheaded human had finally understood what she wanted.

Bo didn't turn on the lamp. Completely exasperated because she wanted to calm down and get some sleep, she threw open her bedroom door, stepped out onto the landing, and practically yelled, "*Morgan!*"

Almost before the first syllable was out of her mouth, there was a burst of movement onto the landing, along with the abrupt flaring of the overhead lights that almost blinded her because her vision had already adjusted to the darkness. She threw up her hand to shield her eyes, then squinted—and found herself staring straight at Morgan crouched in a firing stance. She was looking down the barrel of the big Glock, held in a two-fisted grip, and right above them a pair of piercing, ice-blue eyes boring a hole into her.

Her muscles locked; her blood ran cold. She'd always thought that was just an expression, but now she found that it wasn't. She was staring death in the eye, and her body felt icy from the inside out, as if her blood had indeed frozen. Her heart was slamming against her rib cage so hard she could feel the fabric of her tank fluttering, and all she could do was stand there waiting to be shot.

Delighted, Tricks started for him and Bo almost died from terror, afraid that in his state of hyperalertness he'd shoot the first thing that moved, which was Tricks.

Instead he barked, "What's wrong?" as he straightened and with a short, sharp motion of his wrists snapped the barrel upward and held it pointed toward the roof. Bo's sense of relief was overwhelming, as debilitating in its way as her terror; her vision dimmed for a second, and she almost sagged to the ground before she caught herself.

Tricks was wagging her tail so hard her butt was twitching back and forth. She reached Morgan and licked his kneecap, then thrust her nose into his groin to make sure it was him. He grunted a little but didn't move, his gaze moving swiftly from point to point, searching for the threat.

Bo tried to breathe, tried to suck in a much-needed deep breath. In a thin voice, which was all she could manage to squeeze from her constricted throat, she said, "Tricks."

His face was still set in stern, hard lines as he looked down at the dog, who was looking up at him with bright eyes and an "Aren't you glad to see me?" expression.

"What's wrong with her?" he asked sharply.

Even his voice was different, deep and hard and clear. He'd lost the shallow weakness in his voice he'd had when he first came here, though so gradually she wasn't certain when the quality of his voice had changed. He wasn't full strength but he was still lethal, and for the first time she saw that in a way she hadn't before, not even when he'd accidentally tried to choke her.

"Nothing," she managed, her own voice shaking. She was shaking all over, head to foot, so acutely aware that she or Tricks, or both, could be lying in a pool of blood right now—and the whole situation was her fault. She knew what he was, yet she'd still jerked the door open and yelled his name, without considering what his trained reaction would be. You don't poke a gator and expect it not to snap, but she'd done just that. "She . . ." Her voice trailed off as her terror faded enough that she could see him, all of him and not just the pistol and his eyes. She reeled under a second shock, completely different in nature from the first one but just as devastating.

He wore only a pair of boxer shorts.

She'd thought of him as thin, and he was—but only in comparison to the powerful musculature he'd sported before, going by how his clothes hung on him. His body as it was now looked like a swimmer's body, still muscled, but sleek. Had he retained that much muscle, or had he truly been pushing himself so hard in these past two weeks that he'd already packed some back on?

She had been cold, but abruptly a wave of almost suffocating heat swept over her. She wanted to look away, she wanted to open her mouth and tell Tricks to stop nudging him in the balls, she wanted to say, "Sorry," and go back into her bedroom. None of these were viable options, though, because she literally couldn't move. She was as stunned as if she'd been slammed by some invisible force that had knocked her stupid.

She could see the lines of muscle clearly delineated in his arms, his long legs that still looked powerful. Holy crap, she could see something else clearly delineated in his boxers, and thank God it was sleeping. Swallowing hard, she jerked her gaze upward to the broad plates of his lightly haired chest muscles—and she stopped, staring at the obscenely long red scar that bisected his chest, and other lines that looked shattered and puckered, almost like a broken windshield. The scar—well, she'd seen surgical scars before, even those of heart surgery, and a scar was a scar. But what in hell were those dark lines radiating out from the scar?

She was still so stunned that she pointed at his chest and blurted, "What's that?"

His dark brows drew together in a scowl. If she was still in shock, he was still in attack mode, without any outlet for the adrenaline pouring through his system. "Scars," he said curtly. "You remember. Bullet. Surgery."

She gave her head a little shake. "Not that. Those lines." She moved closer, frowning at his bare chest in the brightness of the overhead light that he'd flipped on as he charged out of his room. "They look like . . . a spider web?"

He glanced down at his chest and grimaced. "Oh, that. That's what's left of my tattoo."

A tattoo! She blinked. Okay, that made sense, even if the pattern didn't. "Why a spider web?"

He scowled again. "It isn't a spider web," he growled. "It's a bull's-eye."

A . . . bull's-eye. She blinked, then blinked again. A freakin' *bull's-eye*?

She snapped from bewilderment to fury so fast she had no way to rein herself in, no way to retreat behind her walls. Her mouth fell open, she hung there motionless for a second, and then she blew. "You drew a damn *target* on your chest!" she shrieked. "You *moron*! Do you have a death wish? Did you think it was *funny* when some knuckle-dragger nearly killed you?"

He moved closer, his chin lowered, squaring up against her like a fighter about to go a round or three. His gaze was locked on her face, fire simmering in his own eyes, but he gave a negligent shrug. "I thought: 'Shit, this messed up my tattoo.'"

She felt as if her eyes might bug out, as if her hair were standing on end. The only other time in her life when she'd been this angry was when Kyle Gooding had punched her in the face and she felt the same, as if her skin couldn't contain her body. In her outrage, she poked the gator again, literally, jabbing his left pec with her forefinger as she glared up at him. "*Idiot!*"

She saw a flash of his eyes, glittering like glacier ice, and then he kissed her.

She had no warning. He wasn't kissing her, and then a split second later he was. His right arm was around her waist, holding her up on her toes against him, and she could feel the coolness of the weapon still in his hand as it pressed into her hip. His left hand cupped her jaw, holding her face tilted up while he lowered his head and slanted his mouth over hers.

Something cataclysmic happened inside her. It felt right, as if every other kiss she'd had in her entire life had been wrong. All of her senses, everything she knew or felt, was swamped by this. The taste of him filled her, the mint of the toothpaste he'd just used underlaid by something raw and hot and powerful, something that made her heart pound and her blood, which had been so cold, sear her veins as it raced through her body. There was the heat of his skin, most of it bare, against her and under her hands. The tank shirt she wore was a single, flimsy layer of cotton between them, inadequate for protection but suddenly feeling rough against her nipples, nipples that were no longer soft but tightly pinched and erect. And below . . . he was erect now, too, a straining hardness pushing against the softness between her legs. There was heat there, his as well as hers, blood pooling and throbbing and burning.

Distantly she was aware that this was just a kiss, one kiss, a kiss that hadn't stopped yet, and she was ready to let him strip down her pants and get between her legs. Even worse, that was what she wanted, wanted as she had never wanted a man before. She wanted him there, inside her, riding her deep and hard.

She was a fool.

The thought was a slap in the face, a dash of cold water, just what she needed to will control back into her arms and legs, steel back into her spine. The first step was to turn her head, breaking contact with his mouth. One kiss, but if he kept on kissing her, she knew he'd have her on her back. She let her forehead rest on his shoulder and that was almost worse, because she could smell the heat of his skin and feel the tug of instinct that urged her to burrow deeper against him, so she could absorb more of that heat and man-scent.

The second step was to stop digging her fingers into the muscled pad of his shoulder, to place her palm flat against his chest and push. Her fingertips flexed on his skin, just for an instant, then she concentrated her strength and put pressure in her touch. She couldn't push him away, he was too strong for that, but the pressure let him know to stop.

Slowly his arm released its hold and he let her drop from her toes, her body moving down his, the hard ridge of his erection momentarily dragging through the soft folds between her legs and sending little fiery arcs of sensation through her clitoris. She caught her breath, bit back a helpless moan even as her hand pushed more insistently against him. Oh my God, she wanted to surge against him and whisper, "Do that again," because she felt so close that if he did it again, she would come.

One kiss. One kiss, and everything else.

Then she was free, stepping back, and hallelujah, her trembling knees came through like champs and didn't fold.

He said nothing, his eyes narrowed, his gaze locked on her. His chest was rising and falling as if he'd been running, and she was savagely gratified that she wasn't the only one wrestling with the effects of that kiss. She refused to let herself look any lower than his face, she didn't want to see how far his boxer shorts were poking out or if they had failed to contain him. What if they had? Would she be able to resist curling her fingers around his penis, stroking it, bringing him to his knees the way he'd almost brought her?

"No," she said, her voice hoarse but firm. "We aren't doing this. Sex is not on the table, not part of the deal." She would keep saying that until she convinced herself as well as him.

He cocked his head a little. "Not part of the deal," he agreed, "but we'll be doing it. Count on it."

Panic raced through her because she was afraid he was right. And if he was, it would be because of *her* weakness. She couldn't let herself be weak, she had to remember that he was leaving and keep her guard up. She'd learned too many times not to depend on anyone else to forget those hard lessons now. She turned away, needing the sanctuary and privacy of her bedroom, where she could close the door and be alone. "Don't touch me again," she ground out. "Good night."

"Wait."

She didn't want to stop, she wanted to get to her bedroom, but her feet halted and she stood with her back to him, waited to hear what he said.

"Why did you call me?"

Call him? She couldn't think; her mind was a big blank mess. Why had she called him, what had started this fiasco? She turned back to face him, confusion written on her face, and she saw Tricks sitting patiently, waiting for the humans to stop acting silly.

Thoughts began forming, memory returning but moving as slowly as molasses. She said, "Tricks."

He glanced at the dog. "What about her?"

"She was driving me crazy. She knew you were up here, in a different place, and she wanted to come visit."

He scrubbed a hand over his rough jaw, the rasping sound arrowing through her. She thought of that beard scraping across her breasts, between her thighs. No, no, *no*! She wasn't going to go there . . . she already had.

He sighed and said, "That was it? That had you yelling as if the house was under attack?"

"No, that had me yelling as if I was exasperated and wanted to get to sleep but she wouldn't let me," she said shortly. "Not every yell means we're being attacked."

"In my world it does."

The truth of that silenced her. The scar on his chest was proof that he lived in a very different world from hers.

She acknowledged that with a nod, briefly closed her eyes. "Anyway . . . that was it. Just leave your door open, if you don't mind, and I'll leave mine open. She'll probably go back and forth between us until she decides to pick her place and settle down. She might get on the bed with you, so if you don't want her in there just say so and I'll keep her with me no matter how much she acts up."

"No, that's okay, I don't mind." He gave her a smile that was like a wolf flashing its fangs, with a total lack of humor. "But just for the record—she's not the one I'd choose."

Chapter 14

Bo lay in bed, curled protectively on her side like a shrimp, so tense every muscle in her body was aching. She'd been rash, she'd been stupid, and the whole incident was her fault. She *knew* to keep her distance from him, to not let him see in any way how attracted she was to him. The kiss wasn't even the worst part. Yes, she'd kissed him back, as hungrily as he'd been kissing her; while that had been a huge mistake, it was one she could handle. The worst part was getting angry at him because he'd had a target tattooed on his chest.

Even a fairly thickheaded man would figure out a woman would get so angry at a tattoo—one that was like daring someone to shoot him—only if she *cared*—and Morgan wasn't thickheaded. She was beginning to fully appreciate how intelligent and cunning he was to have muted his personality to the extent he had so she wouldn't be uncomfortable with him. She'd seen flashes of the unmuted Morgan before, but tonight more of the power of his personality had come through loud and clear.

She wanted to sleep, needed to sleep. But her senses were too on edge, her mind racing as she zigzagged between remembering everything that had happened, how it had felt when he'd touched her, how he'd tasted—and then all the reasons why she should never let it happen again. Tricks, of course, went back and forth between the two bedrooms, jumping up on the bed to nuzzle Bo, then after a few minutes jumping down and trotting to the other bedroom to presumably treat Morgan to the same "I'm happy so no one is going to sleep" routine. Occasionally she'd hear the deep murmur of his voice as he tried to get Tricks to settle down in one room or the other, but good luck with that. Or maybe he was telling Tricks "Good girl" because she'd almost gotten him laid, Bo thought resentfully.

Finally, on about the fifth or sixth return, Tricks licked Bo on the arm and then curled up on her bed on the floor. "Please just go to sleep," Bo muttered, though why it mattered she couldn't say. She wouldn't have been able to sleep even if Tricks hadn't been partying.

For whatever reason, having Tricks back in her room and no longer trotting back and forth allowed Bo to relax. She couldn't change what had happened; she simply had to make certain it didn't happen again. Once she got that thought firmly fixed in her mind, she dozed off.

Tricks woke her up at the normal time by laying her muzzle on the pillow and staring at her. The message was plain: it's morning, and you haven't fed me yet.

She gave Tricks a hug, then lay there for a moment longer. The morning brought a return of mortification. She didn't want to get up and face the day, she didn't want to face *him*. She wanted the whole situation to just go away, which was such a juvenile thought that she mentally slapped herself, got out of bed, and got on with her normal routine.

She hadn't heard him walk by her open door, but he was downstairs, and just coming in from outside as she went down the stairs. He was dressed in one of his regular tee shirts, this one dark green, and khaki cargo pants. He had a cup of coffee in his hand, which meant she'd been so sound asleep that she hadn't heard the coffeemaker. Evidently Tricks had also been tired enough after her back-and-forth exertions of the night before that she hadn't alerted Bo to Morgan's activity.

Morgan, however, looked rested and alert and completely comfortable. It wasn't fair.

"Good morning," he said, going to the coffeemaker
and punching the *brew* button. It began hissing and
spewing, and coffee was streaming into a cup for her
by the time she reached it.

He leaned against the cabinet in what she had come
to realize was his habitual position—he was a lounger—
and said, "I'm sorry about last night."

Thank goodness she wasn't holding the cup of coffee
yet, or she might have dropped it. Of all the things she'd
imagined him saying, that wasn't on the list, not even
at the bottom. She sighed in relief and said, "Thank
you."

"I didn't intend to put you in an uncomfortable position. I'm a guest in your home, and I want you to feel
safe with me here. No matter what a great little ass you
have, whether or not anything happens between us is
your call, not mine."

If three sentences could have been better constructed
to shatter her thought processes, she didn't know how.
A reassurance, a—*he thought she had a great little
ass?*—and then another reassurance. All she could
think was: he liked her ass.

She reached for the coffee, halted, glared at him.
"Don't notice my ass."

"Too late. I'm a man; of course I noticed your ass."

She backed said ass against the cabinets to protect it from being stared at and finally got the cup in her hand. "So much for reassuring me and making me feel comfortable."

"Well, hell, I figure you have to know you have a great ass, unless you've spent your life in a convent."

Truthfully, she'd never considered her ass. She mulled over what he'd said as she swallowed some coffee and finally realized—"You're flirting with me."

A tiny smile quirked the corners of his mouth. "Guilty as charged. I figure you could use a little flirting. Want me to take Tricks out?"

Jerked back to Earth by the question, she looked at Tricks, who was standing by the door staring at both of them as if they'd lost their minds because no one had yet taken her outside.

"Crap," she muttered. "No, I'll take her." She needed away from him for a few minutes, and Tricks wasn't the only one who liked routine. Routine would ground her, give her a break from feeling jerked first one way and then another.

She stepped out into the cool, bright morning and stood sipping her coffee as she watched Tricks. Okay, now what? The subject was officially out in the open, and disarmed, so to speak. He said it was her call, and then he flirted with her.

She felt like a teenager, though that wasn't quite accurate because even as a teenager she'd been wary. But she'd still been excited by the possibilities opened up by flirting; if she hadn't been, she would never have gotten married. Since that bad decision, though, she'd deflected any male attention with a bland indifference, and she'd been so good at it that she couldn't remember exactly when she'd last been on a date. Perhaps she hadn't had a real date since her divorce, and that was *years* ago. She hadn't missed it, hadn't worried about it. She liked how her life was. She liked her privacy, the calm, the sense of control.

So why was her heartbeat getting all fluttery at the idea of Morgan flirting with her? Because she was attracted to him, that was why. Her brain knew he was temporary, but her body and hormones didn't.

The way she saw it, she had two options: she could keep him at a distance, or she could have a fling with him and wave good-bye when he left. Keeping him at a distance would be less wear and tear on her emotions, while having a fling would make her physically very satisfied.

Hands down, she'd opt for protecting her emotions, every damn time.

Tricks finally did her business and got tired of sniffing around, and was ready for her breakfast. When Bo opened the door to let her back inside, the smell of bacon frying hit her in the face and almost made her drool. Really, were there any smells on earth better than bacon and coffee? Well, maybe the new car smell, but that was debatable. She stopped dead, staring at the scene in the kitchen. Morgan had a towel slung over his shoulder while he stood at the cooktop using a fork to flip the strips of bacon sizzling in a skillet. He glanced over his shoulder at her. "I was hungry, so I thought I'd get started. I can do bacon and eggs and throw some bread in the toaster. That okay with you?"

"Wow, you're really trying to get on my good side, aren't you? Yes, thank you, bacon and eggs sounds great."

He pointed the fork at her. "You could have been gracious enough to leave off that first sentence." Then he flashed a grin at her. "Even though it's true."

That grin was a shock, transforming his face with roguish charm. Morgan being charming was also a shock, though she'd seen a bit of it when he'd kissed Miss Doris's hand. In his real life, he probably had to swat the women away. Again, she felt as if he was letting her see more of the real Morgan—or maybe the real Morgan was feeling well enough to make the effort.

Nevertheless, she appreciated both the effort and the food. Cooking wasn't something she enjoyed, though she did enjoy the end result. It was nice to have a hot breakfast that she hadn't cooked, nice to work together in comfortable silence. She fed Tricks, then set the table and got everything ready while he dealt with the food. Within ten minutes, they were sitting down at the table.

Last night, she wouldn't have thought she would ever feel comfortable with him again, yet here she was, sitting beside him and making small talk as he asked what was on her agenda for the day, when the kids would be taking Tricks for another practice ride before the Heritage Parade, how the Emily/Kyle situation was shaping up.

She was wary and on guard, but that morning set the pattern for the days that followed. April slid into May, and the days began warming in earnest, with the cool mornings and evenings becoming only fond memories. Bo stayed as busy as possible when she was at home, working like a fiend on the tech-writing projects and stopping only to take Tricks for walks or to prepare meals. The best thing she could do for herself was keep her interactions with Morgan to a minimum, which wasn't easy considering they were living in the same house—and, despite everything, they were becoming friends.

How could they not? If friendship had been impossible, if he'd been a jerk, she couldn't have tolerated having him around all the time even though she was being paid to house him. But he wasn't a jerk. They talked about various things; he'd been to a lot of places and seen a lot of things. He had a different take on almost any item that was on the news, and conversations with him were simply interesting.

When she was in town, all the goings-on kept her distracted. The Emily/Kyle situation was on track to being resolved. Mr. Gooding had agreed in principle to the town's conditions, though Kyle was reportedly pissed off about the whole thing and his sister Melody was going out of her way to say nasty things about Emily. Emily kept her head and ignored Melody, and her lawyer was getting the papers ready to be filed.

There were also the parade practices with Tricks, who still refused to ride without Bo also being present. She resigned herself to being in the parade. The kids promised they'd figure out a way so she could sit mostly hidden, and she had to take them at their word. Any more practices were impossible because now the kids were tied up with decorating their float and they had no spare time.

Sometimes Morgan went with her to work when he got too bored staying at the house. She could only imagine how that must be wearing on him; he was accustomed to living a high-adrenaline life, jumping out of planes and getting into firefights. He seemed to enjoy the small-town quirks, such as the parade and the divorce drama. Whenever he was at the police station with her, visitors would appear, usually bearing food as the whole town seemed to be on a mission to fatten him up. For whatever reason, he was getting acquainted with a surprising number of the townspeople, somehow becoming part of the warp and woof of local life.

One afternoon when she collected the mail there was a letter addressed to Morgan Rees, plain white envelope, no return address.

The letter had to be from Axel because no one else knew he was here, or the name he was using. When she thought about it, snail mail was the safest way to contact Morgan—no data to trace.

He lifted his eyebrows when she handed it to him. "He wasted a stamp to tell me there's no progress? He must be afraid I'll jump ship if I don't hear something."

"Maybe there's progress, but nothing definitive yet."

He tore open the envelope and scanned the single sheet of paper, then wadded it up and did a three-point shot to the wastebasket. "No progress."

She didn't know if she was disappointed or not. She wanted him gone, but she also knew she'd miss him when he left. "*Would* you jump ship?"

"Only if I had a good reason."

She didn't ask what would be a good reason, but evidently boredom wasn't on the list.

He started going on her walks with Tricks. He always took his Glock, because warm weather = snakes. She had done the same but saw no reason to take her pistol if he was armed, so instead she took only her long, sturdy stick. She might not be able to shoot a snake, but she assumed he could.

At first he couldn't make the whole trek with her, because the hill was too much for him; instead he'd wait at the bottom for her and Tricks to return. Tricks always bounded to him in a paroxysm of delight, as if she hadn't seen him in days instead of less than half an hour. By the fourth walk, he was going partway up the hill. By the seventh, he was keeping pace with her. His rate of recovery astounded her, but of course he'd been in phenomenal shape to begin with, so he didn't have as far to go as the average person would have.

Unfortunately, working like a fiend on the tech-writing projects meant that there were inevitably lapses when she didn't have any to work on because she'd already finished them. She couldn't manufacture projects out of thin air. Very occasionally she'd been able to pick up a last-minute job when something happened that prevented the tech writer already lined up from doing the work, but for the most part the work was something scheduled ahead of time.

Her options then were to sit in her room or watch television with Morgan. She watched television.

She'd always been an on-off watcher; sometimes there would be a program that she liked and watched, but for the most part it was something she'd have on while she read, or worked on a tech project. With the schedule Morgan had had while he was operational, he hadn't had the opportunity to watch much beyond sports and news—or the interest, truth be told. He liked hockey better than basketball, football better than baseball, but shortly after coming to stay with her he developed a passion for women's fast-pitch softball. Thanks to her satellite system, he got to watch a lot of women's softball; because she didn't have a preference for anything else, she found herself also watching softball.

With his move upstairs to the guest room, the sofa had ceased being a bed and returned to seating. Morgan sat on one end, she sat on the other, and Tricks on her special blanket snoozed contentedly between them. She always rested her muzzle on Bo's thigh and turned her butt to Morgan, but he was okay with that; he knew where he was in Tricks's hierarchy of affection.

On the day she got home and found he'd cut the grass for her, she could have hugged him. She didn't because she was smarter than that, but the impulse was there.

Damn it all, she wasn't just attracted to him; she *liked* him.

Now that he was stronger, Morgan made it his mission to walk the hills around Bo's place, getting the topography set in his mind. He wanted to know all the possible routes anyone could take to approach the house; the surrounding hills and mountains were rough going, which was reassuring. There were bluffs, impenetrable underbrush, streams and rivers. From a strategic point of view, he liked that.

He knew it was unlikely anything would actually happen here, but his training said to prepare for the unexpected. He was the bait in the trap, but the rat was never intended to actually get the cheese. The act of looking for his location would trigger the trap.

Still . . . shit happened.

If it were just him, he wouldn't mind, but he had Bo to consider.

The simplest approach usually had the highest degree of success. The more complicated a plan became, the more details could go wrong. In this case, the simplest approach would be to come up the driveway. The very length of the drive itself was part of what made it the most likely; anyone could get far enough from the road to be out of sight from both road and house.

He couldn't turn the house into a bunker; it simply wasn't feasible to bury the entire house, or reinforce walls and windows and doors. Nor was it feasible to dig an underground escape tunnel, not when weighed against the likelihood of anything actually happening, how long it would take, how much it would cost.

There were real-world, more reasonable approaches he could take.

He didn't talk it over with Bo because he knew she'd kick up a fuss—either that or come to the not unreasonable conclusion that he hadn't told her everything she should know about the level of danger. He and Axel had definitely downplayed that part of the situation, but neither of them had exactly lied.

Logically, the townsfolk would be fine. Only an idiot would try to take him out in town, where there would inevitably be a bunch of witnesses and someone to interfere. No, if trouble came, it would come here, to Bo's house.

There were commonsense measures to take that wouldn't involve turning the house into a bunker. He called a security company and made an appointment for a salesman to come out, listen to what he wanted, and give him a price. Because he wasn't stupid, he waited until the day of the appointment to tell Bo.

She was working at her computer, but at his words she swiveled her chair around to face him. "You did what?" she demanded, annoyance in both expression and tone. "Don't you think you should have talked this over with me first?"

"No," he said baldy. "I knew you'd balk, just like you're doing now."

"I already have a security system."

"You have an alarm on the doors and windows. You need more."

Some of the things he liked best about her were that she was logical and reasonable and organized. Unfortunately, that meant she immediately came to the logical and reasonable conclusion he hadn't wanted her to reach. "What aren't you telling me?" she asked, her dark eyes narrowed. "If you can't be traced here, why do I need beefed-up security?"

"Because things can always go wrong. What I'm thinking of is stuff you should have anyway, such as security cameras. You live out here by yourself; you need to be able to see what's in the yard before you take Tricks out at night. You need motion-sensor lights. I'm paying for this, and I'm putting it in. If you don't like it, after I'm gone you can have it taken out."

She glared at him and finally muttered, "Don't be so damn reasonable. Give me something I can argue against."

He knew better.

She had to leave for town before the salesman got there, which frustrated her to no end. She was still scowling as she drove down the driveway. At least Tricks was smiling at him from her normal seat in the front of the Jeep.

The security salesman was the usual sales type: friendly, gregarious, with a knack for overselling. It was his bad luck that Morgan was immune to overselling.

He took the guy on a walk around the property, telling him exactly what he wanted, and where: cameras that covered all of the house exterior, no blind spots, with monitors in the most-used rooms of the house; motion sensor lights; driveway alarm. The driveway alarm was problematic; the best was a buried sensor probe, and that worked on a line of sight, which meant that putting it at the beginning of Bo's driveway, close to the road, simply wouldn't work. There were too many hills, trees, and curves in the way. If he had unlimited time and money, and government resources to work with, he could get something that worked, but he didn't have those three things, so he had to settle and have the probe located at the farthest line of sight, which unfortunately was about seventy-five yards. It would have to do. If anyone approached at night— again, the most likely scenario—they could well turn off their headlights and drive close enough to set off the alarm.

He ignored the salesman's efforts to sell him a maintenance and service contract. He wanted the system, not their monitoring—and he wanted it installed as soon as possible.

Installation was an all-day project, which meant Bo was there for the first part of it. The cameras were installed first, and she was impressed by the clarity of the images on the monitors; he let her choose the location of said monitors because it was, after all, her house, and he wanted her involved so she'd stop glaring at him.

Then she had to go to work, which pissed her off all over again.

He was grinning as he waved to her on her way down the driveway.

"You think you're so smart," she muttered when she got home, still disgruntled. The fact that he was cooking supper—nothing fancy, just grilled steaks and baked potatoes, with a stab at a salad for her—evidently held no sway with her.

"Want me to drive down far enough to set off the alarm, so you can see how it works?"

"Yes." There was no hesitation at all.

So he drove down far enough to set off the alarm, then reversed back to his usual parking spot. When he got out of the Tahoe, he could hear Tricks barking her head off.

He went back inside. "Impressed?"

"It's loud, I'll give you that. Tricks went nuts."

"She'll be a good backup alarm, then, in case we both happen to sleep through it—not likely, but I guess it could happen." No way would either of them sleep through the ruckus Tricks was raising, running around the house looking for the very loud intruder.

Morgan wasn't completely happy, but he definitely felt better prepared in case the shit hit the fan.

Three days before the Heritage Parade, Bo said, "The divorce goes before Judge Harper today. Fingers crossed there's no problem."

Morgan thought seriously about going to town with her, just for the entertainment value, but he had something he wanted to do, so he said, "Want to leave Tricks here with me, in case you get tied up dealing with the Goodings?"

She looked at the golden with regret. He knew she liked having Tricks with her, and God knew the dog was always happier with Bo, but there were practical matters to consider such as Tricks's need for regular outside trips. He was a handy dog-sitter, and Tricks would be more comfortable.

"Okay, thanks. I'll call if I'm going to be late."

She left, and Tricks did the staring-out-the-window-and-looking-forlorn routine. Leaving her to it, Morgan opened the door to the storage area beneath the stairs and spotted the treadmill Bo had mentioned to him. It was folded up, had wheels for ease of moving it, and wasn't blocked by too much other junk. He moved some boxes around and rolled the machine out. The activity pulled on the scar tissue in his chest but—not much. As soon as he built up his stamina some more, he'd start with the weights.

The treadmill was a decent one, electric, had an incline; he could get a good workout on it. Going up and down the hill with Bo and Tricks on their walks was good, but he wanted more.

Intrigued, Tricks came over to inspect the machine, giving it a good sniffing, then she got her ball, went to the door, and stood there looking from

Morgan to the door and back again. He didn't obey her hint fast enough, so she went to him and swatted his knee with her paw, which was her signal that she really really needed to pee and he'd better hurry.

"You're a pushy little shit, you know?" he said conversationally. She didn't care as long as she got what she wanted. She bounced out when he opened the door, dropped her ball, and took off running.

He was anxious to get to the treadmill, but he was well aware that Tricks had to have her fun time before she'd consent to pee, so he threw the ball. Then he threw it again. And again. On the fourth time, he said sternly, "Young lady, you're going to be in a lot of trouble if you don't take a piss this time." He didn't know what trouble she'd be in, but it sounded good. He threw the ball, and Tricks went after it. He could have sworn that she kept a weather eye on him as she retrieved it. She trotted back, still watching him, then paused and bumped her butt on the ground. If she'd held the pose a little longer he might have bought it, but all she did was a quick bump, then she was up again, trotting to him with her tail jauntily waving, certain she had fooled him.

A laugh exploded out of him. All he could do was pet her and praise her, laughing the whole time, because, holy hell, she'd just *pretended* to pee. And she was so gleeful that she'd fooled him, as if she'd played the best joke ever.

Evidently she'd been lying about needing to pee too; all she'd wanted was to play.

He gave up, surrendered, mentally waved the white flag. He was seriously in love with this dog.

He took her back inside and finished setting up the treadmill, then went upstairs to put on his running shoes. Maybe he was being too optimistic to think he'd actually be running much, but he sure as hell was going to find out.

Going back downstairs, he stood on the side rails of the treadmill and attached the safety clip to his shirt. He set the workout he wanted; nothing fancy this time, just a steady fast walk on a few degrees incline, to see where he stood now so he'd know what he needed to do. Tricks came to lie down beside the treadmill, resting her muzzle on her paws.

He turned on the treadmill and stepped onto the moving belt, found the pace.

As soon as the belt started moving, Tricks lifted her head, her ears perked up and her eyes bright with interest. Then she got up and trotted away; evidently she was already bored.

Morgan monitored himself: Legs, good. Breathing, good. Heart rate, good. Of course, he'd barely gotten started, but overall . . . not bad.

Tricks reappeared, tennis ball in her mouth. Damn it, *now* she wanted to go outside. He said, "Sorry, princess—"

She all but danced to the front of the treadmill, and let the ball go.

It shot between his feet and across the room, and she darted after it.

Morgan swore at the top of his lungs as he tried to avoid the ball and keep his balance on the moving belt. For a split second he felt like one of those cartoon characters slipping on a banana peel, with feet and arms going in four different directions. He grabbed the bars and caught himself just before his head made contact with the control panel, but his feet kept going. He gathered himself, braced his weight on the bars, and did an in-air half-jack. His feet landed on the side rails.

Having retrieved her ball, Tricks trotted back to the front of the treadmill while he still stood there spread-eagled over the moving belt, and let it go again.

"Shit! Fuck!" he growled in exasperation and shut the machine off.

When the belt slowed to a stop, he got off the machine and glared at the dog who was back at the front, gently waving her tail as she gave him a quizzical look. It made no sense to her that he'd stopped her new game almost as soon as it started.

Morgan sat down on the floor, and she immediately came to him to be petted. The bad news was that he obviously wouldn't be able to get on the treadmill if Tricks was anywhere in the house.

The good news was that at least he hadn't killed himself.

Chapter 15

The call came in late in the afternoon, right before time to go home. Listening to it over the radio, and to Loretta's responses, Bo muttered, "Shit," and dropped her head into her hands. They'd been so close to making it through the day without any drama.

It was Jesse's day off; Officer Patrick Jones was in the station. He said, "I'm on it, Chief," and was out the door. That was the fastest she'd seen him move in the entire time she'd known him.

Loretta said wistfully, "Man, I'd like to see this."

Bo wasn't of the same opinion. She'd been *this close* to going home. She could feel a headache coming on, precipitated by the drama and long hours she knew were coming at her. "I was hoping everything would go smoothly and the whole town could move on."

"Yeah, but you're not a Hobson. We live for shit like this." Loretta paused. "Want me to call Jesse in? Not that Patrick can't handle it, but Jesse has a way of settling people down." That was because Jesse had perfected the cop's "don't mess with me" stare.

"He'll be on a date with Kalie," Bo replied, but they both knew Jesse would be monitoring his radio anyway, and he was probably already on his way with Kalie beside him. No one would want to be left behind in tomorrow morning's gossip, not even Jesse.

For herself, she'd like to pack it in and go home, but that option was off the table now.

She got her cell phone and called home. Morgan picked up on the third ring.

"Anything wrong?" he said by way of greeting, getting straight to the heart of the matter.

"The divorce proceedings didn't go well. I'll probably be several hours late. Go ahead and eat whatever you feel like eating, and feed Tricks. I'll grab something here when I have time. How's Tricks?"

"She's fine. She nearly killed me, but she's fine."

"Okay, good," she said absently, and hung up. After a few seconds she realized what she'd said and started to call him back but gave herself a little shake and forgot about it. With Tricks, it could be anything. She'd find out later.

Within twenty minutes, the police station was a mob scene. She'd expected to see Emily and Kyle brought in, or at least Kyle, but that wasn't the case. Patrick arrived first, with Melody Gooding handcuffed in the backseat of his cruiser. She was yelling and cussing at Patrick, kicking the seat, and generally raising hell. Then Jesse rolled up, as predicted, and of all people he had Miss Doris in *his* cruiser—handcuffed in the back, while Kalie Vaughan sat in the front passenger seat wide-eyed and shocked.

Miss Doris was spitting fire, yelling at Melody as soon as the officers had gotten the two women out of the cruisers. "I'll kick your sorry ass all over this town!" Miss Doris bellowed. Her normally sweet round face was fiery red and not looking sweet at all, while her mild blue eyes were sparking fire.

Oh, holy shit.

Other people began showing up, crowding into the small police station: Emily and her mother; Mayor Buddy; a few members of the town council; the two lawyers who had been representing the divorcing parties; a couple of the volunteer firemen and a paramedic; Miss Virginia Rose, who must have been in the courtroom sightseeing; Sam Higgins, the school-bus driver; then Mr. Gooding and Kyle came in, with Kyle looking furious and sullen.

Kyle gave Bo a menacing look but then remembered where he was and quickly looked away. No, she thought, he did not want to start mouthing off in here and demanding she release his sister. He'd barely escaped being charged the last time, and that had led to his being forced to sign the divorce papers as Emily wanted them.

Last but not least, Daina arrived with her for-now boyfriend, Kenny Michaels. What on earth were they doing here?

The noise of all the raised voices was deafening, with everyone shouting and no one able to hear what anyone was saying. At least half these people had no business being here, Bo thought, though the paramedic might come in handy.

Daina slipped over to her and said, "I thought I'd come get Tricks, get her out of the way so you don't have that worry."

"Oh—thanks," Bo said in relief. "But I kind of had a feeling this might happen, so I left her at home with Morgan."

"You're good, then?"

"I wouldn't go that far."

Daina smothered a laugh. "We'll get out of the way. Call me when it's over. I want the scoop." Then she and Kenny left, with Kenny giving a small wave as they went out the door.

340 • LINDA HOWARD

There were still far too many people.

Bo climbed up on her desk, clapped her hands, and yelled, "*Hey!*" She didn't like confrontation, but, damn it, she was the chief, and this situation couldn't be sorted out with this many people in the way.

Silence fell, even between Melody and Miss Doris, who had continued cussing at each other the whole time. Bo was kind of stunned Miss Doris knew those words. Everyone in the crowded station turned to look at her.

"I want everybody out," she said. "Even you, Mayor Buddy. Everybody except my two officers, Miss Doris, Melody, Loretta, and me. If you aren't one of the six people named—*out.*"

"Now see here—" Mr. Gooding began hotly.

"No, I won't see here. We can't get this mess straightened out with everyone in here yelling at each other. Emily, Kyle, take your lawyers with you. If they're needed after we talk to Miss Doris and Melody, they can come back. Out. I mean it. Anyone who is still here in sixty seconds will be arrested."

Mayor Buddy beamed at her in pride and said, "I guess I know better than to go against you when you're riled," as he headed out the door. He paused just long enough to give her a wink. He was followed posthaste by Sam Higgins, the firemen, and the medic. It took an additional glare from her and threatening looks from both Jesse and Patrick to get everyone else out. Miss Virginia Rose wore a stubborn expression, as if she wanted to be a holdout, until Loretta stood up and cleared her throat. "All right, all right," Miss Virginia grumped as she went out the door.

As soon as the door closed and silence fell, Loretta humphed. "For a minute, I thought she would deliberately get herself arrested so she could see what all goes on."

Bo jumped down from her desk and shook her head as she stared at the two miscreants. "I can't believe this," she muttered.

"It's this old bitch's fault," Melody said, sneering at Miss Doris.

Miss Doris erupted again, her soft round body bristling with outrage. "I'd slap that stupid look off your face if it didn't go so deep bleach and sandpaper wouldn't take it off!"

Jesse turned his head into his shoulder and managed to turn a laugh into a cough.

"Okay, let's get their statements. Jesse, Patrick, take them into separate rooms so they can't hear each other, and, ladies"—when she paused, both Miss Doris and Melody looked at her—"remember, there are a lot of witnesses to what happened, and we'll be talking to them all. What you tell us should be pretty damn close to what *they* tell us, because you don't want to add making false statements to the list of possible charges." If everything went the way she hoped, they wouldn't need to talk to anyone else, but these two didn't have to know that.

Miss Doris looked horrified at the idea that she might be charged with a crime, while Melody just looked contemptuous. Given that her father had been bailing her out of scrapes all her life, she likely didn't expect this time to be any different. Nevertheless, both she and Miss Doris were obligingly silent as Jesse and Patrick took them to the tiny but separate interview rooms, which were side by side and had only drywall dividing them, which necessitated each officer turning on the noisy box fans in each room that had been bought to prevent eavesdropping. The solution was low tech, but it worked.

The statements didn't take long. Patrick came out first, leaving Melody in the interview room. Bo and Loretta both looked expectantly at him, and he cleared his throat. "The gist of it is, the court proceedings were over, had gone off without a hitch though Kyle didn't look too happy about any of it. On the way out, Emily and her mother and Miss Doris passed by a bunch of the Goodings, and Melody said, quote, 'I'll be glad when this is over and my brother can get a real wife instead of a whore' unquote."

As badmouthing went, that was typical of what was said in a lot of divorces, and not even original. Bo could think of a couple of her mother's divorces that made Melody's trash talk sound like the stuff of Sunday school classes.

"Emily and her mother didn't pay any attention," Patrick continued, "but Miss Doris blew a gasket. She got right up in Melody's face and started yelling, 'You keep your filthy mouth shut about my granddaughter or I'll stuff my fist down your throat,' again, quote and unquote."

"Ouch." Bo winced. Miss Doris was definitely guilty of assault—a misdemeanor, but still.

"Melody admitted to then saying, 'I'll wipe the floor with you, old lady. You won't be so full of yourself when your house burns down.' Which evens out the assault charges if we're keeping score."

Loretta grunted. "Huh." She looked displeased that someone besides a Hobson was using house-burning as a threat.

Bo felt somewhat relieved. Things were looking up. With both of the women having committed the same misdemeanor, that gave her a place to start negotiating. If only one party was guilty, the other would undoubtedly press charges, which would keep this mess going likely for the rest of their natural lives—and beyond, because West Virginia didn't breed people who easily forgot slights.

The trick was getting them both to not press charges because right now they were still fighting mad. There would be lingering resentment, of course, but at least there wouldn't be rap sheets.

Jesse came out, and they all compared the two statements. At least Melody and Miss Doris had been truthful; they were almost word for word what each woman had said to the other.

"What do we do now?" Jesse asked, taking a peek out the front to where Kalie still waited patiently in his patrol car. At least she'd had the sense not to come inside and add to the crowd. Bo thought about reminding Jesse that he wasn't supposed to have unauthorized ride-alongs in his patrol car, but they had more important fish to fry. Besides, she wouldn't be telling Jesse something he didn't already know, and she wasn't going to carp about rule-bending when he'd bent a big one regarding Morgan.

Maybe she wasn't any good at being a police chief because she seemed to have problems sticking to the rules. Well, that was a thought for another time because right now she had to deal with this.

"Why don't you take Kalie home, and we'll let those two sit and think for a while," she suggested. "Half an hour, an hour—they need the time to cool down."

There was a general nodding of heads; cooling down could only be good. Jesse took Kalie home; Patrick took his supper break. Loretta decided there wouldn't be any more excitement and went home to cook supper for Charlie and bring him up to date. Bo sat at her desk and began catching up on the day's paperwork. There wasn't a peep from either of the two interview rooms.

The phone rang once. She prayed it wasn't a call that the remaining family members on both sides were in a brawl. The caller was indeed a Gooding, but she lucked out on the purpose of the call. "I need to know what's going on," Mr. Gooding barked. "Do I need to send our lawyer in?"

"I'm trying to talk both of them into not pressing charges so everyone can walk away clean," Bo said calmly. "Just be patient."

"Oh." He sounded surprised by her position. He paused. "Thank you, Chief. If it'll help, tell Melody I said to go along with your suggestion."

"I will. Thanks for checking, Mr. Gooding." If he could be polite, so could she.

Then she waited some more. Finally she got up and went into the interview room where Melody sat, probably bored to death because there was no TV, no magazines, nothing to look at other than her manicure.

The pretty young woman had a sullen expression, but beneath it all she was also beginning to look tired. Burning that much adrenaline took a lot out of a person. Bo pulled out the only other chair in the room and sat down. She waited until Melody looked up at her before saying, "Here's the deal. Miss Doris won't press charges if you don't. You can both act pissy if you think it'll get you anywhere, but I can tell you up front that all it'll get you is a rap sheet. Your dad called a while ago and said to tell you to take the deal."

Melody opened her mouth, likely to say something smart, but then she closed it again and considered her options. "Okay," she finally said, no arguing, no threats.

Well, hallelujah. Relieved that it was so easy, Bo said, "Where's your car?"

"At city hall."

"You want to walk? I can have one of the officers drive you if you don't."

"I'll walk."

As Bo was showing Melody out, Jesse arrived back at the station from taking Kalie home. He stayed silent until Melody was gone. "Everything work out?"

"Halfway there. I still have Miss Doris in the other room, but Melody's agreed not to press charges."

He sat down. "I'll wait and take Miss Doris home. I know she didn't drive because Kalie said that Emily picked her up."

How on earth had Kalie known Emily was picking up her grandmother? Even though Bo had lived here seven years, small-town ways still sometimes baffled her. Everyone knew everyone else's business. Was the information passed on by some weird osmosis?

"Kalie and Emily are Facebook friends," Jesse explained with a grin, having noted her expression. "Emily posted about it."

Social media to the rescue; at least that made sense. She didn't do Facebook herself, figuring her life was no one else's business. It wasn't as if she had a ton of relatives who kept track of her or were interested in what she was doing.

Finally she went in to Miss Doris. She'd chosen Melody first because she'd judged Melody the most likely to press charges, in which case there would be no deal-making with Miss Doris. Again, she pulled up a chair and sat down. Miss Doris looked both guilty and angry, which meant she could tip either way.

Bo said essentially the same thing she'd said to Melody. "Melody has agreed not to press charges if you don't."

Miss Doris's mouth opened in astonishment, closed, then opened again. "She did?" she squeaked.

Bo shrugged. "She's guilty of the same thing. It makes sense for both of you to drop it and walk away."

"Well, my goodness." Miss Doris paused for maybe half a second. "All right. If she's dropping it, so will I."

"Good deal. Jesse said he'll take you home."

"That's sweet of him. I imagine it's dark by now."

"Yes, it is, but we wouldn't let you walk home anyway."

And that was that. Jesse and Miss Doris went out the back door to his cruiser just as Morgan and Tricks came in, meeting them on the way. They stood in the door for a minute or so, saying hello and exchanging small talk, then the first two were gone and the second two came on into the station. Tricks went immediately to Bo, smiling her doggy smile and putting her paw on Bo's knee.

"I missed you too," Bo crooned, doing some two-handed ear-rubbing as she bent down and rested her forehead on top of Tricks's head. She looked up at Morgan. "Why are you two here?"

"I figured you'd had time to get everything sorted out, short of there being actual blood involved, and thought you might be hungry. We can get a hamburger at the drive-through if you want."

A nice hot hamburger that she hadn't cooked herself sounded great. "Let's go," she said, getting to her feet. She locked the station doors and they all got into the big Tahoe. The hamburger joint was just a couple of blocks away, so there wasn't much time for her to tell him anything other than her food order, which was a small hamburger, small fries, and a bottle of water. Morgan's choice was the deluxe cheeseburger, which was twice the size of her hamburger, large fries, and also a bottle of water. They took their food booty back to the station and arranged it on her desk, then Morgan dragged the chair over to their makeshift table and sat down across from her.

"Your truck driver friend called," he said as he salted his fries and opened packets of ketchup to squeeze over them. "He went through Alabama and stopped to pick you up some Naked Pig; he figured you wanted some, so he didn't bother checking. He brought it over, and I paid him."

"Thanks."

"I also told him to double the next order. If I'm drinking it too, we'll need more."

She hid a smile. "You don't want to get some Miller, or Bud?"

"I'm a convert. Give me the Naked Pig." He paused and squinted at her. "That's a sentence I never thought I'd be saying."

They both chuckled, then he said, "Fill me in on the drama."

She did, glad that everything had been calmed down so easily and without anyone getting hurt. He had a laugh about Miss Doris's language; it was her turn to laugh when he described Tricks's escapade with the treadmill. She almost choked on a swallow of water because she could just see him trying to avoid killing himself while Tricks was blissfully unaware of anything other than chasing her ball.

As she swabbed a fry in a dollop of ketchup, she said, "How long did you make it on the treadmill?"

"Are you kidding? I'm still alive, aren't I? I stopped right then. There will be no treadmill while Tricks is anywhere around." He winked at her and popped a fry into his mouth. "We went outside and walked the hill a couple of times instead."

This must be her day to be winked at, Bo thought. First Mayor Buddy, now Morgan. Hearing her name, Tricks laid her head on Bo's knee and gave her a sad look, letting her know how awful it was that she wasn't getting to share their food. Bo said, "Forget about it, young lady," whereupon she promptly abandoned Bo and laid her head on Morgan's knee, subjecting him to the woebegone eyes.

"She's sharper than a switchblade," he commented before saying, "No," in the same firm tone Bo had used. He'd started doing that, she thought; the same words, the same intonation.

Bo started to reply, but a strange noise from outside caught her attention. It sounded like . . . She didn't know what it sounded like. A party? A ball game? She frowned, cocked her head to listen, but still couldn't nail down the sound. Then, through the window, she saw what looked like a . . . herd? flock? . . . of fireflies coming toward the station. Large fireflies. She said, "What on earth is that?"

Morgan had turned at the sound too. He looked out the window and very matter-of-factly said, "A mob."

A . . . mob? In Hamrickville?

Frowning, she got to her feet. He stood too and put his hand on her arm. All humor had fled his expression and he looked tough and capable. "If you think this is in the least dangerous, you stay here and I'll handle it."

He could, too. He was just one man, but he wasn't a man even a mob should take lightly. She said, "I don't think this mob will amount to much. I wonder what they want, what has them upset? Only one way to see, I guess."

She cast a regretful look at the half-eaten hamburger and remaining fries; they'd be cold and not nearly as appetizing by the time she got back to them. He said, "Okay, but I'm right here at the door if you need me."

She was tired and would rather be finishing up her hamburger, but facing this "mob" was her job. Opening the door, she stepped out on the sidewalk and squinted at the approaching crowd. The overhead street- lights cast weird shadows on their faces, and the light was so ghastly some of them looked like zombies, but there were only a few people she didn't recognize.

"Crowd" was perhaps stretching it a bit. She estimated there were maybe thirty people there, crossing the street toward her—and jaywalking at that, not that anyone in Hamrickville paid any attention to silly rules regarding where they crossed the street. The lights were mostly cell phones, a modern-day nod to flaming torches, though a couple of smokers carried cigarette lighters. A lot of the mob members ran shops here in town, which meant they were friends with Miss Doris. She saw Harold Patterson, the barber; Miss Virginia Rose, who seemed determined to be in the thick of whatever scene was going on; Faye Wiggins, the florist. Even the librarian was here.

Each and every one of them wore a big white tee shirt pulled on over their regular clothing. Miss Doris's sweet face had been printed on each shirt, with black jail bars stamped over her, and printed under her face in big letters was FREE DORIS.

Bo clamped her hand over her mouth and pinched hard so she wouldn't laugh at them. This was so sweet. Really. Her heart gave a little bump, then swelled with emotion.

When she could control herself, she pulled out her cell phone and snapped a photo. The flash, and the realization of what she'd done, stopped them in their tracks. She hadn't done it for evidence, but because she wanted to remember this moment forever. Then she leaned against the streetlight post and crossed her ankles.

"What's up?" she asked casually.

Harold Patterson began sputtering. "What's *up*? I'll tell you what's up! You're holding Miss Doris in jail while you let that Gooding girl free to strut down the street like she owned it. That's not right, it's just not right. We've come to get Miss Doris out of jail."

"We'll sign any bail papers you got," added Miss Virginia Rose. "Whatever it costs to get her out of jail."

Oh, man, they didn't know how a real mob was supposed to work, with violence instead of an offer to put up bail for Miss Doris. This was truly so sweet that Bo thought she could get a little teary-eyed if she didn't control herself. She said, "First of all, I can't decide bail for anyone, only a judge can do that."

"Where's Judge Harper?" someone from the back of the crowd shouted, and they began looking around as if they expected him to be marching with them, or maybe they were plotting a course to his house.

"There isn't any bail," she said, raising her voice.

Harold Patterson gasped. "You mean you're holding her *without bail?*"

"No, I mean there's no bail because there aren't any charges. Miss Doris didn't file charges against Melody, and Melody didn't file charges against Miss Doris."

"Then why is Miss Doris still in jail?"

"She isn't. She's at home."

The barber turned red in the face. He was so upset he seemed incapable of seeing reason. He began shouting, "No, she isn't! No one saw her leave the jail! You've still got her in there and—"

Miss Virginia Rose said crisply, "Don't be a child, Harold." She gave Bo a stern look. "Chief, be square with us. Is that truly what happened?"

It was all Bo could do to keep a big smile from breaking out. God, these people were great; she blessed the day she'd landed here. As seriously as possible she said, "It is indeed. Jesse took Miss Doris home about half an hour ago, maybe a little more. Emily had posted on Facebook that she was picking up Miss Doris for her court date, and Kalie is

Facebook friends with Emily, so Jesse knew Miss Doris wouldn't have her car."

That convoluted explanation evidently made perfect sense to everyone because smiles broke out. She heard several "Thank yous," and "Sorry to disturb you," and a "See, I told you everything would be all right." Then, mission accomplished, the firefly crowd moved back across the street and began dispersing to their own cars and residences.

Bo stood on the sidewalk for a minute or so, watching them, then went back inside the police station.

Tricks was sitting there with a big doggy smile on her face, as happy as ever. Morgan was crouched on the floor, his arms around Tricks. He was laughing, his shoulders shaking, as he fought to muffle the sound by burying his face against Tricks's plush fur. Her heart gave another of those little bumps, and the hairs on her arms lifted in alarm. She didn't want to feel anything for him other than concern over his situation; anything more personal was too dangerous.

Bo pushed emotion away and said, "You better not get snot on my dog."

He lifted his red face from Tricks's fur and managed to gasp, "Free Doris!" before succumbing again, collapsing on his ass on the floor and holding his stomach.

She liked his laugh, deep and rolling. "Wasn't that great?" she asked, beaming. "All of it. And I got a picture." Then she began laughing too because she couldn't hold it in any longer.

He rose lithely to his feet, snatched her into his arms, and whirled her around in a circle. She was astonished by the ease with which he lifted her, but she couldn't stop laughing as she clutched at his shoulders. "Put me down! What if someone comes in?"

He snorted. "What if they do? After what I just saw? There's no one in this town who would even blink an eye." He smiled down at her, blue eyes still glinting with laughter.

She looked up, so close she could see the emerging beard on his strong jaw, the striations, both light and dark, in his eyes that made the blue so brilliant. The muscles in his shoulders bunched under her palms as he set her down.

"You have a good heart, Chief," he said and kissed her forehead.

She could handle a forehead kiss, she thought; it was friendly without being sexual. Not that she wanted to be friends with him, but still—

Then he blew that out of the water by gripping her head with both hands, tilting her face up, and covering her mouth with his.

Chapter 16

I t was like before—the hot taste of him, the thrill of recognition, the instant hunger. But it was different, too, because neither of them was riding the knife edge of anger. There was a slowness to the way their mouths clung together, a laziness to the dip and stroke of his tongue. Did laughter give a different, lighter taste to his mouth? Did it to hers? He wasn't holding her head now; instead his hands were gripping her waist, the heat of his palms burning the softness of her skin as he brought her body close against him.

He nipped at her bottom lip, licked the tiny sting, moved his mouth down to her throat. Her head fell back, as if the touch of his mouth turned her neck to rubber, and holding it upright was too much effort. She didn't even try; she couldn't deny the thrill, the hot chase of lightning from his mouth to her nipples and down between her legs.

She'd been turned on before. She knew the allure of sex, the heat and pleasure of it. But even during her marriage she'd always felt somehow distant from the act, as if her mind couldn't quite engage with her body. This was different. This was scary. Not only was her mind right there, but she felt as if her body had the upper hand, as if touching him somehow made her mental gears shift into neutral. This was more than pleasure; she didn't want to have just the experience, she wanted to have *him*, to feel *him* on her, inside her. That wasn't sex, that was need, and need was a completely different animal. She didn't want to need anyone.

And yet . . . she did. *Him*, for reasons she couldn't pin down. Chemistry, maybe. Propinquity, probably. And he liked her dog.

His erection was a thick ridge against her stomach, inviting her to lift herself up, wind her legs around his waist, and let him do whatever he wanted.

Alarm clanged in her brain, but distantly. They were standing in the middle of the police station. He wasn't mostly naked, the way he had been before when he'd kissed her. They weren't being driven by raw emotion; she wasn't in danger of giving in to the subtle surge of need rising through her body—not here, anyway. She was aware of the alarm; that was all, just as she was aware of his thick hair beneath her palm. But—when she had moved her hand from his shoulder to the back of his head? His hair was cool on the surface, warm at his skull, so soft her fingers curled in it. She was aware of his chest rising and falling with every breath he took, she could feel the thumping of his heart.

His heart—the heart that had come so close to never beating again because he had a job and lived a life that put him in harm's way, because an assassin's bullet had damn near killed him.

The thought chilled her as nothing else could have, and with the chill came a return of common sense, of willpower. Bo pulled her mouth from his, tucked her head; her forehead was resting against his chest, her hand lying lightly over that heart that was still beating strongly, despite all odds, because he'd had the strength to overcome what should have been a fatal injury. She had to keep that reality front and center before she started doing stupid things such as hoping they could have something together. No, face the facts: she was already being stupid by kissing him; he'd been plain about what he wanted, and she'd just underscored her own weakness where he was concerned. He was too astute not to have realized what this episode revealed.

She felt the need to clarify her standing, despite what her present actions were saying, or maybe because of what they were saying. "Rules haven't changed. No sex." As soon as the words were out of her mouth, she winced in embarrassment. Mixed signals, much?

"How about a celebratory kiss?" His tone was low, his breath brushing her hair as he slowly rubbed his lips against the hollow just below her ear, then so lightly, delicately, licked it as if he were tasting her. All the nerve receptors in her skin lit up, and her nipples pinched tight, making her want to rub her entire body against him.

It would be silly to say no to what they'd already done. Just because she had no intention of getting involved with him . . . did that mean she couldn't allow herself the purely physical enjoyment of kissing him? *And that way lies a slippery slope,* she thought, because the same logic, or lack of it, could also be applied to sleeping with him.

Regretfully she made herself release him, step away. "We've just had it," she pointed out. He let her go without effort, and a tiny part of her mourned that, wanted him to persist. How perverse was that? But it was human; she wanted him to want her the way she wanted him.

But he was smiling down at her, a crooked smile that invited her to join in his amusement. "Is there a rule about how many celebratory kisses are allowed?"

"Yes. One."

"What idiot wrote that rule?"

"I did."

"Scratch the previous comment."

His prompt reply had her laughing. The man was a fast thinker. He'd have to be, though, or he'd have been killed long ago.

She sighed as she turned to the desk and gathered up the scraps of their now-cold meal. She wished he hadn't kissed her—but he had, and once again she'd been complicit. At least he'd done nothing more than kiss, though she suspected that was more because he was too damn wily than because his interest had cooled. He didn't strike her as a man who blew hot and cold, but rather as a man who went after what he wanted and was very good at planning his strategy.

That worried her. She didn't want to be the target of any strategy . . . or did she? She had no idea what she wanted. She knew what she *should* want, knew what was safest, but for the first time in a long, long while she wasn't certain she could stay the course she'd mapped out for herself.

He looked around the office. "Are you finished here?"

"I am. I'm getting out of Dodge—or in this case, Hamrickville—before anything else can happen." Maybe, with the court hearing over and both Melody and Miss Doris out of jail, they would have peace again.

She locked up and they went to their respective vehicles. Tricks loaded up into the Jeep, looking very happy to be in her special place with Bo. Bo pulled her thoughts away from what she shouldn't, couldn't, have and concentrated on the very good things that were in her life now. She reached over and rubbed Tricks's neck. "Did you play ball with Morgan's machine? Was it fun?" Man, she wished she had a video of that.

Tricks gave her a tongue-lolling-out-the-side-of-her-mouth grin.

From his vehicle, Morgan motioned for her to lead. Fifteen minutes later, after a stop at the mailbox to retrieve the day's offerings, they parked side by side in the dark driveway. The security lights came on, and he'd left the porch light on to dispel the shadows on the patio. She didn't like going into a dark house, never had, so the light was a welcome relief. She wouldn't tell him that, though; he'd gotten his way about the added security and that was enough.

As she got out of the Jeep and let Tricks out, the mild spring night folded around her, rich with the sweet scents of wild rhododendron and fresh grass. The crickets were chirping, some night birds offering an occasional liquid note. She paused a moment to savor the smell, then joined him on the porch.

They went in together, man, woman, dog. It was almost like a family, she thought wistfully before she caught the recurring theme. Morgan was *not* family. She and Tricks were family, they were the ones who'd still be there when he was somewhere on the other side of the world.

Tricks ran to her bowls and first checked to see if food had magically appeared in her food bowl, then transferred her attention to the water. Morgan dropped into "his" spot on the sofa, propped his boots on the wood and steel coffee table, and turned on the TV. Bo stood there for a minute, absorbing the new rhythms of her life that had become commonplace without her noticing.

"Stop watching me like that," he said without looking at her. "Or we'll have to go upstairs."

Damn it, she should have known he'd be able to pick up when he was being watched. She felt her face getting warm. There was no denying it though she wasn't happy that he'd noticed. Denying her interest would be silly; giving in to it would be downright dangerous. "No," she said. "We won't." Then she added, "You said it's my decision, remember?"

He gave her a sideways glance. "Never said I wouldn't try to change your mind."

Her mind shouted *No!* but excitement fizzled along her veins at the idea. She almost asked him exactly what methods he'd use before catching herself. Physical attraction was a bitch. She knew exactly what she should do, and too damn bad she had to battle chemistry and her own stupid hormones to keep her head straight.

Irritably she said, "Any relationship between us would be a waste of time."

"How is that?" He looped his arms behind his head, linked his fingers. He looked totally at ease, which was at once both annoying and sexy. She didn't want him to feel at ease when she didn't, but his self-confidence definitely called to her. "Wouldn't the relationship be the whole point?"

"Been there, done that, don't see the *point* of doing it again. I'm not—" She started to say "*interested*" but swallowed the word before she made an even bigger fool of herself. "I try to learn from my mistakes. The fact is, I'm better off alone than I am investing time and effort in a relationship that'll be over in a few months at the most, maybe even a few weeks—hell, maybe to-morrow, for all either of us knows."

His eyebrows lifted. "How do you know it would be over?"

"Because you won't be here," she explained with exaggerated patience. "You'll leave, and—"

"And the roads go in only one direction? I can't come back?"

She wanted to smack him out of sheer frustration. If she hadn't already betrayed her attraction to him, she'd have simply lied, but she'd stood there like a fool and kissed him back in a way no man would mistake, espe-cially a man like him who was trained to notice every detail. Now she was cornered, and she *hated* being cor-nered, hated not being in control. Damn it, why did he have to be so persistent and reasonable? He wanted sex; for a man, that was simple, but she wasn't a man.

"You're such a turd," she said sourly and stomped upstairs.

Her feelings weren't helped by the laughter that fol-lowed her.

Morgan smiled to himself as he clicked to a softball game. Normally Bo was as level-headed and contained as anyone he'd ever known; she got angry, but she didn't lose control. He was getting under her skin, and that was a good thing because it meant she wasn't able to distance herself. She *wanted* to—but, damn, their physical chemistry was so hot it kept blindsiding her, getting her flustered and annoyed.

He almost knew how she felt. He wasn't reluctant to get involved the way she was, but almost every day he'd get punched in the gut by the growing intensity of his fixation on her. This was new to him, scary new.

He'd wanted women before, but mostly he'd wanted sex. He hadn't been this focused on one particular woman since high school and his first major crush— and the situation was getting worse by the day. Instead of spending most of his time now thinking about re- gaining his strength, going over and over everything that had happened that last day in an effort to pin- point exactly what had almost gotten him killed, he was thinking about Bo: watching her, evaluating her smallest response, learning her patterns and move- ments and likes.

He wasn't a navel-gazer; when he wanted sex, he got sex. Couldn't get any simpler than that. And after sex, he turned his analytical thinking back to the job. But he felt as if he needed to concentrate on Bo, to get the best read possible on her so he didn't make any missteps. He didn't know why not screwing up with her was so important but it was, so he went about his campaign to get her with the same thorough attention he'd given to planning critical ops. His question about whether or not he could come back hadn't been rhetorical. No matter what happened with his job, he didn't want to lose touch with Bo.

Or her dog. Don't forget the dog.

As if reading his mind, Tricks trotted up to lay her muzzle on his knee and give him the full dark-eyed, furrowed-brows treatment. Then she woofed and looked at the stairs before looking back at him. He chuckled because the message was plain: *Aren't you going upstairs too?* If one of her humans went upstairs, she evidently thought the second one should follow.

He liked the way she thought. And he liked thinking of himself as one of her humans.

But Bo was giving herself time to cool off, and he didn't want to push her too much. She'd be back down in a few minutes. Next time . . . maybe next time he'd get his hands on those little boobs and find out if they were soft or firm. He was betting on firm, and his mouth watered at the thought. Shit, he had it bad. Or good. He hadn't decided which yet, but it was exciting as hell. He said softly, "Not yet, girl," as he stroked Tricks's head.

Chapter 17

The weather had been cloudy for the few days before the Heritage Parade, but parade day dawned clear and warm—unfortunately. Bo had kind of been hoping for rain, which was bad of her on the kids' account. She resigned herself to sitting on a flatbed trailer in the sun, but at least everyone else would be having fun.

She put Tricks in the shower with her, which Tricks actually loved because cavorting in the "rain" was one of her favorite things. There wasn't room for much cavorting, but Tricks didn't care. She whirled, she danced, she tried to catch the water drops in her mouth. Bo tried to stay on her feet with the dog bouncing around like a delirious dervish, and get Tricks clean and thoroughly rinsed. Then she used three beach towels to get the excess water out of the plush golden fur; after that, Tricks stood patiently while Bo finished drying her with a blow dryer, as if she knew she needed to be extra pretty for the day.

Bo huffed out a tired breath when she was finished. She needed to shower, too, and even though she hoped she wouldn't be on display, she wasn't betting the farm on it, no matter how much the kids reassured her. That meant makeup and something dressier than her usual work garb: not a dress, because she'd be climbing on and off the flatbed, but nice pants and shoes, and a pretty blouse. Part of her looked forward to dressing up a little, but being in a parade had never been on her bucket list. Tricks and the kids, though, would have a ball; if Tricks had a bucket list, being queen of a parade would definitely be on it.

She let Tricks out of the bedroom so the dog could visit with Morgan while she herself returned to the shower to begin getting herself ready. She dried her long dark hair into a sleek fall that reached the middle of her back. She put on earrings and makeup. As she dusted blush on her cheeks, she wondered if Morgan would notice—then she mentally kicked herself for wondering. Whether he noticed or not shouldn't matter to her. She couldn't let it matter. Damn it . . . it mattered. She wanted him to find her attractive. She wanted to be pretty for him.

She was as bad as Tricks. But while Tricks was supremely confident that she was the prettiest dog in the world, Bo had no such illusion. She wouldn't break any mirrors, but neither was she a beauty queen. She liked that she had nice thick hair and big eyes, but her figure was nonexistent. If she let herself be self-conscious about anything it would be her lack of boobs; the only cleavage she'd ever have was butt cleavage, and—and Morgan had said she had a sweet little ass.

A wave of heat engulfed her, and her legs were suddenly so weak she had to lean against the bathroom sink. Remembering what he'd said, and the laser focus of his eyes when he said it, leached the strength from her muscles so that all she wanted to do was lie down—preferably with him.

She pressed her palms over her eyes. She was in so much trouble. The only hope she had of coming out of this devil's arrangement unscathed was for Axel to call *today,* so Morgan could leave immediately. The temptation to simply forget about her well-founded reservations was growing every day. And even if he left today, would she be unscathed? Would she be able to promptly forget about him? The answer was no. She might never completely forget him; he might linger for the rest of her life in the area of her heart and soul reserved for regrets.

Before she got so bogged down in *what ifs* and *maybes* that she couldn't function, she shook herself out of the doldrums and finished dressing. It was going to be a long day, and she didn't have time to dawdle.

Long or not, the day should be interesting and could possibly be downright fun, once the parade was over. After the parade there would be a huge picnic in the town park; some vendors had already set up their booths to sell soft drinks, cotton candy, popcorn, and other treats. Every year, something happened that gave the townsfolk something to talk about for months, such as Mayor Buddy falling in the pond, or one of the kids thinking it was a good idea to tie his daddy's car keys to a helium balloon and let go of it. The kid had thought the keys would weigh the balloon down so it would drag across the ground. The balloon had been a big one, and he had been wrong.

Since becoming chief, she'd spent all day at every Heritage event, as did Mayor Buddy, all the town council members, and at least one patrolman. Things usually ran fairly smoothly with only minor bumps, though year before last there had been some excitement when a barbecue grill had caught on fire and also caught the tree shading it on fire. That had caused a rule to be put in place that no grills could be positioned under trees or close to structures of any kind. She was only surprised the town had gone that long without a grill catching something on fire.

She left her bedroom to find the downstairs empty; through the wall of windows she could see Morgan strolling around the yard with Tricks. He was wearing jeans and a white tee shirt, and a pair of brown Vasque multisport shoes instead of his usual boots. As she watched, he squatted down in front of Tricks to say something to her and scratch behind both her ears. Tricks lifted one paw and laid it on his arm, her expression blissful as she listened to whatever he was saying.

Stopping in her tracks, Bo simply watched him for a moment. The way he moved was powerful and lithe, as graceful as a ballet dancer but in a completely different way, as if his balance and strength were so intertwined that he could attack from either left or right without losing anything in speed. His bare arms were roped with sinewy muscle, his skin tanned from all the time he'd been spending outdoors. He'd been with her just a month and his recovery was nothing short of spectacular, especially when she considered how weak he'd been when he got here.

He was completely able to care for himself now. Heck, he was even caring for *her*. He was doing the lion's share of the housework: laundry, most of the cleaning, some of the cooking. If it weren't for the situation he was in, he would likely already be gone.

She had always treasured having her house to herself, her sanctuary where she could shut out the world and be alone, just her and Tricks. But now, when he left, there would be an empty place that she hadn't noticed before, that he'd filled with his grouchiness and humor and *guyness*. The house even smelled different now: a man lived here, and it was obvious. She felt as if she should bring in fresh flowers to offset the musky scent of man, sweat, the leather of his shoes, the oil he used to clean both her pistol and his, plus sometimes the sharpness of gunpowder that told her he'd been practicing while she was gone. She'd never noticed anything like this before, during her marriage, but now all of her senses seemed to be acutely attuned to Morgan in ways she'd never thought possible.

While she was gathering the supplies Tricks would need for the day—food, water, a chew toy, a soft blanket—Morgan came back inside with Tricks. "You ready to leave?" he asked.

"Almost." She put the food, water, and toy in a small cooler and set the cooler on the blanket. "Now I'm ready."

He tucked his Glock inside his waistband, in the slim-carry concealed holster, and pulled a blue shirt on over his tee shirt, leaving it unbuttoned. "So am I."

A little taken aback, she said, "Why the weapon? You've never taken one to town before."

He lifted his brows. "There'll be a crowd there, right?"

"Well, yeah. Most of the people in town try to show up."

"That's why I'm armed. The probability of trouble goes up exponentially, the more people there are."

"We've never had any trouble before—not anything that required firearms anyway." She paused, then smiled. "I take that back; someone had to shoot down a helium balloon year before last."

"Escaping, huh?"

"With some car keys tied to it."

He chuckled. "Wish I'd seen that."

"Watching a grown man jump up and down like Rumpelstiltskin and scream '*Get it! Get it!*' was definitely the highlight of the day." She paused, then sighed. "I suppose I should get my weapon from the Jeep. I hadn't thought about it."

"Firearms are like hospitals. If you have 'em and don't need 'em, that's a good thing. If you need 'em and don't have 'em, that's a very bad thing."

She grumbled inwardly because the pistol would have to go in her bag and would get heavier and heavier as the day wore on. She'd never bothered getting a holster that could clip to her waistband, rationalizing that she was just administration instead of a real police chief, but this last month had made her realize that for better or worse, she *was* the police chief, a real one, and she had to accept the responsibilities that came with the job. She could have used better training when it came to the Kyle Gooding incident, and the "mob" scene could have turned out much worse if the people had been different. She'd been lucky; now she needed to be smart.

Morgan stuffed Tricks's leash in his pocket, then took the cooler and blanket from her. While he was putting everything in the Tahoe and loading up Tricks, she retrieved the pistol from the Jeep and stowed it in her bag, which was now as heavy as she'd anticipated.

The main street had already been blocked off in anticipation of the parade. Morgan had so quickly learned the area that she suspected he'd been studying Google Maps, and without asking for directions he took secondary streets that led them to the staging area along the park where the parade floats and marchers were lining up.

"Holy shit," he said as he got out of the Tahoe and surveyed the scene. "I didn't expect it to be this big."

"I think there's thirty-something entries, but not all of them are from Hamrickville. The Shriners aren't;

they're based in another town, but they do all the parades."

The local VFW led the way, followed by the Shriners on their motorcycles, then the Ladies' Club on a short-trailer float that looked as if they were having a tea party because all the ladies were seated on delicate chairs around an ornate wrought-iron table. One year Mayor Buddy had ridden a Segway at the head of the parade, but it had gotten away from him, dumped him on his ass in the middle of the street, and mowed down a trash can. That was before he'd broken his ankle skiing. After the broken ankle, Mayor Buddy had decided riding the Segway was like asking for trouble so that idea had gone away, to the disappointment of the townsfolk.

The high school seniors' float was seventh in line, and the kids came running when they saw her and Tricks. "This is going to be so awesome," said one of the girls. She was wearing a floaty summer dress and a tiara and had glitter all over her face. They were all dressed in their party best, boys and girls, and the whole bunch wanted to get Tricks "dressed." Despite efforts to get her accustomed to a tiara, no way was Tricks having any part of it, but they'd prepared for that possibility by having a glittery pink bow with long dangling ribbons that they stuck on top of her head.

At least it matched the pink boa they draped around her. Bo swallowed her laughter; she glanced over and saw that Morgan had turned his back, though there was a betraying shake to his shoulders. The kids were laughing too, so she didn't think their feelings would be hurt. Tricks's expression was blissed out; all that attention was right up her alley.

"We tried to hide a chair for you to sit on," one of the boys told Bo apologetically, "but that would make your head stick up out of the decorations, so we put a cushion on the floor for you. Is that okay?"

She smiled. "A cushion is fine." Truthfully, she'd expected to be sitting on the trailer floor, so the cushion was a big step up.

"Want me to take your bag?" Morgan asked.

The thought of him with a purse hanging from his shoulder was entertaining, but she shook her head. "Thanks, but I'll keep it with me. I'll be sitting."

They all trooped to the float to take their places because the parade organizer had blown a whistle and bellowed "Five minutes!" through a bullhorn. Bo prepared to climb onto the trailer, but Morgan forestalled her by clamping his hands around her waist and swinging her on board as if she were a child. While her heart was still pounding in reaction, he picked Tricks up too and placed her on the trailer because all the tissue-paper flowers meant she didn't have a clear shot for jumping up. Tricks darted to Bo and indulged in some excited licking because she was going for a ride. Bo found her place on a fat cushion in front of the raised dais where the male and female class favorites were standing. She could even lean back against the plywood dais. The decorations completely hid her from view on both sides though she could still see what was going on directly in front of her. The closeness of the decorations stopped any breeze from reaching her, but she'd asked to be as hidden as possible. The parade wouldn't last that long anyway, maybe forty-five minutes—an hour if they stretched it out.

Up ahead came the roar of the Shriners' motor-cycles as they were started. The VFW vets in their mismatched odds and ends of uniforms marched out in precision form, and the parade began.

Morgan kept pace with the float, walking on the right; the parade was moving at a crawl, with peri-odic pauses for the marching band to do a dance rou-tine or something. He wasn't certain exactly what was going on up ahead because his focus was on watch-ing Tricks. The crowd was sparse at first, with most people gathered down the main street, but the dog didn't care. As soon as the first applause and calls of "Tricks!" started, she began her routine of woofing as she turned her head left and right, a happy expression on her face. Every woof generated more applause, which brought on another woof, so it was self-perpetuating.

The girls positioned on each side of her were laughing and smiling as they waved, the boys were hamming it up with body-builder poses, the other girls were throwing candy to people. The kids were having a blast, maybe as much of one as Tricks was having.

As the parade turned down the main street and the crowd became thicker, people lined up four and five deep, sometimes more in places, and with onlookers in the upper-story windows of buildings as well as some on the roofs, Morgan felt himself slip into hyperalert mode. Until now he'd been very relaxed in Hamrickville, but crowds always made his lizard brain nervous. People could get into arguments, or do stupid shit that would domino into disaster. The kids were taking care to keep Tricks from getting too close to the edge of the float, but if something startled them, or Tricks, what could happen? What if she jumped off the moving float? What if Bo made a headlong dive after her? He broke out in a sweat at the idea because he knew Bo wouldn't hesitate.

He was just looking for trouble, he knew. The girl on the left had a good grip on Tricks's shortened leash, and the girl on the right was positioned slightly behind but with her leg touching Tricks's side. They were both waving at the crowd, but they were also keeping a sharp eye on the dog. Then the one on the left even knelt down and put her arm around Tricks while still waving. The crowd was eating up having a canine "homecoming queen," judging by all the laughter and applause. The idea was a hit.

The main drag was about eight blocks long. Morgan hadn't thought to ask where the parade would end, but the location didn't really matter because he intended to follow it all the way. He settled into a combat patrol routine, his head moving on a swivel, automatically noting everyone and looking for anything that was out of the ordinary. He cared about both the woman and the dog on that float, and he intended to do all he could to make sure nothing happened to them.

They were in the fifth block when he noticed the man about twenty yards ahead of him—young, tall, longish brown hair. It was his height that let Morgan key in on him because he was taller than most of the people around him. What set him apart was that he wasn't cheering and clapping. Instead he was glaring . . . toward the float. Something had definitely pissed him off, and pissed-off people could be trouble.

Automatically Morgan picked up his pace, threading through and around groups of people, wanting to get closer to the guy in case something happened.

Then the guy turned and started down the sidewalk toward him. Morgan stepped aside, let him pass. The guy passed within inches of him and never glanced his way. Instead he was still watching the float; he was definitely keyed on that particular float, the one Bo and Tricks were on. And there was nothing good in his expression.

The guy was wearing a jacket. Morgan's spine began tingling in warning.

He wheeled, began shadowing his target, working closer despite the milling crowd. People were jockeying for position so they stepped in front of him without looking, or he had to sidestep a kid. The good news was the guy in front of him had to deal with the same conditions and obstacles, so Morgan was gaining on him.

Shit. That jacket was all wrong. The weather was too warm for anyone to be wearing a jacket. Everyone else was in summer clothes: short sleeves, shorts, sandals, lightweight stuff. In his world, people wore jackets when they shouldn't be wearing them in order to hide firearms or bombs.

The tractor pulling the float went past. Now the float itself was beside them, filled with waving teenagers.

Toward the back was a built-up platform with two teens on top of it, and Bo was sitting with her back to the platform, out of sight. Through the profusion of colored tissue paper tucked into the holes of chicken-wire forms, he could see Tricks's pale golden head lifting with each little bark as she woofed from side to side.

The parade stalled again, the float stopped, and behind him the marching band swung into a lively tune. Applause burst out, but Morgan didn't bother looking for the cause. All of his attention was focused on the man who was still pushing his way through the crowd on the sidewalk.

The guy drew even with the end of the float, where Tricks and the girls were positioned, and he stepped off the sidewalk into the street. His gaze didn't leave the float as he put his hand inside his jacket.

Their forward progress had stopped again, but that didn't matter to Tricks. As far as she was concerned, all the applause was for her. Bo had to laugh because Tricks was so into her role. She would occasionally look back to where Bo was seated, reassuring herself that her human mom was still there, but for the most part she was acting like the ham she was.

The bright sun beat down on Bo's head, making her glad for her sunglasses. This would probably last another half hour at the rate they were going. She was actually kind of enjoying it; one of the kids had passed her down a bottle of cold lemonade, and she had nothing to do but sit there, sip her lemonade, and watch Tricks have a blast.

While they were stopped, one of the girls opened a bottle of water, produced a small bowl from somewhere on the float, and filled the bowl for Tricks to have a drink. The other girl held Tricks's pink boa out of the way so it wouldn't get in the water. Bo chuckled and started to take a picture, but Tricks stopped drinking before she could dig her phone out of her bag. She hoped people along the way were taking pictures they could share with her; if she'd thought, she'd have charged Morgan with the job of snapping a few photos. To be on the safe side, when they got to the end she'd take some pictures of Tricks before everyone got off the float.

She settled back against the plywood dais, glad that this was working out so well. The cushion made a surprisingly comfortable seat, and darned if she wasn't getting a little drowsy. She let her head rest on the dais; because of her sunglasses, if she closed her eyes no one would notice. The idea was tempting.

Kyle Gooding stepped into the middle of the street right behind the float, just a few feet from the back of the trailer. She was so astonished she gaped at him. What was he doing, crossing the street in the middle of a parade? Had he flipped out?

Then he pulled a pistol out from under his jacket. His good-looking face twisted into something ugly, and he pointed the pistol—

—right at Tricks.

Bo's blood froze into icy shards of horror, and her heart stopped beating. Her vision narrowed to not much more than a pinpoint. With a guttural, inhuman scream she lunged forward, knowing she couldn't cover those few feet in time to save Tricks, knowing she was going to see that bright little life destroyed, knowing too in that second that she would kill Kyle Gooding with her bare hands unless he shot her before she could manage it. Terrified, savage, she desperately clawed for inches, trying to grab Tricks. The air was molasses, dragging at her hands and feet, slowing her down.

The two girls saw the pistol and screamed, ducking. Bo saw the flicker of Kyle's eyes as their piercing screams cut the air, the split second of hesitation.

Something blue sliced in front of her vision, just as the deep crack of a shot shattered the joy of the day, the peace of the town, her heart.

Tricks yelped, just once.

Still screaming, unable to stop the animal sounds coming from her throat, Bo reached Tricks.

She threw her arms around her, hoping against hope the wound wasn't fatal, searching through the golden fur with hands that were shaking so violently she couldn't control them. Tricks leaned against her and licked her cheek. The awful screams had stopped and Bo heard herself babbling to Tricks, begging her to be okay, *just be okay sweetie I'll take care of you I'll kill that bastard.*

Where was the blood? She couldn't find any blood.

"I'm so sorry!" one of the girls frantically apologized, kneeling on the float. She was crying. "I stepped on her paw!"

Bo couldn't get her thoughts ordered. What did stepping on Tricks's paw matter when she'd been *shot*? But the girl—was her name Christa?—looked up at Bo with swimming blue eyes and said, "I saw the gun and ducked and that's when I stepped on her paw and she yelped. She's okay, isn't she? I didn't cripple her?"

Bo was still caught in that damned molasses, unable to grasp any one thought, with time moving in agonizing slow motion. She turned her head to the right and saw Kyle Gooding, the bastard, face down on the street with Morgan kneeling on him and twisting his right arm up and back in an agonizing hold, if Kyle's screams were anything to go by. "You're breaking my arm!" Kyle howled. "Stop, you're breaking my arm."

Morgan gave the arm a vicious twist and the howl became a scream. He looked up at Bo kneeling with Tricks in her arms, his face set in a savage mask, his eyes blue ice. "Are you okay?"

She wanted to shriek and tear out her hair. How could she be okay when Tricks—but Tricks was sitting there leaning against her and giving her random licks, and Christa seemed to realize what was wrong because she put her arms around Bo. "It's okay, Chief," she said gently, with tears running down her face. "Tricks is okay. He didn't shoot her. Mr. Rees stopped him."

Bo's mouth worked as she tried to form words. She managed to get out, "The shot—" before her throat locked. She felt icy cold despite the sun. Her heart was beating again with heavy, sluggish beats.

Morgan's head swiveled as he looked around at the gathering swell of people, everyone murmuring and asking questions. Bo became aware of shouts and disturbance as others ran toward them, pushing through the milling crowd. She saw Jesse, his expression alert as he ran from the direction of the park. "Is anyone hurt?" Morgan barked. "The shot went wide. Did it hit anyone?"

The shot had gone wide because he'd plowed into Kyle like a bulldozer. He'd been the flash of blue. Like a freeze frame Bo had a sudden clear image of him in the exact moment he hit Kyle, a lethal human missile with murder in his eyes.

At his question people were looking around, calling out, but no one seemed to be hurt. Then there was a sudden outcry of "Oh my God, he's been shot!" and her blood turned cold and sluggish again.

"Ohh, shit, you're breaking my arm," Kyle moaned.

"Shut up," Morgan said, gripping Kyle's hair and giving his head a short, sharp bang against the pavement. Kyle shut up, probably because he was unconscious.

Bo was okay with that. If any questions were asked, she'd swear Morgan hadn't done anything. What the people crowded around them would say was up in the air, but she didn't hear any sympathy being expressed toward Kyle.

She should get down from the float. She should stop holding Tricks and get down from the float, do her job, because she was the chief. But she couldn't, couldn't move, couldn't care. She laid her cheek against the top of Tricks's head, closed her eyes, and tried to concentrate on breathing.

Then Jesse and Patrick were there, Jesse in his street clothes because it was his day off, Patrick officially taking charge. Patrick crouched beside Morgan and handcuffed Kyle, while Jesse stood at the rear of the float and said, "Chief, is everyone up here okay?"

"I think so," Christa replied in a shaky voice, as if she knew Bo was still incapable of doing so. "He was aiming right at us, then Mr. Rees hit him!"

At Tricks specifically, though with the girls so close to her and Bo directly behind, she supposed any of them could have been hit.

The shouts around the wounded person got louder, and Jesse took off in that direction. Bo was gathering herself—thinking about gathering herself—when hard arms closed around her and lifted her bodily off the float. Morgan's scent and heat closed around her, thawing the ice in her veins. She managed a very weak, "No," from her constricted throat, though she wasn't certain what she was saying *no* to. Morgan stood her on her feet, said, "Can you stand?"

She nodded. He took her hand and placed it on the float, just in case. Then he gathered Tricks in his arms and gently set her down on the street too. He looped her leash around his wrist, asked one of the kids to pass Bo's bag down to him. He hung the bag off his left shoulder, scooped Bo up in his arms again, and called out, "Can someone open this store? The chief needs to get out of the sun."

Someone could. It turned out to be the hardware store. Morgan carried her inside with Tricks trotting along beside him. The store was cool and more private than the street. She didn't even mind the somewhat funky smell that hardware stores always had, for some reason.

A battered office chair on wheels was dragged out. Bo sat down, then leaned forward and looped her arms around Tricks, burying her face against the dog's soft ruff. The weight of what had almost happened was so heavy that she could barely breathe, barely force her lungs to pump in and out. Tricks had been targeted because of *her.* Whatever maggot had gotten into Kyle Gooding's brain, he'd known that the best way to get to her was through Tricks. It was common knowledge she doted on her dog, and bright, innocent, happy Tricks had almost been killed because of that.

The realization devastated her, filled her with such pain and remorse she couldn't get a grip on her emotions. She'd handled everything in life that had come her way: instability, betrayal, financial problems, deprivation, but she didn't know if she could handle anything bad happening to Tricks because of her. But what had she done? What had so enraged Kyle that he'd decided to destroy something she loved?

The son of a bitch! She wanted to choke him, she wanted to hit him with everything she had.

She was jerked from her thoughts as Morgan squatted in front of her, his big warm hands cupping her elbows and his dark brows lowered over the blue ice of his eyes as he studied her face. "Bo—honey, everything's okay. Tricks is fine."

He could have been killed, she realized—again. Jumping Kyle the way he had, Kyle could easily have turned the weapon on him and pulled the trigger. He'd risked his life for her, for Tricks, for everyone on the float and everyone lining the street to watch the parade. Kyle could have kept shooting until he was out of ammunition. But despite nearly dying just a couple of months before, Morgan hadn't hesitated.

Sensing something was very amiss, Tricks laid her head on Bo's thigh and looked up at her with worried dark eyes. Gently Bo touched Tricks's head. "Why didn't you shoot him?" she asked in a very low tone, because she didn't necessarily want anyone else to know Morgan was armed.

His hands tightened on her elbows. "I couldn't get a clear shot with all the people around," he murmured.

He was watching her so intently she realized she had to get it together. She was the chief of police; she had to act like it. If Mayor Buddy and the town council wanted her to let Jesse and Patrick handle it because she was too directly involved, she was okay with that, but until they told her so, she had to do her job.

She drew a deep breath, let it out, and firmed her jaw. She still felt like jelly on the inside, but on the outside she would show strength or die trying. "I'm okay," she said, lifting her head and looking around at everyone who had crowded into the store, all the concerned expressions on the faces of people she knew and some she didn't know. "If you can give Tricks some water, I need to get out there and do what needs doing."

Chapter 18

She stepped out into the bright spring day with Morgan close behind her, Tricks's leash in his hand. Tricks had lapped up some water, then refused to let Bo leave the hardware store without her, as if she knew how upset Bo was.

Once again, because of Kyle Gooding, she heard the sirens of multiple patrol cars and medics racing to Hamrickville. This time there wouldn't be any dropping of charges, at least not on her part. She intended to nail him with every possible charge and let the district attorney sort it out.

The street was clogged with people milling around, and the parade floats were blocking traffic in every direction. The VFW guys and the Shriners were trying to clear the street by moving the floats out of the way, which met with some difficulty because in several cases the men who had been driving the tractors had left their vehicles to go see what was going on. But the front end of the parade was beginning to move, so the clearing out had started.

There was a concentrated group around the end of the float where Kyle was, and another one across the street, presumably where the gunshot victim was. With Morgan and Tricks beside her, she started across. She didn't want to see Kyle's face now because if she did she might snap. Not only that, she didn't care if the son of a bitch died.

She waded into the crowd, aided by Morgan's strong arm reaching out ahead of her and moving people aside. Some people glanced at her and said, "Sorry, Chief," as they moved. Some of them glanced at Morgan, then their eyes widened and they muttered, "Sorry," as they too moved away. She didn't have to imagine what his eyes looked like because she'd seen that lethal iciness before. She didn't know if she actually needed his interference, but she was glad to have it.

A man was lying on the ground, his face and shirt a bloody mess. Several people were kneeling beside him, and one woman was pressing some cloth to his head.

The man's eyes were open and he was talking, which was good.

She did what she knew to do: she moved the crowd back, she crouched down and got the man's name—Jeff Simmons. She didn't know him, but his wife, the woman who was holding the cloth to his head, looked familiar. In short order, she discovered that Mrs. Simmons was a teacher at the local school, which explained her familiarity.

Mrs. Simmons was holding it together and began giving Bo a coherent statement, but then she lifted the soaked cloth, and her husband's head wound immediately started pouring blood again. She made an inarticulate sound of distress and burst into tears.

"Let me take over," Morgan said, crouching down beside the wife and angling his body between Tricks and the wounded man. "I have some medic training." He slapped the bloody cloth back over the wound and in about thirty seconds had commandeered someone's tank top to cover that, which he held in place with someone else's tie. Who had worn a tie to a parade?

Bo shoved the errant thought aside and concentrated on the task of getting a statement. Mr. Simmons was remarkably calm. "I don't think I'm shot," he said. "I mean, we all heard the shot, but there was a kind of sharp ping, then something hit my head."

Still holding the makeshift bandage firmly in place, Morgan looked around. "Were you standing beside that light pole?"

"Yeah," Mr. Simmons affirmed.

"I think the bullet hit the pole and a big splinter of wood tagged you in the head. Maybe not. The bullet could have ricocheted and grazed you. Either way, this isn't a penetrating wound."

"Oh, thank the Lord," sobbed Mrs. Simmons. She wiped her eyes and face, which was a waste of time because she was still crying. Someone passed her a handful of tissues.

Then the real medics arrived; they'd parked on a side street and run the rest of the way. Bo and Morgan stepped back. Tricks pawed Bo's leg and whined; the atmosphere was far different from the parade, and she didn't like it. Either that, or she needed to pee. Looking down at her, Bo broke into a wobbly smile; it was a definite "I need to pee" signal because if a dog could be said to be squirming, Tricks was.

"You need some time alone with her," Morgan said, having followed the unspoken communication. "Take her to the side of that building. I need to see about something. Where will you be?"

"Right here," she said, stepping up onto the sidewalk. "I figure I should stay far away from Kyle."

"I'll be right back. Fifteen minutes, tops." He hooked his hand around the back of her neck and pressed a quick kiss to her forehead, regardless of who might be watching. At this point she didn't care, and she didn't think he ever had. All she wanted to do was what had to be done so she could go home.

Morgan threaded his way through the crowd; Hamrickville wasn't a big town, but most of the population seemed to be standing in the street. That slowed him down some, but not by much. He had something to take care of, and he wanted to do it now. The look on his face had some of the more perceptive citizens moving out of his path. He could feel the ice settling in his veins, the hyperawareness of all his senses, the way he always reacted when things went to shit and it was fight or die.

Jesse and Patrick were still at the float, though Kyle Gooding was now sitting on the ground with blood dripping from his nose and chin. Morgan eyed him dispassionately, wishing he'd put more force into slamming the asshole's head against the pavement. If he had, this would be finished already, so that had been a slight miscalculation on his part.

Patrick had pulled up his patrol car, easing through the crowd with his blues flashing and occasionally tapping the horn. Morgan waited while they hauled Kyle to his feet and opened the back door of the cruiser, easing him into it even though Morgan suspected they both would have liked to drop-kick him into the seat. Kyle sat sullenly, staring down at his feet.

Morgan approached Jesse. "I need a private word with the asshole. Okay for me to get in the car?"

Jesse turned, eyed him, studied his face. "You can't kill him."

"Don't intend to." *Not yet anyway.*

"You can't even touch him. I'm not giving him any avenue to get off the hook this time."

"Don't intend to touch him either."

"Okay, then." A faint wintry smile touched Jesse's face. "I would say record everything on your phone, but I probably don't need to know. Tap on the window when you want out." He nodded; Morgan opened the back passenger door on the other side and slid onto the seat beside Gooding. He closed the door with a controlled thud.

Kyle lifted his bloody face and snarled at him, "Who the fuck are you?"

I'm your worst nightmare. The line from the movie popped into Morgan's head, but he resisted the temptation. Looking out the window instead of at Kyle, he said offhandedly, "I'm the man who plans to kill you."

"What? Who—?" The words were kind of blub-bered thanks to the swelling of Kyle's mouth, which gave Morgan a great deal of pleasure.

Now Morgan looked at him and smiled. He knew it wasn't a pretty smile because Kyle visibly recoiled. "You tried to kill the chief. I happen to be in love with her." He was distantly astonished at the words coming out of his mouth but went with it anyway. He'd think about it later.

"Wasn't trying to kill her," Kyle mush-mouthed sullenly. "The dog. I was gonna shoot the fucking dog. This was all her fault; if she hadn't jumped me, I never would have hit her, and my family wouldn't have made me sign those fucking divorce papers to keep from being arrested. I lost my house, she should lose her dog. Nobody cares about a dog, you can't even sue for 'emotional harm,' or anything like that. I looked it up."

"Well, see, that's the law—but I don't give a fuck about the law. I happen to be real fond of the dog myself. She's smarter than you are. Better looking, too."

"Fuck the damn dog. You're threatening me. That's against the law." Blood and spittle dripped down Kyle's chin. "I'll have you arrested."

"Good. I can arrange to be in the same cell with you." Casually, Morgan looked back out the window. "Here's how it's going to be. You're not going to say a word about aiming for the dog, you're going to say you were trying to kill the chief—"

"Bullshit!"

"—and you're going to plead guilty," Morgan continued as if Kyle hadn't interrupted. "You're going to go to prison. And that's the only way you're going to stay alive. You don't make bail, you sit your sorry ass in a jail cell until you're sentenced, and you serve your time. When you get out, you move far away from here and never come back to this area again."

"Do you know who I am? My father—"

"Fuck your father. The problem is, you don't know who *I* am. I'm a man who knows how to kill you seven ways from Sunday, and I'm just itching to try all those ways out on you, you motherfucker. You set foot outside the jail, you're dead. Remember that. You want to know how I plan to kill you? I think skinning you alive would give me a lot of pleasure. I can make it last a long time, and you'd be alive and screaming right up until the end. Yeah, I like the idea of that." He thought of Bo's white face and wild eyes, the inhuman sounds coming from her throat as she lunged toward Tricks, and the truth of what he was saying was plain in his savage expression.

Kyle jerked back so hard he banged the back of his head against the window. His eyes were wide with fear, whites showing all around the irises. "You're crazy as hell!"

Morgan considered that, then shrugged. "Possible," he said casually. "But I'm also a man of my word. The only place you're safe from me is in jail—and you'd better pray nothing bad ever happens to the chief or her dog because if it does, I'm going to assume you paid for it to happen, and I'm coming after you, jail or not. There's no place you can go that I can't get to you, no way you can hide even if you change your name. And I know how to get away with it, even if you tell a hundred people to look at me if anything happens to you."

Kyle's eye were all but bugging out. The stupid fool couldn't back down though, had to cling to the idea that he was smarter and badder than everyone else. He sputtered, "I don't believe you."

"Your funeral," Morgan said. "I look forward to attending." He tapped on the window. Jesse opened the door, and Morgan gave Kyle another chilling smile before he got out of the patrol car.

"If he says I threatened him, he's lying," Morgan told Jesse.

"I figured as much."

Morgan reappeared well within the fifteen minutes he'd allotted. Bo had let Tricks pee, then simply knelt beside the dog and hugged and petted her for several minutes, so grateful to still have her that she almost broke down and let loose the flood tide of tears that were threatening to overflow the dam of her control. She was still there when he circled the building to find her.

"We can go home," he said, putting his hand on the small of her back when she stood.

"No, we can't, not yet. We have to give statements."

"Fuck that. Jesse can come out to the house." He looked hard and implacable and as if he didn't give a damn whether or not they gave statements.

Thank God he'd been here. If he hadn't been—she couldn't even think the thought. Even afterward, he'd been a rock she could lean on, capable of acting when she herself had been almost frozen by that debilitating sense of horror that lingered deep in her bones.

"It's my job," she said, and braced herself to get through the coming ordeal. It wouldn't be traumatic, just exhausting, when she wanted nothing more than to curl up and not think for a day or two.

"Just let me know when you've had enough, and I'll get us out."

He would, too; regardless of how many questions still needed to be asked and answered, if she said she had to go home, he'd take her there.

A little buoyed by that knowledge, she waded in to what had to be done. Police work was always much slower than people thought it was; television had given the nation a false idea of how long it took to process a crime scene, to interview witnesses—in this case, a *lot* of witnesses, upward of fifty people who had actually seen something as opposed to the couple of hundred who only thought they'd seen something. Going home wasn't on the books for several hours—the rest of the day, in fact.

Jesse took her statement, and Morgan's, and that of everyone else who had seen anything. Of all the kids who had been on the float, Christa's statement was the most coherent and thorough, but then she'd been the one kneeling with her arm around Tricks, staring at the pistol in Kyle's hand.

No mention was made of Morgan banging Kyle's head against the pavement, and if Kyle had made any such accusation, Bo hadn't heard about it. Kyle wasn't there; he'd been taken to the county lockup—again. But the police station was as crowded as it had been the day of the Melody/Miss Doris incident, with people coming and going. The parade had been aborted, of course, but the picnic in the park was happening. Once the snarled traffic had been straightened out, there was nothing the townsfolk wanted to do more than gather in the park where everyone could talk about what had happened or what they thought had happened.

Someone brought her some food from the picnic, and a cold beer. Bo really wanted the beer, but she was too tired and on edge to decide if she was on duty or not, so she settled for water. Morgan drank the beer and smirked at her while he did it. She didn't care if he smirked. He'd saved Tricks, so as far as she was concerned, he could smirk at the world.

Daina came to take care of Tricks; Bo let her go even though every cell in her body protested letting the dog out of her sight. Tricks liked the crowd and people, but she was getting tired and needed a nap.

Finally the day wound down. Jeff Simmons was being kept hospitalized overnight for observation; the word came in that he had indeed been hit by the ricochet, but he'd be okay. Daina arrived back with a refreshed Tricks, who bounced from person to person to announce her presence, with repeated trips back to Bo to touch base with her center of security.

And enough was, finally, enough. "I'm going home," she announced tiredly.

Mayor Buddy, unusually solemn, had been there through all the aftermath. He patted her shoulder. "You've had a hard day. I think you should take off a couple of days, get everything inside calm again. Unless all hell breaks loose at the park tonight, Jesse and the rest of the men can handle everything, and call you if all hell *does* break loose. I mean it. Stay home."

Normally she'd have soldiered on, but this wasn't normal. She gave a brief nod. "At least one day." She'd take that one, then reevaluate. She was exhausted. She felt hollow, and frighteningly fragile, as if she might shatter without warning. She needed to just be home.

"I'll go get the truck," Morgan said, and only then did she remember that he'd parked at the other end of town, where the parade began.

"No need for that," Mayor Buddy said, evidently realizing exactly where they had parked that morning. "My car is here, hop in and I'll take you to it."

"Thanks, but we have Tricks," Bo pointed out. A lot of people didn't want a dog in their car; she'd been one of them, until Tricks.

Mayor Buddy looked down at Tricks, who was lying with her muzzle resting on Bo's foot, and a spasm crossed his face. The official word going around was that Kyle had been about to shoot Bo, but she knew differently, and evidently some other people did too. "She can ride in my car any time," he said. "In the front seat, if she wants."

Bo managed a smile. It was weak, but it was a smile. "Don't give her any ideas."

The ride to the park was a matter of a few minutes; the park was filled with people finishing the day the way they'd planned it, with picnics, food trucks, balloons, games, and fireworks to close out the festivities after dark. For most of them, the morning's excitement had been a momentary distraction that hadn't touched them at all other than giving them something to talk about while they ate their grilled burgers and hot dogs. No one paid any attention to them when Mayor Buddy stopped beside Morgan's big black SUV.

"I'm riding in back with her," Bo said when Morgan opened the back door for Tricks to leap into her seat. He gave a brief nod and opened the other door for her.

He started the engine so the air conditioning would run, then said, "I'll be right back," and strode across the green to one of the food trucks. When he returned, the brown paper sack he carried filled the Tahoe with the smell of grilled hamburgers and onions. With vague surprise, she looked at the clock on the dash and saw that it was well after their normal time for eating dinner. She'd eaten about half of what had been brought to her at lunch, too gut-punched to manage more, but now she was actually a little hungry. The funny thing was, if he hadn't thought of it, she probably wouldn't have eaten at all.

Tricks had great interest in the smells coming from that paper sack, but the seat harness prevented her from jumping into the front seat to check it out. Nevertheless, she leaned forward as far as she could go, her dark eyes focused on the sack. Bo put her hand on Tricks, sinking her fingers into the soft fur, needing to feel the warmth and life still there. She needed to touch her.

Morgan glanced at her in the rearview mirror. "Gooding will probably plead guilty."

She stirred herself, made a small scoffing sound. "Kyle? His father is probably in touch with every judge and lawyer he knows right now, trying to make it go away."

"I'm fairly certain that won't happen this time." He didn't say any more, but she wasn't stupid, and she definitely remembered his expression—as well as the fifteen minutes when he'd had "something to do." She could see an echo of that expression on his face now, in the iciness of his eyes. She was fairly certain that if Kyle *did* plead guilty, it would be because he was afraid not to. She was good with that, and she didn't intend to ask any questions.

Now that they were alone, she could feel the fatigue setting in, coming at her fast and heavy. The draining emotional upheaval left her as empty as if she'd run a marathon. Sliding over, she let her head rest against Tricks's side for the comfort of being close to her.

"I know she's a dog," she murmured, not knowing if Morgan could hear her but not caring because she needed to say it anyway. "But I love her." She didn't add any qualifiers such as *like a child* because love was love and didn't need measuring.

His gaze flicked to the mirror again. "I know," he said quietly.

Finally, finally, they were home. Tricks bounded out, her energy restored; Bo climbed out as if she hurt in every bone of her body, which she kind of did, but mostly she was so tired she could barely move. Morgan checked the sky, said, "There's enough daylight left for me to take her for a walk. You go inside and put your feet up, eat one of those burgers. I'll eat when we get back."

"I'll go with you," she said, unable to bear the thought just yet of letting Tricks out of her sight. She'd let Daina take her because she knew that was best for Tricks, but that was the only reason, and she'd been on edge every minute Tricks was out of her sight.

He seemed to get that because he gave a brief nod and held out his left hand to her. She didn't know if he meant for her to take it or if it was a "come on" gesture, but she seized it and held on tight. "Thank you." She should have said it sooner, would have if she'd been able to gather her thoughts. She was trying so hard to function and not give in to the terror that still roiled deep inside her that function itself was getting shortchanged. "It was lucky—more than lucky—you were there."

He squeezed her hand, then laced their fingers together so their hands were palm to palm. The touch of him, the strength she could feel in his hand, held her steady when she was feeling increasingly fragile, as if she might shatter into a thousand shards.

"It wasn't luck," he said briefly as they strolled across the yard to the trail she and Tricks had worn in the earth. "I'd already spotted him." Bo was watching Tricks dance along the trail as enthusiastically as if she hadn't gone that same route multiple times a day for most of her life, but at Morgan's statement she glanced questioningly up at him.

"I didn't know who he was," he explained, "but he was wearing a jacket and that made me suspicious. When he moved, I followed."

"What's suspicious about a jacket?" Then it hit her, and she said, "Oh." Why would anyone wear a jacket on such a warm day unless they were hiding whatever was under the jacket? She wouldn't have noticed that, at least not at first.

Those few awful moments flashed in front of her, as vivid as if they were happening again. She saw the hate in Kyle's eyes, the sheer viciousness, and the sick enjoyment of what he intended to do. "He was aiming straight at Tricks," she said in a low tone and swallowed with difficulty because her throat immediately tightened at the memory.

"I thought he was. He could have been aiming at you, given that you were directly behind her, but I was fairly sure she was his target."

"I knew I couldn't get there in time." Her voice had tightened to a thin thread of sound. "But you did."

"Hey." He squeezed her hand again, which brought her stricken gaze up to his. "I wasn't going to let anything happen to either of you."

But it could have. Who else but Morgan would have noticed something odd in someone wearing a jacket? His training, his level of expertise in taking people down, had put in him a unique position to stop Kyle, but what about when he was gone? She couldn't think about that now, she simply couldn't.

"I don't understand it. Why hurt her? She's so innocent—" Her voice broke.

"He blames you for making him give Emily everything she wanted in the divorce."

"*Me?*" Indignation saved her, gave her back some control. She stopped in her tracks to stare at him in astonishment.

"His reasoning—or lack of it—is that everyone was so angry at him because he punched you, and he wouldn't have punched you if you hadn't jumped him. Ergo, it's all your fault."

She had nothing to say to that, too stunned by that monumental lack of logic to even try to get her mind around it. Silence was good, requiring no effort. Pretty much the only things keeping her going were watching Tricks go about her routine untouched by the day's happenings, and the feel of Morgan's hot palm pressed against hers. Tricks did her business and they turned around, retracing the path through the purpling twilight.

Their hamburgers were cold, but she nuked them just enough to get them warm, while Morgan opened a Naked Pig for each of them. If it hadn't been for the beer helping the food to go down, she never would have been able to swallow. When Tricks was fed and they were fed, the day crashed down on her. She let Morgan handle what cleanup there was and dragged herself upstairs, made herself shower. Afterward, she went to the balcony rail and called down to Morgan that she was going to bed.

He was sitting on the sofa watching television. He tilted his head back so he could see her. "You okay?"

"No," she said honestly. "But I will be."

And she would. She knew she would. Just not tonight. Tonight, it was all still too close, her nerves were still too raw. When she got into bed, Tricks jumped up and snuggled against her, as if she somehow knew Bo needed comforting.

The need to touch Tricks was overwhelming. Bo stroked the soft fur, trying not to think how close she had come to losing her. "Sweet girl," she whispered, remembering Tricks as a puppy, a lightning-fast ball of white fuzz hell-bent on attacking life and sampling everything she could, tripping over her own paws, diving at Bo's shoelaces, splashing wildly in the plastic wading pool Bo had bought for her. She tried to hold on to that line of thought, to make herself smile and use the good memories to keep the bad ones at bay.

She couldn't do it. The fragile smile in the dark faded, and the other memories rushed in. Lying there, she was swamped by that horrible moment when she'd been fighting to get to Tricks, knowing she was too late. For a few minutes that were so devastating she could barely think about them, she'd thought she had just seen Tricks killed in front of her. That yelp—what if it had been the last sound Tricks ever made?

The raw sound of anguish tore from her throat. She buried her face against Tricks's neck as sobs shook her. She hated crying; she kept her emotions battened down and buttoned up, because viewing everything pragmatically and evenly was the best way to get through life. She wanted to stop, wanted to put this behind her and get back in balance.

She had always tried so hard to keep Tricks safe, and today she hadn't been able to. If Morgan hadn't been there, Kyle would have killed her.

She was so mired in distress that she didn't hear the bedroom door open, but she wasn't startled when the bed gave under Morgan's weight as he sat down with his hip against her back. "Hey," he murmured as he smoothed strands of hair away from her wet face. "It didn't happen. Keep that thought front and center: it didn't happen."

"I know," she said, her voice thick with tears. "But it was so close. I couldn't get to her. I saw what he was about to do, and I couldn't move fast enough. I felt as if my feet had been *glued* down."

"For what it's worth, in a crisis like that how things feel and how they really are are two different things. You were moving like you'd been shot out of a cannon."

"And I still wouldn't have been there fast enough." Heartbreak was plain in her tone. She would have failed. Tricks would have died.

The bedroom wasn't dark because of the light from the landing coming through the open door; she could see Tricks's brows quirking quizzically at this unusual behavior from both her main human and her auxiliary human, her face so expressive she might as well be speaking. Bo's heart swelled as she trailed a tender finger down the golden head to rub between Tricks's eyes.

For all of Tricks's life, Bo had done everything she could to keep her safe and healthy, to give her a happy, secure life. Dogs didn't live that long; every day was precious. But despite everything she'd done, all the precautions she'd taken and the care she'd given, she could have lost Tricks today, and it had been out of her control. Things happened. Some people were stupid-ass idiots. She couldn't anticipate everything, couldn't control everything, or even most things. Loss happened. It was random, striking without warning and despite all efforts to ward it off. Lightning could strike a hermit alone on a mountain as easily as it could someone in a town.

"Don't," Morgan said, and she realized she was sobbing again. She could no more stop the tears than she'd have been able to stop the bullet.

She could have lost him today, too. He wasn't hers to lose but . . . she cared. She couldn't deny that she cared.

Tricks hadn't been the only one in danger; Kyle could have turned the gun on Morgan just as easily. Today had all but slapped her in the face with a hard truth: there were no guarantees. She could safeguard her emotions to the best of her ability, and still be blindsided by events she couldn't control. She could have lost Tricks today. She could lose Morgan tomorrow. Whether or not she slept with him, let herself show how much she cared for him, wouldn't affect the amount of pain she would feel if anything happened to him. She would instead bear the extra burden of regret, regret that she hadn't made the most of their time together.

He might stay, or he might go. She had no control over that. The only thing she could control was how fully she lived *now* because now was all she had. That realization was almost as terrifying as that moment when she thought Tricks was going to die. She had been protecting herself with an illusion.

Silently he got up from the bed and went out onto the landing. The light went out. His absence speared through her, and she started to call out a strangled plea for him to come back when she saw his dark shape moving back to the bed.

He stood on the other side and she heard the rustling of fabric, the sound of his belt hitting the floor. Her heartbeat began a hard, thumping pace, sending heat through her body and banishing the cold. His voice came in the darkness, deep and firm. "C'mon, Tricks, find some other place to sleep." He snapped his fingers, and Tricks, the treacherous hussy, bounced up as if she'd been longing to get on her own comfortable bed but had been keeping Bo company while she was so upset, but thank you very much for relieving her of the duty. Her paws hit the floor and she trotted out with great purpose, as if she had something important to do.

Bo made a strangled sound at her own thoughts, half sob and half chuckle. She swallowed and managed to say, "What?" Not very coherent or eloquent, but it was the best she could do.

He sat down on the bed to remove his shoes. "You know what. The only question was *when*. The answer is *now*."

That was succinct enough.

She wanted this. She wanted him, specifically. But she didn't want him here out of pity, and all this crying might be a major turnoff to him. Morgan didn't strike her as a man who had a lot of patience with weakness. "Are you sure?"

He was lifting the covers, and he paused. "You're kidding, right?"

"I'm a mess." She was a tangled turmoil of emotions, grieving when there was no need to grieve, crying when she hated to cry, so over-flowing with thoughts that she couldn't get a handle on any of them long enough to know for certain what she was feeling.

"I'm a guy," he said prosaically as he got into bed beside her.

She was surprised into laughter and surprised that she *could* laugh. "Does that mean guys don't mind messes?"

"Pretty much." He slid his arm under her neck, urged her closer so that she was lying completely against him, her head snuggled onto his shoulder. The heat of his bare skin engulfed her, warming her through the fabric of her clothing. Under her fingers she could feel the crispness of his chest hair, grown back enough to be somewhat soft.

"I just don't want you to do this because you feel sorry for me," she confessed almost inaudibly.

For answer he took the hand lying on his chest and moved it down to the front of his shorts. His erection jumped at her touch, pushing into her palm. "Does this feel like sympathy?"

No, it definitely did not. Excitement speared through her; when he lifted his hand she left hers where it was, and trailed her fingertips up and down the hard length before folding her hand around his penis to get a good feel for the size of him. A little purring sound vibrated in her throat before she could catch it. He was so thick she had a pang of doubt before her hormones smothered it. *Yes,* she wanted him, she wanted this. She had always been alone, stood alone, and now she didn't want to.

At her touch he went rigid and gave a rough groan. Firmly he grabbed her hand and moved it away. "You aren't the only one with problems," he growled, his voice sandpapery. "I haven't had sex in so long I'll last maybe fifteen seconds. I have to think about the tactical aspects of this."

The darkness made it easy for her to relax, to smile. "You're looking at me the same way you would a military mission?"

"Damn straight. I have territory to conquer, like these points of interest." He slipped his big hand inside the loose neck of her tank top and gently rubbed his palm over her nipples, making them tighten. The rasp of his rough skin sent a sharp twinge of sensation from her nipples straight to her groin. Her back arched in response, her fingers dug into his shoulder. Primal excitement lit up her nerve endings, firing off such a multitude of responses she instinctively turned into him to seek more of them. His heat seared her from head to toes, drawing her in, comforting and enticing.

"Hills and ravines," he murmured, pressing his lips to her temple as he moved his hand to the small of her back and deftly slipped under the elastic waistband of her sleep pants to stroke the curves of her ass and slide a finger along the cleft there. Helplessly she arched again, her body knowing what it wanted and curving into his touch. Her heart was racing, her breath coming in rapid puffs. Just like that he had her skin so sensitized she felt as if a mild electric shock was running through her. Just like that she was ready for him—but then, she'd been ready for him since the first time he'd kissed her.

"Interesting tight places," he continued, sliding his hand farther down to curve it between her legs. Two big fingers pressed into her; the sensation of being penetrated and stretched was almost overwhelming. She clutched at his broad shoulders, digging her fingers into the pads of muscle. When he moved, he moved fast. There was something she needed to think about, but as long as he was doing what he was doing, she seemed incapable of thought, only of feeling.

Then his fingers were gone, and he deftly turned her onto her back; the sudden emptiness was so sharp she had to fight the irrational surge of anger at the absence of all those sensations. But at least that gave her a little breathing space, and she remembered what she'd wanted to tell him.

"I'm on the pill." She blurted it out, too distracted to think of a lead-in. She had been taking the pill for years—not for birth control, but because otherwise her periods were horribly irregular.

"Good deal. I'd hate to get out of bed and make an emergency run to town to buy condoms. You might not let me back in." She could hear the smile in his voice.

She might not, simply because she might panic. She hadn't made love in years, not since her divorce because in the bitter aftermath she had concluded that sex made women stupid. The obvious solution was to not let anyone close enough that she was even tempted— and she hadn't been, until Morgan.

When she didn't argue with his supposition, he gave a rueful laugh and kissed her. Until he did, she hadn't realized that in the middle of all the great-feeling things he was doing to her, she had really wanted to be kissed. She looped her arms around his neck and gave him back as good as she got, matching his tongue stroke for stroke, loving the taste and hunger and urgency of him. His hands clenched on her sides and he drew back, yanked the tank top off over her head, then came back down on top of her.

Oh. That was the only thought she could muster. He was heavy and warm and the hair on his chest rubbed her tender nipples to achingly tight points.

The weight of his legs nudged her thighs apart and he settled between her legs to push the hard ridge of his erection against her soft cleft. She made an incoherent noise, lifted against him. She had never before felt so . . . *overwhelmed,* so completely undone and turned on. He was big, he was dangerous, and he was about to do things to her she had thought she was done with, likely for the rest of her life. Instead, in his hands, she had gone from zero to ready so fast she was dizzy.

Being made love to like a military campaign was a novel experience. He was thorough in his tactics, laying waste to any possible skittishness she might suffer, overwhelming her with pleasure and moving on to new territory before she recovered enough to protest any particular liberty he might be taking. She tried to reciprocate, but he was having none of it. "No touching," he ordered when she tried to caress his penis through his boxers. "My fuse is too short—"

"Doesn't feel short to me," she murmured, earning a chuckle from him.

"Just save that for next time."

Maybe, she thought, and maybe not. She took her arms from around his neck, stroked them down the muscles in his back, down to his hips where his boxers clung. She slipped her right hand beneath the waistband, drew back enough to murmur, "Why don't you take these off?"

"Not yet."

His refusal only made her more determined to get the boxers off him. Swiftly she tugged them down as far as she could reach, baring part of his ass; he reached for her hand and while he was distracted by that she lifted her left leg high around him and slid her foot down his side until she hooked the waistband and could drag it downward.

He gave a smothered laugh. "Fighting dirty, huh? Guess I'll have to show you what fighting dirty really is."

In a flash he had her sleep pants jerked down and off. His strength was so effortless she could only imagine what he was like when he was in top shape; even now he put most men to shame. She had a momentary qualm about being nude while he wasn't, more vulnerable, but she didn't have time to dwell on it because he slid down between her legs, lifted her thighs over his shoulders, and put his mouth on her.

Oh, God. She arched, her fists knotting the sheet. He definitely knew what he was doing. Oh—*God!* He licked at her, sucked at her. She was flooded with sensation, pleasure that spiked and ebbed, only to spike again. Her muscles clenched and relaxed, clenched and relaxed, caught in a rhythm that grew steadily stronger until she was shaking from the force of it, her body drawn bow-taut and aching. Heat seared her from the inside out until she felt molten.

Her climax roared at her like a freight train, fast and relentless. She gave a hoarse cry when it hit, the pleasure so all-encompassing she could only endure and try to ride it out. At her cry he surged upward, covered her, reached down to fit the head of his penis to her opening and pushed inside while the spasms were still wracking her. She cried out again, a guttural sound of both shock and ecstasy because he was big enough to stretch her to the point of pain, and feeling the bulk and heat of him so deep inside her intensified the rhythmic clenching of pleasure. She needed something to hold on to, to keep from spinning away, and the only rock she could find was him so she locked her legs and arms around him and clung through the tempest triggered by his hard, deep thrusts.

Maybe he did last only fifteen seconds; she didn't know, didn't care. All that mattered was that they were both caught, riding out the fury together. She was in his arms and he was in hers as he shuddered and bucked in release.

Then it was over and they lay there like storm wreckage, breathing hard and trembling, unable to muster the strength to separate. Their bodies were sweaty from exertion, glued together. That was good, she thought dimly, managing to lift one hand and put it on his side. He'd finally shed those damn boxers, though she couldn't have said when. Didn't matter. *Now* was what mattered.

"Holy shit," he muttered weakly, started to lever himself off her, and instead collapsed back with a groan. He was so heavy she could barely breathe, and she didn't care. She turned her face against his neck, inhaling his hot male scent and drawing it deep inside her.

"Stay here a minute." She loved the feel of him on top of her, inside her. Had sex felt like this before? If it had, she didn't remember. She couldn't remember feeling stretched and invaded and possessed; she never would have allowed herself to be possessed. And yet . . . Morgan had done all of that, and she had reveled in it. As intense as the pleasure had been, it had also been mutual, and she had possessed him in turn.

Slowly their heartbeats returned to normal, their lungs stopped heaving in search of oxygen. Her body felt heavy and relaxed, resembling marshmallow more than muscle. He braced himself on his elbows over her, letting her breathe more easily, and nipped at her lower lip. She nipped in return and he threaded his fingers through her hair and began kissing her, slow deep kisses that impossibly ignited a subtle but unmistakable flare.

No way. Even if he was capable, she wasn't. Maybe in an hour or two. Right now she wanted to sleep, though the need to clean up was becoming more pressing with every second. She might need to change the sheets if she had the strength to care.

He stretched an arm upward and turned on the lamp. She blinked against the flare of light, then smiled at the expression on his face. His hair was damp with sweat, his eyes heavy-lidded from pleasure explored and sated, his mouth curved in pure satisfaction. If ever there had been a perfect picture of masculine sexual triumph, he was it. Her own mouth curved in a smile because the triumph was hers; she had put that look on his face, and she didn't care if he ever realized it because this wasn't about keeping score, it was about making each other happy.

Her heart gave a hard thump of recognition, and she curved her hand around his neck to pull him down for another kiss.

Just as their mouths were about to meet, he froze. The look of satisfaction on his face changed to consternation.

Bo frowned in puzzlement. "What's wrong?"

He was motionless, as if he'd come face-to-face with a rattlesnake. Slowly he cut his eyes to the left.

Bo turned her head. Tricks was standing with her muzzle resting on the edge of the bed, her brows beetled above her dark eyes as if she simply couldn't believe what she'd seen her humans doing. The accusation in her eyes as she stared at Morgan was plain: he had to be the instigator because Bo had never done such a thing before.

"Ah, shit." Morgan gently disengaged from Bo's body and rolled to lie beside her, staring up at the ceiling. "I may never get another hard-on in my life."

Chapter 19

He was, happily, very wrong about that.

Bo woke naked in his arms, with her head on his shoulder and her legs tangled with his. The bedcovers were evidently somewhere on the floor, given that they were nowhere in sight. She hadn't been cold at all, not with a living furnace lying next to her. She put her hand on his chest, feeling the crisp hair, the raised scar tissue, the padding of hard muscle. Looking down his long body, she followed the trail of hair down his taut abdomen to his penis and testicles. Men were so interesting, she thought sleepily, with everything out in the open to get in the way and have to be constantly adjusted. How did they even sit down?

His penis twitched, and she blinked in interest, watching closely. Then it began to swell and lengthen, and she smiled. At this signal he was awake, she tilted her head up to find him watching her. "Good morning," she said, then nestled her head back on his shoulder.

"Morning." His morning voice was always deeper than normal, and rusty. His hand smoothed down her bare back. "Damn, I like your outfit. You should wear it more often."

"I wear it every day," she pointed out.

"Yeah, it's the extra layers I don't like."

Just as he was beginning to show her how much he liked her outfit, he jumped and said, "Shit!"

The tone of voice and word choice were dead give-aways. Bo turned her head, knowing what she would see; Tricks once again was standing beside the bed with her muzzle resting on the mattress, staring accusingly at them.

Morgan rolled onto his side and stared at the ceiling. "This has to be what parents feel like when they're getting it on and then see their kid standing there watching them."

She snickered. "Not quite. Tricks won't ask what we're doing."

"Yeah? Look at that expression."

"It's past her breakfast time." Her regular mealtimes were very important to Tricks.

He glanced at the clock. "Just five minutes!"

"She doesn't care. She knows the numbers on the clock, and she knows we're late."

Once he would have scoffed at the idea that a dog knew numbers, but not now. He rolled out of bed and paused to vigorously rub Tricks's ears, which she enjoyed but which in no way got her attention off of food, before going on to the bathroom. Bo sighed in appreciation of the scenery, because such a tight, muscular ass was worthy of an in-depth study.

Then she realized—well, hell; she needed the bathroom too, and she was disconcerted by his occupation of hers. She hadn't shared a bathroom in so long the logistics hadn't occurred to her.

All she could do was roll out of bed, grab some clothes, and trudge down to *his* bedroom and bathroom. Already he'd marked the territory as his: his scent, his clothes, his toiletry items . . . his pistol on the bedside table. She stood in the middle of the room and simply absorbed the excess of testosterone. Yeah, she was loopy this morning, no doubt about it.

Tricks made short work of her inaugural trip outside that morning because she was behind in her schedule. If a dog's attitude could say "hurry up," then Bo was being dog-nagged . . . not that it was the first time. Tricks didn't deal well with tardiness when it came to her food. Still, Bo bent down and hugged her close, closing her eyes in gratitude that she still had Tricks with her, thinking that she might never completely recover from those moments of terror.

By the time Morgan came downstairs, Tricks had been fed and Bo was sitting at the bar sipping her first coffee. Morgan fetched his coffee, straddled the barstool beside hers, clasped her neck, and gave her a long, leisurely kiss. He hadn't shaved, and his stubble was rough on her face. Morning stubble was such an ordinary thing, but she laid her hand along his rough jaw and cherished the prickling against her palm. She leaned into him, enjoying the kiss, the touch, his presence. She felt at ease with him in a way she hadn't since she'd first been attracted to him and tried to fight it. The fight was over, and she'd won. Or lost. Or both. She couldn't make herself care, not today.

He lifted his mouth but kept his hand on her, stroking it down her back. "Do you want to do anything special today?" he asked

She shook her head, a little suspicious. She didn't want him, or anyone, to be "careful" with her, as if she were frail and in danger of going to pieces. Okay, so she'd gone to pieces a bit the night before, but she'd held it together until she was alone in her room. She had cried; she hadn't had a full-bore meltdown.

"I don't need the kid-glove treatment," she said.

He shook his head, a little grin quirking his mouth and his blue eyes glinting at her. "You're the hardest woman to court I've ever seen."

Court? Bemused, Bo considered the idea. First, to stay with his terminology, why would he be trying to court her *today*? He'd gotten what he wanted last night. That was what courting was, wasn't it? An effort to have sex? If he meant it in the old-fashioned sense of the word then . . . then she was at sea, because it meant a focus on the future that she couldn't quite get her head around—not yet, anyway. Deciding to enjoy the moment didn't mean she was completely changing how she approached life, just how she dealt with *him*.

"You've done my laundry," she finally offered.

He laughed as he rubbed his hands up and down her arms. "See what I mean? How many women would consider someone doing laundry to be courting?"

"Probably most women. Laundry's a pain in the butt."

"Well, hell, then throw down a load of underwear and I'll get right on it."

She laughed and said, "I'd rather think about breakfast right now. What sounds good to you?"

Bo was oddly at peace as they went through the morning routine. She had made a decision and she was good with it, whatever happened. Yesterday had taught her that there was no way she could isolate herself from life and the bad things, and she couldn't predict or prepare for them; all she could do was live.

She might not have the future with Morgan, but she had the now, and that was sufficient. Suddenly she felt free: free to touch him whenever she wanted—which was often—free to walk around in whatever state of dress or undress she wanted, free to *want*. Wanting and denying herself had been a brand of torture; wanting and being able to fulfill that want was delicious.

They had made love twice more during the night; he was very good at it, and very focused and disciplined, all of which translated into something great for her. She was a little sore this morning but also infinitely relaxed. She didn't torment herself wondering if it was just sex to him while it was making love to her because knowing wouldn't change a thing. She could analyze something to death without a single detail being affected. Tomorrow might be different, but today was today.

After they'd had breakfast and cleaned up the kitchen, she putzed around tidying things that weren't very messy to begin with, then she went upstairs. Taking him at his word, she threw a load of laundry down. By balling several garments together she got enough heft and weight to get some distance on it, and a pair of jeans landed neatly across his head as he sat in front of the TV, feet up and channel-hopping in classic male form. She expected him to bolt upright, but instead he laughed, leaned his head back, and said, "I wondered if you'd jump on that."

"Consider it jumped on."

While he started the laundry, she changed the sheets on the bed, a little amused and turned on because they definitely needed changing. The dirty sheets went over the balcony too; he'd know what to do with them. Delighted by the game of throwing things over the balcony, Tricks began running and barking, then grabbed a stuffed animal and slung it around to kill it. Everyone else was having fun, so why shouldn't she?

Morgan grabbed one leg of the toy and began playing tug of war with her; while they were occupied, Bo wandered to her desk and stood looking down at it.

She had a tech-writing project she could work on. She studied it, thought about it, but couldn't make herself plant her butt in the chair. For the first time in forever she had absolutely no interest in work. As traumatic as the day before had been, and as eventful as the *night* before had been, she thought she needed a day to do nothing but relax and enjoy the life she had . . . somehow. Doing something. The question was: what?

She was saved by Tricks, who abruptly abandoned the game with Morgan, went to the door and gave Bo her "Well?" look. The first trip outside in the mornings was for necessity, not walking, and now it was past time for her first walk of the day.

Morgan armed himself, she got the house keys and cell phone, and out they went.

The day seemed to call for a long, rambling walk, much longer than usual. At first they didn't talk; the morning was warm but not yet uncomfortably so, the greenery was still fresh and damp from last night's dew, and the sky overhead was a clear blue except for cotton-ball clouds drifting by. It always amazed her how noisy nature was; the birds were singing so wildly they sounded drunk, the bushes rustled with what she hoped wasn't a rabbit because she didn't want Tricks to give chase, the trees swayed in a light breeze. Bees droned, insects buzzed, arguments broke out between birds.

Morgan took her hand and they walked side by side when they could; when they couldn't, he kept hold of her hand but walked in front, his head swiveling back and forth as he looked for trouble in any form, reptile, rodent, whatever might take Tricks's attention. Though she'd been walking this path without incident for years, he used his grip on her hand to steady her as she stepped over logs and rocks.

She felt vaguely guilty, as if she was playing hooky.

"I don't know how to relax," she confessed after thinking about it for a minute. "I feel as if I should be doing something."

He laced his fingers with hers. Having him hold her hand felt new and exciting as well as . . . comfortable. She was comfortable with him. That struck her as sexy, which told her she had it bad when she could equate even comfortable with sexy. She suspected that if he had knock- knees, she'd find that sexy too.

He brushed aside a bush branch for her to pass. "You've worked hard since you moved here, digging yourself out of a hole. That takes guts. But I've noticed you aren't a sit-down-and-veg-in-front-of-the-TV kind of woman."

"Vegging in front of the TV drove you nuts in no time, so you can't say anything."

"I'm not much for staying indoors. When I did get some down time, I'd try to go fishing, but that's not on the table for now."

Tricks darted out of sight behind a mossy boulder, and Bo pulled her hand free to run forward to keep her in sight, make sure she hadn't found a snake or a skunk. Instead Tricks was standing in front of a weed with a yellow bloom on top, staring at a bumblebee as it droned from one flowering weed to another. "Come here," Bo said. "Don't eat the bee." Tricks ignored her and continued to watch the bee until Bo said sternly, "Young lady!" That warning was the second tier leading to getting into serious trouble, and with a wag of her tail that said she'd seen enough, Tricks trotted back to the trail.

"Did you know bumblebees can't fly if their muscles are colder than eighty-six degrees?" Morgan said; he too was watching the bee. He folded her hand in his again as soon as she rejoined him.

Bo blinked. "I've seen them fly when the weather is colder than that."

"They warm up their thoracic muscles by shivering. Can take up to five minutes."

"Supposedly they shouldn't be able to fly at all."

"That was an error in calculation. Bumblebees go into dynamic stall—they create a little vortex—plus their short wings displace a disproportionate amount of air."

That was interesting, but the subject matter made her squint up at him. "And you know about the aerodynamics of bumblebees because—?"

"Just something interesting that was covered in flight school."

She was silent a moment as she digested this new insight into him. Going to flight school logically meant he was a pilot. "What do you fly?"

"Helicopter and small fixed-wing. Flying's okay. I don't like it as much as I do the water." He answered as casually as if it were no big deal, as if flying helicopters and small airplanes were commonplace. Maybe it was in his world; it wasn't in hers. In her world, people drove. She knew only one other person who could fly small planes. But she wasn't surprised by this facet of him, or the scope of his experience; she'd known from the beginning that he navigated very deep waters. Was this how a military wife felt? Or the wife of a firefighter, or a cop? As if his experiences were so dramatic and diametrically opposed to hers? How did people find common ground?

She could drive herself crazy trying to find the answer—because there wasn't one—or she could just let things be. She opted for her new zen attitude. They had slept together; that was the extent of their relationship. For now, that was enough. She might not feel the same way tomorrow, but she'd find that out tomorrow. In the meantime, she wanted to know more about something he seemed enthusiastic about.

"Where do you fish?"

"The Potomac, when I'm home from a mission. I try to get back to Florida a couple of times a year, do some deep-sea fishing, hit some bass lakes. Not that I get that much down time, because even when we aren't on missions, we're training our asses off, but I still hang on to my boat."

"What kind of boat do you have?"

"Just an old fishing boat I named the *Shark*. When I get released to go back out in public, we'll take her out if you like fishing." He tilted his head back, eyed the pieces of sky visible through the tree limbs. The woods weren't so thick that walking was difficult, but the shade was nice.

"I don't know about fishing, I've never tried it, but I love the water." She kept her tone casual despite the leap her heart rate made at his reference to the future. She wouldn't bet on it—but she liked that he'd offered.

"That's right, you're a swimmer. You don't get much swimming around here, do you?"

"More than you'd think," she replied, thinking about the secluded lake where she took Tricks in the summer.

"Yeah? Where?"

"I'll show you later." The lake would be a nice surprise for later in the day, maybe with a picnic lunch. It was a pretty place, and the lake was big enough for some serious swimming, though the water was so cold she could stand it only during the hottest weather. Tricks didn't care, she just loved to swim. The cold water was probably what kept snakes away, because she'd never seen a snake around or in the lake. If she had, likely she'd have enrolled Tricks in the nearest Y—or tried. Given Tricks's track record, she was betting on her girl getting people to bypass rules and regulations.

"Do you own all this land?" he asked at one point. They were at least a mile from the house, probably more, though they'd walked at least twice that because their route hadn't been a straight line.

"No, I own ten acres. I *think* this belongs to some-one who lives in Charleston, but I'm not sure. Mayor Buddy owns a chunk of land close to here, and to the east the land belongs to Kenny Michaels's folks. You've met him; he's Daina's boyfriend."

"I remember. So . . . we're trespassing."

"Technically. The land isn't fenced or posted. I'll walk it until the owner, whoever it is, tells me not to walk it, and then I'll stop. I'm careful not to leave trash or anything like that."

He tsked. "And you an officer of the law."

"I know, it's shameful." She smiled up at him, which for some reason made him stop, plant his hands on her hips, and pull her in to him for a long, hungry kiss.

With a picnic in mind, Bo made some sandwiches, packed a small cooler with bottles of water and Naked Pig, added some chips and Oreo cookies, and said,

"Come on, let's load up the Jeep. There's a place I want to show you."

He looked at the cooler. "We're going to be gone long enough that we need supplies?"

"I plan on eating while I'm there. I thought you might too." While he loaded the cooler and, at her request, two folding camp chairs, she packed up some food and water for Tricks, and got a quilt and several towels. She folded the towels inside the quilt so Morgan wouldn't see them.

Mindful that Tricks would insist on the passenger seat, Bo tossed the keys to Morgan. "You drive, and I'll crawl in back."

"Tricks wins again," he said, grinning.

"You bet."

When they were all settled, with Tricks looking very pleased at being in her seat after mostly riding in the back of the Tahoe since Morgan had started driving again, Bo pointed across her yard. "Go that way."

A blue glance slanted her way. "Cross country, huh?"

"It's a fairly easy drive, though I wouldn't try it in a car."

He handled the Jeep off-road as if he'd done it a million times, which he probably had, in various vehicles. There were no truly challenging areas, just places where he had to angle the vehicle to cross a dip, and one section where the only option was to thread the Jeep through a jumble of boulders that they couldn't go around because the trees were too thick.

In ten minutes, they topped the crest of a rolling hill and there was the lake, shiny and blue, about twelve acres in size. To the north, at the shallow end, was where the cold spring fed into the lake. Large sycamores and black oaks provided plenty of shade on the banks, which was nice during the worst of the summer heat. The weeds were knee high in some places, because the lake wasn't a manicured and maintained area. To the east a large rocky outcropping rose like a wall, blocking access from that direction.

Morgan stopped the Jeep and just stared at the lake for a minute. "Water," he said finally, with something like reverence in his tone. "You didn't tell me there was a lake."

"It's a cold-water lake, so I don't let Tricks swim until about this time every year. It's still too cold for me; I'll give it another couple of weeks before I try."

He still hadn't looked away from the water. "I'm going in."

"Don't say you weren't warned. If you want to freeze your butt off, that's your decision." She, however, was going to sit on the quilt on the bank and throw the ball for Tricks to retrieve.

He set the Jeep in motion, bumping down the hill. When he got closer to the bank, he drove back and forth several times to flatten the weeds in a nice-sized area so the way to the water was clear and they had a place to spread the quilt. Tricks recognized where she was and knew she was going to swim, so she started woofing in encouragement. Morgan began playing into it, wheeling the Jeep in wide sweeping turns while Tricks played cheerleader. Bo sat in back wondering if they were ever going to get out of the Jeep.

Finally he stopped by a sycamore tree, and they unloaded the Jeep. Tricks raced back and forth between Bo and the lake bank, barking to show she was ready for her tennis ball to hit the water. "Just cool your jets," Bo advised her. "I'll get your ball in a minute."

When the quilt was unfolded and Morgan saw the towels, he grinned. "You knew I'd be going in."

"I suspected," she said drily.

"Any snakes?" He was stripping his shirt off over his head as he spoke.

"Not that I've ever seen," she replied as he dropped his shirt on the quilt and began pulling off his shoes and socks. His bare shoulders gleamed in the dappled sunlight there under the big sycamore. A lot of times his expression was either blank or guarded, but not today; enjoyment shone in his eyes, and his mouth was curved in a smile.

"Underwater snags?"

"Stay away from the south end, it's rough there." She paused. "I don't know about turtles, so be careful of your dangly parts."

He laughed as he shucked down his jeans and stepped out of them, leaving him clad only in his boxers. "I'm keeping my dangly parts corralled. I can't set up a secure perimeter to make sure we're completely private, so no skinny dipping."

Tricks was still impatiently dancing around. Bo got the tennis ball and walked down to the water with man and dog. "I fully expect you'll push yourself," she said to Morgan, "so give me a signal to look for if you get in trouble." From her own competitive swimming experience she knew that people who were truly drowning couldn't yell for help because they couldn't breathe.

His eyes narrowed at the idea that a big, bad, whatever-he-was might need help in the water. She imagined a lot of his training was in the water, and normally he could probably swim rings around her, but despite the sleek muscles she could see rippling in his mostly bare body, she hadn't been shot and he had. He might think her offer was funny—or insulting—but she didn't care.

Opting for diplomacy, he said, "Babe, I never want you to risk yourself trying to help me."

She snorted. "Oh, how sweet. Let me check my give-a-shit meter to see where that registers. Nope, nothing there. Sorry." She crossed her arms and stared at him, gaze level. The "babe" wasn't going to distract her, though she suspected he'd thrown that in to either piss her off or soften her, and he didn't care which. Too bad: this wasn't about whether or not she was capable, it was about whether or not he could admit that he might still need help. When he'd first arrived, he hadn't had any choice about accepting help, and she suspected that made him a little touchy about it now.

He could simply ignore her and wade into the water. She couldn't stop him, and they both knew that. But last night . . . last night had either forged a bond between them, or it hadn't. If it had, he would acknowledge that she needed to have a signal to look for. If it hadn't, she needed to know that too.

She could feel herself getting chilled inside, waiting for his answer. Okay, so she wasn't completely zen. This wasn't an ultimatum though; whatever he answered, she would still enjoy him while he was here. The only change was that she would *know* it was temporary, and somehow she would manage.

He stepped closer and cupped her chin in his palm, his thumb rubbing along her jawline. She looked up at him and had one of those moments of acute awareness of how big he was, over a head taller than she was. The blue of his eyes darkened as he studied her face. Leaning down, he brushed his mouth over hers, light as a whisper. "I'll hold up a clenched fist," he said, then released her and turned away.

When he waded into the water, Tricks bounded in beside him with a surplus of enthusiasm that sent up a huge splash, then she began swimming strongly for where she was certain Bo would throw the ball. Obediently Bo threw the tennis ball so it landed just ahead of her; Tricks grabbed the ball in triumph and started back for the bank, but then her golden head turned sharply as she noticed that Morgan wasn't coming with her. Instead he was stroking smoothly through the water, his dark head sleek as a seal's. His arms pistoned steadily, but there wasn't a lot of splash, just the flash of his skin and a small bit of turbulence in his wake.

Alarmed, knowing what was about to happen, Bo called, "Tricks! Here!"

Ignoring Bo, Tricks turned and went after him, swimming as hard as she could. She even dropped the tennis ball and left it floating in the water.

"Crap," Bo said sharply to herself. She knew exactly what Tricks was doing, but a dog couldn't swim as fast as a human who was fairly good, and Morgan was more than fairly good. He wasn't going for speed, but his strokes and kicks were powerful and smooth, eating up distance.

She began jerking off her shoes and jeans, steeling herself to go into that cold lake, because her in the water was the only thing that would pull Tricks away from Morgan in the water. Trying again, she cupped her hands around her mouth and yelled, "*Tricks!*" as loud as she could.

Morgan was already over a hundred yards away, maybe two hundred, but he must have heard her because abruptly he stopped and turned in the water to face her. She doubted he paid any attention to her, though, because Tricks was coming right at him, swimming so hard she was leaving a wake.

Tricks reached Morgan, and though Bo didn't have binoculars, she didn't need them to know what happened because she knew her dog. She gripped her head with both hands as Tricks latched on to Morgan's arm and began towing him toward the bank. She was "saving" him. She'd done the same thing to Bo the first time Bo had gone swimming with her, and it had taken several trips to the lake before she relaxed her vigil.

"Oh, good Lord," Bo muttered. She could only imagine what Morgan was thinking.

After living with Tricks for two and a half years Bo was seldom surprised anymore by anything that the dog did, but there was still the occasional mind-boggling moment. In retrospect, she could follow Tricks's reasoning: when Morgan had arrived, he'd been weak and unable to take care of himself. There-fore, he was someone Tricks needed to watch over. Seeing him in the water, without realizing how much he had recovered, had triggered her protective instinct and she had gone after him thinking he was literally in over his head.

Bo waited anxiously for them to reach the bank. That was a long way for Tricks to swim without a rest; she could retrieve her tennis ball thrown in the water for hours, but that was with her feet touching ground at the end of every retrieve. As they got closer, she could see that Morgan was helping her, stroking with his free arm and keeping an eye on her. If Tricks got too tired, he'd make sure she didn't get in trouble and made it safely back.

Finally they reached shallow water and he stood, but he kept Tricks close until she was touching the bottom too. Tricks kept pulling on his arm, insisting that he get out of the water. When they waded out onto the flattened weeds, Tricks finally released his arm so he could straighten. He wiped the water out of his face with his free hand, then Tricks showered him again as she vigorously shook and slung water everywhere.

His chest was rising and falling with deep breaths as he looked at Bo. She shrugged and willed herself not to get teary-eyed, but really, Tricks's valor made her feel misty. "Such a good girl," she crooned, bending to pet Tricks and praise her.

Morgan petted her too, telling her thank you, then he shook his head as he met Bo's eyes. "I've been saved," he said wryly. "Reckon she'll let me go back in?"

Chapter 20

Before Bo could answer, tricks realized she'd left her ball in the water and went charging back into the lake. Bo started after her, taking two steps into the water—damn, it was cold!—but Morgan put his hand on her arm. "She looks okay. If she gets tired, I'll go get her."

Bo stepped back out of the water but kept her gaze on Tricks. Morgan stood beside her, keeping watch too. He said, "Has she done that before?"

She nodded. "The first time I swam with her. She got such a look of horror on her face when she saw me in the water. She was only about four or five months old, but she swam like a champ. Thank goodness I wasn't very far out, because she was still just a puppy. I don't know if her strength would have held out."

"Don't you know she was thinking, 'Oh shit, Mom's in the water and if she sinks I'm screwed.'"

Startled, Bo laughed out loud. "She doesn't know swear words."

"Betcha."

The idea of puppy Tricks swearing to herself was priceless. Bo was still chuckling as together they watched Tricks retrieve her ball and turn, swimming for the bank. She wasn't going as fast as she normally did, but neither did she seem to be in any distress. Now that she had Morgan safely on land, she wore her normal jaunty, happy expression. It was amazing how a dog could smile with a ball in its mouth.

"The guys would rag my ass forever if this got out," Morgan observed.

"Oh, good, I have something I can blackmail you with." Tricks was touching the bottom now and bounding out, sending water flying everywhere, so Bo backed up out of the spray area. Morgan stayed where he was because he couldn't get any wetter. Tricks gave him a quick look of disdain—evidently for being so foolish as to go swimming—and took the ball to Bo.

Morgan scratched his jaw. "I think I've been dissed."

"Most definitely." Bo didn't take the offered ball, instead saying, "You need to rest a few minutes, princess, that was a long swim. Just a few minutes, okay?

Nose around and see what you can smell." After a few seconds Tricks dropped the ball and trotted off to sniff out something interesting.

Morgan had turned back and was looking out over the lake. Bo could feel him wanting to get back in the water, but he waited, not knowing how Tricks would react. For Bo's part, she was content for him to stand there, because just looking at him made her hormones whisper, "Oh man, he's *fine.*" As good as he looked now, with water dripping off his lean, muscled body, she could only imagine what he was like at full strength. For him, "weak" was most people's normal.

The scar on his chest wasn't the only scar he bore; there was a white slash across his right triceps, a dark discoloring along his left thigh that looked like road rash, a jagged scar under his left shoulder blade, even a raised white slash of scar tissue on top of his left foot. She wondered if all the injuries on his left side had occurred at the same time. And all she could see right now were those on his back; she hadn't noticed any on his front last night, but then she'd been preoccupied with other things—plus the light had been off.

Her gaze lingered on the way his wet boxers were hanging low on his hips and clinging to his ass. The muscle definition in his legs was mouthwatering. Come to think of it, there wasn't anything about him that wasn't mouthwatering, but those legs looked as strong as trees. Thick pads of muscle lined the indentation of his spine, laced along his ribs. She remembered that when he'd arrived his arms had looked thin; they certainly didn't now. She didn't know what he'd been doing while she was at the police station, but she suspected he hadn't rested much, not to fight his way back this far.

He had the body of a warrior. She didn't *try* to forget what he was, but in the day-to-day normality of the routine they'd established, one reality would sink out of sight below the other reality. Yet every time she'd almost forgotten, something would happen to remind her. Yesterday it had been that moment when he'd taken Kyle down, the savagery in his gaze, the almost absent way he'd slammed Kyle's head into the pavement to knock him out. Today it was seeing the scars he bore. Since the moment when he'd choked her, he'd been careful to keep himself under control and on low intensity, but by then it was too late. The people in town might have bought it, but she knew the truth.

"You've been really careful since you've been here, haven't you?" she asked as she bent down to retrieve her jeans. "Simmer instead of boil. You walk a tightrope when you're stateside, don't you?"

He didn't have to ask what she meant and he didn't deny it. He shrugged and said, "For the most part I don't have to because I'm with other men who are the same. That's my job. But when I'm in the real world, I can ratchet it down with no problem—except for the minor slip when you shook me awake."

"Minor." She made a scoffing noise as she shimmied into her jeans. He'd scared the crap out of her, and he could so easily have crushed her throat. "You could have killed me."

"*Could* have. But I didn't, and I didn't hurt you, so that makes it minor. Scared you, though. I'm sorry about that."

His tone was absent. She looked up from zipping her jeans to see that his attention was riveted on what she was doing. His expression was so hungry that her heart skipped a beat and she froze, trying to get a handle on her immediate response to nothing more than that, just an expression. She felt breathless and turned on; a minute ago her wet feet had been cold from the lake water, but one look from him was all it took for heat to wash over her from her toes to her head.

Her cheeks were hot as she got her shoes. She wasn't shy but she'd never been a flirt, never wanted to flirt. Why not just be up front and save everyone time and trouble? But now she wanted to tease him and get him as revved up as she felt, though if she went by his actions last night he didn't need much revving.

She took a deep breath and composed herself, remembering that he'd wanted a long swim. "If you want to go back in the water, I can hold Tricks to keep her from saving you again. For all I know, if you go back in the water, she might write you off as wasted effort."

"She would, too," he muttered. "But, yeah, I'd like a longer swim. I'm way out of shape."

"How long could you swim before?"

"Fifteen miles or so. Like I said, we trained our asses off."

Fifteen . . . *miles*? He could swim farther than it was from her house to Hamrickville? She said faintly, "Yeah, I can see how just swimming a couple of miles would be disappointing."

"The first couple of miles is just fun. After ten miles, it stops being fun and starts being work."

She called Tricks to her and held her firmly while Morgan waded back into the lake, made a shallow dive, and began crossing the lake with strong, smooth strokes of his arms. Tricks strained against her hold, whining low in her throat with her dark gaze fixed on Morgan's disappearing form, but Bo reassured her that he was all right and after a minute she took her cue from Bo's attitude.

While keeping a weather eye on Morgan for the raised fist that would signal distress—and, oh shit, she hoped she didn't have to go into that cold water, though she would if she had to—she began throwing the ball into the lake for Tricks to retrieve, combining her two favorite things, retrieving and swimming. After a while the sun got too hot on her face and arms and she called Tricks out, let her shake, then toweled her off and spread a dry towel next to the quilt for Tricks to lie down on. Morgan had stopped swimming up and down the lake and was gliding toward them, his arms moving steadily, so she guessed the aquatics were at an end for the day.

He was breathing fast as he waded out. She met him at the edge of the water with a towel. "Thanks," he said, rubbing it roughly over his head, then swiping at his chest and arms and legs. Going to where he'd dropped his clothes, he stepped out of his wet boxers and pulled on his jeans commando. His movements were economical, not giving her much time to enjoy the view, but she took what she could get and what she got was an eyeful. Boy parts weren't pretty but good God almighty, Morgan's were impressive. She felt breathless remembering lying pinned beneath him while he stroked in and out of her body. What was she supposed to do with this feeling? They'd had sex; neither of them had made any promises, however vague, to each other.

He dropped down on the quilt and lay spread-eagled, his chest rising and falling with his deep breaths. "God, that felt good."

She supposed some things just needed to *be*, without any great introspection or examination, so she knelt beside the cooler, opened it, and pulled out a couple of Naked Pigs. "Here, you can celebrate with a beer. Ready for a sandwich?"

"Or two," he said, sitting up to take the beers from her and open them while she got out the sandwiches. He turned up his bottle and drank deep. He'd been out long enough that the sun had brought deeper color to the tops of his shoulders and his arms. He sat with his legs drawn up and his arms draped over his spread knees, looking out over the lake with his gaze narrowed against the sunlight glinting on the water, the neck of the beer bottle hooked between two fingers. His posture couldn't have gotten any more "guy," and it was startlingly attractive.

She sat tailor-fashion at an angle to him, getting the food out of the cooler and dividing it between them. She poured Tricks's food into a bowl, and the sound brought Tricks jumping up from her towel, tail wagging. For a couple of minutes there was silence except for the sounds of man, woman, and dog paying attention to their food.

Food always tasted better on a picnic, Bo thought, even when the food was just a sandwich and a cold beer. Whether it was the sun, the fresh air, or the peace and quiet, her taste buds were either more sensitive, or more easily satisfied. And she had Morgan, and Tricks—for now, for today.

Tricks was too tired to try to guilt them out of their food, so she returned to her towel and curled up for a doggy nap, completely satisfied with her day so far. Morgan wolfed down his first sandwich but took his time on the second one. Bo was comfortable with the silence; she finished most of her sandwich, ate a cookie, then stretched out on the quilt with a sigh of contentment. She could take a nap, she thought drowsily, rolling over to pillow her head on her crossed arms.

"Did I take advantage last night?" Morgan asked, his deep voice taking command and snapping her out of her soporific mood. She opened one eye to study him, found him watching her with that piercing, intent look of his.

She considered that, rejected the idea that she hadn't been capable of knowing her own mind. "I could have said no if I'd wanted to. I didn't want to." She yawned.

"That's kind of how I was looking at it, too, but I wanted to make sure."

"I won't lie; yesterday was a nightmare. I was upset, I was grieving—"

"Grieving?" He looked surprised at the word.

She waved it away. She didn't want to explain that she'd been grieving the loss of her blinders, that now she saw how she'd deluded herself into thinking she could keep her heart and Tricks safe, that every day they were perched precariously on the cliff of chance, and chance could send them toppling over. Instead she said, "In my mind, she was dead. Even when I knew she wasn't, getting over it wasn't easy. For a minute . . . for a minute I was in hell. But—" Her tone got stronger. "But crying didn't turn me into a weakling. I was crying, that's all."

He reached out and wrapped his big rough hand around her ankle. "I never thought of you as a weakling. But I've never said I understand how women think, and I had to allow for the possibility that you thought . . . shit, I'm confusing myself. If you're okay with last night, then that's good."

"I'm okay with it." Because she could, she laid her hand on his bare shoulder, then rubbed it down his back. "More than okay." She paused, then said, "So . . . why are you blowing sunshine up my skirt? If I were wearing one, that is."

He released her ankle and in silence finished his sandwich, then lay back on the quilt beside her and rested his beer bottle on his bare stomach. "What makes you think I'm blowing sunshine?" he asked as he got comfortable, just when she'd thought he wasn't going to answer.

"Please. When was the last time you were uncertain about anything, especially a woman? You think I haven't been paying attention to how you operate since you've been here?"

He patted her thigh. "Can't put anything over on you, can I?" He didn't sound worried about it; in fact, there was a definite note of satisfaction there.

"So what was the point?"

"Just trying to make you think you had a little bit of control," he said, then burst out laughing when she swiftly pinched him. "Ow!"

"You deserved it." She gave a contented sigh and closed her eyes again, basking in the peace, the light breeze rustling through the tree limbs overhead and changing the dapple pattern of the sunshine. Tricks was sound asleep, resting after her exertions. Morgan was stretched out just inches away, and his presence let something relax deep inside her, as if she knew he was on guard and she was safe. She moved her hand so she was touching his side and went to sleep.

Morgan didn't want to move and maybe wake up Bo, but he still managed to lift his head enough to take the occasional sip of beer. No way was he letting the Naked Pig get warm on him. It felt nice to just lie there, pleasantly tired from the three times he'd made love to Bo last night as well as the strenuous swim he'd taken. He'd definitely been pushing himself, but he was still happy with the distance considering how long it had been since he'd done any training.

When he was on the job, the physical and skill training was almost nonstop. You didn't learn how to shoot and keep the same level of skill without constant practice. You didn't swim fifteen miles, not get in the water for three months, and assume you could still swim the same distance. Staying on top in skill and condition required constant training. Now that he knew about the lake, he intended to be in it almost every day, preferably with Bo here to keep an eye out because even expert swimmers could get in trouble. On the job, he didn't bat an eye at always having a teammate to back him up, but part of him rebelled at the idea of Bo possibly putting herself at risk to help him if he cramped up or something like that.

His reluctance to endanger her, even in theory, said something. He'd worked with women before and not once worried about them because they were women; he worried about the welfare of his team in general. Of course, they'd been professionals who knew the possibilities and odds. Bo wasn't in his line of work; she was one of the ones he served to protect.

He turned his head to look at her, sleeping by his side with her hand just touching him. That light touch made his chest feel too full to hold his heart; the realization was startling, and a little bit panic-making. Damn. Maybe he'd been telling the truth when he'd told Kyle he was in love with her, though he wasn't sure he knew exactly what love was or what it felt like. He liked her; he liked her probably more—no, *definitely* more—than he'd ever liked any other woman. He'd been hot for a particular woman, sure, but hot for and liking were two different things and the way they combined now knocked him for a loop.

He'd been engaged, but he hadn't been in love. He'd even been vaguely relieved when things had gone off the rails, which said a lot. Still, he wasn't a navel-gazer and he'd never spent a lot of time thinking about what had gone wrong or what he wanted in a woman, or if he would ever truly want to spend the rest of his life with one particular woman. He had the GO-Teams for money and excitement and purpose, he had female companionship when he wanted it, and sex when that was all he wanted. If anyone had asked, he'd have said that wasn't a bad way for a man to live.

Except—now there was Bo, and it mattered. All of it. If he wanted sex—hell to the yeah—he wanted it to be with her. If he wanted companionship, he wanted it with her. He liked the routine of her orderly house, the lack of fussiness with which she met life. She didn't do dramatics, she held it together, she coped. That was why her devastation at almost losing Tricks had hit him so hard. He'd have done anything to take that look out of her eyes. He hadn't been certain she wouldn't kick his ass out of her bed, considering how hard she'd been working to keep him at a distance, but instead she had turned to him so . . . well, hell, *sweetly* was the only word he could come up with to describe it. The woman was turning him into a fucking poet.

Okay, he could deal with that—as long as he got her again.

Today . . . something was different today. She was softer, more relaxed, more content. If last night had been the cause, then he'd have a great time keeping that look of contentment there, but his ego wasn't big enough for him to assume his dick was a magic cure-all. Whatever was going on with her, it was something she'd worked out for herself, and whether or not she'd ever tell him about that "something" was up in the air.

That was another thing: she hadn't wanted to rehash what had happened last night, hadn't gone over every detail fretting about what meant what. In his experience, women did, and it drove him nuts. Fucking meant fucking. End of story. But not Bo; she hadn't brought it up at all, which had forced him to do it.

Maybe it all meant something.

He wasn't worried about figuring things out; he had time. Correction: He hoped he had time. He hadn't heard from Axel except that one letter, but truthfully that had been one letter more than he'd expected. He had no way of pointing Axel in any direction, so they had to wait for the bad actors to make a move—and so far they were sitting tight. Why wouldn't they? Unless they knew he'd remembered whatever it was he didn't remember, they had nothing to lose by waiting. They wouldn't move until they had to move, which left him and Axel sitting on their thumbs.

What if he got a call from Axel tomorrow that the trap had been sprung, the assholes caught, and he should report back to the teams ASAP? For the first time ever, he didn't want to go. He wanted to have more time with Bo.

If Axel knew, he'd shit bricks. Despite some logical reasons for sending Morgan to recuperate at Bo's, mostly he'd done it out of spite, and Morgan knew it. That was Axel. He was mean and immature and vindictive to everyone he perceived as being against him, which was balanced by being very good at his job and almost pathologically loyal to "his" men. He would never have sent Morgan here if he'd had any inkling that it might cost him one of his team leaders.

His own thought startled Morgan. Would he leave the GO-Teams to be with Bo? Would he have to? Some of the team members were married, and they made it work. Some of them got married and then divorced, but didn't that happen to people no matter what kind of job they had?

Okay, double fuck, was he really thinking what he was thinking?

He looked at her sleeping face, the wide mouth relaxed and soft, her dark lashes fans beneath those big dark eyes that were closed now, but he wouldn't be a bit surprised if she opened them and smiled at him. And if she did, he knew what his reaction would be. He'd have her naked in no time, and Tricks would probably be giving them that reproachful look again.

Triple fuck, since he *was* thinking what he was thinking, he had a big decision to make: did he come clean about Axel's plan to set up him as bait that could backfire and draw some real danger here, or did he hope it never came to that? The last option was the easiest, but it was probably the stupidest.

It was his call, and he had to make it.

Chapter 21

When bo woke up, she gave a little hum of relaxed contentment, stretched, then sat up and raided the cooler for a bottle of water. As she twisted the cap off, she asked Morgan, who was lying with his arms crossed behind his head, "How long did I sleep?"

"About an hour." His mouth quirked and his eyes glinted with humor. "You don't snore, and I didn't see you drool, but I can't rule that out."

"Everyone drools," she replied comfortably and took a deep drink of water. "Do you snore?" She stretched to get Tricks's water bowl and poured some water into it because Tricks had raised her head at Bo's voice, signaling that her nap was at an end too. Tricks immediately got to her feet and came over for a drink.

"Depends." He ran his hand down Tricks's back. "If I'm on a mission, no, probably because I never go into really deep sleep. But when I get home after crossing so many time zones that I don't know what day it is, I definitely snore."

"Huh. I guess snoring could be dangerous when you're on a mission." She'd never thought of snoring in those terms before; how odd and disturbing and a little sad that something so human could, under the conditions he considered normal, be a threat to his life.

"Depends on where we are. Sometimes we're in a safe house in a city, so snoring isn't a big deal."

"Can you tell me what you do?"

"Some of it. Most of it is classified." He squinted at the lake as if considering what to say, how much he *could* say. "I'm the leader of a GO-Team. GO stands for global offensive; we get sent wherever we're needed, whether it's legal or not, which is the main reason it's classified. Maybe we have to defuse a developing situation, take a power player out of action, things like that. Don't ever Google anything I'm telling you or it could land you—and me—in a world of shit. But mostly you."

"Promise." She didn't ask what taking someone "out of action" entailed, but she had a good guess, and Googling anything about the GO-Teams would be an act of idiocy.

That was what his life was like, where the least thing could trigger extreme action and reaction. She couldn't imagine the pressure and stress, though probably every person who was in that line of work was an adrenaline junkie, which meant the man beside her likely was too. To test that theory she asked, "Do you jump out of planes?"

"If I have to. Not my favorite thing."

That was kind of reassuring; she'd always wondered what brain fart drove people to parachute for pleasure.

She thought of something else. "Set explosives?"

"Got an expert who does that, but I know how."

"Ride motorcycles?"

"*Hell* no! Those fuckers'll kill you."

His vehemence made her burst out laughing. "And those other things won't? And, uh, are you forgetting why you're here in the first place?"

He scratched his nose. "I guess it depends on what you're used to." Shrewdly he added, "If you're trying to find out if I like the action, the answer is: to some extent. It can be a hell of a lot of fun, kicking ass and blowing shit up. Mostly I like knowing that what I do makes a difference, but I like a lot of things about being stateside too. Plumbing that works. The food. We have the best junk food, you know that?"

He was definitely a connoisseur of junk food; his fondness for it approached fervor. "Speaking of junk food, we have Oreos."

"Bring 'em on."

Alerted by the rustling of the package, Tricks ran over to check out the cookies, but they were a no-no for her. Bo distracted her with a doggy treat, a nice edible chew bone. Tricks snatched the bone and returned to her towel to devote herself to its destruction. Morgan wolfed down a couple of cookies and chased them with a beer, then said, "We need to talk."

His tone, his expression, both made her uneasy. She looked down at her cookie to hide her foreboding. Experience told her conversations that began this way were never good; that was how her ex-husband had begun his explanation of how he needed more than she could provide, how a stepfather or two had said good-bye, how her mother had announced her first remarriage. Was now when Morgan told her not to get too attached, that anything they had was temporary and he'd be going back to his exciting job when the time came? She knew that; he didn't have to spell it out. And knowing it was one thing, but she didn't want to *hear* it, she didn't want him to say, "We'll have a good time, baby, but then it's *adios.*"

"No, we don't," she said briskly. "I get it."

"Trust me," he growled. "You don't."

She rolled her eyes. "So this isn't the part where you tell me you'll be leaving—"

"I want to—"

"—and that's good because I really don't want to hear it!" she ended, the words clipped off hard and flat.

"Bo. Shut up."

At his hard tone she looked up, her eyes flashing with temper, but he seized her by the back of the neck and kissed her, his mouth hungry and fierce. For a second she held herself stiff, not responding, but he wasn't having any of that and dragged her across him so her butt was on the quilt between his thighs and her legs were draped over his. He tilted her head back and kissed her until she softened a bit; she still didn't kiss him back, but she was accepting his mouth. His hand delved under her shirt and closed over her breast, deftly pinching her nipple until it formed a tight bud, the sensation sharp but not quite painful. Pleasure arrowed straight down between her legs, making her tighten and clench as if he were inside her, damn him.

She didn't want to flash back to how all of that had felt, but she couldn't stop the memory or her response. She had wanted him all day—not a gnawing need but a constant low heat. She had wanted to touch him, to feel his weight pressing her down, the heavy sensation of him pushing between her legs and into her. She hadn't indulged because waiting was its own sort of perverse pleasure, feeling the craving slowly grow. She liked the anticipation, the knowledge that when they finally came together again the pleasure would be more intense for the waiting.

And the way he was kissing her now . . . She began to think that perhaps the "This is temporary" talk hadn't been on his mind after all. His mouth was too hungry, his touch too . . . possessive? She'd never had anyone feel possessive of her before, so she wasn't certain.

She bit his lip and murmured, "Don't tell me to shut up," mainly because she didn't want him thinking he could get away with it.

He drew back a little to look down at her, his eyelids heavy and color deepening the sun bronze on his cheeks. "If I do, will you bite me again?" he asked, and bent to nuzzle her temple.

"You bet."

"Shut up."

The air between them changed and sizzled. She laughed and bit him, and ended up flat on her back with her shirt jerked up and his mouth clamped over her nipple. She took a deep breath and closed her eyes, sinking and floating in the sharp, prickling sensation that pulled at her. He slid his hand between her legs and cupped her through her jeans, rubbing the heel of his palm against her clitoris. Bo's eyes flared open and she stared up at the bits of blue sky she could see through the gently swaying tree limbs. Her gaze was unfocused because all of her attention was focused inward, on her body and what he was doing. *I'm going to come,* she thought dimly, then she said it, and then she did it.

He fought her out of her jeans while she was mostly comatose, unable to help him because her body was limp and heavy and still faintly pulsing. He didn't get her shirt off, but it was shoved up under her arms anyway. He hooked his hands under her thighs and pulled her legs up and apart, settling solidly between them. The light breeze briefly cooled her hot damp flesh, then he was there, reaching between them to set the thick head of his penis against her opening and stretching her as he slowly pushed inside. He made a rough sound deep in his throat as he lifted her legs once more so he could seat himself as deeply as possible. Bo roused enough to wind her arms around his shoulders and her legs around his back, and held on as he began thrusting.

He didn't take long, about a minute, but it was a tumultuous minute. The heavy push and drag of his shaft inside her just did it for her, so fast and so hard that within that minute she was feeling the coil of desire again. His orgasm hit and he bucked and shuddered through it, then slowly sank down on her until she was bearing his entire weight. Almost immediately he struggled up onto his forearms so she could breathe, but his head hung down so his forehead rested against hers. "You kill me," he muttered almost soundlessly. "Bo."

Was that good? she wondered woozily, because he made her feel drunk, drunk on pleasure, on him. She smoothed her hands up and down his sweaty back, either to soothe him or to satisfy her own need to touch him. Maybe the two were mixed together; maybe somewhere along the line her needs and his had stopped being so defined and separate.

When they could manage the effort, silently they pulled apart and cleaned up with the napkins she'd brought, and some of the water. Morgan gave a low growl of laughter because Tricks had turned her back on them while she finished off her chew bone. When they were dressed again—halfway, at least; she had on her shirt and underwear, and he had on his jeans—he pulled her to sit between his drawn-up legs and wrapped his arms around her. "Now," he said. "We talk. I have something serious to tell you, about me being here."

She thought about that a minute. "Will I like it?"

"Probably not. But if you and I are going to do this thing we've got going, then I'm going to be straight with you. You might kick my ass to the curb, but that's a chance I have to take."

Okay, so it definitely wasn't a don't-get-serious-because-I-have-one-foot-out-the-door talk. Bo leaned her head back against his shoulder, laid her arms on top of his where they wrapped around her stomach. Her mind raced, trying to think what could be so dicey about his situation here, which led her immediately to Axel. "Damn it!" she said irritably. "I knew I should have been more suspicious of Axel. He's behind this, right?"

"Mostly right. I have my share of responsibility. The deal is this: what he told you was correct, as far as it goes—"

"But, because he's Axel, he didn't travel too far down the truth road, did he?" She felt like growling. Any time Axel was involved, her irritation level shot through the roof. She didn't like him, didn't trust him, and so far her instincts had been dead on the money.

Morgan grunted. "He has other priorities, and they're damn important priorities. Likely he chose to send me to you partly out of spite, because that's Axel. But he had other criteria for choosing you, such as the relative isolation of the town, the small population that would make it easy to spot strangers, the relatively short distance to D.C. He was setting a trap."

Bo absorbed that, rapidly sorting through and discarding scenarios. She wasn't schooled in subterfuge, but she was intelligent and observant, and this additional information clicked in a way Axel's original argument hadn't. Oh, she'd been swayed—by Morgan's condition, by the money Axel had offered, by the surface logic of what he'd said. The logic even went deeper than one layer because of the probability that their organization had been compromised from the inside. And yet . . . she should have been more suspicious.

She asked the most important question first: "Is it possible anyone in town could be in danger or hurt?" That had been one of her original concerns, and she'd been fool enough to believe Axel when he'd denied it. The town and the people in it were her responsibility; more than that, the people were her friends. If anything happened to any one of them—she didn't know if she'd be able to get past that. On the one hand she appreciated that Morgan was telling her the truth, but on the other hand this was so potentially big that she didn't know if she'd be able to handle it. How ironic that she'd been so worried he might leave, and now she might *make* him leave. But she would hear him out, and she wouldn't make a hasty decision. There were a lot of things to consider, circumstances to weigh.

He sighed and rested his chin on top of her head. "My guess? Almost zero. But anything is possible. We don't know who we're dealing with. The idea was to hide me away in a place that was safe but not inaccessible, leak info that I'm recovering my memory, and trigger the bad actors into making another hack—but this time with a trigger on the information so we'd know who was doing the hack."

"And if that fails, Hamrickville is small enough, isolated enough, that it would be easy for us to spot an outsider," she finished. "There's a flaw in that, though; the town is small, but it's also big enough that I don't know everyone, or even have a good idea who at least half the population is. It's four thousand people; a stranger wouldn't necessarily stand out." People who lived in large cities seemed to think everyone in a small town knew everyone else, but that just wasn't so.

"But there aren't a lot of roads coming to Hamrickville, so intercepting someone would be more feasible than if you were on an interstate. Hamrickville was a secondary consideration, and a convenient one. Axel's money was on catching the hacker and following the Judas twig all the way back to the Judas tree."

"Except nothing has happened, despite his 'leaks.'" Normally she loved for things to be calm; drama wasn't in her wheelhouse. But in this instance, she thought her reaction should be more . . . forceful, more angry, yet going off half-cocked wasn't her way. She was angry, yes—at Axel. He was a champion asshole. He hadn't turned a hair at possibly endangering the townsfolk, or herself, come to that. His sole consideration was finding and eliminating the threat to the GO-Teams specifically and to Morgan as a . . . well, Morgan had said it perfectly himself: he was a secondary consideration. Maybe that was why she wasn't throwing a total fit at Morgan, why she wasn't screaming and telling him to go screw himself the next time he got a hard-on.

"Exactly. He hasn't had a nibble. So we're dead in the water because I still don't have a fucking clue why I was targeted. If it helps, anything happening in town would be damn stupid on the part of whoever is behind this. If they slip past Axel's trap, more than likely they'll come to your house."

"Ah," she said neutrally. "That definitely explains your insistence on all the security upgrades."

"I think the chance is small, but I can't discount the possibility. I'd rather be cautious than unprepared. Until and unless we hear from Axel that the trap was sprung and the jerks caught . . ." He shrugged.

"Nothing to do but wait," she said.

He was silent a minute, then said carefully, "Does that mean you aren't going to kick my ass to the curb?"

"I don't know," she said honestly. "There's a lot to think about. I know Axel, remember? He came up with the idea, and you were probably half-conscious at the time, juiced up on pain medication—" Considering how weak he'd been when he'd arrived, she could only imagine how serious his condition had still been when Axel cooked up his plan. And then the bastard had put him on the road from wherever to drive here on his first day out of the hospital. Most people would have collapsed before they got halfway here. Morgan had gutted it out, but then, Axel had likely known he would.

"Don't give me a full pass because I've had plenty of time to think about it since I got off the funny flying stuff."

"I'm not giving you a full pass," she said testily. "This is serious, so don't rush me, okay? I need to think about things." One of those things was how he didn't try to sidestep the issue or pass blame off on Axel, which would be laughably easy.

"I'd rather you punch me in the nose and get it over with."

"You don't get to choose. I'm pissed, but I'm still deciding how to allocate the pissery."

"Oh, God." His arms tightened around her. "Serves me right, falling for a reasonable woman. I'd rather you yell and get it over with."

Bo sat quietly in his embrace, letting his words seep through her. She was cautious enough, suspicious enough, about romantic relationships that her first cynical thought was to wonder if he'd said he was falling for her as . . . manipulation, maybe. He was sharply intelligent, as witnessed by the way he'd so rapidly and correctly assessed Jesse's character and adjusted his attitude and approach on the fly. He could read people, knew how to say what he needed to say to get what he wanted.

On the other hand, except for the information that he'd omitted at the beginning, as far as she knew, he'd always told her the truth. He hadn't hidden anything from her, he'd answered all her questions . . . and yesterday he'd risked his own life to protect her and Tricks.

She watched the lake, seeing the ripples that probably signaled small fish coming to the surface, watching the bank reeds sway in the breeze. Tricks nosed around, following one interesting smell to another interesting smell, her extravagant tail swishing happily back and forth. Morgan's arms were around her, his strength between her and the world. She didn't know what to think about that because she'd always stood alone, handled things alone—until she'd come to Hamrickville.

She knew there wasn't anything special about the little town, except maybe the fond blend of admiration and fear in which everyone held the Mean-As-Shit Hobsons, that she could have found friendship and caring in almost any place she chose. Except she hadn't chosen, being here had been forced on her by her finances, and it was what it was. They were her friends. They were hers to protect.

That line of thought led to her wondering if Morgan thought of her, and them, as his to protect. He'd been there when she needed him. He'd gone above and beyond. For better or worse, he was becoming part of the town. People greeted him with a "Hey, Morg!" as if he'd become one of them. Jesse treated him with respect, and Bo had to admit that weighed big in Morgan's favor because Jesse was nobody's fool.

If she was going to sit here and think of reasons why she shouldn't blame Morgan for the situation, there were several. He treated her with respect; not once had he ever made her feel less than capable. He didn't second-guess her, he didn't question her decisions, he made it plain that he considered it her-house-her-rules and he was willing to do whatever he could to help her. He treated her as an equal, which, considering the kind of man he was and what he did, was quite a statement.

And, if she wanted to keep going down this particular road, he was as completely under Tricks's paw as she was. He'd fought it, but now he made no pretense of being indifferent. Maybe she needed her head examined to base a decision on whether or not someone loved her dog, but Tricks was so important to her that she couldn't discount it.

On impulse she called Tricks to her. "Tricks! Here, sweetie." She clapped her hands. "Come get a hug."

Tricks whirled and came bounding to her, a big smile on her face. The sunshine glinted on her pale gold coat, catching the iridescent threads in the soft fur and making her glow. Enthusiastically she pounced, licking Bo's face and hands, her tail wagging so hard her entire body was wiggling back and forth. "Pretty girl," Bo crooned, warding off some of the swipes of Tricks's tongue while engaging in her own hugging and petting. "You're such a smart girl. What do you think of Morgan, huh?" She held Tricks's head still and went eye to eye with her. Tricks stilled, her expression becoming one of intent listening as if she knew Bo was telling her something important.

Bo jerked her thumb at Morgan. "He did something I don't like, and I can't decide if I should keep him or not. Mostly it wasn't his fault."

"Son of a bitch," Morgan muttered. "No pun intended. You're asking a dog to decide—"

"Whether you get probation," Bo finished coolly. "Yes. She's an excellent judge of character, in case you haven't noticed. She doesn't get the final vote, but I want to know her opinion. Tricks, is Morgan worth keeping?"

Tricks turned her dark gaze on Morgan as if considering. Bo felt him tense, and part of her wanted to laugh. She was only half serious, but the half that was, yeah, that half wanted to know what Tricks thought. The thing was, Bo couldn't remember asking her such an abstract question before; she *thought* it was possible Tricks would at least partially understand, but she wasn't sure. Either way, watching the faint alarm with which Morgan awaited Tricks's verdict was amusing, and she could use some amusement now.

After a few seconds, Tricks moved forward and licked Morgan on the cheek. Then she backed away, wagged her tail, and returned to her own pursuits.

Bo and Morgan sat in silence, watching her. Eventually he said, "I've been blessed."

"Not quite the same as coming from the pope, but yeah."

"Do I get probation?"

She let the sentence lie between them for a while, but the truth was that she wasn't ready to make a final decision, couldn't make one. "I guess so. There's a lot weighing in your favor."

He laid his cheek against the side of her head. She didn't have to spell it out for him; he knew that she was pissed and might stay pissed for a while, but she wasn't kicking him out and they'd work through it. That was what people in real relationships did, she thought with a sharp twinge of terror. Dear God, was this a real relationship? Part of it felt real, felt like more than sex. They'd been living together for weeks, building a routine and meshing their lives together.

"Maybe it's real," she said faintly.

"I guess I'll need to work on making up your mind for certain," he said, then threw a thumbs-up toward Tricks. "Thanks, girl."

Chapter 22

B o was good with leaving things up in the air for a while until she was able to give the situation more thought or until something actually *happened*. She'd have felt a lot worse about being pressured to make an immediate decision because this was too important. She could think of this thing she and Morgan had going on, as he'd put it, though it felt strange to regard herself as half of a couple. She could imagine him being a part of her life for a while, perhaps even quite a while. She could embrace what they had now without regret despite what he'd told her. Those were the things she *could* do. What she couldn't do was bring herself to think in terms of permanency because that meant she'd have to deal with more than she was ready for. She could handle the near future, she could handle the now, but she couldn't handle more of a commitment than that.

She wasn't blind to the circumstances that had shaped her; she had deliberately made the decision to close off the romantic part of life and be solitary. She'd liked being solitary, liked the security it gave her. It had required a traumatic event to get her to change her mind, one that had shaken her to the core and that she would rather have not experienced, but yesterday had happened. It was real, and she dealt well with reality. Things were different now. She had rearranged her priorities, willingly and deliberately.

On the drive from the lake back to the house, she sat quietly in the back, occasionally glancing at Morgan as he expertly steered the Jeep through the huge granite boulders, around trees, and angled it across dips. She liked the solid set of his head on those broad shoulders, the sure grip of his big rough hands on the steering wheel, the alertness with which he noted every detail, his head constantly turning. Nothing would surprise him, she thought.

She watched as he reached over to stroke Tricks's neck and was rewarded by a quick lick. Tricks was practically beaming; she'd had a great day. She had ridden to and from the lake in the front seat, gone swimming, and retrieved her ball until she was too tired to chase it anymore. She'd had a good nap and a chew bone. Looking at that happy, innocent creature made Bo's heart fill with love and tenderness, and she had to smile.

"Thank you for her," she said quietly.

He gave her a swift glance in the rearview mirror. "I couldn't let anything happen to either of you. I'd have killed him with my bare hands first."

He would have too; that wasn't an empty boast, it was a flat statement of what he could and would do. She accepted that, was even comforted by it. She wasn't certain what it said about her that she liked having his lethal ability standing between her and the world. She'd never before felt the need to be protected, but yesterday had proved that bad things could happen anytime and anywhere, and men like Morgan stood ready to step in. Jesse would have done the same, or any of her officers, but even though they would have known Kyle, would they have recognized that something was out of whack simply because he wore a jacket? Maybe, maybe not; they hadn't dealt with that type of situation before. Morgan had immediately recognized the threat and taken action, and no matter what happened between them in the future, she would love him forever for what he'd done the day before.

When they reached the house, he got out and went around to unclip Tricks's harness and let her out, then waited for Bo to climb out of the backseat. When she was mostly out, he gripped her by the waist and lifted her out the rest of the way, set her on the ground.

"Thanks," she said, pushing her hair back, then looked up when he didn't immediately release her.

He pulled her in and bent his head, taking her mouth in a kiss that was too long and too deep to be comfortable for either of them. She responded with so much warmth and passion that she surprised herself, but that was the "thing" between them, and she accepted the strength of it. When he drew away, she let her head drop forward to rest against his chest, and he stroked his hands up and down her back, down to cup her ass and hold her against him.

Oh, God, she enjoyed this, the freedom to touch him and be touched. It was enough for now. He was here, Tricks was here, and Bo was a little surprised to realize how happy she was despite what he'd told her. Annoyed, yes . . . but happy.

They unloaded the Jeep and he took the cooler; with his free arm around her they walked to the house and she unlocked it. Again she had the sense of family, the three of them, with Tricks dancing around their feet while she and Morgan emptied the cooler and put things away.

Bo hadn't taken her cell phone with her, wanting to ensure that their peace wasn't disturbed, and when she glanced at the big industrial wall clock in the kitchen, she was a little startled to see that it was after three o'clock. Either she'd napped longer than Morgan had estimated, or their lovemaking had taken longer than she'd guessed—maybe both. The time at the lake had flown, so what had felt like just a couple of hours was twice that.

There would be more days spent at the lake. She intended to make an outright habit of it.

She checked the answering machine: no messages. There weren't any missed calls or texts on her cell either. She had to suspect that Mayor Buddy had laid down the law and told everyone not to bother her today, which made her want to give him a hug. Just as she had the thought, her phone played a fanfare, her text signal. That was what she got for tempting fate by thinking about the lack of calls. This text, however, was from Daina, who was pretty much immune to Mayor Buddy's benign tyranny. The message said: *You okay?*

Bo texted back: *Pretty much.*

Daina: *Want me to bring dinner?*

Bo started to say no, then reconsidered: *What's on the menu?*

Daina: *LOL. Any takeout you desire.*

Just joking. Thx for the offer, but we've got plenty of food.

Daina: *K, let me know if you need anything.*

I will.

Daina: *Is Hot Stuff taking care of you?*

Bo smiled. When had Morgan become "Hot Stuff"? To tease Daina she texted, *Who?*

Daina: *Oh, pls. The hunk who looks at you like he could eat you up.*

She texted back: *Oh, him.* But she was taken aback, because—really? Morgan looked at her like that?

Daina: *Snort.*

Bo deleted the texts because she always did, on the theory that she could never be embarrassed by something that wasn't there. She smiled a little as she put the phone down, glad she had friends, glad she was no longer so solitary. Despite her best efforts to not let anyone matter to her, they did. Slowly and surely she had developed relationships, even if there hadn't been any romantic ones—until Morgan.

Because that was the way she rolled, she went to the computer and sat down. She needed to carefully consider all aspects of the situation; to that end, she set up a chart of pros and cons, so she could clearly see and balance each item.

"You're working?" Morgan asked from the kitchen. She thought he might be about to cook something, but she didn't look over to verify her hunch.

"Not exactly," she absently replied.

Under the con heading she listed: *Put town at risk.* She sat there another minute or so, thinking, but to her surprise she couldn't come up with anything else. Yes, he had lied by omission, but that came under the risk to the town. He also thought any risk to the town was negligible, that trouble was more likely to come here, to her house. Maybe that also came under the same heading, and he'd taken steps to minimize that risk.

Other than that . . . what?

After fruitlessly staring at the blinking cursor for a while, she moved over to the pro column. The first thing that came to mind was that as soon as they had moved into an intimate relationship, he'd come clean. He hadn't tried to hide it, hadn't made excuses. His honesty there completely counterbalanced the whole lied-by-omission item. He was a man, not a man-child. He accepted responsibility for his own actions, as well as the actions of others.

He'd risked his own life to protect her and Tricks.

He stood willing to back her up any time she needed it but was confident enough that he didn't have to make a production of it. He trusted her to handle her life and her job.

Those were big things.

Out of the corner of her eye she saw him moving toward her and knew he was about to be nosy given that she'd said she wasn't working. She hadn't entered any of the things she'd been thinking in the pro column, and an imp of mischief prompted her to quickly type: *Has a big dick.*

He moved like a ghost, without making a sound, but she felt his presence like a mild electrical charge as he stood behind her.

There was a short pause as he read the headings of the columns, then the two items listed. He gave a quick snort of laughter and pulled her up from the chair, turning her to face him. His eyes were dancing with amusement, his hard mouth quirked in a grin. "All I need to know is, does the pro outweigh the con?"

She looped her arms around his neck and nestled her head against his shoulder, sinking into his warmth and strength. "No, but all the other stuff I didn't write down does." She had needed to think it out, but now that she had, there was no doubt, no hesitation. She knew this man, knew the steel that made him, and the fact that he was a surprisingly nice guy was the cherry on top.

"I won't ask what the other stuff is. I will ask if spaghetti with a salad and garlic bread will suit you for dinner."

"Yes, it will, and why ask when the sauce is already cooking? I can smell it."

"I needed an excuse to come see what you're doing."

She smiled against his shoulder. "Daina called you 'Hot Stuff.' She also said you look at me like you could eat me up."

"Yeah? How about that. Seems to me I already have." His voice dropped a couple of notes and memory sent a frisson of pure sensual pleasure up her spine. "I plan on doing it again too."

He was seducing her before she'd even had the promised spaghetti. Bo tried to remember if she'd ever been seduced before; she didn't think she had. Two days ago she'd have said she didn't want to be seduced, but that was two days ago.

She was happy, she thought with a little shock. *Happy.* She'd have said before that she was happy, certainly that she was content, but the fizz of euphoria in her veins showed her the difference.

Happy. It would take some getting used to.

Going back to work the next day, and taking Tricks with her, was more difficult than Bo had anticipated.

As the clock ticked toward time to head to town, her sense of dread grew. She started to ask Morgan to keep Tricks at home for her, but when it was time to leave, he joined her. "I'm not ready to let you out of my sight," he said flatly, scowling. "It'll take me a while to get over seeing that son of a bitch pull his weapon and knowing I couldn't take a shot."

She'd felt much the same way, knowing there was nothing she could do to save Tricks. She looked at the dog, who was bouncing at the door in anticipation. "I've always felt she was better off with me, but being with me may put her in danger."

"Only from Kyle Gooding, and the bastard won't be poking his head out of a jail for quite a while."

"He'll get bail."

"He could. But he won't. He knows better."

That was all Morgan said, but Bo got a clearer picture of why Kyle was going to plead guilty—and now she had no doubt that he would. Morgan was waiting for him if he got out of jail.

The citizens of Hamrickville had become accustomed enough to Morgan's black Tahoe that any time they saw it, they expected Bo and Tricks to be inside. Morgan let down the windows so the people could see Tricks, and Tricks could collect her accolades. There seemed to be more people in town today than usual, so there were more calls of "Tricks!" and more waves. Tricks, of course, acted as if it were a continuation of the parade and began woofing happily, turning her head from side to side to include all her subjects.

Seeing that, seeing Tricks's enjoyment and happiness, helped soothe Bo's heart. She smiled back at Tricks, grateful that the dog was untouched by the terror that had so devastated her. She wanted Tricks to be happy and confident every day of her life.

Morgan parked behind the police station as he always did, and they went in the back. Bo was in front; she skidded to a stop when she saw what was at her desk, and Morgan bumped into her from behind, sending her lurching off balance. His arm immediately locked around her to support her, holding her against him until she was steady again.

A huge bouquet of balloons was anchored to her office chair, gently swaying and bobbing in the office air currents. Tricks froze, staring at the balloons for a moment before darting forward, her tail wagging madly as she planted herself under them, looking upward with such intensity Bo thought she might be plotting the trajectory needed to get to them. There had to be at least thirty of the things, in all colors, and they were definitely within Tricks's leaping range.

"Those balloons are about to be toast," Morgan said as he eased himself between Tricks and her target. He untied the strings from Bo's chair and re-anchored the balloons to the handle on the top drawer of a tall filing cabinet. Tricks followed him, her dark gaze still locked on the tantalizing arrangement, then she turned her head and stared at the chair positioned beside the cabinet.

Bo said urgently, "Move the chair!" and Morgan whisked it away just as Tricks was gathering herself to leap into it, and from there to the balloons. Thwarted, Tricks gave a disgruntled huff and trotted to Bo's desk, where she raised her nose to the edge and sniffed at a mystery box perched in the middle.

"Mayor Buddy brought the balloons," Loretta announced, a disembodied voice rising from her cubicle across the office. "Daina brought the cookies."

"Cookies," Morgan said. He was fast; he reached the desk before Bo did and opened the box to examine the contents. "Chocolate chip for sure, probably sugar cookies, and what looks like sugar cookies with something reddish in them."

"Snickerdoodles," replied Loretta, still out of sight. "Don't you know cookies?"

"I know Oreos. That's all a man needs." He offered the box to Bo. "They're for you, so I'll let you have first choice."

"Gosh, that's so big of you," she said and took one of each variety. Tricks began bouncing up and down at the sight and smell; because it was evidently a day for treats, Bo broke off a bite of a sugar cookie and held it down for her.

Looking at the pile of paperwork on her desk, Bo sighed. That was what taking a day off work got her: double the paper. There was nothing to do but get started, so she did, with her chosen cookies lying on a napkin to the side. Morgan brought a cup of coffee and set it next to the cookies, then took himself over to have a chat with Loretta.

Then the parade started.

There was never a crowd, usually just one visitor at a time, but the police station door might as well have been a revolving one. Miss Doris came bustling in with several boxes, which Morgan immediately took control of so he could investigate. "Cupcakes," he announced, and slanted a fierce blue-fire glance at Bo. "Don't lick the icing," he growled, pointing a finger at her for emphasis.

What? She stared at him in bewilderment. "I always lick the icing."

"Don't."

Miss Doris giggled, and Bo looked over to see the older woman blushing. She looked back at Morgan, and his expression spelled it out for her. She felt her own face getting warm. "Okay," she said, forcing out the word because her throat was suddenly tight from the heat wave sweeping up from her toes. She felt like a high schooler—or what she imagined a high schooler would feel like because her own high-school years hadn't involved any relationships other than friends on her swim team.

Morgan returned to the box. "We also have dog-shaped cookies. Just to be on the safe side, Miss Doris, are these people cookies or—"

"Oh no, they're for Tricks," she said before he could try them out himself. "I made up my own dog-safe and healthy recipe for her, you know."

"I'll know for sure you love me when you make man-shaped cookies," he said and winked at her, which left Miss Doris in a blushing, giggling mess.

A little while after Miss Doris left, Patrick brought in a dozen doughnuts, a mixture of chocolate-filled and lemon-filled. "Hey, Chief," he said, setting the box on her desk. "I figured you could use some sugar therapy. Are those Miss Doris's cupcakes?"

"They are. Help yourself," Bo invited. Holy hell, she was going to die of sugar shock, but she felt obligated to try one of everything that had been brought. "Those are for Tricks," she added, when Patrick began nosing around in the box of dog treats too. They wouldn't hurt him, but Tricks might hold a grudge if she noticed someone else eating her treats.

Jesse and Kalie came in with a fruit basket; at least that sugar came with some vitamins. Bo began to wonder if the whole town thought she had collapsed from the trauma, then realized she damn near had. If she'd been the one Kyle had tried to kill, she'd have been frightened, but not devastated. Not only that . . . it dawned on her that even though they weren't saying a word, evidently they all knew Kyle had been aiming at Tricks and not her. Christa, who had been beside Tricks on the float, knew the truth; Bo assumed she'd been interviewed, and she would have told them the truth. It didn't matter. Kyle was pleading guilty to trying to kill the police chief, and that's how it was going to stand.

Evan Cummings, the school principal, came by with a flower arrangement from him and his wife, Lisa. He apologized to Bo over and over, as if the whole thing were his fault for talking her into letting Tricks ride on the float. Bo was so grateful he hadn't brought more food that she almost hugged him; instead she reassured him they were all right, asked if he'd heard from Mrs. Simmons how her husband was—he was fine, had spent the night at the hospital but was released yesterday morning—and tried to press some of the overflow of goodies on him. He took a chocolate-filled doughnut for himself, then escaped.

After Miss Virginia Rose finished her shift at the supermarket she brought a box of chocolates; by this time even Morgan looked as if he'd had his fill of junk food, but Bo enthused over the chocolates anyway. They might not get eaten right away, but they *would* eventually, for sure. And the more people who came in, to ask how she was and to pet Tricks, the more touched and teary-eyed she became. These people cared about her, about each other, about their town. She wasn't alone, hadn't been alone for far longer than it had taken her to realize.

If she hadn't had such a wall around her in high school, would she have made close friends then? She'd never know, she couldn't redo the past, but she had to wonder. People were pretty much the same, big city, small town, or rural; they made friends, and they protected their own.

Eventually the procession dwindled and she settled down to work in earnest. Morgan took Tricks out for a walk. As soon as they were alone, Loretta got up and left her cubicle, coming over to give Bo a pat on the arm. "Congratulations," she said.

Startled, Bo looked up. "What?" she asked in bewilderment.

"Morgan. That's more man than most women could handle, though if it weren't for Charlie, I wouldn't mind giving it a shot," she mused and went back to her cubicle.

Well, hell. Evidently that was something else the entire town was clued in on. She thought about it for a minute, then shrugged mentally. She wasn't embarrassed. She hadn't even thought of telling Morgan to keep their new involvement on the down low, which said something about how drastically things had changed for her.

The days slipped from May into June, easing from late spring toward summer. The wheels of law weren't in any hurry and Kyle was still in jail, waiting arraignment so he could enter his guilty plea. Bo half-expected Warren Gooding to pay her another visit, but all of the Goodings seemed to be making themselves scarce. Melody wasn't seen shopping in town, and neither was her mother. The people who worked at the sawmills had no gossip to report, nothing overheard, no threats made. Perhaps Kyle had stepped so far out of bounds this time that his parents knew there was no making this go away; Bo wouldn't bet the farm on it, but she'd take what she could get.

Morgan began working out like a fiend. He swam every day that it didn't rain, and some days when it did. His reasoning was that "wet's wet." As long as there was no lightning, he swam. He ran; he started out with what he called an "easy hour," which seemed to extend every day by five or ten minutes. Of course she knew he'd already been doing some running, but it was astonishing how fast he built his endurance. She could almost see the difference every day as he began packing on hard-toned muscle.

One day he took Tricks out for a walk to give Bo some uninterrupted time to finish a tech job. She pushed hard, her concentration aided by caffeine, and finished just in time to grab a bite to eat before leaving for town. She got up from the desk, stretched, turned to say something to Morgan—then noticed that they hadn't returned. She checked the time; they'd been gone well over an hour.

Alarm shot through her, her stomach bottoming out. Had Morgan tripped, maybe hit his head or broken his leg? Had Tricks gotten hurt? The ideas of eating and work vanished, and she ran to the door, only to skid to a stop so fast she almost slammed into it. Through the glass she saw Morgan and Tricks in the yard. Tricks was nosing around, her tennis ball forgotten on the grass, and Morgan was doing push-ups.

Just that fast Bo went from panic to admiration as she watched his shoulders and arms bulge with each rep. His gray tee shirt was dark with sweat, which meant he'd either been running with Tricks or he'd been doing push-ups for a while. While she watched, he stopped, lying on his stomach, and called Tricks to him. She pranced over and when he patted his back she seemed to know what he wanted, because she daintily stepped onto his back and lay down. Morgan began doing push-ups again.

Bo's mouth fell open. Tricks wasn't a huge dog, her weight staying around sixty-two or sixty-three pounds, but still—that was sixty-two pounds! Push-ups were tough enough, at least Bo thought they were, but Morgan was popping them off as if he could keep going for hours. How long had he been using her dog as added weight?

Long enough for Tricks to be comfortable with it, evidently. Her tongue was lolling out to one side as she half-closed her eyes in bliss. She liked new things, she liked Morgan, she liked going for rides. Being on his back while he did push-ups hit a lot of her likes.

Bo opened the door. She was intending to just stand there for a few minutes—the scenery was fine—but as soon as she moved, Tricks noticed her and gave a welcoming bark. She shot straight off Morgan's back and over his head, her paws digging into him for purchase, as she rushed to get to Bo. Morgan yelped, because those paws had to hurt, not to mention that he was startled by the way she bolted over his head. Bo laughed as she knelt down to welcome Tricks into her arms, hugging her and receiving a few enthusiastic licks.

Morgan rolled to a sitting position and used his sleeve to wipe off his face. His dark hair was black with sweat, all visible skin glistening. He'd smell pretty rank, she thought, and didn't care. She wanted to throw herself against him despite how sweaty he was, wanted him to take her down to the ground and get on top of her. Her lower body clenched at the thought and she tightened her muscles against the temptation to do exactly what she wanted to do. She had to go to work.

"How long have you been using Tricks as weight?" she asked, getting to her feet and stepping to the edge of the patio.

He squinted up at the sun. "A week or so. She caught on fast. I need to up the weight, though, so you're on board next."

She gaped at him. He wanted her to get on his back while he did push-ups? "Are you nuts? I weigh a lot more than Tricks!"

"You don't think it'd be fun?"

Okay . . . that put a different slant on the idea. She gave Tricks one final pat and tilted her head. "I'll think about it. How many push-ups do you do?"

"You don't want to know. Hell, *I* don't want to know. A lot."

"More than a hundred?"

The look he gave her as he got to his feet and strolled toward her told her she'd underestimated by a lot. "A thousand?" She couldn't imagine doing a thousand push-ups. She was healthy and strong, but push-ups had always challenged her.

Again the look.

"I can't deal with this," she muttered. "The idea of that many push-ups makes my head hurt. What am I supposed to do while you rip off fifty thousand push-ups with me on your back? Nap? File my nails? Read *War and Peace*? You should go to the gym and lift weights like normal people."

"Not quite the same thing, but I see your point." He went past her into the house and she realized she'd been right about his smell. She was also right that it didn't matter at all.

Oh, shit. *She didn't mind if he stank.* She'd accepted that she was in lust with him, accepted that he meant way more to her than she'd felt comfortable with, even accepted that he could cause her a lot of heartache, but until now she'd managed to avoid admitting the truth to herself. Not minding if he smelled like a bear was the kicker, and she couldn't dance around with her emotions any longer.

She was in love with him.

Chapter 23

Toward the end of June, another letter arrived for Morgan. It came on a day when he'd gone to town with Bo, and while she dealt with things in the police station, he'd ridden patrol with Jesse. He'd become friendly with all her officers; she suspected it was some guy instinct, that they sensed that his level of expertise in weapons and explosives and hand-to-hand far exceeded theirs even though she knew he wouldn't have talked about it, and they gravitated to him. After her refusal to sit on his back while he did push-ups, he'd started working out at the small gym in town, and whoever wasn't on duty had begun working out with him. Her guys made an effort to stay in pretty good shape, but Morgan's idea of "in shape" made theirs look like kids playing in the yard. Sometimes she marveled that they didn't all choke on the testosterone levels, but they were trying to keep up with him.

He executed the U-turn and pulled up to her mailbox, retrieved the mail, then passed it all to her to sort while he wheeled into the driveway. Bo sifted through the catalogs and sales papers, extracting her lone credit card bill and the plain envelope without a return address that was for Morgan. Silently she held it up to catch his attention. He gave it a quick look. "Open it. It won't say anything you can't read. If there was any news, he'd have called your cell."

She tore open the envelope and extracted the single sheet of paper, on which had been typed two whole words: *No news.* No one would ever accuse Axel of being chatty.

Morgan scowled in frustration. "Shit. It's been over three months. I know Axel, know he's been spreading word that I'm recovering my memory, but no one is moving. Whoever it is is playing a waiting game, but that's dangerous."

"Or they suspect a trap," she pointed out.

"There is that. Anyone who knows Axel knows how devious he is."

"In which case, they don't really believe you're recovering your memory—which you aren't, given that you never lost it to begin with, but let's not quibble."

He reached over the console and patted her thigh. The familiarity of the gesture made her smile. They'd been sleeping together for a month now, and she didn't know if she'd ever stop going off like a rocket every time he touched her. On the side of fairness, he seemed just as hot for her. She knew she was attractive, in a noncurvy kind of way, but she'd never felt sexy—until Morgan. She'd look up and find him watching her with an intensity so hot her skin felt seared. She didn't even have to *do* anything, at least not anything special. As far as she could tell, just watching her load the dish-washer turned him on. She honestly thought he'd made love to her more often in a month than her ex-husband had in the almost-year they'd been married.

She was happy. She was peaceful. What they had was so great she thought it was worth the pain she'd feel if/when he eventually left. Every so often he'd mention something they could do in the future, but it was always near future, not long-distance future. She didn't make any assumptions based on that, because assumptions led to expectations and expectations led to disappointment. She simply accepted, and lived—more joyously than she'd ever lived before.

When they got to the house, he tossed the envelope and letter into the trash with the rest of the junk mail. The weather was hot enough that they were waiting until closer to sundown to take Tricks on her last walk; she fed Tricks, then she and Morgan began throwing together a quick supper. He was quiet, and whenever she glanced at him she saw the narrow-eyed intensity of his expression, meaning he was mentally attacking his situation from every angle, trying to worry loose some detail he hadn't noticed before. His work was dangerous but important, and until this situation was resolved, he couldn't do it, couldn't live under his own name, couldn't drive his own vehicle or live in his own home. *She* was happy, but he was in limbo, his real life on hold.

Perhaps she was part of his real life now, but she'd never know for certain until he got his real life back. Her instinct was to let the issue lie untouched, to take what she could get of him while circumstances still favored her, but—was that fair to him? He'd built the life he wanted, put himself through inhuman training and lived on the knife edge of danger in order to do what he did. If he chose to walk away from it at some point, that was different—because it would be his choice. Being locked out would eat at him.

She knew that he had mentally gone over and over the details of the day he'd been shot, knew that he and Axel would have analyzed it all down to the nth degree, and come up with nothing. Going over it again likely wouldn't accomplish anything, but she did have an orderly mind and could listen, and sometimes a little back and forth could knock something loose that he'd realize was significant.

"You want to do a rundown of that day, start to finish?" she asked, keeping her tone even so he wouldn't be able to read how much she really didn't want to do this.

He frowned down at the salad he was tossing. "I've gone over it until I want to punch the wall. It's frustrating, knowing something is there but damn if I can see it. What the hell are these little green things?" he asked, poking at the salad.

She leaned over and looked. "Capers."

He filched one out of the salad and tasted it. "What exactly is a caper?"

"Pickled flower buds."

"Who the hell ever thought of pickling a flower bud?"

"Someone hungry."

He laughed and popped another caper into his mouth. "Yeah, that'll do it. I've eaten some weird shit a time or three because that's all there was. Okay, let's go over it; a fresh point of view can't hurt."

She braced herself to stay noncommittal, to just ask questions and let him sift through the details. "Start at the beginning. What did you do when you got up?"

"Called a teammate, asked him if he wanted to go fishing. He said no. He had companionship of the female variety, and that'll outweigh fishing with him every time."

She arched an eyebrow. "Only with him?"

He hooked his arm around her neck and pulled her over for a hard, hungry kiss, one that involved tongue, lingered, and ended with them both breathing a little harder. He lifted his head and wiped her mouth with his thumb. "I didn't say that. If I had you naked in bed—yeah, I'd skip fishing, too."

"Oh, thank you so much." She slid her hand along his ribs, feeling the hard layers of muscle, then re-gretfully eased away in the interest of keeping up the conversation because if they kept kissing, then dinner would go on hold and they'd end up naked. That had already happened too many times for her to think oth-erwise. "Did he know where you were going?"

"No, but he knows where I live so he wouldn't have had to hack any database to get my address."

"That could have been to fake people off."

"That's what Axel said."

Bo scowled at him because she didn't like thinking she had anything in common with Axel the Asshole.

Morgan grinned and tapped her chin with his finger but continued, "I don't see it, myself. Kodak is a friend, has been for a long time. If I got crossways with him during the mission we were on—and I didn't—he had plenty of opportunity to take me out and make it look legit. I've trusted him with my life a lot of times, and vice versa. My gut says no."

"Okay, I trust your gut. What happened next?"

"I went to the marina where I keep my boat. On the way I stopped for breakfast—drive-through fast food—but didn't see or talk to anyone other than the kid in the window. At the marina I said hello to the marina owner. He made a phone call immediately afterward, but Axel checked that, and the call was to his wife. Nothing there."

"Unless his wife is some kind of master spy and you saw something you shouldn't have seen at the marina."

She expected him to laugh again, but he said, "I checked out the marina, sure, like I always do. Everything looked normal. There weren't any piece-of-shit boats with an expensive antenna array, no unusual license plates, and Brawley—the marina operator—has been there since before I started renting a boat slip. He doesn't click for me."

She blew out a breath, trying to get her head around the mindset and level of alertness required to check out a familiar place *every single time he went there*. It was mind-boggling. After a few seconds she gave up and shook it off. "Does *anything* click?"

"Not really. Next up: I saw a congresswoman and her husband on the river in their boat, went over to say hello. I know them both—not well, but their son was kidnapped and we got him back alive, so I'd say they're both kindly disposed toward me."

"I don't remember anything in the news about a kidnapping involving a member of Congress," she said as she took a pair of baking potatoes out of the microwave. Yes, it was heresy to zap potatoes instead of baking them, but so what; she was going for speed.

"It wasn't in the news. The whole episode was kept dark."

"Was anyone else on the boat with them?"

"Not that I saw."

She had put pork chops in the slow cooker that morning; she got a platter and dished out the chops. "If you don't know them well, how did you recognize their boat?"

"I didn't. I recognized her hair. It was Joan Kingsley."

"Oh," Bo said, thinking hard. A face flashed into mind. "I know who she is! White hair. She's big time."

"Yep. She's on the House Armed Services Committee."

"Do you think she's behind this whole thing?"

"In my experience, politicians are to blame for almost everything, so that's what I default to. Her husband is a D.C. lawyer, which is almost as bad because in that town they're all in bed with each other. But even with that tilt, I can't make it work." He took the salad to the table, then got the plates and silverware.

"You know what Sherlock Holmes said: eliminate the impossible, and what's left is the truth no matter how improbable. Paraphrasing, of course."

"All of it's improbable. Every possible suspect."

"Except for the one who isn't. Okay, how far from the congresswoman's boat were you when you spotted her? Did you know it was her?"

"Not for certain, but that hair's distinctive. I was about a hundred yards away, give or take. Their boat was anchored in a fairly open stretch of water, though it was a long way down the river toward the bay." He paused, thinking. "Where the boat was positioned, no one could come up to them from any direction without being seen from some distance away. That's good safety strategy."

They took the food to the table, sat down, and began serving themselves. Bo ate quietly for a minute, thinking about what he'd already told her but also taking the time to savor the fork-tenderness of the pork chop.

God bless the inventor of the slow cooker, was all she could say.

"Would she need to be so safety conscious?" she asked, when their immediate hunger had been satisfied.

"She isn't the speaker, but she's important in D.C. Plus her son had been kidnapped, could have been killed. I'd say the answer is yes."

"So the position of the boat wasn't suspicious?"

"No. If I'd anchored, I'd have done the same."

"What did you see as you drove toward her?"

"She was standing at the railing, waving. Her husband was on the deck with her, but he went below."

She put her fork down, tilted her head at him. "How do you know it was her husband, if you weren't close enough to know for certain it was her?"

Morgan paused, thinking, his gaze absent as he looked into the past. "I didn't, not from that distance, but he was wearing a blue shirt and when he came back on deck he was still wearing it—*Fuck!*"

"What?" Bo asked, so startled by his verbal explosion that she dropped her fork; it hit the plate with a clatter. She grabbed for the fork to keep it from bouncing to the floor.

"He was buttoning the shirt when he came back up." Morgan's tone was grim, as rough as ground glass.

"Over a white tee shirt. But I didn't see any white when he went below."

"What's wrong with—Oh. I see. Why was he buttoning it if he'd already had it on?"

"Exactly." He sat silently, mentally tearing the details apart. "The man who went below deck had gray hair, as far as I could tell. Dexter Kingsley's hair isn't gray. I couldn't swear to that, because the angle of the sun can mess with hair color, but . . . yeah." This was resonating with him, the way something did when you knew instinctively it was right.

"Then there was someone on the boat they didn't want you to see. She's a politician, so I have to say that isn't completely unexpected. What happened then?"

"I pulled up close to their boat, shut mine down. We chatted. She asked me to come aboard for a drink."

"Well, that doesn't make sense. Why would she ask you to come aboard if she didn't want you to see who was on the boat with them?"

He flashed her a look that chilled her; his eyes were blue ice, his jaw so hard she knew his teeth were clenched. "To kill me," he said flatly. "Even though they pulled a switch, they couldn't be sure I'd bought it. If I'd been someone else, maybe, but she didn't know who was coming toward them until I got my boat closer. I work in counterterrorism, I'm supposed to notice every detail, but I missed that one. They couldn't know that, though, so they had to take care of me."

This time she didn't drop her fork; she put it down carefully, all appetite gone. She'd thought dragging out every detail for examination might help, but she'd kind of hoped it wouldn't. Now she had to deal with the fallout; everything would change fast, and whatever happened, she had to focus on how this would help Morgan. Her emotions were secondary, and something she would simply have to handle, though it was hard to get around the reality that someone had so coldly planned to kill him.

"But couldn't you have already reported it? What good would killing you do?"

"Reported suspicious behavior, yes, but she knew that I couldn't have recognized the other man any sooner than she recognized me—not as soon, actually. I was driving a boat, concentrating on where I was going and what I was doing; traffic on the river was heavy that day, with a lot of boats crisscrossing. Besides, thinking something is suspicious isn't the same as knowing something bad is going down."

"But you *didn't* know," Bo insisted. "Even if you'd reported something suspicious and questions were asked, all they had to do was deny anyone else was onboard. There was no proof."

"My best guess? Because of what I do, even if I hadn't seen the other man well enough to recognize him, I have the resources to do some digging. There are cameras everywhere in the D.C. area, plus a lot of places have private security cameras; they wouldn't be sure they were completely under the radar. If they showed up anywhere on camera with the other guy, Axel could likely find it if he simply knew the direction to start looking."

"Then Axel would be able to identify the other man."

"Possibly. That would depend on whether or not he's in any of our databases, or if we could get a license plate or credit card receipt that would tell us." Then he shrugged and said, "Yeah, the odds are we'd find something. As it was, even if I had noticed something, I couldn't have started looking while I was on the water. My boat is just an old fishing boat, not set up for anything like that. If I'd wanted to do some digging, it would have had to wait until I went back ashore. They got my boat registration numbers and set things in motion. Probably they couldn't find which marina I used, so instead of waiting for me there, they had to get my home address and set up an ambush."

"But you had a cell phone, didn't you? Why couldn't you have called whoever you would have called, and gotten the ball rolling before then?"

"I can only guess that they had no means of taking a long shot at me, plus the shooter would have to be a trained sniper to hit someone in a moving boat. I was heading down river, instead of back toward D.C., so likely they assumed I wasn't immediately suspicious. If I started thinking about it and called in before they could get to me—nothing they could do unless they wanted to chase me down on the river and have a gunfight there, with potentially hundreds of witnesses. They played the odds that I hadn't noticed anything, and they were right. If they'd left it like that, I'd never have given that meeting a second thought."

Bo got to her feet and took her plate to the kitchen. She was a logical person, but this was taking strategic thinking to a degree that was foreign to her; her head was actually aching a little from trying to think of all the possibilities, probabilities, ins and outs, and angles. "But they tried to kill you and failed. So now you have them arrested—crap. You can't. You have no proof they did anything."

He got to his feet too. "Now I call Axel and get the ball rolling. The first step is trying to identify the other man on the boat. At least now we don't have to wait for them to trigger an electronic trap by trying to hack the system again to find out where I am."

"And then what? You still have nothing."

"We have a string to pull. Eventually the ball of yarn will unravel—one way or another."

Bo watched him bound up the stairs to get his burner cell phone to call Axel, almost afraid to consider what that "one way or another" would entail. No, she was definitely afraid because the only clear way she could think of to draw them out and force them to commit some act that would get them arrested was to stick with some version of the original plan, which was to use Morgan as bait.

Morgan pulled out the burner cell—not a smartphone, just a simple phone that didn't have GPS—and called Axel. When he heard the familiar voice, he said, "I got it. Call when you can." Meaning use a burner on that end too, or get to a phone away from any agency network that could be hacked. However he made contact was up to Axel, depending on how paranoid he was feeling that day. Morgan didn't bother leaving his name because not only had they been making phone calls to each other for years, on the off chance Axel hadn't recognized his voice, he would still recognize the burner number. The bastard was crazy good at things like that.

Axel must have been either in a meeting or feeling very paranoid because it was over half an hour before he called back. By then Morgan and Bo were sitting on the couch watching TV, waiting for the sun to get farther down in the sky before they took Tricks for a walk.

"Who was it?" Axel asked in his usual brusque tone.

"Congresswoman Kingsley. There was someone else on the boat with them, a man. When they saw me coming toward them, he went below and when Dexter Kingsley came up, he was buttoning up the other guy's shirt."

"And you're just remembering this now because—?"

Fuck you, Morgan thought without heat. If he took offense at everything Axel said, he'd have beat the shit out of him a long time ago. Because it amused him, he looked at Bo and said, "Axel wants to know why I'm just now remembering this."

As he'd halfway expected her to, she snatched the phone out of his hand. "Because I had the sense to ask questions about the details when he wasn't fighting for his life and loopy on painkillers," she snarled.

Good girl. He couldn't think of anything he could have said that would have gotten Axel's goat the way he knew Bo just had. He gave her a thumbs-up and took the phone back.

Axel was still sputtering curses, then he broke them off to say, "If you're so smart, why did you wait two damn months to start asking those questions, huh?"

"I'm back," Morgan said, grinning because he'd never before seen Axel knocked off balance.

"Was that Bo? It had better be Bo. You wouldn't have told anyone else. What did you tell her?"

"Everything."

"*Everything* everything, or a sanitized version?"

Knowing what he was asking, Morgan said, "Everything everything. God, Mac, when did you turn into a teenage girl?"

"Fuck you too. Listen, are you certain?"

"Absolutely. Start a database search. The guy could be domestic, but I think the shooter is a link. He was Russian, so I'd start looking at Russian operatives first. They'd have the contacts with the Russian mob to find the guy. Who was in the country at that time? Who has gray hair? Weight—" He thought back, measuring his memory of that figure heading below with that of Dexter Kingsley as he came up on deck—"one eighty-five to two hundred, height five eight to five ten. If you can come up with some possibles, we might be able to find a withdrawal for twenty K if it came from a domestic bank."

"Don't tell me how to do my job," Axel growled. "Okay, got it. What else?"

"That's it."

"I'll get back to you."

Morgan ended the call and tossed the phone onto the couch.

"How long will it take him to get some photos for you to look at?" Bo asked.

He shrugged to indicate there was no way to tell. "Could be an hour or so, could be days. There'll be a lot of gray-haired Russian guys, but he can neck it down by the height and weight, then he'll have to start pinpointing their known locations for the time frame. For that he'll have to check records, human intelligence, cell phone grids, traffic cameras—and that's just off the top of my head. The ones who are left, the ones he can't definitely say were somewhere else that day, are the possibilities. And there's no way I can make a positive ID, just a probable one that will help him narrow his focus even more."

"And unless they do something else, such as hack the agency files again, you have nothing on them," she pointed out—again. And she was just as correct this time as she had been the first time she said it. He leaned back and hooked his hands behind his head, smiling as he studied her.

"What's so funny?" she asked, looking down to see if she had spilled something on herself.

"Nothing's funny. I like looking at you." And he did. He liked her sense of humor, but he also liked the seriousness that was such an important part of her makeup. Those big dark eyes were so solemn when she was concentrating on something, such as when she'd been asking every question she could think of to prod more details out of his memory—and son of a bitch if it hadn't worked.

He was relieved that he'd finally pinpointed the detail that really mattered, relieved to the point that he felt like laughing. A burden had been lifted, and a new purpose had been born. Not knowing *why* had eaten at him, knowing there was an enemy out there but not knowing who. He couldn't defend against someone he didn't know was coming after him. But now at least he knew who, though the why of it still had to be discovered.

For the first time, he could foresee an end to the situation. Until things were settled he'd been hamstrung with Bo, not knowing what he could or couldn't do, how long the current state of affairs would hold, if he'd ever be tracked down to Hamrickville. Now he didn't have to wait. They could take the offensive, get this thing settled.

He grabbed her and pulled her across his lap, ignoring her startled yelp to catch her chin and kiss her with all the fire he felt whenever she was in his arms. "You did it," he murmured, trailing his mouth down her neck to her fragile collarbone. He knew she wasn't really fragile, but everything about her felt fragile to him; her bone structure was so fine that his wrists were twice as thick as hers. He'd almost been anxious about crawling on top of her—almost, and definitely not enough to stop him. But she always met him with such enthusiasm that in the heat of the moment he'd forget, and the next thing he knew they'd be locked in the down and dirty and she'd be wringing him out. God, it was great.

He loved the honesty of her. There were no games being played, no pretense, just an open giving and taking. He *thought* she loved him, though getting her to ever admit it to him could take some doing. Given that, and knowing she didn't expect a future with him despite how she felt, she had still done what she thought was best for *him* rather than herself when she'd decided to undertake that direction of questioning. Sure, it had been a long shot, but she'd taken that chance.

"I don't know what was different about how you were asking the questions because Axel asked for every detail too, but you pulled out the one thing I needed."

"I told him," she said absently, her fingers moving to the back of his neck. Her tone said she was concentrating on touch, not the conversation. "I asked when you weren't doped up."

"Good theory, but I haven't been doped up for a couple of months now, and I still hadn't hit on the significance of that shirt. I've gone over and over that day plenty of times too. I just missed it."

He was annoyed, but hell, shit happened. Even if he'd remembered about the shirt on the day he first regained consciousness, as Bo had twice pointed out, they would still have nothing on the congresswoman. Even when they eventually identified the mystery man—and he had no doubt they would—*proving* something illegal was going on was going to be a bitch. The guy could be the head of Russia's SVR, but meeting with him on a boat to talk wasn't a crime—suspicious, but not a crime.

Axel would be looking though. Now that he had a name, he'd be turning over every rock Joan Kingsley had ever stepped on.

But how long would that take? Whatever was going on, they'd already had three months to cover their tracks. Morgan wasn't inclined to wait.

An idea began turning over in his head, one that would bypass finding any elusive evidence about whatever had been going on that day and provide a whole different crime with which the Kingsleys could be charged. Once investigators had a foot in the door, so to speak, the evidence for the other crime could well turn up.

He'd have to think about it, work out the angles. A lot of things could go wrong, but the advantage of the plan was that he wouldn't be a sitting duck waiting in Hamrickville and possibly endangering Bo and his other friends.

Chapter 24

At five-thirty in the morning, Bo's cell phone chimed the arrival of a text. The sound woke her out of a deep sleep, and she raised her head to growl, "What the hell!" If there had been an emergency in town she would have been called, not texted.

Morgan snapped on the lamp and reached across her to snag her phone off the bedside table. "It's from Axel," he muttered, squinting at the partial text showing on the lock screen. He swiped his thumb across the screen and tapped in her passcode, then went to the full text.

Bo yawned and stretched, reveling in the feel of his naked body stretched across hers. She hadn't realized he knew her passcode, but she wasn't surprised—or concerned. He'd seen her use it often enough to know the pattern. "What does it say?"

"He's sent some photos for me for me to look at," Morgan replied absently. She knew that tone, and her heart leaped the way it always did. He was looking at her bare breasts as if she were a gazelle and he was a starving tiger. He dropped the phone on the bed and snaked his hand under the sheet to stroke up her thigh, over her belly, then down between her legs at the same time he closed his mouth over her nipple to give it a sharp tug. A low sound hummed in her throat as his big finger pushed into her.

Even after a month, things still went fast between them, as if neither of them wanted to wait. She knew he wasn't going to leave her behind, and her response to him was fierce enough that he'd have to hurry if he did. The way he fit inside her, big enough for her to feel stretched, long enough to feel deeply penetrated, sent her over the edge. It was perfect, as if their bodies had been made to be together. Logically she knew that was impossible, but when they were making love, logic flew out the window, because "perfect" was how it felt.

"He'll call any minute now," she said breathlessly as Morgan settled on top of her. She stroked his ribs, his shoulders, opened her legs to him and latched them around his hips. His entry was careful, but as soon as the head of his penis was inside her he stroked deep the way she liked.

"Won't be the first time I've ignored him." He rested his weight on his elbows and cupped her face as he moved inside her, watching her with that eagle gaze as if he wanted to catch every flicker of expression. He did that a lot, his focus locked on her as if nothing else was going on in the world.

She was self-conscious enough of her bed head and general early-morning scruffiness that she put her hand across her face. "You're watching me."

"Yeah." His voice was low and rough. His rhythm inside her was slow and steady. "I want to know if I do anything that hurts you, or that you don't like. Or if I do something you really like, so I can do it again."

She pretty much liked everything they did, so she had no protests. On the other hand, she did like to return the favor; she put her hands against his chest and said, "I want on top."

He wrapped an arm around her hips, anchoring her in place as he rolled to the side. She sat up, feeling him push so deep inside there was a pleasant ache. Sighing in pleasure, she absorbed the sensation, moved her hips searching for more.

"Tell me if you like this," she murmured, bracing her hands on the bed on each side of him and rising to a crouch so their only point of contact was his penis inside her. Slowly she rose and sank back down, watching his face.

He sucked in a deep, shuddering breath. "God almighty."

She did it again, slow rising, slow falling. "Does that mean yes?"

His fists clenched on the mattress beneath them. "It feels like you're going down on me." His voice was restricted, as if he could barely talk.

"I am," she purred. "Just not with my mouth."

Then she concentrated on the task at hand. At some point the phone did ring, but she and Morgan barely noticed. He wasn't the only one getting pleasure from the position; every time she sank down on him, her nerve endings erupted in small explosions of pleasure. Her climax edged closer with every downstroke, and she slowed to draw it out, to wring out every ounce of sensation.

It was torture, but the most pleasurable kind imaginable. Her nipples tightened and stood out, chills of ecstasy running over her skin. Such mutual pleasure sent her mental walls tumbling; the words "I love you" trembled on the edge of her consciousness, thought but left unsaid because such words were either a gift or a burden and she wasn't certain which they would be to him. Rather than take the chance she said them silently, acknowledging how much he meant to her, letting herself savor the moment, just this moment, of loving.

But no matter how much she slowed, eventually the pleasure built to such a point that she was almost paralyzed, trembling on the edge of climax. Morgan was a taut, muscular arch beneath her, his teeth clenched as he fought not to come before she did. Her inner muscles were clenched so tightly around him that moving either up or down would likely end it for both of them. She moaned, deep and shaky.

He broke, clamping his big hands on her hips and driving her down to the hilt on his thick penis. She gave a quick, gasping cry as her orgasm gathered and then surged, swamping her entire body with sensations so intense she was lost to everything else. His hips bucked beneath her, intensifying the spasms. She thought he was swearing through his clenched teeth but the words were muted by her fast, heavy heartbeats pounding in her chest, her ears, throbbing in her throat.

The spasms began to subside, coming slower and slower, her body jerking with each one. Gradually she folded over, wilting on him, until she was lying draped on top of him as limp as a ragdoll kitten. His breathing was fast and heavy but so was hers, and within seconds their bodies had synchronized, breaths and hearts.

After a minute he managed to move his hand, stroking it over her back and ass.

"Damn, woman," he muttered. That was all, but she felt those two words down to her bones.

Getting enough strength built up to get out of bed took another few minutes, then they did a quick cleanup and headed downstairs to her desktop for Morgan to view the photos. At least she assumed they were on the desktop because looking at photos on a phone wasn't the best way to make an identification.

She took Tricks out and returned to find Morgan with a cup of coffee in his hand and one ready for her. He was waiting for her before he began looking at the photographs. Hurriedly she fed Tricks, then they went to the computer.

He'd turned on the burner phone and slipped it into his pocket, because there wasn't any way to anticipate which phone Axel would call: her home phone, her cell, or Morgan's cell. "Be my guest," she said, gesturing to the desktop. He sat down, pulled up her email, and clicked on the one with an attachment. She leaned over and looked at the address of the sender: it was a woman's name, using a Gmail account.

"Is that Axel?" she asked.

"I assume so. I'm guessing he set up a separate account from some hole in the wall he has, or some phone registered to God only knows who." He clicked to open the attachment, and the little wheel started spinning to show the command was processing. Then photos started opening up on the screen, and Morgan began scrolling down.

The photos had been taken in a variety of environments: on the street, in restaurants, in a courtyard of what she suspected was an embassy, going by the flags. She didn't ask how the photographs had been attained. Another man had been Photoshopped into each photo, a dark-haired man in a suit. The Photoshop was obvious because the image was the same in every instance.

"Who's that?" she asked, leaning over his shoulder to tap the screen.

"Dexter Kingsley. This way I can compare heights, going by what I remember from the man in the blue shirt going below on the boat, and Kingsley coming up. I have good spatial memory."

She just bet he did. "These are the foreign agents whose whereabouts can't be accounted for that day?"

"Mostly. I'd guess there are a few domestic troublemakers in here, knowing Axel; he'd throw in anyone he found suspicious."

He took his time looking at each photo, comparing the two men's heights and, she supposed, such things as shape of head, whatever he could have noticed at such a distance. She didn't see how he could make a definitive ID under such circumstances, but this was about narrowing down the possibilities.

Each image was numbered, twenty-three in all. There was no identification of the people in any of the photographs; he wasn't concerned with that. Axel would know who they were. Morgan paused at image number eight, scrolled down through nine, ten, eleven, twelve, paused at thirteen, then scrolled through the remaining nine. He went back to thirteen, then back to eight. Thirteen again. Eight. He went back and forth a couple of times, then tapped the screen. "Eight."

She had no idea what parameters he was using. To her none of the men resembled each other, though they did all have gray hair. Number eight's hair was kind of iron gray, neatly cut and shaped to his head.

"That's the most likely prospect, huh? What made you decide?" Eight and thirteen looked nothing alike facially, so there had to be something else that had made him go back and forth between the two.

"The shape of the head, and the way his ears are set."

"Damn, what kind of eyesight do you have?" she said, both startled and amazed. From the distance he'd said he was at, detail had to be at a minimum—at least for her, and she had twenty-twenty eyesight.

"Twenty-fifteen in my right eye, a little better than that in my left eye. Comes in handy."

"Wow. I can see that. I can also see I need to put on makeup every morning before you get up."

He slipped his hand around her right thigh. "No, you don't. You look great. Besides, if you're naked, I'd never notice if you have on makeup or not." He didn't look up at her, but she could see a grin tugging at his mouth.

She rolled her eyes and gave him a light slap on the shoulder, though inwardly she was pleased that he liked her naked. "Thanks a lot. Anyway, back to business. Do you know who this guy is?"

"Not a clue. I'm not in the information-gathering side of the business." He reached for his cell, and it rang right on cue. He hit the button and put the call on speaker.

"Why the fuck didn't you answer the phone?" Axel barked.

"Couldn't get to it," Morgan said neutrally.

There was a pause, then Axel erupted in a yell: "You son of a bitch, are you screwing my sister?"

The surge of rage made Bo feel as if her eyes were popping out of her head. He'd always had that instant effect on her. She leaned over, slammed her fist down on the desk and yelled back, "I'm not your damn sister! And, no, he isn't screwing me! *I'm* screwing *him*! I've worn him down to a dried-up husk of his former self! I—"

"Did you put this call on *speaker*?" Axel interrupted, his tone aghast.

"She's the woman you trusted to save my life," Morgan retorted. "Damn right I did. Plus she's in it now, so she deserves to know what's going on." Annoyance and laughter were fighting in his expression, though Bo was at a loss to guess exactly what was triggering what. She'd called him a dried-up husk. Axel had called him a son of a bitch. The call could go either way. "Are you interested in which photograph I identified, or are you going to continue butting into something that's none of your business?"

"It's my business if—which photograph was it?" Axel's tone changed in mid-sentence, illustrating exactly what was most important to him.

"Number eight."

"Shit."

"Shit, what?"

"Of all the possibilities I sent, that's probably the worst outcome. Are you sure?"

"Not a hundred percent. I'm going by the shape of the head, the ears. I'm sure that of the pictures you sent, that's the closest match."

"Okay, good enough. Those are the ones we couldn't get a definite location on for that time frame, so I'm calling it a hit."

"Russian?"

"Yeah. Keying on them was a good idea. He's Foma Yartsev, high-ranking SVR. A secret meeting with someone on the HASC is definitely something they'd kill to cover up."

"Maybe Yartsev was the one who ordered the hit if he didn't want it known who *he* was meeting."

"Possible. Definitely something I'll look at. But if so, we have an even bigger problem because that means the SVR has penetrated our data system."

"You still haven't been able to trace it back?"

"If I'd been able to trace it back, I'd have a lead, now, wouldn't I?" Axel said irritably. "Hell, no, whoever did it was genius. And when we catch him—or her—we'll likely recruit the bastard." He sounded aggrieved at the prospect; even when he was younger, negotiation had never been his first choice. He preferred to hammer home his point, go for the most drastic punishment.

"Or the person you have looking for the hack is the hacker," Bo couldn't resist pointing out, knowing her comment would drive him crazy.

The absolute silence on the phone told her she'd guessed right. His brain had flipped into squirrel mode, worrying the possibility from every angle.

Morgan lifted his brows at her and she smirked, shrugging. "You could be right," he murmured. "Nothing is impossible."

"Shit!" Axel's expletive was sharp. "I'll have to go out of house, have someone else recheck my guy. I can't see him being a bad actor. Of course I did some deep checking on him, but if he's good enough to be the hacker, he could build any background he wanted."

"Okay," Morgan said. "While you're doing that, I say we move forward. I've been thinking."

"Go on."

"We have nothing on them. Even if you can tie Yartsev to Rykov, prove that he hired the shooter, and even if you can prove it was Yartsev on the boat with the Kingsleys—which I don't think you can because his craftwork will be too good—we still have no proof that the Kingsleys did anything wrong or that they knew about the hit being put out on me."

After a pause Axel said, "True. I'm listening."

"But we can bait them into coming after me again, which is essentially what you'd planned to do anyway. You expected them to spring the trap when they were looking for my location, but they're too smart for that because they expect a trap from you."

"I'm too good at my job," Axel said sourly.

Bo rolled her eyes but suppressed a snort.

"So I need to go to them," Morgan said.

There was a short pause, then Axel said interestedly, "What's on your mind?"

"Just thinking out loud here, but maybe give me a medical discharge, or just put in my files that I'll need to be reevaluated due to physical problems. Whatever. I initiate the contact with the Kingsleys, let them know I remember, say I need money."

"Blackmail."

"Without actually saying it."

"That's entrapment."

"I'm not a law officer."

"Yeah, but now you're breaking the law and they still haven't."

"They will when they come after me and try to kill me again. Do you honestly think they'd be willing to quietly make blackmail payments for the foreseeable future?"

"No. A politician like Kingsley couldn't let that kind of threat hang over her head."

The three of them were silent as the possibilities and probabilities ran through their heads. Bo stood quietly beside Morgan, half of her wanting to shriek at him for putting himself in danger again and the other half knowing he had to do whatever he could to resolve the situation. She put that aside and tried to think strategically. If the Kingsleys—or, more likely, another hired killer—came after Morgan, they'd be coming here because Morgan was right, and here at her isolated home would logically be the best place for any attempt on him to happen. Any halfway competent killer would figure that out in short order.

But . . . what if the killer used a rifle? That would be almost impossible to defend against. There were a lot of hills surrounding her house on which a patient assassin could silently wait for a good shot. Her blood ran cold as the truth of that thought sank deep into her bones.

There was no way to know whether or not Morgan would ever have noticed the significance of the blue shirt if she hadn't questioned him, but her actions had definitely set events into motion. If anything happened to him, it would be her fault, and she didn't know if she could live with that.

Therefore, she had to do whatever she could to keep that from happening.

Morgan said, "Let me know when you've doctored my file and re-checked your computer geek." He disconnected the call, turned around, and pulled her down on his lap. "Stop," he commanded.

"Stop what?"

"Fretting. Blaming yourself."

She leaned against him, let herself enjoy how big he was so that their faces were on a level rather than her sitting above him; enjoying, also, how attuned to her he was. That in itself was a revelation because she'd always worked so hard at keeping herself hidden. But Morgan *saw* her, and apparently liked what he saw. "Fretting is a natural part of the situation," she said. "And, yes, I have part of the responsibility for whatever the outcome is. If it works, yay me. If it doesn't . . ." To her dismay, her voice wobbled, and she had to blink fast to vanquish the tears that threatened. She firmed her mouth and lifted her chin, refusing to give in. What they had to face was best done with logic and preparation, not tears and emotion. She'd save those for afterward.

A small scowl pulled his dark brows together. "Listen. Part of my job is anticipating all the possibles. If I fail at that, it's on me. But there are things we can do. For instance, whatever phone I use to contact the Kingsleys, Axel can transfer the trigger to that number so when they trace the phone's location, we'll know to start looking for movement. Likewise, now he knows to start tracing all their calls, to put eyes on them, so if they have a personal meet with anyone we'll know it."

It was reassuring to know they wouldn't simply be sitting there waiting for someone to take a shot at him.

"What if the Kingsleys are innocent?" she asked. "What if it *is* the Russian—Yartsev—and he's betraying Russia to us, via the Kingsleys?"

"That's the best possible scenario. If that's the case, as soon as I contact the Kingsleys, they'll have Homeland Security on me so fast my ass will be in jail before I can blink twice. That's when Axel will have to come to my rescue before I get locked in some hole."

Her horror must have shown on her face because she didn't trust Axel to do anything. Morgan chuckled and said, "It won't come to that. I'll be held while my story is checked, sure, and there'll have to be some high-level powwows, but then the various agencies will get things settled. I have a top-secret security clearance and was reinvestigated just last year; that'll settle down most of the dust."

"But even if that's the best possible situation, Yartsev still tried to kill you. Wouldn't the Kingsleys have told him what you do, who you are?"

"They *should* have, if that were the case, but that doesn't mean he'd necessarily trust their assessment. If he's betraying his country, he's probably seeing knives coming at his back from every angle."

"Why wouldn't he try again?"

"I imagine the issue would be discussed with him," he said drily. "But that's all supposition. Until I know for certain they aren't involved, I'm going on the assumption that the Kingsleys are in this up to their asses. In the meantime, we'll start making preparations and taking precautions."

"Such as?"

"Perimeter security. I like what's already been done, but there can be more, and Axel can find the budget to pay for it. FLIR systems—that's forward-looking infrared cameras, which will spot body heat—wireless transmitters, an escape route. I can get one put in fairly fast if you don't mind tearing up a section of the floor. Beef up the windows. Of course, the best thing would be for you and Tricks to stay in town—"

"No," she said fiercely, then immediately realized no way would she let Tricks stay in any danger zone. "Well, Tricks can stay with Daina. But if I'm not going about my routine, wouldn't that be a heads-up to anyone watching?"

"Only if they've been watching long enough to *know* your routine."

"I don't care about the floor," she said, ignoring his point because she wasn't about to give ground on hers. "Tear it up. Start tomorrow."

"We don't have to move quite that fast. The clock won't start ticking until I contact the Kingsleys, and I won't do that until Axel doctors my file with the fake medical disability and finishes checking out his hack-hunter. You burned his ass with that one," he said, grinning.

"And now I've caused a delay because he's paranoid."

"It isn't paranoia if it's real. The world he lives in, it's real. I know he's checked his guy out so thoroughly he probably knows the placement of every freckle, and I figure the guy's clean, but Axel will take a hard look at him again." He paused. "I suggest we bring Jesse into the loop. We may need his help, his and the rest of your officers. I want to do everything I can to mini-mize any danger to you and the town."

She thought about that, running through things like scheduling and the budget—things that, as chief, she had to think about. "It would have to be on their own time. I don't think their involvement could be on the town dime."

"I don't expect them to do it for free, and I'll handle their pay." He shrugged. "I'm always gone too much to spend my paycheck, so it accumulates."

Privately Bo thought he might have to fight the men to get them to take money, given the way they were all but hero-worshipping him, but that was a problem for later.

Instinctively she knew that Morgan was slipping into his zone now, that he was going on the offensive instead of waiting for someone else to make a move. She could sense his focus sharpening, all but feel the electricity zinging through his veins. This was his world, a world of strategy and violence, and he was at home in it.

Chapter 25

Inviting killers to come after him meant Morgan had to do some serious strategizing, not just for himself but for Bo and any of the Hamrickville officers who elected to help. He went for a run, needing the automatic physical activity that would free his mind to worry and pick at the situation like a wolf picking at a carcass. He put on his shorts and running shoes, told Bo how long he'd be gone, and set out over the hills, pushing himself to a dead run.

He was afraid Bo was going to be a problem. His instinct was to make sure she was far away from any potential harm, and he expected her to fight him every inch of the way. He respected that, up to a point—the point at which he turned hairy and started dragging his knuckles on the ground. The bottom line was that she was precious to him and he'd do anything and everything he could to keep her safe, no matter how much of a battle she put up.

One step at a time, though; if he'd learned anything from all his missions over the years, it was that events never played out the way they were originally anticipated.

That was worrisome because it meant that no matter how he strategized, he couldn't cover everything. He had to play the odds and plan for the most likely avenue of attack while staying alert for something— anything—different.

This could go down several different ways. Yeah, it would be great if Homeland Security showed up and arrested him, because that truly would be the best outcome for both him and the country. He wanted Congresswoman Kingsley to be innocent, to be working for the country rather than against it. He liked her. She seemed warm and genuine. Big deal. He went with facts, not emotion.

At any rate, he didn't have to make any preparations for Homeland Security—likely the FBI. He was good there.

The possibilities after that were trickier, and far more likely.

The bad guys might use the Russian mob again, but he'd bet against that for a couple of reasons. One, they'd already tapped that asset, and it hadn't worked out well. Using them again established a pattern, one that pointed to Russia, which could lead to Yartsev. And while the Russian mob could blend in with a large metropolitan population, it was a different story in Hamrickville, West Virginia. A Russian would stand out like a hyena in a wolf den. Hell, someone from *New York* would stand out.

Which left the Kingsleys and Yartsev with two or three options: hire a home-grown hit man—which had a higher probability of success but meant bringing in a stranger who might or might not be reliable and who would represent another possible security risk—or involve the SVR, which had taken the place of the KGB.

If Homeland Security and FBI involvement was Morgan's best-case scenario, the SVR was his worst. The organization could bring to bear measures he'd have a difficult time countering: FLIR imaging, for one, which could literally tell them how many warm bodies were in the house and where. Overwhelming force was another possibility, in which every living thing in the house would be obliterated. A massive explosion was another possibility, as was a trained sniper taking him out any time he ventured out of the house.

On the other hand, if the Kingsleys were dealing state secrets to the SVR, the Russians wouldn't want to call attention to the organization or the connection. If anything went wrong—and something almost always went wrong, in some way—the repercussions would far outweigh the benefits.

Morgan mentally rolled the situation around, decided the SVR's involvement wasn't likely. Neither was the Russian mob's. Higher on the probability scale was a professional, but when secrecy was essential, involving others was a risk.

The most likely move they'd make was much closer to home. One of them personally would come to do the job.

Again, he necked down the probabilities. Joan Kingsley was the least likely, with her husband only slightly more likely, because he knew both of them on sight. Then again, maybe they both had unsuspected skill with weapons, which they would count on to take him by surprise. Yartsev himself was another possibility. He for certain would be weapons trained, and likely also trained to disguise himself. Though Morgan would have photographs and possibly video to study soon, he'd seen Yartsev in the flesh only once, and at a distance.

So—Yartsev was the most likely, followed by Dexter Kingsley, then Joan Kingsley. Or Yartsev and Dexter working together. Or all three of them.

Despite Yartsev's training, Morgan thought that was something he could handle. His own training was far beyond anything Yartsev would have experienced, at least in weapons and strategy. The SVR man dealt with espionage and intelligence; Morgan dealt with devastation—two very different disciplines.

He would prepare for three shooters; if only two, or even just one, tried to take him out, he'd be overprepared, which wasn't a bad thing.

While he'd been mentally sorting through all the details he'd been running full out, and now he slowed to a jog to cool down. A glance at his watch told him he'd been running for an hour; he was soaked with sweat, but all in all he felt pretty good. He was all systems go, heart and lungs working hard but smoothly. His legs weren't up to snuff yet after enduring two months of enforced inactivity, but every day he was adding distance to what he'd done the day before.

If they came here expecting to find a broken-down wreck, they were in for a surprise.

That said, he couldn't afford to feel cocky about his chances. His good physical condition would be easy for them to find out if they did even the most rudimentary fact-finding before acting. He had to assume they would if Yartsev was involved. The Russian wouldn't walk blind into his own bathroom. The Kingsleys . . . maybe, if they were acting on their own.

He took an easier pace heading back to the house, and halfway back ran into Bo and Tricks on their walk. As soon as she saw him, Tricks whirled and raced toward him, barking happily. He knelt down and gave her some vigorous ear rubbing and chest scratching, which evidently felt so good she almost collapsed in bliss.

Bo approached at a slower pace, Tricks's pink leash hooked through her belt loop out of her way, her green tank top baring the gleaming skin of her shoulders to the bright morning light. She was smiling as she watched him and Tricks. "Did you get everything worked out?" she asked, and when he stood, she linked her arm through his despite his sweatiness.

Morgan looked down at her and everything coalesced inside him in a blinding moment of light, the color around him flaring in brilliance before fading back to normal. In the trees a mockingbird began running through its repertoire of trills, whistles, and warbles, the sweet tone sinking into his bones. "Not yet," he said, feeling as if he were in an alternate universe and liking it. "The main part is up to you."

"Me?" She looked both puzzled and pleased. "I thought you didn't want me to help. Okay, what can I do?"

No hesitation, he thought, just a willingness to throw herself into the fray and do whatever she could. "You can marry me," he said.

She froze and actually turned white. Her big dark eyes widened until they eclipsed her face. Her mouth worked, but nothing came out.

He figured the turning white wasn't a good sign, but he knew the battle he had to fight was also one he had to win, and he was ready to go to war, right here and right now, to get this woman. "I've been playing it cool," he said, "not putting any pressure on you because I know you've dealt with some shitty people who let you down, and I wanted to give you time to realize you can trust me. But now I may be running out of time, and I want you sewed up and locked down, legally, in case this thing doesn't have a good outcome."

If anything, she went even whiter, standing stock-still on the narrow trail in the woods. The mocking-bird sang some more, and a few other birds got in their own whistles and calls. Tricks dropped her ball at his feet and backed up, tail wagging, inviting him to throw it for her. For once, the humans in her life ignored her.

Bo's mouth worked again, and this time words came out. "That's not fair," she croaked.

He clamped his hands around her waist and turned her to face him. "I don't give a shit about fair. I give a shit about you. Oh hell, that wasn't very romantic, was it?" He bent his head a little to peer into her eyes. "Do you want romantic? I can try. I'm more of a see-it, want-it, go-for-it type of guy, and I did: see you, want you, go for you."

Her chin wobbled, and alarm spiked through him. "Are you going to cry? Don't. Please don't. Just say yes, and we're good."

She looked around wildly as if expecting to be rescued by a bush or a tree, but his hands were firm on her waist and he wasn't about to let her go. Finally she half-shrieked, "You want me to marry you because you might *die*?" but at least she was talking and not crying.

"No, I want you to marry me because I'm . . . I'm—" To his consternation, the words clogged in his throat, and it was his turn to look around for one of those rescue bushes. Damn it. He thought he'd said them before, when he'd been engaged, but if he had, it was because they'd been expected and he couldn't remember for certain. This was completely different. This was important. This was the rest of his life.

He looked down into those big dark eyes, so solemn and so scared, and his pulse leaped through his body. He grabbed a deep breath and went for it. "I'm crazy in love with you. That's *why* I want to marry you. I want to marry you *now* so if anything happens to me, everything I own will come to you, no question. I'm not rich, but I have some savings and a good pickup truck, plus an old boat. What do you say?"

Annoyed that they were ignoring her, Tricks gave an indignant bark. He glanced down at her; she used her paw to bat the ball to his foot in case he couldn't figure it out. He gave a rough laugh. "I just hope you love me half as much as you love your dog."

The seconds ticked along in silence, going on and on until Morgan began to wonder if he'd overshot his target. Then her lips moved, and she said in a low voice, "I do."

He knew he had it bad when he didn't balk at coming in second to a dog. He was already used to it. Besides, Tricks wasn't an ordinary dog.

"So you'll marry me?"

She gave a jerky nod. "Though you could just make out a will leaving everything to me."

Yeah, she'd think of that.

"I'll do that, too. But I want to marry you, and you nodded yes, so it's a done deal. Is there a waiting period in West Virginia?"

She shook her head. Then she said, "You'd have to use your real name. But West Virginia isn't an open-record state, so marriage certificates won't turn up in an online search."

"That's convenient. I was already working out how I could finesse the timing, but it's good that it doesn't matter. I'd like to get it done tomorrow."

"I can't," she said, still looking dazed and more than halfway panicked.

"Why the hell not?"

"People."

"What people—oh. The ones who would be mad at you if you didn't tell them, right?"

She sighed. "Like Daina and Loretta and Jesse and half the town."

"Yeah, like them."

"I can't plan a wedding overnight anyway."

"Then we'll get married and have the wedding later." Shit, had he just said that? He'd been off the hook until he opened his big mouth. What had he let himself in for? Men looked forward to big weddings with less enthusiasm than they did a visit to the dentist. On the scale of things he didn't want to do, weddings might rank above seeing a proctologist. Maybe.

"I don't want a big wedding," she said, still in a tone that said she was in shock.

If anything, he fell even more in love with her. "I don't either, but what will the town let us get away with? I can tell you straight up they'll want Tricks to be a bridesmaid."

She gave a choked laugh. "You're probably right." She looked down at Tricks, who had abandoned her ball to sniff around some undergrowth. "What about you? Your mother, for instance. Will she want to be here? Come to think of it, have you been in contact with her at all?"

"*I* haven't, but we thought of that. Axel has sent a couple of emails that she thinks are from me, telling her I'm all right but busy, that kind of thing."

"Does she even know you were shot?" Bo asked, her tone a little shocked.

"No. I'm fine with her never knowing." He rubbed the side of his nose. "You think I should tell her I'm getting married? Ah, hell, don't bother answering. But I'm still not waiting; she can come to the after-marriage wedding. What about your parents?"

She looked off, thought it over. "I'll let them know, but really, there's no point in inviting them. They won't come. An announcement after the fact will do."

"If you want them here, they'll be here." If he had to twist arms and break heads, they'd be here. He'd have them escorted under armed guard, if necessary. His friends weren't the type of people who messed around.

She shook her head and gave him a wry glance. "You'd make them be here, wouldn't you? I appreciate the thought, but—no. Having them here would just stress me out. I'd rather be happy."

Making her happy was his new life's mission. He released her to lean down and pick up Tricks's ball, then linked his hand with hers and headed back down the trail toward the house. Her slim fingers felt as fragile as a bird's bones in his rough hand, and for the first time in his life he was acutely aware of the trust being offered to him as a man. His previous relationships, abbreviated and fairly uncomplicated as most of them had been, had been straightforward and based mostly on sex. This was more. She was giving him something incredibly special—herself, her trust, inviting him into her life.

Pragmatically she said, "We can't get married yet anyway. We have to get the license here in this county, where we live. Even though the courthouse isn't in Hamrickville, too many people know me. The people we'll tell will keep it quiet, but the average person in the county courthouse won't know they shouldn't Google your real name, and trust me, at least one of them would."

He said something very graphic and pithy, not at all happy to see his plans put on hold.

She gave him an amused glance. "In a hurry to get me into bed?"

"You bet. I've never had married sex before. I wonder if it's different."

She laughed, and he used his grip on her hand to tug her closer and drape his arm around her shoulders. "Okay. I'm not happy about waiting, but I don't see any way around it. I'll be busy the next few days anyway: get a bank account set up in the Caymans. Bring the guys up to speed. Ammo to buy, security to set up, things like that."

She digested all of that and asked only one question. "The Caymans?"

"A blackmail attempt won't look legitimate unless I'm asking for serious money, which brings up the problem of how I'd report that to the IRS. They'll expect me to know about things like that, which I do; I can't have them wire the money into a regular stateside bank. The blackmail has to look real from every angle, so I have to have an offshore account for the money to be paid into."

"How will you avoid getting into trouble over it?"

"Everything I do will be coordinated with Axel and documented. Yes, there are gray areas, but what matters is stopping them. I'm assuming their guilt until I'm proven wrong." He paused. "I don't expect they'll ever appear in a court of law. This will be handled on the down low."

"Meaning . . . what?"

"Meaning they may negotiate their way out of trouble by double-crossing the Russians, though they may not be in any position to do that. The flow of information may be all one way, in which case their asses are in a sling. However it ends, that's not my problem. My job is to stop them."

"*Our* job," she corrected quietly. "We're in this together." She gave him a crooked smile. "That's what being married means."

They weren't quite a mile from home; they strolled, they threw the ball for Tricks whenever they were in a clear patch. There was plenty of time before Bo had to go to work, so they weren't in any hurry. He enjoyed holding her hand, teasing a grin out of her, watching the sun dapple her face as they walked through the trees.

He felt both drunk and sober, elated and nervous, numb and so hyperalert he was aware of everything, every bird song, every breeze, every rustle of the trees.

Damn. This must be what being in love felt like. No wonder it made people act like fools. The guys would never let him live this down—and he didn't care.

Of all the things that had happened since Morgan Yancy turned up in her life, this morning had left Bo with the biggest sense of unreality. She couldn't believe he'd asked her to marry him, but even more startling was that she'd said yes. But he had, and she had, and she still hadn't recovered from the shock.

There were a lot of questions that needed to be asked and decisions that had to be made, but for now she couldn't concentrate on any of them. She would deal with those later—after she'd come to terms with the fact that she was getting *married*. And not just married, but married soon, as in whenever he was freed from the need to conceal his real name. To him the delay was annoying; to her, events were progressing at breakneck speed. She was both dazzled and terrified; they were going from strangers to lovers to *married* in just two months? Well, a little over two months, by the time they actually got the deed done. Dear God, what was she thinking?

She was thinking that she loved him. She was thinking that living with someone was different from the on-off of dating, that she had gotten to know him faster than she would have from a year of dating. She was thinking that she relied on him, that he'd risked his life for both her and Tricks, that he always stood ready to back her up if she needed him. She didn't know his birthday, or his mother's name, or about a million other things about him—but she did know the important stuff, and she'd learn about the unimportant stuff as it came up.

When they got back to the house, he said, "I'll grab a quick shower and help you with lunch."

"Are you going to town with me today?"

"Not today. I'm going to do some thinking about beefing up the security here, walk the hills behind the house again to see if I overlooked anything, that kind of thing."

He was serious about the security, and given that he was setting himself up as bait, she was all for taking any precautions they could. The thought of danger coming here, to this place she'd made her own, sent chills up her back. He truly could die. He'd nearly died before she ever met him, but he wasn't hesitating to wade back into the fray, risking himself yet again. That was what he did, and who he was. She might fear what he did, but she wouldn't change what he was.

She put some bacon in the oven to bake, then began tearing up lettuce and dicing fresh tomatoes into it. Morgan came down the stairs two at a time as she salted and peppered the mixture. "I smell bacon," he said.

"BLT wraps. The tortillas are in the refrigerator. Hope you like them."

"I've never seen a BLT I didn't like, except for one that had avocado on it."

"You like avocado."

"I like guacamole. Two different things. And it's called a BLT for a reason, not a BLAT."

"With that kind of reasoning, you'd leave off the bread."

"Bread is understood. And it starts with a B, so that's taken care of. Even when it's a tortilla, it's still bread, just flat."

His guyness when it came to food never failed to amuse her. On the other hand, he wasn't picky, which would have driven her nuts.

He set the table and kept watch on the bacon while Bo finished up with the lettuce and tomato part. Tricks stood watching it all with intense interest, positioned by her bowl as a reminder not to forget her when the food was doled out.

"As if I'd forget," Bo chided gently, keeping one eye on the clock because she didn't want to feed Tricks early. Tricks looked at her bowl and back to Bo, then nudged the bowl with her foot.

"It isn't time." Though it was just two minutes early, a rule was a rule, because if you bent it Tricks would devote herself to bending it even more. When the digital numbers changed, Tricks barked.

"Scary," Morgan commented, having watched the performance yet again. When the numbers changed,

Tricks recognized the magic ones that signaled Food Time.

Bo measured out the food and set it down. Tricks wagged her tail in approval, then began eating. Bo petted her, then a thought struck and she straightened to give Morgan a narrow-eyed look. "Are you marrying me just to get my dog?"

"It's a thought," he replied without hesitation, then laughed. "As if marrying you would make any difference. She's yours and as far as she's concerned, no one else is even close. I know how she feels." He winked at her. "I'm yours, too, remember?"

The silver-tongued devil, he knew just what to say. She chuckled and returned the wink, a little amazed at how easy it had become to flirt with him. She didn't think she'd ever winked at another soul before Morgan.

After lunch she noticed she was running a little tight on time, so she hurried to take a shower and get ready. Morgan would be busy, which meant Tricks was going with her. She would tell the important people in her life about her and Morgan, and put her head together with Daina to start making plans. Now that Morgan's desire to get married *tomorrow* had been thwarted, there wasn't any need for both a quick marriage and then a ceremonial wedding later. They could make some quick plans, Miss Doris would bake them a cake—nothing fancy, but when something tasted as good at Miss Doris's cakes, it didn't have to be fancy—and she could go shopping for a dress. A simple ceremony, maybe in the park; simple refreshments and treasured friends. His mother could be here for the actual ceremony. What could be better? But if the situation with Morgan hadn't resolved itself by then, they'd have to be extra careful and not have the ceremony outside.

A chill went down her back. How many weddings were planned with the idea that a sniper might take out the groom?

Thinking of that precaution led her to think about the larger security areas they had to address. Both she and Morgan would have to be extra careful. As soon as he was cleared to make his "blackmail" call to set events in motion, she would have Daina keep Tricks. She couldn't bear the idea of Tricks being in danger again—Morgan, either, but this was his show, his job, and his decision. Tricks was as innocent as a child. Being separated would be difficult for them both, but better that than Tricks being harmed.

Because all that was on her mind, she felt uneasy as she went downstairs. "Be extra careful," she said to Morgan, her brow furrowed. "Take your cell phone, and your weapon."

He nodded to the Glock lying on the kitchen counter. "Planning on it. How about you? It's never too early to start getting in the habit of taking extra precautions. Where's your weapon, Ms. Chief of Police?"

"In my bag." She'd bought a holster that she could clip to her waistband, but the only time she ever used it was if she and Tricks were going on a walk by themselves, something that seldom happened these days.

"Takes too much time to dig it out of a bag. Get it out, and keep it handy."

His voice always took on a matter-of-fact coolness when he slipped into what she thought of as action mode, but he knew what he was talking about so she didn't argue. She got the holstered weapon out of her bag and clipped it to her waistband. "I feel as if I'm masquerading as Lara Croft, Tomb Raider," she muttered as she pulled her shirt down over the bulge.

"Naw. You're way cooler," he said with a quick grin, though his hard gaze swept down her form. "Carry your bag on your right shoulder, and no one will be able to tell you're packing."

She got her cell phone and Tricks's leash. Tricks bounced to the door and stood there looking eagerly at the door handle, concentrating as if she could open the door by force of will alone. Bo figured that in Tricks's mind that usually worked because if she stared at the door long enough someone would open it for her.

"I'll call you when I leave," she told Morgan, stretching on tiptoe to kiss him.

His arm went around her and he pulled her close for more than one kiss. "Drive safe. Love you. See you tonight."

She hesitated, then said, "I love you too," a little shyly, because saying the words still felt so strange, because feeling free to say them was nothing short of earth-shattering. She could feel herself blushing as she went out the door, with Tricks darting ahead of her, barking in an excited frenzy as she dashed around the vehicles.

"Tricks, load up!" Bo called as she used the remote to unlock the doors. She opened the passenger door for Tricks and tossed the leash onto the console. Tricks was still barking, and Bo started to turn to call her again.

Something hard jabbed painfully at the back of her skull, and a man said, "Don't make a move, or I'll blow a hole in your damn head."

Chapter 26

Bo froze. Her skin prickled as if ice cubes had slid down her spine. Her knees wobbled like gelatin. Her throat and lungs seized, her heart rate leaped into a full gallop.

But while her body was reacting to the twin bombs of terror and adrenaline, her mind somehow distanced itself, fought for clarity. Two thoughts occurred. One, the voice and accent were American, which meant this was likely Mr. Kingsley. Two, she'd been right about the hacker being right under Axel's nose. How else could they have been located so fast, when they had talked to Axel just last night?

Tricks was still barking; she was surprised Morgan hadn't already stepped outside to see what was up. Because he hadn't, maybe he'd glanced outside the window and was already in action. She had no idea what form that action would take, or what direction he would come from.

Kingsley grabbed Bo's hair in a painful grip and jerked her head back. "Shut the dog up, or I will. Now!"

Galvanized by the threat, Bo managed to say, "Tricks, sit." Her voice was thin, but at least it worked.

Her head was at such an angle that she could barely see Tricks out of the corner of her eye, but Tricks stopped barking and her butt hit the ground, and she looked up with her big doggy grin, expecting to be praised and petted. "Good girl." To Kingsley she said, "She's a golden retriever. They're very friendly." God, don't let him mistake Tricks's barking for aggression and shoot her; most likely her barks had meant *Someone new to pet me!*

"No shit," he said, jabbing the pistol harder against her skull. "Do I look stupid? But she's a pretty dog; I might take her with me when I finish here."

How pathetic was it to feel grateful that Tricks might survive even if she and Morgan didn't?

Think! She had to think. There was a pistol in the holster at her waist, hidden by the bag slung over her shoulder, if she could get to it without him noticing. Pulled tight against him as she was, he'd notice any movement. Then it didn't matter because he switched hands with the weapon held to her head and swiftly frisked her, immediately finding the pistol and jerking it off her waistband. "How about that," he said sarcastically. "Who would ever think the chief of police would have a gun? Did you think I wouldn't check?"

They knew who she was. She doubted the Kingsleys would have been able to find out both the location of Morgan's cell phone and her identity without using government assets, so they had—just not the United States government.

She wondered how long he'd been out here. Had he seen them go in, but perhaps hadn't been close enough to get an accurate shot? Pistols weren't distance weapons. On the other hand, maybe he'd simply been waiting to catch one of them alone. If it were Morgan, he could kill him and leave, but Bo was the one who had come out of the house first. She knew damn good and well he intended her to be the shield between him and Morgan.

Her thoughts raced feverishly. How good a shot was he? He was a lawyer, right? How likely was he to be expert with a pistol? Competent, maybe, but when people like him went hunting, they were more likely to do game hunting with important clients they needed to impress. Shooting with a scoped rifle was a far cry from being accurate with a pistol.

But what if he was? Unlikely people took up target shooting.

And target shooting was very different from shooting at people, who didn't just stand there unmoving. One of the classes Jesse had insisted she take had emphasized always running when faced with a pistol, that the odds were you wouldn't be hit. Okay, if she could pull free—

That thought was interrupted as he tightened his hand in her pony- tail, wrapping it around his hand and jerking her toward the house. "Keep your mouth shut, open the door, and don't try anything. Where is he?"

"He . . . he was in the kitchen when I came out, but he was going to change clothes so . . . I don't know for sure."

"When we go in the door, where's the kitchen?"

So he either hadn't had a chance to reconnoiter and look through the windows, or he'd been too afraid to try. Walking up to someone's windows during the day and peering in was kind of noticeable. "To the left," she said, letting her voice quiver. That was kind of accurate: ahead, and somewhat to the left, but definitely not directly to the left.

"Which way does the door open?"

"Ah . . ." She actually had to think about that, because she opened the door both going and coming and either direction seemed natural to her. "To the right."

He pushed her forward.

Surely Morgan had seen them. Surely he'd slipped out the back door and was easing around the side of the house. *But what if he had gone upstairs for something?* She had no way of knowing. She stumbled to buy time; it wasn't much of a pretense because of the way he had her head pulled back. She couldn't see where she was putting her feet. If she hadn't known every foot of her property so well, she really would have stumbled and fallen.

"Stand the fuck up," Kingsley snarled, pushing her forward another foot or so.

Morgan would have heard Tricks barking, in any event. She had to trust that he'd at least looked out the window.

Tricks barked again, that joyous, welcome sound that she gave when she saw just two people: Bo and Morgan.

"She likes to be petted before she'll eat," she said jerkily, unable to think of anything else to say but hoping she could distract him from Tricks, both her barking and the possibility that she might be dancing toward Morgan.

Dear God, please let Morgan be coming toward them. Please don't let this asshole jerk force her inside the house and catch him unawares. If that happened, they were both dead.

"What?" Kingsley sounded startled, as if he couldn't put her words in any context. That was good. That was what she'd wanted.

"Tricks. When she gets fed at night. She likes to be petted."

"Forget the damn dog. Don't open your mouth again."

He pushed her once more, his hold on her hair pulling her head slightly to the right. At the very edge of her vision she saw movement, movement that wasn't Tricks. A pistol was jammed against the back of her skull but she had to do something to keep him from seeing Morgan. If she startled him he might pull the trigger anyway. She had no way of knowing whether or not she was signing her own death warrant but there was nothing else she could do. At least Morgan and Tricks would be okay.

The two beings she loved most in the world would be okay, and that was all that mattered.

She simply lifted her feet and let herself drop heavily to the ground.

Hot pain seared through her scalp. Her whole body jarred as she hit the ground. Shots, both a sharp crack and a deeper roar, shattered the morning, the world.

Her head and neck burned as Kingsley's grip on her hair jerked her head around. Moisture, hot and red, drenched her.

Then everything was quiet except for her ringing ears. She felt odd; her focus was both blurred and sharpened, a series of images flashing in great detail while everything else blurred. She was lying on her side without knowing how she'd gotten there, staring at small pieces of gravel and blades of grass, the first post on the porch, the concrete. Everything was sideways, which puzzled her until she realized why. Oh, right; lying on her side would cause that.

She knew she was alive, but wasn't sure how. She couldn't order her thoughts enough to . . . Kingsley . . . where was Kingsley? He wasn't gripping her hair any longer though she tried to move her head and couldn't. Maybe he was the bulk she could feel at her back. Maybe he was still using her as a shield.

She saw Morgan charging toward her, big black Glock in his fist. She saw Tricks right at his heels, heard her barking. She said, "Tricks, be quiet," afraid Kingsley would shoot her. Then she realized there was no point in being quiet now, nothing to be gained from it, because obviously he already knew Morgan was there. Why wasn't Kingsley shooting? And why was her voice so weak and distant?

Then Morgan skidded to his knees beside her and shoved away the heavy mass that had been resting against her back. His eyes were pale blue fire in his strangely white face as he gently eased her flat on the ground. "Let me see, sweetheart," he said softly.

She frowned up at him. "See what?"

"Your neck."

He was pulling at her clothes. Tricks was whining, nosing her arm. Bo lifted her left hand and gently stroked Tricks's leg, which seemed to be about all she could reach.

"What about my neck?"

"Kingsley shot you."

"He did?" she asked, surprised. "I don't feel shot."

"Trust me on this." Morgan turned her head to the side, his touch tender, and he blew out a breath of relief. "It's more than a graze, more like a deep gouge, but no important veins or arteries were hit."

"That's a plus." She managed a scowl, though she wasn't certain why—maybe to reassure him that she was okay because grumpy meant okay. "Are you sure you didn't shoot me? By accident, of course." Kingsley's pistol had been against her head. How could he possibly have missed enough to just graze her neck? Or gouge. She couldn't quite picture the difference.

"I'm certain," he growled, shucking his tee shirt off over his head and tying it around her neck, cinching it almost painfully tight with the knot right over where her neck was beginning to burn.

"How? I heard two shots."

"Because my shot hit him."

That made sense, so she stopped arguing and instead grappled with the logical conclusion. "He's dead, right?"

"Very."

She was fairly certain "very" meant something grisly. She didn't want to look. She kept her head carefully turned away as Morgan slipped his right arm under her knees and his left one under her back, lifted her, and easily stood with her cradled against him. Her head swam from the movement, and she clutched at his bare shoulder. He carried her inside the house, pausing at the door to call Tricks in a sharp tone that had her trotting obediently to him, as if she knew this wasn't a time for mischief. She whined as Morgan carefully laid Bo on the sofa.

"Don't try to sit up, that'll put pressure on your neck and make the bleeding worse," he said as he grabbed up the phone.

"Wait," Bo said, lifting a hand toward him. She was surprised to see blood on her arm, her hand. "I'm not critical, right?"

He hesitated, his expression still fierce and set as he stared down at her. "Right."

"Get in touch with Axel first. That's more important."

Morgan's jaw set, then he started tapping the screen of her phone. "I'm sending him a text. If the hacker is capturing all his calls and hears my voice, he'll know it's all gone to hell and bolt, alert Congresswoman Kingsley. 'Ha ha, big brother, I was right,'" he read to her. "He should be able to figure that out, because you'd never call him big brother."

After the zipping sound that signaled the text had been sent, he tapped the screen some more. "I'm calling Jesse direct, instead of 911. I want to keep this as quiet as possible, give Axel time to throw a net over his hacker," he said to Bo, then, "Jesse, this is Morgan. We've had some trouble at Bo's house. One man dead, Bo's injured, not critically. Get some people out here, but keep it quiet. Nothing over the radio. This is all tied in with why I'm here." He listened for a minute, then said, "Okay," and thumbed off the call. "Jesse's getting everyone rounded up," he said, then eased down to sit on the edge of the sofa with his hip against hers.

"I almost had a heart attack," he growled. "I heard Tricks bark, looked out the window, and saw him jab that barrel against the base of your skull. I grabbed my weapon and went out the back door, but I expected to hear a shot every second."

"I had some use as a shield," Bo said drowsily. Her neck burned and throbbed, but overall she just felt sleepy and very fuzzy. "That was the only reason. Thank goodness it wasn't Yartsev."

"Yeah. He'd have had a better plan."

She would likely never have seen Yartsev, she thought. She'd have driven off, he'd have killed Morgan as soon as Morgan stepped outside, then perhaps he'd have waited for her to return. Probably not; she'd have simply returned home to find Morgan's body, and she would never, never have recovered from that. Kingsley, on the other hand, hadn't had the skill or the experience to pull it off. But she was tired of thinking about it, tired of fighting to stay awake. "I'm so sleepy," she mumbled, and closed her eyes.

"Baby, no, you can't go to sleep." He put his hand on her shoulder and shook her.

Her eyelids cracked open just enough for her to give him a baleful look. "Did you just call me baby?"

His lips twitched. "I did. And you can't do anything about it."

She managed a smirk. "The joke's on you. I don't mind at all. Just let me rest, okay?"

"You are resting. You're flat on your back."

"But you keep talking, and I want to take a nap. Just a short one."

"No dice."

"Then get a washcloth and get some of this blood off me, okay?"

As soon as his weight left the sofa and he disappeared, Bo closed her eyes and went to sleep.

She was roused by the slow slide of a warm, wet washcloth over her arm. "Tricked me, didn't you," he said without heat, his touch firm but tender.

She didn't feel guilty. "Just for a minute. I'm so tired."

"Adrenaline crash and blood loss."

"Where's Tricks?"

"Lying right here. She's fine."

Her phone signaled an incoming text, and Morgan picked it up. "He said, 'Gloat, why don't you? 10-4.' He understands."

She didn't see how he could tell that, but he was the one who worked with Axel so she took him at his word.

She was silent for a while as he carefully cleaned as much of the blood off her as he could. She'd have loved to change out of her bloody clothes but didn't feel like going to the exertion of taking them off. No doubt she'd be taken to the nearest hospital where they'd be cut off her anyway. She didn't care; she never wanted to wear them again.

Despite her fatigue she began thinking of practical matters. "I'll need some pajamas and fresh underwear," she murmured.

He gave her a startled look. "Right now?"

"In the hospital. There's no way I can get out of going, is there?"

"None."

"Then gather some things together for me. Pajamas, underwear, robe, toothbrush and toothpaste, hairbrush. Also some jeans and sandals, a shirt and a bra. Make that two pairs of underwear, just in case. And anything else you see that might come in handy."

He leaned over and kissed her. "Now I know you'll be all right."

"Yeah? How?"

"You're giving me orders, just like when I first showed up here."

"Someone had to. You weren't taking care of yourself."

"And you aren't taking care of yourself now. I think I'll wait until reinforcements get here before I get your things," he said, proving that he was smarter than the average bear.

"I'm lying here, aren't I?"

"Yeah, but I can't tell the difference between asleep and unconscious, so I need you to be awake."

"All right, all right." Her neck was hurting worse by the minute; she wasn't certain she could go to sleep anyway.

"I think I'll get a tattoo of a bull's-eye on my neck," she threw out to see what kind of reaction she could get out of him. Given that she currently didn't feel like doing anything, not even sitting up, that was about the limit of her entertainment.

"Bullshit," he said, frowning down at her.

"Hey, you did."

"I got the tattoo before I got shot."

"I can pretend I did, too."

"All right, so 'Mom' on my triceps would have been less in-your-face, but the GO-Teams are an in-your-face group of guys. One time we—" Whatever tale he was about to get into was halted when he lifted his head at the distant sound of sirens. Tricks jumped up but didn't run to the door as she normally did whenever she heard something unusual. Instead she stood by the sofa and gave her tail an uncertain wag; the expression on her face was the same one she'd gotten as a puppy whenever she broke something and didn't know exactly what had happened but figured she was guilty anyway. She whined softly.

Bo cautiously shifted enough that she could touch Tricks, slide her fingers deep into the soft fur. "It's okay, princess. I smell bloody, but I'm fine." To Morgan she said, "I expect you'll be heading to D.C. as soon as I'm hauled off, right?"

"It's my job," he said, not even hesitating.

She hadn't expected him to stay and wouldn't have asked that of him. What was going on was a lot bigger than what had just happened here, despite the dead man lying in her yard.

The sirens rapidly got closer and louder. Morgan stood to look out the windows as the parade of vehicles roared into the yard. "Jesse's leading the posse," he said. "Medics right behind him." He opened the door to let the medics in and went out to meet Jesse.

From that minute on, Bo had no control at all— not that she'd had a lot before. Within a minute her house and yard were swarming with crisis personnel. Medics surrounded her, their bodies preventing her from seeing anything other than them. Morgan's tee shirt was cut off from around her neck, but part of the fabric stuck and they left that, bandaged over it. It said something about how she felt that she made no protest at the blood pressure cuff, the light in her eyes, the IV line that was started almost immediately. Jesse came in to see her, his face that combination of carefully blank eyes and nothing-going-on-here expression that cops used to keep events at a distance so they could function.

"You're leading an interesting life lately, Chief," he said.

"I keep interesting company."

"Tell me about it. He filled me in. We'll handle things on this end. Don't worry about it. Nothing will hit the news until he gives the okay."

She managed a truncated nod because the thick bandage kept her from moving her head very much. "Can you take care of Tricks? Take her to Daina?"

"No problem. If Daina can't take her tonight, I'll take her home with me."

With all the people grouped around her she hadn't seen Morgan come back in, but he appeared beside her as she was being loaded into the back of the medic truck, one of her suitcases in hand. He'd taken the time to pull on another shirt. "Here's your purse, too," he said, putting the suitcase inside the truck and setting her bag on top of the stretcher with her. "I put your phone in it." He leaned down and kissed her, his blue eyes intent as he studied her. "I'll call you when I can."

"Go do what you have to do," she said, lifting her hand to touch his jaw. "I love you."

"I love you back. Remember that." He gave her one more fierce kiss, then was gone.

From inside the medic truck, she couldn't even watch as he drove away.

Sometimes things just went to hell and there was nothing you could do about it except pick up the pieces and deal with what was left. He hadn't anticipated—no one had—the hacker actually being the one guy Axel had gotten to set up the trap and try to trace the hack. They must have had a big laugh about that, picturing Axel anxiously waiting for a trap that was never sprung because they knew it was a trap.

Dexter Kingsley had moved so fast Morgan hadn't had time to put in more sophisticated security measures, and the ones he *had* installed had been useless. Kingsley had evidently driven partway up the driveway while they'd been on their walk. Then he'd simply waited, maybe crouched out of sight behind Morgan's Tahoe, until someone left the house. If Morgan had been first, he'd have been shot on sight. But Bo had been first, and Kingsley couldn't shoot her without alerting Morgan, so he'd decided to use her as a shield.

God save him from amateurs. They were unpredictable, they did wild shit that anyone with half-assed training would never do, and sometimes it worked. What if Kingsley had thought to use a silenced weapon? He'd have shot Bo, maybe Tricks too, then waited until

Morgan came out. Kingsley hadn't thought of it, and the dumbass plan hadn't worked out, but Bo had come so close to being killed Morgan had lost ten years off his life. Only his training had kept him moving, kept him thinking, all the while he was almost insane with gut-wrenching fear.

He wanted the hacker—Devan Hubbert—in a bad way, but Hubbert had given them the slip. At least Axel had been able to secure Hubbert's personal computer and currently had a whole computer forensic team breaking it down to the code. Whether or not they could find anything incriminating against the Kingsleys was up in the air. The bad news was that street cams showed Hubbert entering the Russian embassy, which meant either he had asylum or he was a deep plant. They couldn't touch him, at least not without the Russians' permission—which wasn't going to happen. In the meantime, they were digging as deep into his background as they could to determine if he was a deep plant or a home-grown traitor.

When Morgan had entered the GO-Teams headquarters, everyone he met looked surprised to see him. There were a lot of people on the support side who he knew on sight but whose names he didn't know. Everyone knew his name, though, and knew something really bad had gone down a few months before. The place looked like a fire drill, with everyone rushing around and a sense of urgency permeating the air.

He'd gone straight to Axel's office; though they hoped Devan Hubbert wasn't still able to monitor Axel's conversations, until they knew for certain, they were maintaining strict protocol over the phone, so nothing much had been said. Axel's office, his car, his home were all being swept for bugs. They were routinely swept anyway, but this time everything was being checked down to the wiring. All computers were being checked for any keylogging program. The damage Hubbert could have done—likely had done—was enormous.

"Let's step outside," Axel said sourly, indicating how worried they were about the entire building being compromised. There was a safe room, completely shielded from electronics, but evidently he wasn't trusting even that right now.

From the street the building looked like a nondescript, slightly run-down office building in need of some repairs. There was secure parking from a discreet entrance in back, and adjacent was a public parking area where Morgan had parked since he didn't have his security ID with him.

The three-hour drive had put him there in the late afternoon, when the D.C. heat was oppressive, the humidity close to a hundred percent. Because of that, as well as the possibility of a parabolic mic being aimed their way—who the hell knew?—they got into Morgan's Tahoe and he cranked up the air conditioning as well as the radio.

"What happened?" Axel brusquely demanded.

"Dexter Kingsley showed up. Good thing it wasn't Yartsev, or the outcome would likely have been different. I didn't have any fancy security in place yet; it's sheer luck Bo and I aren't both dead. He grabbed her when she left for work. I heard the dog barking, saw what was going down, and flanked him from the rear. He was holding Bo with his pistol to the back of her head," Morgan said tersely, his face tightening as he relived the sheer dread and, yes, terror, that he'd had to fight through so he could function. "She lifted her feet and dropped straight to the ground. He shot but his aim was off, got her in the neck."

Axel's sour expression didn't so much as flicker. "Is she dead?"

"No. He didn't hit anything vital."

"I assume he's dead though."

"Correct."

Axel said, "That's something, then. We still don't have shit against the congresswoman. Maybe there'll be something on Hubbert's personal computer, but until then we can't overtly move against her."

"Overt" was the operative word. What was done in private was a different animal from what was said in public.

"I suggest we pay Congresswoman Kingsley a visit," Morgan said, glancing at the time. "I wonder if she's still in her office."

"No. I put a tail on her. She went home twenty minutes ago." His smile was cold and mirthless. "I think talking to her is a good idea. Unofficially, of course."

"It will be a pleasure." The long drive had taken Morgan from a hot murderous rage down to a cold murderous rage, driven by the knowledge that he couldn't do what he wanted to do. His instinct was to walk up to the door and when Joan Kingsley opened it put a bullet in her forehead. He couldn't do that. He didn't give a damn about the law, but he did give a damn about whether or not he'd be free to spend the rest of his life with Bo. That mattered. Personal vengeance was one thing, but stupidity was another. Axel would take care of Congresswoman Kingsley, whether that action involved something catastrophic to her health or was restricted to removing her from a position of power—or a combination of both. Things happened. Sometimes those things were truly accidents. Sometimes they weren't.

"Let me drive," Axel said. "I know the way." They swapped seats, though Morgan wasn't crazy about it because Axel was a shitty driver. But when they arrived at the Kingsley residence in Bethesda, he saw why. The house was a gorgeous Georgian mansion, three stories, thick columns. A gated drive prevented casual access to the property. Axel let down the window to press the button. From his vantage point Morgan couldn't see a security camera, but there almost assuredly was one, and Axel would have known that. He preferred to keep Morgan in the passenger seat, out of sight. Morgan aided in that by looking down as if he were fooling with his phone in case there were multiple cameras with different viewpoints.

"Yes?" came a voice, without identifying the residence.

"Axel MacNamara to see Congresswoman Kingsley."

There was a short pause, then the gates began smoothly sliding open on their tracks. When there was enough room, Axel pulled forward. Watching in the side mirror, Morgan saw the gates slide together again.

There was a lot of money represented here, in the three-car garage, the security, the house, the manicured grounds. Morgan remembered their cabin cruiser, which wasn't a small one. He guessed it would run a couple of hundred thousand, at least; he'd never priced a boat that big or that fancy. Congresswoman Kingsley's salary wasn't anything to sneeze at, but neither was it sufficient for this. Dexter Kingsley must have been a hell of a lawyer—either that, or they'd been raking money in on the side for quite a while.

Axel got out and closed the driver's door. Morgan waited a little bit longer, watching the curtains to see if he detected any movement. Axel continued without pause up the sidewalk to the front door. Morgan thought he saw a slight twitch of the curtains, enough that whoever had peeked out had seen only Axel going to the door.

Quickly he exited, vaulted a piece of shrubbery, and was standing beside Axel when Congresswoman Kingsley opened the door, a calm smile on her pretty face, her silver-white hair immaculate.

He hadn't accomplished anything except surprise, but it was worth it to see the absolute shock on her face when she recognized him.

She began, "Morgan! It's wonderful to—" Then she stopped, realizing the pretense was no good because she knew that he'd remembered what he'd seen that day. She knew because of the hacker. She knew because her husband had gone to silence him. What she didn't know was what had happened to her husband.

"Congresswoman," Axel said into the abrupt silence. "May we come in?"

She didn't say anything, simply opened the door wider and stepped away, leaving them to follow her or not.

She went into an elegantly appointed living room, the furniture upholstered in a yellow-and-white-striped fabric that was probably silk. "Please, sit down," she said, her voice only slightly strained.

Morgan planted his ass on the striped silk, impassively watching her. He waited for Axel to speak but when Axel didn't and she didn't, the silence grew and deepened until all the color had leached from her face except for the artificial hues of her makeup. Morgan was accustomed to being the weapon, the point of the spear, but he realized that this time Axel was content to let him take the lead.

"Ma'am," he said, "I regret to inform you of your husband's death."

She flinched, an instinctive move that was swiftly conquered. She straightened her shoulders. "I see. May I ask . . . the circumstances?"

"Head shot," he replied laconically. "While he was attempting to commit murder."

Joan Kingsley wasn't made of steel, she was made of titanium. She sat quietly, watching them, waiting for one of them to betray exactly how much they knew. She wasn't going to give them anything, not a single detail.

Axel spoke up. "We believe Foma Yartsev left the country this morning. A full-press search is going on for Devan Hubbert, but we have his personal computer, and a team is doing a thorough forensic investigation of it now."

She had gone even whiter as she listened, but she didn't break. She folded her hands, said calmly, "I don't know what you're talking about."

"I'm sure you don't. Let's be frank, Congresswoman. We know. We can't prove it—yet—but we know."

"Does this have anything to do with my husband's death?" she asked, still not giving an inch, determined to play her hand as long as she could. If they couldn't prove anything, she was for damn certain not going to confess.

Axel ignored the question. "You won't be allowed to leave the country. The FBI will be watching every move you make. I suggest you resign from the Armed Service Committee immediately. In the short term, that might be beneficial to your health."

She glanced swiftly at Morgan. He met her gaze with all the icy menace he felt.

"And in the long term?" she asked.

He didn't blink. "You have to take your chances," he said finally.

"I see." She stood, lifted her chin. "Thank you, gentlemen, for stopping by to give me the . . . bad news. If you don't mind, I'd like to be alone now. May I ask when my husband's body will be released to me?"

"We'll let you know," Axel said, and they left.

Chapter 27

Letting congresswoman Kingsley walk—at least for now—went against the grain, but Morgan accepted that he'd have to let Axel do what he did best, which was handle crises. In an earlier time he'd have stayed, resumed his training, reintegrated into his team. But this was a different day, and he had to get back to Bo.

"You know how to get in touch with me," he said as he let Axel out at the GO-Team headquarters. Darkness had fallen; even driving hard, he couldn't make it back to Hamrickville before midnight. He could have gone to his condo and spent the night there, started out fresh in the morning, but he didn't want to go to the condo. He wanted to look into Bo's solemn dark eyes for himself, reassure himself she was all right even though he knew Jesse would have contacted him if anything went wrong. That was what he knew. What he felt was entirely different.

Startled, Axel said, "Where are you going?"

"Back to West Virginia."

"Yeah, I guess you need to get your stuff."

"No, I need to check on Bo, make sure she's all right. We're getting married."

Axel's eyes literally bugged out. "What? What? Are you crazy?"

"Team members can be married."

"It isn't that. It's—are you *crazy?* This is my stepsister you're talking about. She's a vindictive viper. She'll drive you nuts. She—"

"Yeah, she feels the same way about you." One thing about it, those two were never going to reconcile their differences and become friends. Morgan didn't much care; it wasn't as if they were going to be spending their Christmases together.

"But—"

"But, nothing. We're getting married. I asked, she said yes. You can be there if you want, but I warn you, you'll have to be on your best behavior or the people in that town will take you apart on her behalf."

Seeing that tactic was going nowhere, Axel shifted. "You need to get medically cleared, get back into training." He paused. "I'm assuming you can pass the physical. You can, can't you?"

"I wasn't sure at first that I'd ever be able to get back into action, but yeah, I could pass the physical. I've been doing a lot of work on my own. That isn't the point. The point is, I'm going back to Hamrickville. You take care of the congresswoman."

That jerked Axel back to where his attention naturally focused. "She might walk," he snarled. "We might not find a thing on Hubbert's computer."

"Taking care of problems is in your wheelhouse," Morgan said. "Handle it."

Axel closed the door, and Morgan put his foot to the gas pedal.

The first number he tried was Bo's cell phone, but it went straight to voice mail, which told him it wasn't turned on. The next number was Jesse's.

"I'm on my way back," he said. "How's Bo?"

"She's good. She'd lost enough blood she had to have a transfusion, but unless there's a fever or something, she can go home in the morning." Jesse sounded tired. "It's been a shit-storm around here today. How are things on your end?"

"We didn't get all the loose ends tied up, but we're working on it. You don't have to keep the lid on any longer. I'll read you in on the details when I get there."

Better not say too much on a cell phone, which was about as private as an open door in a motel room.

"Got it. Are you coming by for Tricks?"

"You have her?"

"She's here at the police station with me. I'm still working on the paperwork. I hate paperwork," Jesse growled. "And there's a shitload of it."

"Sorry about that."

"Uh huh. How far out are you?"

"Just got started. About three hours."

"I'll probably still be here."

Relieved about Bo's condition but needing to hear her voice anyway, Morgan ended that call and tried Bo again. Got voice mail again. He figured she was asleep, aided by some happy juice. He remembered too well how that went. But he'd rather she sleep than be in pain, so he settled in for a fast, hard drive, pushing to get back to her.

He made it in under three hours; he wheeled by the police station and saw the lights were still on, so he whipped into the rear parking lot and went in. Jesse looked up when he entered, leaned back in his chair, and yawned. "I finished just a few minutes ago."

Tricks had been snoozing on her bed, but she woke and lifted her head. When she saw Morgan, she shot over to him, her tail wagging madly as she greeted him with a wiggling body and licking tongue. He went down on one knee and rubbed her ears, stroked her thick fur. "It's been a long day for you too, hasn't it, girl? Want to go home?" He shot a glance at Jesse. "Via the hospital. What room is she in?"

"308."

"Is it one of those hospitals with strict visiting hours?"

"No, people pretty much come and go as they want. Relatives sit up with their sick folks, things like that."

He stayed long enough to give Jesse a quick rundown of events and fill him in on what was going on. "Shit, that isn't good," Jesse said, after finding out that Congresswoman Kingsley might be untouchable. "If she sold out the country once, she'll do it again."

"If she were in any position to do it, but she won't be. She'll have a hard time now going to the bathroom without someone watching her. She might not be in prison, but she won't be free."

He had to be content with that too. It was a tough pill to swallow, but he'd let Axel do what Axel did.

He thought about taking Tricks home first, but the need to see Bo, see her for himself, was riding him hard. The night temps were cool enough that he could leave Tricks in the Tahoe with the windows down a bit and let her snooze while he paid a fast visit. He walked her around first, then she happily bounded into the Tahoe and settled down. He didn't have her seat harness with him so he drove carefully, even though traffic was almost nonexistent.

He hadn't been to the hospital before, but he programmed the GPS and followed the directions. Half an hour later, he pulled into the hospital parking lot and found an empty slot under a light. There was a surprising number of cars there, given that the hospital wasn't particularly large even by small-town standards, so Jesse was likely right on target about people staying with their relatives.

He lowered the windows down an inch or so, letting the cool night air seep in. He said, "I'll be back in about fifteen minutes. You don't let anyone in, okay?"

Tricks woofed softly. It wasn't until he was inside the hospital, taking the interior stairs two at a time, that he realized he'd been talking to her as if she were human and understood every word he'd said. He gave a mental shrug. He'd bet on Tricks understanding more than some humans he'd met.

He exited on the third floor, checked which way the room numbers were running, and strode to room 308. The nurses' desk was down the hall, a small center of activity, but he didn't have to go that far down. There was no point in knocking, not if Bo'd been given happy juice, so he simply pushed the lever-style handle and went in.

The room wasn't completely dark, for the convenience of the nurse who would be coming in during the night to check on her. The head of the bed was raised a little, and Bo was turned slightly on her left side, her legs curled and her left hand tucked under her cheek. A big, thick bandage covered her neck and part of her right shoulder, but from what he could see in the dim light, her color looked good. An IV needle was in the back of her right hand. He checked the bags hanging from the rolling stand: an antibiotic and standard saline solution for hydration. Anything she was getting for pain was in the form of an injection or a pill.

"Hey."

The word startled him. Her voice was low and sleepy, a little slurred. Swiftly he turned to see her half-smiling at him, her eyelids barely cracked enough for her to see him.

"Hey," he said softly, rubbing the back of one finger against her cheek. "I hear you're getting sprung from this place in a few hours."

"So they say, as long as I don't have a fever. I'm hoping all these antibiotics they're pouring into me do the job."

"How do you feel?"

"Sore. Let me amend that: *very* sore. I don't know what they did to patch me up but I think I remember the nurse saying something about staples."

"Those are a bitch," he said feelingly. He remembered staples too damn well.

The more she talked, the more he could detect a slight difficulty in her speech. He suspected her throat was swollen, probably up into her jaw. Yeah, she was going to be unhappy for several days.

He'd come so damn close to losing her. The realization, held at bay while he did what had to be done, slammed him hard, hit him where he lived. His eyes suddenly burned and blurred. "Shit," he muttered, going down on his knees beside the bed.

"Morgan?" She was struggling to sit upright, reaching out toward him.

He caught her left hand and cradled it against his cheek. "You better fu—you better be okay," he growled, amending what he'd been about to say and leaving out the obscenity, because it seemed out of place with what he was feeling. "You hear me?"

"Back at you." She turned her hand so she was stroking his cheek. "I was terrified you hadn't paid any attention to Tricks barking, that he was going to kill you in front of me. Kill both of us, actually," she sighed. "I figured I was dead regardless of what happened.

All I could hope was that he wasn't a very good shot, and that you'd heard Tricks . . . Where is she?"

"In the Tahoe, waiting for me. Jesse kept her with him at the station. I stopped by to find out where you were and picked her up."

"Don't keep her waiting long," she instructed. "Anyway, I thought I saw movement out of the corner of my eye . . . the way he had my head jerked back I couldn't be sure. I couldn't think of anything to do except drop to the ground and keep his attention on me."

She'd expected to die. She hadn't been trying to save herself, she'd been trying to save him. His eyes burned again and his throat clogged. "I love you so damn much," he said tightly, closing his eyes as he gripped her fingers. "I thought my heart was going to stop when I saw he had you."

"I love you too." The words were simple, offered as a gift from a woman who had spent most of her life barricading herself from emotion, refusing to let anyone matter too much to her. When he thought how difficult it had been for her to tear down her walls, he felt doubly blessed, doubly honored. He had to wonder, if Tricks hadn't come first, if the dog hadn't made a huge chink in Bo's walls, if she'd ever have let him in. He figured he owed the dog, and the town, more than he could ever repay.

"One good thing came from it." The words were soft and sleepy, and her eyes drifted shut.

"What?"

She barely managed to lift her eyelids again. "We don't have to wait to get married." She sighed and went to sleep, with him still holding her hand.

No, they didn't, he realized. They damn well didn't.

Their wedding day was ten days later. They waited that long only because of Bo's injury. She didn't want to have a huge bandage on her neck in her wedding photos, however informal those photos were. They decided not to go to the expense of hiring a professional photographer, but as it turned out Brandwyn Wyman not only swung a mean chair, she dabbled in photography and volunteered to take pictures at her cost, just for the practice. So there would be photos, and Bo didn't want her bandage to be the focus of every one of them. By the time ten days rolled around, a bandage was still in place but it could be covered by a ribbon of lace tied around her throat and dangled down her back. The effect was Victorian, especially combined with the simple ivory gown she wore, and the way Daina had arranged her hair in a kind of modified Gibson Girl, with tendrils framing her face and neck. Sparkly earrings completed her wedding outfit. Her flowers were three ivory-white roses tied with some of the same lace ribbon that was around her throat.

She was still cautious about the way she turned her head, but overall she'd healed well. The staples had come out the day before, at her insistence, a few days sooner than the surgeon had wanted, but he wasn't the one getting married. She was, and she wanted the staples out. When he'd removed them, he'd admitted that the area looked good. He'd simply wanted to be cautious.

As expected, all their friends in town had really gotten into the whole wedding deal. Miss Doris had insisted on baking a cake, gratis, and Bo had had to argue with her, refusing to say what kind she wanted until Miss Doris grudgingly agreed to accept payment—a discounted payment, but still payment.

Morgan seemed cool as ever about the never-ending stream of details on which people wanted decisions, yesterday if possible. Between the two of them, they swatted away their friends' inclination to turn this into a huge production. There was no wedding party, no groomsmen or bridesmaids—just him, her, and likely Tricks, because they were prepared for her to refuse to stay quietly seated beside Daina.

Bo wasn't as sanguine as he was. Getting married was a big deal, so big that sometimes she thought she might have a panic attack at the idea of the huge step she was taking. Then she'd look at Morgan, so big and lethal and intelligent, and hell no, she wasn't letting him get away, panic or no panic. He was hers. She'd do this.

By the time she'd been released from the hospital, her house was no longer a crime scene, probably because Jesse and Morgan between them had been ruthless in moving things along. It hadn't been a normal crime scene anyway, not under the circumstances. The FBI had gotten involved and kept everything very quiet. The official word was that Mr. Kingsley had died in an auto accident. If Congresswoman Kingsley wanted to dispute that and bring the true circumstances out in the open, that was up to her. She hadn't. His funeral service had been remarkably quiet.

So far Axel's computer forensic team hadn't unearthed anything that would incriminate the congresswoman; perhaps she knew he wouldn't, perhaps there was a degree of separation that kept her in the clear. At any rate, she had been going about her life, handling her husband's death and funeral, accepting condolences. She *had* resigned from the HASC, so at least she was no longer in any position to know and pass along crucial military details. That was one small victory— too small, but Axel hadn't given up.

Sometimes the good guys won. Sometimes they didn't.

Bo put that terrifying day behind her. In an odd way, she was less upset about it than she had been the day Kyle Gooding had tried to kill Tricks. The most dire threat had been to herself; she'd had hopes that Morgan would be able to handle himself, that Tricks would be okay. She could handle that. She'd had a couple of dreams about it, but the dreams hadn't risen to nightmare status, and that had been in the first couple of days when she hadn't slept well because of her neck.

Still . . . if it hadn't been for that day, she'd have liked to get married at her home, in her yard. Though everything had been cleared by the time Morgan brought her home from the hospital, even the bloodstains washed from the grass and concrete, the patio pressure-washed to remove the splatted brain tissue—something she refused to let herself think about, though she immediately began planning to have that section of grass replaced with new sod, have new gravel brought in for the driveway, the patio posts restained—she didn't want her wedding memories to mix with those memories. It was best to keep the two separate. So they were getting married in the town park, in a little gazebo that had already seen several weddings.

"Brace yourself," Morgan said the day before the wedding as they were on their way home from the surgeon's office. His mother and stepfather had arrived the day before, and his mother—Theresa—had insisted they stay in the small motel so they didn't get in the way, thereby earning Bo's eternal gratitude and friendship. They were going to attend when Morgan and Bo had a quick walk-through of the ceremony that night. Other than eating out with them and having getting-to-know-you conversations, for now she and Morgan were going about their regular routine—almost. Though she'd gone back to work a week after being wounded because paperwork waited for no man—or woman— she didn't intend to work the day before her wedding, and everyone seemed to be totally on board with that.

"Why?"

"Axel's coming to the wedding."

"*What?*" Her head snapped around so fast the healing tissues and tendons in her neck howled a protest, and she slapped her hand over the bandage. "*Ow!* Damn it! What do you mean, he's coming to the wedding?"

"He's coming to the wedding, that's what I mean." He gave her a concerned glance. "Don't jerk your head around like that."

"No joke. Why's Axel coming? Who invited him?"

"No one invited him. This is kind of an open deal, remember? Whoever wants to show up will? My team happens to be between missions right now so they're all coming, and he decided to come along with them."

"Crap. I'd rather have my parents than him." She scowled out the windshield. "Just keep him away from me, all right? Have your guys sit on him or something."

"He'll be on his best behavior. With Axel, though, that isn't anything to brag about."

"I know. We'll make sure he's seated beside Loretta, and we'll give her a heads-up. If he starts anything, she'll cold-cock him. Problem solved," she said with satisfaction.

Morgan laughed. "I'm impressed. That's top-notch strategy. Now I'm actually hoping he gets out of line."

"Yeah, me too." She fantasized for a few minutes about how satisfying it would be to see Loretta lay Axel out with one punch. If she did, Bo would definitely start lobbying the town council to give Loretta a raise.

The big day itself went smoothly, mainly because they weren't making a lot of fuss about the details. A couple of churches and the community center volunteered folding chairs for the wedding guests to sit on and arranged them all in neat rows. They didn't have fancy covers over them, or bows tied to the backs, but no one cared.

Long tables were set up along one side for the wedding cake and punch, as well as the cases of Naked Pig fetched by a couple of Morgan's guys, whom he'd had make an emergency run to Alabama to the Back Forty Beer Company. Some inroad into the supply had been made before it arrived in West Virginia, but he'd ordered extra with that in mind. There were also sparkling water, tea, and soft drinks for those not inclined to try out the Naked Pig.

Daina and Kenny Michaels and a few others, including Emily, Brandwyn, and Kalie, had strung white lights in the gazebo and on the surrounding bushes and small trees. Even though the wedding was during the day, the white lights looked great.

The rest of Morgan's guys, and Axel, showed up well before the ceremony. Bo and Morgan were already in town—she was getting ready in the bathroom at the police station, so he had custody of Tricks until it was time for him to change into his suit. It was a new suit because, in his opinion, none of his old ones did justice to the occasion. Bo had bought a new dress, therefore he bought a new suit. Worked for him.

His guys didn't pay much attention to Tricks at first, other than commenting that she was a pretty dog, which was like saying Einstein was fairly smart. They were all standing around outside shooting the bull while

Morgan threw the tennis ball for her. After a while, of course, she deigned to allow someone else to have the honor and deposited her ball at Kodak's feet.

Morgan kept his mouth shut, let Kodak give it a muscular throw, then filled him in on what he'd done wrong when Tricks retrieved the ball, and on her return gave Kodak a disdainful look before giving the honor to one of the other guys. Morgan instructed him on how she liked the throw, and on cue she caught it on the first bounce and posed for him until he told her it was a great catch.

From then on, the guys were hooked. Tricks had all the attention she could possibly want—maybe, because she had a large capacity for handling attention. She was petted, she was played with, she amazed them with her understanding of people language, she demonstrated that she knew *exactly* what the numbers on the clock meant when it was time for her lunch. Even Axel was impressed. "Maybe we could use her," he muttered.

"Stay your ass away from her," Morgan said. He was only glad Bo wasn't around to hear that comment or she'd have cold-cocked Axel herself, then sent the Mean-As-Shit Hobsons to burn down his house.

For her part, Tricks disliked Axel on sight, which only proved her excellent character judgment. She turned her head away from him every time he tried to pet her. Probably the best pet for Axel was a snake.

Finally it was time for the ceremony. Morgan and Bo walked together to the gazebo, her hand resting in the crook of his arm. She was as graceful as a willow, her gown flowing around her thin, supple body, her skin and eyes glowing, her thick mane of hair currently remaining in Daina's style creation.

Morgan's mother and stepfather sat in the front row of folding chairs. Daina was also in the front row, with Kenny on one side of her and Mayor Buddy and his wife on the other. Tricks was sitting in front of Daina, her leash firmly held, an expression of doggie bliss on her face because of all the attention she'd had that morning. Jesse and Kalie sat on the other side of the aisle, also front row. Morgan's buddies took up the second row. As Bo went past, she saw Loretta give her a thumbs-up. Axel was seated beside her, and he looked positively cowed. It was a great day.

When the minister said, "Isabeau Rebecca Maran, do you take this man—" he was interrupted by a sharp bark from Tricks, who had impeccable timing. Morgan and Bo both burst out laughing, as did everyone else in the audience. Tricks took advantage and pulled loose from Daina, dashed over to Bo, and wormed her way between Bo and Morgan where she stood beaming for the rest of the ceremony. She was happily tucked between her two people, right where she belonged.

Of course Tricks was in all the photographs, except for the artsy close-ups of their wedding rings, Bo's bouquet, and things like that.

Afterward, when the Naked Pig had been drunk, cake and other goodies had been eaten, Bo and Morgan had danced on the grass before others joined in, Tricks had finally decided to take an exhausted nap, and the cleaning up had begun, Bo noticed that Morgan, Axel, and the other GO-Team members were gathered in the shade of one of the big trees, evidently having a serious discussion.

She herself was talking with Theresa and Daina, and she wasn't going to go over. One, this was probably GO-Team business. Two, she didn't want to be that close to Axel. But, hell—as of a couple of hours ago Morgan was her husband, and if he was leaving tonight, she wanted to know. She had taken him for better or worse, so she was prepared for his job to take him away for long periods of time. She hoped it wasn't tonight, and she intended to find out.

She strode over, as authoritatively as one could stride in a gown, and insinuated herself into the group. "Has something come up? Do you have to leave?" she asked, not whining about it and ready to help him pack if he wanted her company.

Morgan looked down at her and smiled as he slid his arm around her. "No, nothing in particular. I was just resigning from the GO-Teams."

Her mouth fell open in shock. "What?"

"This is your fault," Axel said in his typical surly, sour tone.

Bo looked around. "Loretta!" she called, having spotted her friend still lingering as she and her husband, Charlie, talked to some friends. Loretta looked up, excused herself, and headed toward them with an air of purpose.

Axel actually blanched and began edging away.

Morgan said sharply, "Bo hasn't asked me to quit, hasn't said a word about it. This is my decision. I'm not too old yet, but I only have a few good years left while I can stay in top shape, so I'm making the move now. I want to be here, I want to start a family—"

"A *family*?" Bo squeaked, so obviously shocked that all the guys chuckled. Well, all of them except Axel.

"With your permission." Morgan grinned and tightened his arm around her. "So I'm resigning."

"Damn it," Axel said in frustration. "I knew I shouldn't have let you come here."

"You *sent* him here, asshole," Bo growled, and just like that they were almost in each other's faces, with Morgan holding her back because she wasn't in any shape for another brawl. Out of the corner of his eye he saw Loretta pick up speed, and he said, "Stand down, Mac, or be mowed down."

Axel saw the wisdom in that and immediately backed away. He even tucked his hands behind his back. Loretta slackened her pace, but her gaze was locked on him like a guided missile.

"You're one of my best leaders. Hell, you're *the* best." Axel looked as if he'd throw a temper tantrum if it weren't for the pressing need to behave.

"Give it up," Kodak advised, grinning. He loved scenes like this. "Promote one of us, and deal with it. And hire Morgan as a consultant so we don't lose him completely."

At that Axel looked thoughtful. Loretta reached them then and looked down at Axel from the almost six-and-a-half feet height her high heels gave her. "Is the runt causing problems?" she asked. It was amazing how a woman in a green dress with little white flowers on it, wearing makeup and jewelry and high heels, could look so intimidating, but Loretta managed. She had it down to an art form. It also helped that Morgan had recounted the scene between her and Warren Gooding, so all of them knew her reputation and that she generally took no prisoners.

Bo was the only one who laughed outright. The men all hid their grins. Axel looked both outraged and terrified. He wasn't a runt, maybe medium height or a little better, but Loretta definitely made him look runtish.

"He's trying," Bo said, not about to let him off the hook.

Loretta simply waited, her gaze locked on Axel. He fidgeted. He turned red. He ran a finger around his collar. Bo could tell he wanted to go into one of his classic Axel scenes, but the bottom line was he was afraid of what Loretta might do. She was an unknown quantity to him, and he was on her territory. If she knocked him into tomorrow, everyone, even his own men, would swear he'd tripped over a tree root.

Finally he focused on Morgan. "Would you stay on as a consultant?"

"We can talk about it," Morgan said, though Bo knew that would be the perfect solution. He wasn't about to give Axel power going into the negotiations though.

"All right." Axel looked relieved. "Come see me Monday. Uh—unless you're going on a honeymoon, or something like that." He shot a glance at Bo that said he still couldn't believe Morgan had actually married her.

"No honeymoon yet," Bo said. "We're waiting for when it will inconvenience you the most." Beside her, Tricks stopped staring balefully at the man she disliked to give a woof of agreement.

Perfect.

Morgan went through security at the county courthouse and slipped into the courtroom where Kyle Gooding was being arraigned. The process had taken long enough to get to this point, but Kyle had remained in jail the whole time, so that didn't matter.

What he assumed was most of the Gooding family was in the courtroom. The district attorney was there, the Gooding lawyer, and a couple of reporter types, some just out of curiosity. Morgan took a seat away from the others, choosing to be as isolated as possible. He wanted Kyle to see him.

The county deputies brought Kyle in. He'd had his hair cut and he wore a suit for all the world as if he was expecting to walk out of the courtroom free instead of going back to jail. There was a hum of anticipation from his family group. He looked at them and gave them a small cocky grin. In that moment Morgan knew for sure that Kyle intended to back out of their agreement.

He sat motionless, his gaze locked on Kyle. After a minute Kyle felt himself being watched, even as insensitive as he was to everything other than himself. He turned and looked over his family group, then turned the other way to survey the rest of the courtroom audience.

He saw Morgan, and his eyes widened. He swallowed nervously. Morgan just stared, never blinking, every ounce of malice he felt burning in his eyes. This son of a bitch had tried to destroy the woman he loved, and no way was he letting him get away with it. He might not do anything about it today, but the reckoning would come, and soon. The time and circumstance would be of his choosing—and he'd get away with it.

Under the weight of his gaze, Kyle turned pale and jerkily faced forward again.

When the charges were read and the judge asked how he pled, in a tight, shaking voice Kyle Gooding said, "Guilty."

His family erupted in a muted uproar because that wasn't what they'd expected. His lawyer looked at him as if he'd lost his mind. The judge began banging his gavel, shouting for silence. Morgan sat motionless, merely watching as the hubbub died down and the proceedings came to a close. As Kyle was led from the courtroom in handcuffs, he looked back over his shoulder at Morgan.

Morgan didn't move, didn't blink, didn't break eye contact.

When the door closed behind Kyle, he got up and quietly walked back to his pickup, which he'd retrieved from his condo the weekend after he and Bo were married, eight days ago and counting. They had also retrieved the *Shark* from the marina, and it was now at Bo's house.

As he exited the courthouse, he glanced up at the blue sky and thought it looked like a great day to get in some fishing.

Want More Linda Howard?

S ix of Linda Howard's classic tales of suspense and romance are now available digitally for the first time ever:

DIAMOND BAY

DUNCAN'S BRIDE

HEARTBREAKER

MACKENZIE'S MISSION

MACKENZIE'S MOUNTAIN

WHITE LIES

Available now from Avon Impulse.

HARPER (LUXE)

THE NEW LUXURY IN READING

We hope you enjoyed reading
our new, comfortable print size and found it
an experience you would like to repeat.

Well – you're in luck!

HarperLuxe offers the finest in fiction and
nonfiction books in this same larger print size and
paperback format. Light and easy to read, HarperLuxe
paperbacks are for book lovers who want to see
what they are reading without the strain.

For a full listing of titles and
new releases to come, please visit our website:

www.HarperLuxe.com

HARPER (LUXE)

SEEING IS BELIEVING!